Storm Constantine's Wraeththu Mythos

Songs to Earth and Sky
Stories of the Seasons

Storm Constantine's Wraeththu Mythos

Songs to Earth and Sky
Stories of the Seasons

Edited by Storm Constantine

IMMANION
PRESS
Stafford, England

Cover art and Wraeththu Mythos logo: Ruby
Editor: Storm Constantine
Interior layout: Storm Constantine
Interior illustrations: Ruby: pages 6, 10, 79, 131, 268; Helen Walne page 107, photo 'Namaqualand Flowers'

Set in Garamond

IP0135
ISBN 978-1-907737-84-8

First edition by Immanion Press, 2017
An Immanion Press Edition
http://www.immanion-press.com
info@immanion-press.com

Contents

Preface:
Who and What are Wraeththu?

For the benefit of those picking up this book who might not have come across the Wraeththu Mythos before, I'll include enough information here so it's not necessary for new readers to read any previous story or novel in the mythos to enjoy this collection.

The first Wraeththu trilogy (*The Enchantments of Flesh and Spirit*, *The Bewitchments of Love and Hate* and *The Fulfilments of Fate and Desire*) was published in the 1980s, and has since been reissued in a revised, author's preferred edition. The initial trilogy, known as *The Wraeththu Chronicles*, was followed by two further trilogies, (*The Wraeththu Histories* and *The Alba Sulh Sequence*) and also standalone novels and story collections written by me and by other writers.

The Wraeththu: A Brief Description of Their Origin

Humanity is in decline, ravaged by insanity, natural disasters, conflict, disease and infertility. A mysterious race has risen from the ghettos and ruins of the decaying, dying cities. The young are evolving into a new species, which is stronger, sharper and more beautiful than their forerunners. They are the Wraeththu. Androgynous beings, Wraeththu hara transcend gender and race. They possess keen psychic abilities and the means, through a process called inception, to transform humans into creatures like themselves. But they are wild in their rebirth, and must strive to overcome all that is human within them in order to create society anew.

When the first book in the mythos was published, my exploration of the fluidity of gender, and an androgynous state, was ground-breaking and often misunderstood. Some readers and critics were uncomfortable with the idea, and expressed that explicitly. While intersex characters had appeared in science fiction before, (less so in fantasy), their sexuality and psyche hadn't been explored in depth – often the science was emphasised more than characterisation. Times, culture – and genres within fiction – have changed since then, and the idea of fixed gender within strict confines is no longer regarded as the norm, in reality and in fiction and film. Gender politics is also examined more frequently in science fiction nowadays.

My early novels and stories focused upon the rise of the Wraeththu and were very much influenced by the alternative music and culture of the 1980s and 1990s. However, as time's gone on, I've become more interested in how hara have developed, now that humankind have almost vanished from their world. The earth is renewed and nature has reclaimed much of it. Both Wraeththu and I are older and wiser, and it fascinates me to explore what their world has become.

A proportion of them live in small tribes – or phyles of tribes – and lead a bucolic lifestyle, having headed into the wildernesses of the world to escape the 'Devastation', as the upheaval and destruction that accompanied the demise of humankind was described. Hara have evolved in these communities, in tune with the land rather than trying to subdue it or fight against it. This is an idyll of mine – a favourite fantasy – and I enjoy writing about such communities. They are inherently magical, for being close to the land means being close to its spirits, its life force, and also the power of the seasons as they change throughout the year. Different influences hold sway at different times.

This anthology comprises nine stories, each involving one of the Deharan festivals, and the deities and customs that surround them. Nerine Dorman, who lives in South Africa, and who has contributed two stories to this book, has set her tales in her native land, providing a fascinating counterpoint to the stories set in the northern hemisphere.

All the authors are regular contributors to the Wraeththu Mythos, with short stories and novels. Wendy Darling also co-edits the 'Para' anthologies with me – Wraeththu stories with a theme. A list of all the Mythos publications can be found at the end of this book.

Within the Wraeththu Mythos, hara are referred to as 'he', since back in the 1980s, when I first started writing seriously about Wraeththu, this pronoun seemed to me less gender specific than 'she'. A lot has changed in both culture and language since then, but to glue a new pronoun over all the stories would feel at best clunky and contrived. I ask readers to look beyond the loaded meaning of the male pronoun, and to read it as non-gender specific.

As the mythos develops, so more terms are coined by me and other writers that depart from gender specific words and phrases. There are new ones within this anthology. A glossary of terms is provided at the back of the book for readers unfamiliar with them.

Storm Constantine, Samhain 2017

Introduction
The Wheel of the Year and its Festivals

Storm Constantine

The stories in this collection are based around the seasonal cycle, known as The Wheel of the Year. The Wraeththu version is named Arotohar.

In compiling this anthology, I wanted stories that reflected how the seasons affect the land and the people who live upon it. If a winter is too harsh, or a summer too hot, livestock and crops may perish. The festivals were one way in which people sought to appease and venerate the gods who controlled the seasons, in order to attract divine fortune. For those who aren't familiar with the concept of the 'yearly round', here is an overview.

Still observed by modern practitioners, The Wheel of the Year is a Pagan concept, in which the year is divided into eight portions, each celebrated by a festival. The spring and autumn equinoxes and the summer and winter solstices are significant dates in this system, and in between them are four 'cross quarter' days. These derive from ancient pre-Christian festivals. It's clear that these dates were appropriated by Christian religious leaders and placed in the calendar of holy days, in order for their new faith to be accepted more readily by potential converts. Commonly, the eight festivals of the year originally marked or celebrated significant events or tasks in farming.

Yule (the winter solstice), falling around 21st December, equates to the Christian Christmas, (which falls a few days later), and is the shortest day of the year. This is the great winter festival in both traditions. In Pagan belief, it is when the sun is believed to be reborn as an infant god. From this day onwards, light and heat return to the northern hemisphere and the days grow longer. Christianity appropriated this festival for the birth of Jesus, so the ancient rite could be placed comfortably within its belief system. To early Christians, the meaning of the festival, in terms of the seasons, was no doubt more important than the names and myths that the priests attached to it. Yule was also associated with the Norse god Odin, and his Wild Hunt, which was said to ride across the night sky. Another Pagan myth involved the Holly King and the Oak King, deities who represented winter and summer respectively, and who fought continually for dominance throughout the year. At the solstice, the Holly King was killed by the Oak King, thus ensuring that summer would come round again. To farmers, the solstice meant that winter was half way done, and heralded the eventual arrival of spring.

Imbolc, (or Imbolg), on 1st February, (Saint Bridget's Day), lies midway between the winter solstice and the spring equinox. It marked the start of spring, and its name is thought to derive from the old Celtic term *oimelc*, which means ewe's milk, or else *i mbolc*, which means 'in the belly', and is believed to refer to pregnant ewes. The festival originally revolved around the goddess Brigid, who was eventually Christianised into St Bridget. Brigid was believed to visit people's houses on Imbolc eve to bless them; perhaps she might even leave a message in the cold ashes of a hearth. She was seen as representing the part of the year when the sun grows stronger, so was a powerful symbol of light coming back into people's lives after the harshness of winter.

Eostre, (or Ostara), around 21st March is the spring equinox when light and dark are balanced. This relates to the Christian festival of Easter, when Christ is believed to have been crucified and resurrected. Eostre was a Celtic goddess, whose names means 'to shine'. She was connected with the dawn and was regarded as a bringer of light. The hare is seen as her sacred animal. Eostre was a time when spring had settled in and the ground had been prepared for eventual harvest. Its festivals were light-hearted and playful, reflecting the joy the people must have felt at the returning sunlight and warmth.

Beltane (or Bealtain, Beltainn), on 1st May, lies midway between the spring equinox and the summer solstice and is traditionally a fire festival. It marked the first days of summer, when the cattle were driven out to graze in the summer pastures. At the festival, cattle were driven between two bonfires, in the belief this protected them from disease. Beacon fires were set upon hilltops on this night. Beltane was regarded as a 'liminal time', when the boundaries between the material world and the otherworld became thin and interaction was possible between the denizens of these worlds. This is also a time associated with fertility rites, such as dancing around the May Pole, and with the mating of the god and goddess of nature.

Midsummer's Eve (or Litha – a modern Pagan name for the festival) is the summer solstice, around 21st June, and marks the longest day of the year. To the early Christians, it became St. John's Day. This was another festival strongly associated with bonfires, which were lit to drive off evil spirits, who were believed to walk the land once more, as the days became shorter again. As farmers would now be waiting for the fruit of the forthcoming harvests, and would want these to be bountiful, it was important to keep mischievous otherworld entities away, so they could wreak no harm.

Lughnasadh, (or Lammas, Loafmas), on 1st August, lies midway between the summer solstice and the autumn equinox. It's the first harvest festival of the year, marking the first cutting of the grain crops. The name derives from Lugh, a Celtic god of light. At Loafmas or Lammas, the Christianised version, farmers would take loaves made of the first crop into church to be blessed. This is another example of how older beliefs continued into the Christian era.

The Autumnal Equinox, (named Mabon by modern Pagans), falls around 21st September. This has no official corresponding Christian festival, although Harvest Festivals may be celebrated in churches around this time. To Pagans, this is the second of the harvest festivals, when the fruits of the trees have ripened. Many of the crops would already have been gathered. Feasts were held to celebrate the earth's bounty, and this was a time when 'corn dollies' would have been made. These were small effigies made of straw, traditionally from the last of the crop to be harvested. They represented the spirit of the corn and would be kept safe in people's houses throughout the winter, in the belief this would ensure a good harvest for the following year.

Samhain (All Hallows' Eve or Hallowe'en) on the 31st October, lies midway between the autumn equinox and the winter solstice. In the Christian tradition, this was All Saint's Eve, when the hallowed dead were venerated – predominantly saints. To Pagans, this festival marks the end of the harvest and the onset of winter, when preparations have to be made to provide for the cold, dark months ahead. Like Beltane, across from it on the Wheel of the Year, Samhain was a 'liminal time' when the denizens of the otherworld could cross into our reality. Hallowe'en particularly was renowned for stories of ghosts and apparitions, when spirits walked the earth or dead ancestors visited their living relatives. It was also regarded as the Celtic New Year.

In addition to the familiar Pagan festivals, the Deharan version of the Wheel of the Year also includes Adkaya, which falls two weeks before the festival of Natalia (the winter solstice) on 7th December. This reflects the harish life cycle, since Adkaya marks the delivery of the sacred pearl of the dehar Elisin (the harling of light) by his hostling Solarisel. The pearl hatches at the solstice two weeks later.

Within the Deharan tradition, a large communal festival rite is known as an arojhahn. A majhahn is a ritual of lesser significance, or of smaller scale, and because Adkaya is usually observed within the family or among small groups of friends, its celebrations are generally referred to as majhahns.

As the seasons change, the influence of the forthcoming dehar might begin to make his presence felt before the official 'changeover' at the festival. A dehar's influence is at its strongest at the moment he takes on the mantle of custodianship of the Wheel. Thereafter, his influence slowly begins to wane. A few of the stories within this collection focus upon this phenomenon.

Arotahar

The Seasonal Cycle of the Dehara

The festivals and images of the seasonal cycle represent the birth, death and rebirth of all life throughout the solar year. The name of this cycle is Arotahar; the endless rotation of the seasons, the planets, the moon and the sun.

The theme of Arotahar is the life story of the dehara – the Wraeththu deities – as hostling and harling. For the first half of the year, they reign together, and eventually, as transformations take place within them according to the season, they become lovers. This is not to suggest incest, as the dehara change into completely different entities within their cycles – and relationships dissolve and reform. As the year progresses, the original hostling of Elisin, the Child of Light, transforms into a dehar with a more ouanic – or masculine – aspect and becomes the growing Elisin's lover. Together, they create a pearl, hosted by Elisin, who is destined to become in turn the dark dehar of Shadetide. At midsummer, Elisin's lover dies in the fields, leaving the remaining dehar, for a turn of the wheel named Shadolan, alone through the dark months. During this time the pearl matures, to be dropped at the minor festival of Adkaya in early December. The pearl hatches at the winter solstice, and the cycle begins again.

The Western Tradition of Paganism focuses upon male and female deities – the god and goddess of nature. In the Deharan system all deities are androgynous, and only their names and aspects might shift throughout the year. Panphilien's name means 'the lover of all'. Every year, he is born, dies and is born again, giving himself in sacrifice to the land to ensure that life continues. He has twelve aspects, and is known by the names applied to him during the different seasons over which he reigns.

The Wheel of Arotohar and its Dehara

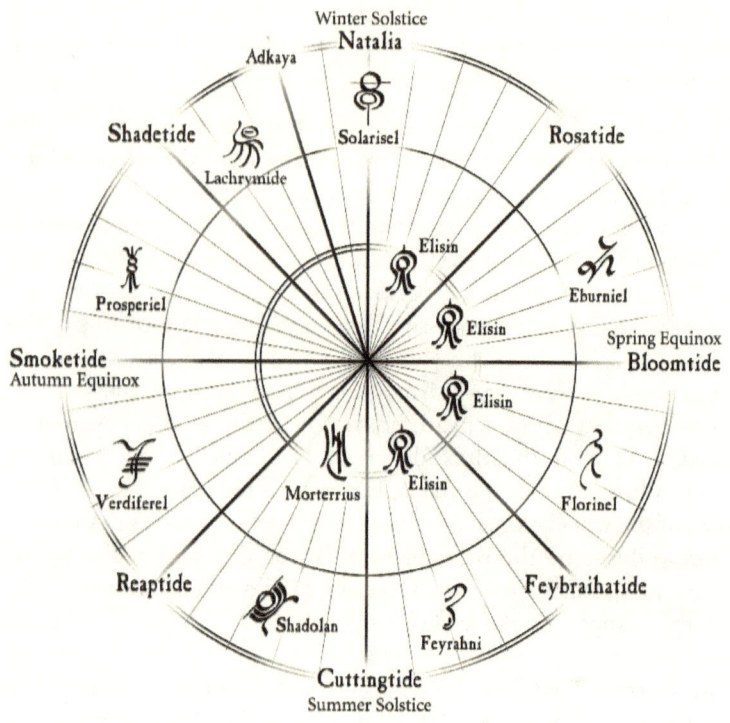

Winter Solstice
Natalia

Adkaya

Solarisel

Shadetide

Lachrymide

Rosatide

Elisin

Eburniel

Elisin

Prosperiel

Smoketide
Autumn Equinox

Spring Equinox
Bloomtide

Elisin

Florinel

Verdiferel

Morterrius

Elisin

Reaptide

Feybraihatide

Shadolan

Feyrahni

Cuttingtide
Summer Solstice

16

The Calendar of Wraeththu

The Months:

January - Snowmoon
February – Frostmoon
March - Windmoon
April - Rainmoon
May - Flowermoon
June - Meadowmoon
July – Ardourmoon
August - Fruitingmoon
September - Harvestmoon
October - Vintagemoon
November - Mistmoon
December – Adkayamoon

The Days:

Monday – Lunilsday
Tuesday – Miyacalasday
Wednesday – Aloytsday
Thursday – Agavesday
Friday – Aruhanisday
Saturday – Pelfazzarsday
Sunday – Aghamasday

Natalia

December 21st

This is the festival of the Winter Solstice, the longest night of the year. At this time, the deharling Elisin emerges from the pearl that nurtured him. The pearl was dropped two weeks previously, at Adkaya, by the dehar Solarisel, and now the deharling comes forth from it. He represents the reawakening of nature and the return of the sun. This is the night of the new year for hara, when the solstice heralds the return of the light and heat. From this point on, the days grow longer, until the summer solstice. Natalia is therefore regarded as the most propitious time to initiate changes in one's life, as the influence of the season, the return of plenty, nourishes the seeds of intention.

Solarisel, the deharling's hostling, is a benevolent dehar of great beauty, visualised as dressed in gold and white, with a mane of golden hair. His aspect is essentially soumic, as he represents the archetypal hostling. He grants the gift of a light heart, of fortune, promise and opportunity. He is the dehar of abundance, whose cauldron of creation offers up the ultimate potential. His is the celebration of the new sun. His plants are the holly, the ivy and the pine. He is accompanied by sleek white hounds, who at the moment of the deharling's emergence, fly through the sky, yelping out the news. To hear the hounds of Solarisel on the solstice night is a fortuitous omen for the coming year.

The deharling is named Elisin, the child of light. He retains this name until the moment of his hostling/lover's death at Cuttingtide.

As with all winter festivals, Natalia is a time for socialising, hospitality and the exchange of gifts.

Summer's End

Fiona Lane

Autumn died and the days grew short, but still the snow did not fall and the rivers did not freeze.

It was not that Aisa missed the cold, but the lack of ice in the river meant that he was unable to construct the altar for the forthcoming Natalia Arojhahn. Every year since he had first come to Forra as High Rehuna, to preside over the festivals of Arotahar, he had carved the blocks of ice from the frozen river that bounded the northern edge of the town and transported them to the same place under the pine trees behind his house. Here, he would sculpt them into an altar, piling block on top of block, and pouring water between the cracks, watching it run and freeze and bond them solidly together. He would polish the ice until its surface was so smooth that to the touch it felt like liquid once more. Then he would set out on it the small collection of objects required for the ceremony – the golden *vakei* – a small tool used for directing energy, inherited from his predecessor – the tall white candles and the glass bowl of glittering gold flakes, which Aisa enjoyed sprinkling over himself and other hara more than he would ever admit.

But this year there was no altar, and only a layer of brown pine needles beneath the trees, instead of the customary soft blanket of snow. When hara from the town went to collect firewood and hunt for game, they still had to use the unsteady wooden bridge to cross to the forests on the northern bank of the river, instead of being able to take the Ice Road directly across its frozen surface and enjoy the illicit thrill of walking on the river.

Aisa stared disconsolately out of the window at the place at the bottom of his garden, where the altar should have been. The shadows from the pine trees were long, and reached almost to the house itself. Through the trees, the low rays of the setting sun glimmered weakly. The light was fading and, without snow to brighten the surroundings, a dismal gloom seemed to settle on the house and garden.

Aisa shivered. It was only just past midday, but the sun did not rise for long at this time of year. His morning's chores were often completed before its first rays broached the horizon, and most days he tried to spend the short period of daylight outside, either tending to the garden, walking to the town, or shovelling snow from where it had drifted inconveniently. But today he had felt like doing none of those things, even if there had been snow to shovel.

He wondered if it was worthwhile to start cleaning the windows of the house, a job he had been putting off for a while because he did not enjoy it, but the low winter light picked out all the grime in heartless relief, and he did not want to be thought slovenly by any unexpected visitors. Of course, he could allocate this particular chore to one of the house-hara if he chose – it was their job after all – but he harboured the conviction that a har ought to be at least partially responsible for keeping his home environment clean and tidy.

He was saved from the prospect of having to spend the next hour or so in the company of a bucket of dirty suds by a knock at the door, and for a moment he felt a small, unworthy twinge of pleasure at having a valid excuse to put off the window-cleaning again. But then he heard the visitor's voice, and his heart sank. Plainly the dehara were not about to let him forget that the universe must remain in balance, and for every unwanted chore successfully shirked there must be an equal and opposite retribution in the form of an audience with Tualenn

Aisa was used to unannounced visits from Tualenn. As Archon of Forra, Tualenn considered it his duty to ensure that the town's High Rehuna was working diligently to guarantee the dehara continued to bestow their blessings upon the hara who lived there. Aisa could freely acknowledge that Tualenn was a hard-working, conscientious and virtuous leader of the community. It was just that sometimes he wished Tualenn would go and be hard-working, conscientious and virtuous somewhere else, and today, he knew, was going to be one of those days.

Tualenn swept majestically into Aisa's small sitting room, unpinned his long fur cloak and handed it to the waiting househar, who received it without a word and immediately spirited both himself and the cloak from the room, leaving Tualenn and Aisa alone together.

'Good afternoon, Tiahaar.' Tualenn's greeting was regal, and Aisa's heart sank a little more, as he knew from experience that the degree of formality which Tualenn employed in their interactions was invariably inversely proportional to how agreeable Aisa would find the subject about to be discussed.

'Tualenn. How nice to...'

Tualenn ignored Aisa's attempted cheerfulness and marched over to the window, frowning, and pointed accusingly with one elegantly manicured finger. For one surreal moment, Aisa thought he was about to complain about the state of the glass, but no such luck was to be his.

'There is no altar,' Tualenn stated bluntly, the tone of his voice indicating, in case Aisa had been unaware of it so far, that he was far from happy.

'No,' Aisa admitted, 'there isn't. That's because there's no snow. Or ice.'

'I can see that. I'm not blind! The question is, Aisa, what do you intend to do about it?'

'What do you expect me to do? Ask the dehara to make it snow?' Aisa's reply was intended to be sarcastic, but he watched in fascination as the minute expressions, which fleetingly crossed the Archon's face, revealed him considering, contemplating and then dismissing this idea within less than a second.

'No, that would not be an appropriate request to make of the dehara. What I mean, Aisa, is what do *you* intend to do? What is your backup plan?'

'My... *backup plan*? I... haven't really got one,' Aisa admitted rather sheepishly.

'Well, you need to do something! Natalia is in three days' time, in case you hadn't noticed!'

'I had, actually.'

'Natalia is the most important festival of the year! Many visitors come to Forra for Natalia. Many *important* visitors!'

To emphasise the significance of this fact, Tualenn folded his arms belligerently and stood with his face scant inches from Aisa's own, close enough that Aisa could see the slight flaring of his nostrils. By sheer effort of will alone, Aisa stifled the laugh he knew was highly inappropriate. Sometimes, Tualenn could be quite ridiculous.

21

'I know. I *will* sort something out. Don't worry.'

Tualenn sniffed, partially mollified, and tucked a stray wisp of hair behind his ear that had come free from its binding. The presence of this insubordinate lock alone gave a clue to the Archon's agitation. Tualenn had hair the colour of the brown nuts found in autumn inside their spikey green shells, but he wore it pulled back tightly from his face and knotted so firmly at the nape of his neck that it seemed to pull his face back with it and gave him an expression of permanent surprise. Tualenn had worn his hair like this for as long as Aisa could remember. The Archon did not like change. If something worked, he saw no reason to alter it.

'I do not have the luxury of not worrying, Aisa. I have to worry about everything, so that other hara don't have to.'

Aisa thought that Tualenn sounded tired, and felt a twinge of pity, which was immediately swept away by the Archon's next statement.

'I need this sorted out by tomorrow. Kindly present yourself at the High Chambers first thing tomorrow morning. There are three hara who wish to speak with you, and I do not want them to be given a bad impression of our town. I will see you there. My cloak, please.'

Without waiting for Aisa's agreement or otherwise to this demand, Tualenn marched towards the door, and the housahar who had previously relieved him of his cloak instantly materialised back into existence in a flurry of agitated attempts to drape the Archon's cloak over his shoulders and pin it into place as he swept out.

Aisa exhaled slowly in the sudden, silent void left by the Archon's departure. Tualenn was a force of nature, and any attempt to argue with him was as futile as standing in front of an oncoming avalanche with a hand raised to halt its progress. But it was Tualenn's determination that had seen Forra prosper over the years. He was a high-caste har, Nahir-Nuri, of the kind that the Gelaming were fond of recruiting for their own, whether the har in question desired such a singular honour or not, yet he had resisted their blandishments and their attempts to persuade him to depart for far-off Immanion, proving to be as immovable an object as the Gelaming were an irresistible force. He was not wrong to say that Natalia was the most important time of the year, because it was Forra's reason for existence, and the source of its well-being. Here, at the boundary between light and dark, was the very nature of the cycle of the seasons revealed, stripped bare.

Natalia was both the end of the old year and the beginning of the new. It was the hope of a summer yet to come, born in the despair of winter's darkest day. On that day, the deharling Elisin, the Child of Light, emerged from the pearl to take his place with his radiant hostling Solarisel and began anew the cycle of life. And death. For at the opposite cusp of the year, in the endless light of midsummer, Solarisel would die, struck down by his own son, that his blood might fertilise the earth and return the life to it.

The cycle of nature was cruel, to hara and dehara alike. It was impossible, Aisa thought, to fully experience the true meaning of Natalia unless one had experienced the true nature of Winter. Other tribes also celebrated Natalia – the mighty Gelaming themselves among them – but Aisa had experienced winter in Almagabra, and he could almost laugh at its benign temperament there. Though a storm may occasionally blow in from the sea, and anxious hara might pull their fine, silk clothing tighter around their lithe bodies and shiver, they knew that the sun would shine again soon enough. Winter did not bring fear to the hara of Almagabra, as it should. To know the true fear of winter, a har must visit Forra and watch the light die a little more each day and the darkness gain, feel the wind bite with a true menace, and see the rivers and streams frozen into glacial immobility.

In Forra, winter was a beast that could kill, and a har who forgot that would forfeit his life. Aisa still recalled the young har who had become lost returning from the woods one evening, whose body he had found the next morning, frozen hard, only a short distance from the safety of the town. The snow had been deep that year, and drifting, and in the fading light there would have been no contours or landmarks to guide the young har. He had come from a southern tribe to visit the town. No local har would have been so foolish, for to live in Forra was to be on intimate terms with the Winter and the Fear and to respect them both.

Aisa shivered, for the light was going, early as it was, and with it the temperature was falling. He went over to the fireplace and, from a basket sitting on the stone hearth, took a handful of pine cones and dropped them into the fire. Though they wouldn't provide much heat, he enjoyed both the sound of them crackling and popping in the flames, and their resinous odour as they burned. He lit some candles, and their golden glow seemed to warm the room instantly.

He remembered that he still had to bring in some more logs from the outhouse where they were stored, and mentally chastised himself for not doing this earlier, while there'd still been enough light to see. Hurriedly, he took his own fur cloak from a peg on the wall and fastened it with the ornate metal cloak-pin, but the pin broke as he was adjusting it and fell in two halves onto the floor at his feet.

Annoyed, Aisa invoked a minor household dehar and one of his less useful recreational proclivities. A bolder har might have simply gone out to collect the logs without his cloak, but Aisa was not that har. He thought for a moment, then went over to his writing desk and opened a small drawer in the front. He rummaged around for a moment, until he found what he was looking for. From the back of the drawer, he pulled out a brooch fashioned from gold and mother-of-pearl and stared at it thoughtfully for a moment. He remembered clearly the day his High-Hostling had given it to him...

You can have this now, Aisa, but keep it safe. You can wear it when you're grown-up.

He had kept it safe all these years, waiting to be grown-up enough to wear it. Instinctively, his hand went to the chain around his neck, and his fingers sought and found the crystal hanging from it that his High-Hostling had given him that same day. Its facets and contours were as familiar to him as his own face. Almost reluctantly, he put the brooch back in the drawer and pulled out instead a large clip normally used for binding sheaves of paper together. With a bit of adjustment, he managed to secure the edges of his cloak together, even if the results were not exactly elegant. Then he took an empty basket from the fireplace and went to fetch more logs for the fire.

Outside, the gloom was deepening, and it was almost dark inside the outhouse as Aisa loaded logs into his basket. The sky was clear, with a single bright star visible where the sun had recently left. It would be a cold night, but there would be no snow. His basket filled, Aisa picked it up and turned to go back to the house, almost tripping over The Skogga as he did so. He muttered a curse under his breath.

'What are you doing here?' he demanded accusingly.

The Skogga looked up at him, unimpressed by Aisa's rebuke, green eyes glowing in the dark. Aisa sighed. Normally at this time of year, The Skogga would be found indoors, lying stretched out in front of the fire, belly up, or lazily grooming herself on Aisa's bed, but the lack of snow and true cold had tempted her out to her summer haunts to see if anything needed doing. Skogga were well-equipped to deal with the winter, with their thick fur and broad, tufted feet, but when not about their mysterious Skogga-related business outdoors they could be indolent.

Not all Skogga were the same. This one had come early to the appreciation of a warm bed and a fish-based diet, and the realisation that fish could be had from hara without the bother of wet feet that getting them from the river entailed. This one was also a she-Skogga. In the summer, she would retire for a time to the outhouse and drop a litter of four or five kits, which would stay around the outhouse and gardens for a while and then depart about their own lives and business. Aisa did not understand why Skogga continued to divide themselves into male and female, rather than adopt the harish solution, but he assumed that they had some good reason for it to which he was not privy.

Nine (or was it ten?) Skogga had come and stayed during Aisa's tenure as High Rehuna and, after a good life profitably spent catching vermin and sleeping in the sun, they were all buried under the tallest pine tree at the bottom of the garden. Aisa did not know where they came from, but after a short period of respectful remembrance for the previous incumbent, another Skogga would show up and take over the position. The she-Skogga would not join her predecessors under the pine tree for some years yet, but already she had decided that the fireside was a better place to be on a chilly night than the outhouse, so she followed Aisa back as he carried his logs to the house, both har and Skogga anticipating with pleasure a warm evening spent in front of a crackling blaze, while outside the wind and the winter held the town in its grasp.

Aisa had created a dehar once. Or, at least, he had discovered one that already existed and named it. It was the dehar of the frost-flowers and his name was Kerankua. Kerankua's only job was to inscribe the ferns and cabbage-roses, which appeared on every pane of glass after a frosty night, and for half the year he attended to this duty with both dedication and precision. What he did the other half of the year Aisa did not know; whether he lay sleeping deep under the permafrost, along with the long-dead southern har, or whether he took himself off to Almagabra, there to bask under its warm sun on golden shores, feeling the grains of sand beneath his naked feet, as he created new designs for each snowflake that would fall that winter, it did not matter. Aisa welcomed him back each year like the old, beloved friend he was, and said farewell to him with reluctance as the green shoots of Bloomtide appeared.

There was still no sign of Kerankua that morning.

Instead, the dim half-light of the pre-dawn was eclipsed further by a thick mist, which hung heavy on every building, fence, tree and shrub. From the low eaves of Aisa's house, spiders' webs drooped, their invisible artifice now revealed by an array of tiny droplets of moisture. They were intricate and beautiful, in their own way, but Aisa missed the frost. He missed the way the grass crisped underfoot, the way his breath issued forth in steaming clouds, the intense blue of the sky, and the miracle of the frost-flowers, drawn everywhere with casual profligacy by Kerankua.

Aisa encountered few other hara as he made his way from his house to the High Chambers. At this time of year, most hara preferred to retreat to the comfort of their own homes and enjoy the days of Adkaya – the period between the dropping of the pearl of the new deharling and its hatching – with family and friends, as they made their preparations for the celebrations that would take place at Natalia. Aisa was glad of this. As High Rehuna, he was known to all the hara of the town, and they would often stop him in the street to greet him or wish him the blessings of the season, for this was held to be good luck. While Aisa, on the whole, appreciated their goodwill, there were times when he could wish for a little more in the way of the solitude of anonymity, and this was one of those times.

By the time he reached the High Chambers in the centre of the town, he was wet from the all-pervasive mist, damp and chilled to the bone in a way that the hard frost never found a way to do. He handed his dripping cloak to one of the few staff who were on duty, arranged his hair in what he hoped was a more orderly fashion and entered the Archon's private offices.

Inside the spacious room, a fierce fire was burning in the grate, for which Aisa was grateful. He resisted the urge to go over to it immediately and warm his backside at the flames, aware that this would be deemed rather indecorous for a har of his status.

On the opposite side of the room stood Tualenn and three hara whom Aisa did not recognise. Hot drinks had obviously been served at some point, but it appeared that, as the last to arrive, Aisa was not going to receive a similar courtesy.

Tualenn greeted him with a scowl. However, as this was Tualenn's default expression at this time in the morning, Aisa tried not read anything too ominous into it.

'Aisa, how good of you to join us.'

Aisa wondered if he ought to interpret this as a rebuke, but decided against it. Tualenn was not a subtle har, and if he had considered Aisa to have committed some sort of breech of etiquette by arriving later than the others, then he would have said so.

Tualenn turned to the other three hara beside him.

'Tiahaara, may I introduce our High Rehuna, Aisa har Kalls.'

The three hara studied Aisa carefully, as if he were some exotic pet brought forth for their entertainment. Aisa returned the compliment. Two of the hara had the same pale gold hair as himself, and their faces a familiar cast. Although he was not personally acquainted with either individual, he was sure he recognised them as being from the same northern tribe as many of the town's residents. The other har was dark of hair and skin, but he evinced nothing outwardly that would give a clue as to his tribe. Possibly Gelaming, from his superior expression, Aisa thought.

'Greetings to you.' One of the gold-haired hara addressed Aisa formally, although his expression was sympathetic. 'I am Mailainn har Mailaa. This is Katko har Mailaa and this is Mousebane har Sulh.' He indicated the fair-haired and dark-haired hara in turn. Aisa felt less than surprised to discover Mousebane was of the Sulh, for in his experience they were they only hara who could give the Gelaming a run for their money when it came to notions of their own innate superiority. Nevertheless, he smiled politely in return.

'And what brings you to Forra, Tiahaara? Have you come to celebrate Natalia with us?'

Mailainn did not reply immediately. He studied Aisa gravely. Aisa could not read his expression, but he did not look like a har who was anticipating the joys of Natalia.

'In part, Aisa. But our primary mission involves you.'

Aisa did not think he had ever heard a har describe his visit to

Forra as a *mission* before, and he felt slightly uneasy, for reasons he could not quite put his finger on. But over the years he had met many hara who possessed their own unique customs and habits, and he was used to accommodating them.

'I am honoured, Tiahaar, that you have travelled so far to meet with me. Do you wish to take aruna with me?'

This was by far the most common reason that visiting dignitaries to Forra would seek out Aisa personally. Some hara, however, were rather hesitant to state this directly, and he had found that it could save a lot of time and misunderstanding if he just addressed the issue in a forthright manner.

Mailainn, however, simply shook his head rather regretfully. 'Tiahaar, while I do not doubt that it would be a delightful experience, there is something else I want from you.'

Aisa smiled to cover his confusion. 'And what would that be?'

Mailainn glanced at Tualenn, who had been listening to the exchange carefully.

'Perhaps we should be seated, Tiahaar Tualenn,' Mailainn said, almost apologetically. 'It's… complicated.'

'Of course.' Tualenn indicated the array of low sofas and chairs near the fireplace, and allowed the visitors to take their seats before seating himself opposite. Aisa sat next to him, perching primly on the edge of the seat. Aisa was sure the last thing Tualenn wanted at that particular moment was to listen to some strange har's convoluted tale, but he took his duties as Archon seriously, always. This could be a blessing or a curse, depending on the situation.

Mailainn folded his hands neatly on his lap and gazed at Aisa thoughtfully for a moment before he began. 'Tiahaar… You are aware of the nature of the dehara… and what they represent?'

'Of course,' said Aisa, rather stiffly. As High Rehuna, he had dedicated his entire life to serving the dehara, acting as an intermediary between them and ordinary hara. It seemed a strange question to ask him, of all hara.

'You are aware that they are created by hara themselves. They are a manifestation of harish energy and harish nature and essence. Both hara and dehara are inextricably linked; one cannot exist without the other.'

'Indeed.' Aisa smiled thinly. It was going to be a long morning if Mailainn intended to lecture them on Wraeththu theology for the duration.

Mailainn leaned forward towards Aisa, a note of urgency creeping into his voice. 'Tiahaar... Not all harish nature is as pure and enlightened as some would have us believe. While Wraeththu have evolved further than humankind, we still have a long way to go before we achieve perfection. We still know hate and greed, and anger and resentment, and pride, and a whole host of other undesirable conditions, and these are sometimes reflected in the dehara we create.'

'What is it you are trying to tell me, Mailainn?' Aisa asked, filled with a growing suspicion that he wasn't going to like the answer to his question.

'Tiahaar, once, a long time ago, a dehar came into being who was a manifestation not of the best qualities of Wraeththu, but of its worst. He was a cruel and wanton dehar, who destroyed, but did not create. Once brought into being, he could not be unmade, but through the efforts of many powerful hara, he was contained and bound, so that his malevolence might not be unleashed upon this realm.'

'All has ended well, then,' Aisa said, hoping that this was true, and knowing that it was not.

Mailainn shook his head. 'Unfortunately, with the passing of time the bonds that hold him have weakened. He has begun to wreak his malice again, not only in this realm, but in others, and against the dehara who protect and nurture Wraeththu. Tiahaar, we are now at the very point in the turning of the seasons when the deharling of the new year will emerge from his pearl and begin the cycle of life once again. If Elisin does not come forth, the cycle cannot continue. Winter will not turn to spring, spring will not turn to summer, summer will not turn to autumn and autumn will not turn to winter. All life will stagnate and die.'

Aisa closed his eyes and felt a cold shiver pass through him. Never again to feel summer's warmth on his skin, or experience autumn's golden melancholy. Never again the miracle of the frost-flowers. Gone forever the promise of spring in the radiant countenance of the newly-hatched Elisin. Suddenly, the absence of the snow and the cold took on a more sinister aspect. The seasons were disrupted by a malign force, that much was obvious.

'What must we do?' he asked, pretending that he did not already know the answer, and hating himself for the coward that he was, avoiding the inevitable for a few seconds more.

'The hara who bound the dehar knew this day would come. All things end, and then begin again. They created a weapon to bind him, and passed it down through generations. And now that weapon must be used again. You know what I am speaking of, Aisa, for you have a part of it. As do I.'

Mailainn reached under his heavily-embroidered shirt and brought out a crystal on a chain. Without having to look, Aisa knew it to be the twin of the one he wore himself, the one he could feel burning with new intensity against his skin, under his clothing. Deep within the heart of Mailainn's crystal burned a greenish flame, flickering and becoming more intense as it sensed the presence of the hara around it.

At the same time, both Katko and Mousebane produced a crystal on a chain around their necks, one golden yellow and the other suffused with a pure violet light, and held them out as if for inspection. Aisa knew what was required of him, yet a last vestige of cowardice remained, and he hesitated for a moment before conceding defeat and pulling his own crystal out from under the layers of clothing that concealed it. It glowed with an icy blue light that matched his own eyes.

Tualenn, who had been uncharacteristically silent during Mailainn's revelations, now pulled himself forward on his seat and studied intently the objects held by the other four hara.

'Would one of you good hara kindly explain to me what exactly these things are? Aisa?'

He looked at Aisa enquiringly, but Aisa found that the words of explanation would not come. Instead, Mailainn answered the Archon's question.

'They are... sources of power, of energy, created during aruna between capable hara, and stored in these crystalline formats, which you see. The energy exists in many dimensions simultaneously; the crystal is the form in which it projects itself into this particular dimension.'

'And these can be used to control the rogue dehar?'

'The energy required to bind the dehar is split into five frequencies. By combining these frequencies, it may be possible to overcome him. Nothing is ever certain, however.'

Tualenn stared at the four crystals in front of him for a few moments, then, as was often his way, he made a particularly obvious comment. 'Five. You said five. I only see...'

'...four. Correct, Tiahaar. The energy crystals must form a symbiotic relationship with a har to release and direct their potential. It requires a har of power and ability to do this, and to be able to withstand the force of the crystal. And also to gain the co-operation of the crystals, for they are not always obliging creatures.'

'Are they... *alive*?' Tualenn's curiosity won out over professional decorum, and he stretched out his hand tentatively towards Mailainn's crystal.

Mailainn closed his fist around it and tucked it back under his shirt before Tualenn could make contact with it. 'In a way. They possess a degree of sentience. They have a will of their own. In order to control them, the will of the harish partner must be at least as great, or greater, than that of the crystal.'

Mailainn took a small leather pouch from one of his pockets, pulled open the drawstring at its neck and tipped the contents out onto the low table in front of him, being careful not to touch it. It was another crystal, similar in size and shape to the others, but lacking any light in its heart. It lay cold and seemingly inert on the table's surface.

'This crystal has no har. Once, it did. In fact, several hara have... *owned* is the wrong word... formed a *relationship* with this crystal, since it first came into being. But it is a particularly capricious entity. And picky. It has rejected more hara than it has chosen. Nevertheless, we will need its contribution, and we will need a har to direct it.'

'You are surely not suggesting that Archon Tualenn should become the partner of this crystal?' Aisa found he had spoken rather more sharply than he intended, but Mailainn did not seem perturbed. He looked up at Aisa with questioning eyes.

'Why not, Tiahaar? Archon Tualenn is a high-caste har of considerable ability.'

'The crystal is dangerous.'

'Of course it is.' Mailainn's voice hardened almost imperceptibly 'But that is the way of it. We live in dangerous times, Tiahaar, and risks must be taken.'

'There must be other hara who would be more suited to this task,' Aisa persisted.

'No doubt, but time is not on our side, Tiahaar. Tomorrow is Natalia Eve. And besides, the crystal makes its own choice. It appears that it may already have chosen.'

Aisa looked across at Tualenn, who had left his seat and crouched down in front of the low table where he stared in fascination at the crystal. Deep within its heart, a small red glow had come into existence, growing stronger even as Aisa watched.

Aisa knew what Tualenn was feeling at that moment, for he had felt it himself, many years ago. He knew that the crystal was singing its song inside Tualenn's head, whispering his name and calling to him.

He remembered his High Hostling holding out the glittering blue jewel, which dangled from its silver chain, and the almost unbearable urge to hold it, to possess it, to be one with it.

Be careful, Aisa, his High Hostling had warned, as Aisa reached for the crystal. *Don't let it overpower you. Don't let it have its own way. Be strong, Aisa.*

Mailainn spoke directly to Tualenn. 'Tiahaar, I will not lie to you. This crystal has killed before, and it may do so again. You must overcome it with your will and join your life-force to its own. If you cannot do that, it will kill you and seek another who can. You do not have to do this. You may refuse and nohar will think the less of you.'

The words were scarcely out of Mailainn's mouth before Tualenn scooped up the crystal from the table's surface, closing his fist tightly around it, as if he feared it might be taken from him. At once, a red glow appeared all around Tualenn's body, flickering like flames and shot through with hints of purple and magenta. The colours rippled ever more agitatedly for a few moments, then gradually steadied, to become a uniform red. Slowly, the glow faded until nothing was left except a spark of intense fiery red deep within Tualenn's dark brown eyes.

Aisa realised he had been holding his breath, and he let it out carefully, hoping neither Tualenn nor Mailainn had noticed.

Tualenn turned to Aisa, with an expression on his face that reminded Aisa eerily of The Skogga, when she had successfully liberated a fish from the long-suffering househar's supplies, using nothing but her own wiles.

Aisa successfully resisted the temptation to smack Tualenn across his face.

'The crystal accepts you,' Mailainn told Tualenn, rather unnecessarily. 'It will remain with you now until your death.' He turned to Aisa, who found himself fiddling unconsciously with the chain around his own neck. 'Tomorrow, you must conduct the ritual to bind the dehar. We must use the power of the crystals and the energy of our own life force to overcome him. We can only hope that it will be enough. Where do you usually hold the Natalia majhahn?'

'In the garden of my own home, but there is no altar, the river has not frozen…'

'It will not matter.' Mailainn cut Aisa off with a wave of his hand. 'All that matters is the energy we can summon. I suggest you return home now, Tiahaara, and prepare yourselves in the way you think most appropriate. We shall do likewise. Tomorrow, we will meet in the garden one hour before midnight. Be sure that everything is made ready.'

Mailainn and his two companions rose from their seats as one and glided noiseless from the room, their long winter robes dragging a little on the floor behind them. Tualenn looked at Aisa as if he were about to say something, but then he too unfolded his long limbs from the chair and followed the three hara out of the room without another word.

Aisa watched him go, then sat and stared at the door, seething inwardly, not sure entirely who or what he was angry with. He felt that Tualenn should have stayed and said something. Anything. He didn't know what.

The burning log in the fireplace spat a shower of sparks as it split and slumped. The room grew darker. After a while, Aisa got up and left.

The morning mist had turned to afternoon drizzle, and signalled its intention to become proper grown-up rain as evening closed in. There was a miserable greyness over the world that even the yellow flames of the candles could not hold at bay. Aisa stared out of the window morosely, but there was nothing to see – he could not make out the pines at the bottom of the garden, or even the outhouse. All was hidden by the grey curtain of rain. He was filled with a sense of loss, which he could not explain.

He had always found there to be something beautiful and almost sacred about this part of the day, at this time of the year, as the light ebbed away, and the snow began falling, silent and implacable, covering familiar shapes, deadening all sounds and bringing with it a sense of isolation from the world.

Many times, he had stood at this window and watched as the heavy flakes fell, and the stillness outside echoed his own thoughts. At such moments, he could feel again the presence of Elisin, the Child of Light. The dehar who had called to him and spoken his name, asking for a service which Aisa had been happy to give if it meant he could hear that voice for the rest of his life. He had kept this experience to himself, hidden like the crystal around his neck, revealing it only to one other, when it had become apparent it could no longer remain secret...

The sound of a visitor being shown into the next room interrupted Aisa's reveries. He knew who it was, and had been expecting him, but this was a conversation he did not want to have. There was no getting away from it, though. With a sigh, he left his station at the window and went through to the small, cosy sitting room where Tualenn was observing The Skogga, who was stretched out luxuriantly and belly up on a rug in front of the fire, her soft, furred pads turned skywards in supplication.

'That animal looks inordinately pleased with itself.' Tualenn noted.

'So would you if you constantly got the best seat in the house. Since that is already taken, may I offer you the second-best seat in the house?' Aisa gestured to one of the chairs on either side of the Skogga-covered rug.

Tualenn smiled graciously and sat down, drawing the chair in closer to the fire. He held his hands out towards the warmth, rubbing them briskly together.

'I hate this time of year,' he said, 'It's so dark and miserable. But at least after Natalia the days will be getting longer again.' He gave Aisa a wry smile, which Aisa returned. It was an article of faith among the hara of Forra that Natalia signified the end of winter, when in fact it was only the beginning – the coming months would see its icy grip tighten further, even as the light began to return.

As the days lengthen, the cold strengthens.

Summer was an entirely different matter in Forra. At Cuttingtide, the days stretched endlessly towards a perpetual twilight, when the sun merely dipped below the horizon for a brief moment, like a stone skipping across the water. Aisa could remember, as a harling, playing outside in the fields long after his official bedtime, oblivious to his hostling's entreaties to come inside, wishing that the summer would never end. These past summers, though, the endless daylight had left him unsettled and exhausted. He felt exposed, with nowhere to hide, and he had found himself longing for the silence of midwinter, and its comforting, concealing darkness.

He was tempted for a moment to ask Tualenn why he stayed in Forra if he hated the winter so much, but the question stayed wisely unasked, there being some use for experience after all.

Tualenn regarded him carefully, and Aisa knew what he was going to say, although he distracted himself by watching the thick dark lashes around Tualenn's dark eyes, marvelling at their length and no longer even feeling the envy that had been so long embedded in his soul.

'Why, Aisa?' Tualenn did not sound angry, which was quite unusual for him, and somehow Aisa found this unsettling

'Why what?' Aisa knew this was disingenuous, but he couldn't quite bring himself to answer Tualenn's question directly.

Tualenn made an irritated *tsk*-ing noise, which reassured Aisa that the Archon had not entirely had a personality transplant. He pulled the crystal from around his neck and held it on his palm in front of them both. The red glow within its depths seemed to have deepened and strengthened since the last time Aisa had seen it, as if it was drawing sustenance from Tualenn's own life force.

'You never said anything. All these years. You never even mentioned it. Not once. Why?'

'I...'

Didn't think it was important? Didn't want to tempt fate? Didn't want to give you something else to use as a weapon against me?

'... didn't think I would ever have to use it. I didn't think it would ever come to this point. Many hara have kept the crystal before me. It passed in and out of their lives, and on to others. I thought it would pass me by too. I thought it would pass to some other har, and then some other after him and it wouldn't be my responsibility, and it wouldn't be me who would have to use it, and now, apparently, it is.'

Aisa looked at Tualenn helplessly, unsure if this was a plea to be excused from his past transgression or from his current situation, but Tualenn said nothing, merely stared down at his hands clasped in his lap, as if they could be forced to give up the secret of how to resolve the unresolvable, if stared at hard enough. Long seconds passed, and a costive silence filled the air around them, condensed and solidified.

Aisa wanted desperately to explain, but he knew it would do no good. Tualenn was too stubborn; he always had been. Tualenn needed to control every aspect of his life, to have a rational explanation for everything, to make sense of the world. It was there, in every line of his body, from his stiffly-held posture to the tightly tied-back hair coiled at the nape of his neck. Aisa could still remember a summer, long ago, when that hair had loosed down into his lap, and they had fallen together in the long grass, laughing, sharing breath, so sure of themselves and what the future would bring. They had argued not long after, and it had seemed so important at the time, but the distance between then and now had blurred the lines and softened all the edges, so that some things seemed to matter less than they used to, and some things seemed all the clearer for the passing of time.

'I didn't lie to you,' he said quietly. 'The crystal... It was never about that. I wanted to be a rehuna. *Needed* to be. I had to serve the dehara. I had no option; it was what I was meant to do. And if I had my life to live over again, I would still make the same choice, and gladly, even knowing what I would have to give up. I never took a chesnari, never blood-bonded with another har, but if I had, Tua, it would have been you.'

He reached over and put his hand on top of Tualenn's, as if the physical proximity could convey the truth of his words in a way that speaking could not. Tualenn only nodded, quickly, clasping his other hand on top of Aisa's. They both sat and stared into the red embers and flickering flames of the fire for a while, caught between the half-remembered past and the very imminent future.

'Things rarely turn out as you expect them to,' Tualenn said, straightening his back and grimacing, 'However, it is gratifying to learn that we are neither of us too old to be surprised by an unexpected turn of events. I will leave you now, Aisa, so that you might spend the night preparing, in whatever ascetic way you think fit. Tomorrow will bring some challenges, I imagine. For myself, I intend to have a hot bath and more than one glass of wine. Possibly even gorge myself on some of those spiced cakes the househara have been so industriously producing these past days. Wouldn't want them to go to waste, would we?'

Tualenn rose, a little stiffly, and gave Aisa a mock-bow, and the one free tendril of his hair fell across his face. He pushed it back absent-mindedly, and seemed about to say something, thought better of it, then simply smiled and departed.

After Tualenn had gone, Aisa remained seated for a while. Not for the first time, he wondered about the life that might have been his. The harlings he might have had. His hand strayed automatically to the crystal around his neck, and he thought about the two hara who had created it during the ecstasy of aruna. Had they created a child at that moment too? He would never know. He would never know what it felt like to conceive and create another har, to bring it into the world and guide it on its journey to adulthood. That path was closed to him now, but he had chosen to nurture another child, the Child of Light, and come the morrow he would do everything within his power to ensure that Elisin would be safely born and grow to adulthood. It was all he could do. It was what he was meant to do.

He stretched out his foot and prodded The Skogga, who was now basking indolently with belly towards the dwindling embers of the fire.

'Come on, lazy, time for bed.'

The Skogga twitched the very tip of her tail, but otherwise did not move, so Ailsa bend down and picked her up, her furry body a dead weight that offered no resistance, and carried her off.

Among the hara of Forra, Natalia Eve was traditionally a time of both cheerful celebration and quiet reflection. Although many hara took the opportunity to begin their observance of the festival as early as possible, the day to day business of the town still needed to continue, and therefore it was unsurprising that the High Rehuna had spent the entire day in his study preparing for the festivities, admitting no visitors, speaking to no-har. The sun rose and set in short order, as was the way of things at this time of year, and an almost palpable hush of anticipation fell over Forra as its inhabitants awaited the events that would signal the beginning of a new cycle.

Still Aisa did not emerge from his study. He had requested that the househara bring him food on a tray, but he had no appetite, and merely picked at what had been prepared. Neither could he settle at his desk to write in his diary, as was his custom every evening. The book was almost full, each page from the beginning of the year to the end covered in his rather untidy handwriting. Yesterday's events were described in full, along with Aisa's thoughts and feelings on the matter, but today, this last day, this last page, remained a blank and Aisa could think of nothing whatsoever to write on it.

He sighed and laid down his pen. A new diary with empty pristine pages lay in the desk drawer, awaiting its baptism tomorrow. Perhaps when the sun rose again, he would have a story to fill those pages, but for now there was no more time. He opened the desk drawer and carefully put the old diary inside, on top of the unused one. Next to it was the gold and mother-of-pearl brooch, still patiently awaiting the time when Aisa might be grown-up enough to wear it. He took it out and fastened it to his overshirt, pushing the curved pin through the fabric. It lay against his shoulder, gleaming gold and nacreous in the light from the candles, and Aisa admired it, as if seeing it for the first time.

The clock on the wall said it was an hour before midnight. The sound of voices and footsteps could be heard from the garden outside, so Aisa took his thick cloak from the hook on the wall, arranged it around his shoulders and went out to join Tualenn, Mailainn, Katko and Mousebane, leaving The Skogga asleep and dreaming of inflicting sudden death upon innocent small creatures.

It was cold outside, yet not cold enough. A wind was blowing from across the river valley, making the tall pines sway and hiss overhead, their tops lost in the darkness above. Mailainn, Katko and Mousebane bowed politely to Aisa when he appeared, but Tualenn gripped his arm in a more intimate gesture than Aisa would have expected from him, and he found himself oddly glad of the reassurance it provided.

'You have the crystals?' Mailainn asked, retrieving his own from around his neck and holding it out as if for inspection. The others did the same. As they did so, the light contained within the jewels grew in intensity, as if they recognised each other, and drew strength from their proximity. A rainbow of colours illuminated the darkness, and it seemed to Aisa that they converged on the radiant blue gem he held in his own hand.

Mailainn closed his eyes and muttered a few words in a language Aisa did not understand.

'The Will and the Weapon,' Mailainn said slowly, 'The Weapon and the Will.' He looked at Aisa directly. 'Tiahaar, I have not been completely honest with you. We have a weapon to defeat the rogue dehar, it is true, but that is not enough. The crystals are like a sword, or a knife – beautiful and useless without somehar to wield them with intent. A weapon is of no use without the will to use it. *You* are the will, Aisa. The will is yours and yours alone.'

Mailainn drew a small sigil in the air in front of him.

Aisa felt strangely disorientated, as if the world had just subtly rearranged itself while he wasn't looking. 'What do you mean *I* am the will? I thought we had to combine the energies of the crystals… I thought this was a group effort?'

That was a lie, thought Aisa. He had assumed that Mailainn was in charge of this venture, and would be its leader. It was slowly dawning on him that Mailainn would not be assuming this position.

Mailainn shook his head slowly. 'Tiahaar, it is no trivial matter, to kill. Most hara are incapable of it. It scars the soul and leaves a stain that will not wash away. And yet, there are a few whose will is stronger than the pain. You are such a har, Aisa, even if you do not know it; you have a strength that will allow you to do this deed. To kill a dehar.'

Am I a killer? thought Aisa to himself, aghast. *Could I really take a life, however otherworldly?* But even as the thought entered his mind, he knew it was true. If it was what he had to do in order to protect Elisin, he would do it. No matter the cost. He had sworn to serve the Child of Light, and that vow was unbreakable.

'Then let's do it,' he snapped, 'while we still have time.'

Mailainn nodded gravely and took the hands of Katko and Tualenn, who had been watching the proceedings intently, but had said nothing. Katko joined hands with Mousebane and they stood there linked together in a chain. The crystals around their necks blazed with unearthly light. Aisa stood facing them, his crystal glowing brighter than any other, its icy blue radiance bleaching away his vision, but behind the light he sensed a darkness. A malign presence.

The sentience within the crystal seemed to recognise this presence and its attention was immediately drawn to it, quick and sure, the way The Skogga would instantly detect the slightest movement indicating the presence of a mouse. Aisa could feel its strength growing, and he wondered what sort of thing he had carried with him all his life without ever knowing its true nature.

The darkness grew as well, a monstrous, nameless thing. This malign dehar had no name, or none that was known to any har. Aisa felt tiny and impotent in its presence, but the power of the crystal flowed through him, fed by the energy of the other crystals. He tried to imagine himself as a weapon – a knife with an edge sharpened to a mere molecule of thickness, harder than steel or diamond. Unbreakable.

Still the darkness grew, and what he had thought before was monstrous was revealed to be only the tiniest part of something much, much larger. The realisation grew within him that the crystals' energy alone would not be enough to defeat this foe; it would require more. It would require his life-force itself. For a moment, Aisa felt his will falter, his resolve weaken.

Can I do this? he wondered *Am I strong enough?*

He thought of Elisin, tried to picture the dehar within his mind. No image came to him.

Focus, focus

He could see nothing. The light from the crystals was blinding, and his body now blazed with a searing aura as he poured his own life-force into the weapon that was forged from the combined energies of the crystals. Still, it was not enough. Still, the darkness grew. Aisa felt every atom of his body vibrating with energy and light. He could give no more. The darkness was stronger. He could not win.

He could feel the despairing efforts of his companions to force more energy through him from their crystals. Vision was gone from him, but he sensed Tualenn letting go of Mailainn's hand, Mailainn's sharp cry of warning, then the touch of Tualenn's hand in his own, the warm flood of Tualenn's own life force pouring into him, merging with his own, bolstering and strengthening it, fuelling it, increasing it beyond any point of endurance until finally – finally – the dark force blinked, stuttered, became a soundless scream, and was unmade by the light.

The raw energy burned away everything mortal from Aisa. His mind and soul were released. And as the molecules of his body flew apart to re-join the cosmos, at the very last he was aware of both the presence of Tualenn, soul to soul, and the face of Elisin smiling down at him, content. And he knew that he had won.

Under the pine trees, an intense silence reigned, broken suddenly and shockingly by the baying of celestial hounds, ringing clear across the midnight sky. Where once had stood two hara was now only a vacant space, and two small crystalline objects lying amidst the pine needles.

As Mailainn bent to pick them up, he turned his face skywards and felt a cold, feathery touch against his face as the snow began to fall, soft, silent and slow.

Yed patted the last of the packed snow into position, then stood back to admire his handiwork. He tilted his head and bit his lower lip critically. It wasn't bad – for a first attempt. The altar he had created was sturdy and functional, but, he felt, he had also managed to add a little artistry to its construction in the form of a few wave-like ripples decorating its supporting sides.

Considering that he had never seen snow until three months ago, he thought that it was a good effort. He experienced once again the thrill he had felt when those first heavy flakes had begun to fall out of the sky, spontaneously appearing in the air above him as if from nowhere and landing on his nose, forehead and out-stuck tongue with a brief, freezing kiss before vanishing.

It was a magic he was sure he would never grow tired of. The delicate flakes landed on the ground, one by one, until they achieved the seemingly-impossible and covered it entirely, and then more and more, until it came past his knees and he had to wade through it, as though he were walking through the sweet white icing on top of one of his hura's delicious Rosatide cakes. To his delight, he had discovered that the stuff was malleable and could be moulded into any shape or form a har could imagine, including the altar he was now so proud of.

For a moment, he felt a brief pang of homesickness as he thought of his family, so far away, and wondered again if he had done the right thing when he had agreed to go with those strange hara who had appeared in his town from the Otherlanes half a year ago, bringing with them the freezing air and alien scents of another clime, back to this strange place with its unreliable sun, which stayed out too late in the summer and sulked below the horizon in winter.

And yet – when they had asked him to return with them to Forra to become its High Rehuna and serve Elisin, the Child of Light, he had suddenly known – *known* – in the very depths of his soul, in that instant, that it was the right thing to do. That it was what he wanted to do. That it was what he was meant to do.

And so, he had abandoned his previous life in his sunny home by the warm sea, and had left behind his family and friends, and he had never felt happier or more fulfilled in his life.

Now, after scarcely two seasons as Forra's High Rehuna, came the most important day of the Great Cycle. It was Natalia Eve and tomorrow Elisin would emerge from his pearl and begin the cycle of life and death once more. It would be the first time that Yed had conducted the ceremony. It was an enormous responsibility, and he wanted everything to be just right.

He arranged the small collection of items on the surface of the altar – the golden *vakei*, the tall white candles and the glass bowl of glittering gold flakes, (he had no idea what those were for, but he was sure he would find out soon enough).

In the centre, he gently placed another object. A metal pin, made of gold inlaid with mother-of-pearl. The pin was bent and twisted, and the mother-of-pearl broken in several places. It would never again be of use, yet it was a sacred item.

Yed knew the story of what had happened to the previous High Rehuna of Forra. The hara who had brought him here had told him everything. And he had wondered to himself whether he, Yed, would be capable of such a sacrifice, if the need arose. He did not know. No-har knew, until the moment came, what he was or was not capable of. Perhaps Yed, in his turn, would be called upon to discharge his duty to the utmost. Perhaps not. In many ways, it was a good thing that the future was uncharted, for what har could face each day with courage if he knew what lay in store for him?

In the meantime, there were many other things to occupy his time and his mind. He placed the last item on the altar – a handful of gold coins, a gift from the town's new Archon. Yed had been surprised and rather overwhelmed to be given such a valuable disbursement – he did not feel he had quite earned it yet – but Gull, the househar, had laughed at him and shown him that the metal was very thin and could be peeled back to reveal a delicious sweet treat underneath.

Gull had also informed him, with a slight twinkle in his eye, that the proffering of this type of sweetmeat was very often a romantic overture. Yed wasn't entirely sure that Gull wasn't teasing him, but if it were true, then it would be one more thing to enjoy about life in Forra, because the Archon was a delight to behold, golden-haired and long of limb, and Yed could quite easily see himself making a few romantic overtures himself in the Archon's direction, leading dreamily in his imagination to a highly satisfactory and pleasurable conclusion for both of them.

Filled with the anticipation of all the good things that the future seemed to hold for him, Yed gave the altar once last inspection, then turned to go back to the house – and almost tripped over the creature called The Skogga, who had performed its usual trick of appearing from nowhere and looking as if it would continue to make a nuisance of itself until food was forthcoming.

The Skogga had been the companion of the previous High Rehuna. *Belonged to* seemed the wrong words to use, as least as far as The Skogga was concerned.

Yed found himself pleased that some aspect of the previous High Rehuna's life still remained here, in the home where he had lived. It felt to him like a connection to a har he had never known – a memento of a life not terminated but completed. A thread unbroken, and a promise that life would continue, the seasons would turn in their eternal cycle, and though summer ended, spring would come again.

With an encouraging noise to The Skogga, he headed back towards the house and the warm fire and the supper that awaited them, each in their own way filled with the joy and contentment of being a har and a Skogga in this place, at this moment in time.

In the distant town, a bell pealed and voices sang in praise of the birth of a new year, as once again the snow began to fall.

Rosatide

February 1st

This festival is named for the fact that the trees become rosy with new growth at this time. The last grey white days of winter are marked by the colour of blood as life begins to rise and surge from the earth.

Elisin is now beginning to grow and his hostling has transformed from his soume (female) aspect into Eburniel, the fur-clad dehar of the snow-covered earth. All early spring flowers, especially those with white petals, are sacred to him. He has nurtured Elisin, borne him from his body and now devotes himself to teaching the deharling the lessons necessary to maturity and eventual solitude. Eburniel teaches Elisin how to imbue the earth with his life-giving energy to encourage new growth.

Traditionally, this is the Festival of Torches, as hara seek to bring the growing light of the sun into their life. Eburniel is also the light of the candle flame. On Rosatide eve, candles and lamps are lit in every window. The shadowy figure of Eburniel, dressed in a cloak of snow white fur, walks across the fields and through the forests. His animal is the white wolf, whose breath is freezing mist.

The wistfulness sometimes associated with this festival derives from the fact that, in assuming a more ouanic (masculine) aspect, Eburniel faces the prospect of his own death at Cuttingtide. If the early spring flowers are found sprouting from snow, they are Eburniel's tears. Despite this aspect, Rosatide is a time of hope and promise. As light fills hara's homes, so they banish the bleakness of the short days and cold weather.

A Message in Ashes

Storm Constantine

The woods and the town covered in snow,
All transformed to a fairy tale,
Like the fresh page of a book opened up,
Ready, waiting, for the story to begin,
For you're all in a scene.
Objects in black ink, fringed in white,
Breathing and living,
And anticipating
A colour.
All transformed to a fairy tale,
Unreal and inviting, inviting you to step in
And follow the path never ending

Red running over white
Red running over white…

From 'Red Over White' by Siouxsie and the Banshees

I was no more than six years old when I met the dehar Eburniel in the forest. This was long before I'd realised I'd share my see'ver's calling as a dryadhar, and until that moment the dehar who'd most fascinated me was Elisin who, my parents told me, was the growing sun. As Elisin was a harling like me, albeit a *de*harling, I loved him above all. As he grew and transformed through the procession of the seasons, taking on different names and appearances, and became fierce, tricksy and/or melancholy, my interest dwindled. To me, the best festivals were when Elisin walked among us as the harling of light. He, after all, persisted through four turns of the year's wheel, whereas all the grown dehara reigned only over one.

That day, a week or so after we had celebrated Rosatide, I was out alone in the winter forest. Where my tribe lived, it was perfectly safe for a harling to do so. My family were part of a small phyle of thirty-eight hara affiliated to the Unneah, who had settled in this isolated corner of the northern, tree-bristled mountains decades before, to escape the last of the Devastation further south. Our nearest neighbouring phyle lay to the west, over seven miles away. Others were scattered throughout the high forests; we met them sometimes at communal gatherings. We traded with phyles in the valleys, whose lands were more suited to farming than ours. But mostly we kept to ourselves. Our way was to live in harmony with the earth, taking nothing more than we needed, and giving as much as we gave. My hostling said we owed this to the world.

So there I was, out in the wilderness, with ice cracking in the lofty branches above me; the forest otherwise silent. I carried a staff my hostling had fashioned for me, and was swathed to my nose in a heavy, fur-trimmed cloak. Thick boots came up to my thighs, and within the watertight leather my feet were swaddled in socks that kept out most of the cold. Around me, as I followed a perfect, crunching path, the immense, motionless pines were heavy with snow, and the silence was unearthly. I saw tracks in the white that revealed the path of snow hares and foxes. I could walk almost without sound; only a deer might hear me – or somehar using senses other than hearing. But I was not here to hunt. My see'ver had sent me to search for Eburniel's Tears, those brave little bells that poke through the snow, white as winter's breath, but with veins of green within the bloom. For Rosatide magic, when life first begins to stir within the earth, the Tears are crucial; they are the essence of this season.

I hummed a song beneath my breath as I walked, my eyes scanning the snow beneath the trees, but my mind elsewhere, making up stories as I usually did when alone, for later recital around a communal fire.

I recall exactly how I was jolted from my reverie. There was no sudden sound, no birds clattering up, no change of temperature or anything else to sense directly. I simply became alert and wary, and stooped into a posture of defence by instinct, my staff held in both hands across my body.

I was on a wide path between the trees that disappeared into a misty haze ahead of me. From this mist, a tall figure emerged. I didn't sense familiarity, and thought at first it must be a har from Gnarly Root in the west, perhaps hunting or even coming to speak with us. I couldn't yet see his face, because he was some distance away and also wore a cloak with a concealing hood. I called a formal greeting, but he didn't respond. Gradually, I began to wonder whether this was a propitious meeting or not. I felt threatened, and in my experience physical threat lay only in the weather, the landscape or predatory animals, not in other hara. So this feeling was unusual and unnerving. I began to back away, deciding that once I felt comfortable with the distance, I'd turn and run, fleet as a hare, back to safety. Yet as I walked backwards, the har approached me swiftly. He did not stride, but somehow seemed to float above the snow. As he drew nearer, I thought he must be a spirit, and they can be hostile, sometimes. But then he threw back his hood and smiled at me. Once I could see his face, my misgivings simply evaporated. He was beautiful and his expression was benevolent.

'What do you want with me, spirit?' I asked, touching my brow with the fingers of one hand, as a gesture of respect and good intention.

He appeared solid and real to me. His skin was dark brown, his hair black, and woven with ivy and crow feathers. He was, like me, covered by a thick, dark cloak, but he carried no weapon. There was a feel of the warrior about him – a sovereignty of ouana perhaps – yet his eyes held the softness of a hostling's nurturing glance.

'Will you not answer me?' I asked in a voice that now faltered.

He had come to a halt some feet away, still regarding me steadily. Spirits don't manifest like this unless they want something, or perhaps sense wanting in a har who doesn't realise themself they have a yearning.

'I'm looking for my son,' he said, in a voice that sounded like three voices, of different timbres, speaking all at once. My see'ver had once told me of ghosts who wandered the land, who were the essence of several hara – sad, lost creatures from the time of war. Was this what I was facing?

'I've seen nohar,' I said.

'He is everywhere,' said the har and moved towards the trees to my right. 'He was here. Come.'

Curious, I followed and looked to where he pointed. There, among the roots, where the snow was thin, the bells of Eburniel's

Tears broke through the earth, defiant of the season, flowers blooming in a cold so fierce it should wither such delicate petals. He had brought me to the end of my search. I bent down to pick some of the blooms. As I looked at them, so more were coming up through the hard ground, determined, narrow green leaves, and then buds, opening to flowers in seconds. Water dripped onto them, which I took as a sign of thaw.

I looked up at the spirit har. 'Thank you, Tiahaar,' I said and saw that he was weeping silently. His tears alone conjured blooms from the cold earth. I knew then who he was. Strangely, I was not surprised, but merely awed – grateful, even.

'Born to die,' he said, in his strange, layered voice, 'and to be reborn, to grow and die.'

'I know, Tiahaar,' I murmured, 'that we might live.'

'You made us this way,' he said, and his voice was resigned rather than resentful. I knew at once he spoke the truth, because my parents had taught me well. The story of the seasons has its moments of joy, but death is never far away. In the spring of life, we carry the inevitability of winter. When we welcome the sun as it grows strong, we are aware always of its decline, the cold darkness.

'I'm sorry,' I said, because I could think of nothing else to say. I might live hundreds of years, yet a dehar lives only a season, like a shimmering, delicate insect.

There were some moments of quiet, as he stood beside my crouching form, a peace between us; an immense yet tiny understanding. 'I will think of you,' I said at last, but realised I was speaking only to empty air.

After gathering up the sacred flowers, I ran home. For a few moments, I had felt like a wise hienama, far older than my years; now I was a harling again, excited and desperate to share my adventure.

Amberfall, our sett, was surrounded by a high wall of wooden pikes, covered with branches and moss. The gates, though, were always open. My parents' dwelling – a low stone house of one story with a domed thatch roof – was in the middle of the sett, next to an open space where rites and celebrations were held.

When I reached home, my parents were both in the kitchen. I flung open the back door, and warmth billowed out to enfold me, the warmth of hearth and hearts.

'What is it, Nooni?' my see'ver Balani demanded, hurrying towards me. He took me in his arms, kissed my head. 'What's happened?'

I pulled away from him and offered the gift of flowers. 'Eburniel gave me these,' I said.

I described what I'd experienced and my assumptions about it. They didn't question my story, because while I was certainly the kind of harling to invent stories, I never lied about reality.

My hostling, Corva, had remained seated at the long kitchen table, where we could seat eight guests if necessary. Now, looking up from his work of mincing herbs for his philtres, he said, 'You went in between. The snow, the quiet, the rhythm of your feet against the ground – these things can conjure a trance. You met Eburniel in a place beyond where you usually are.'

I accepted this explanation without argument, although privately believed it was more as if Eburniel had stepped into our world than I had stepped into his. Despite his calling, my hostling was a realist.

My see'ver said, 'Corva, this is a sign he follows our path.' And to me he said, 'Do you feel this too, Nooni?'

I'd not been aware they'd been waiting for a sign. My hostling was the phyle hienama, my see'ver the highest of its dryadhara. I'd always believed, when I paused even to think about such things, my future would lie in a similar occupation. Their way of life was what I knew.

'Don't rush things or put ideas into his head, Bala,' said my hostling. 'Now is his time to be a harling. Let him be.'

My see'ver grinned at me, but said nothing. He was not in the mood for a quarrel.

Eburniel, I later – long later – realised, had not come to me to indicate a path, but for another reason. He was a foretelling.

In the spring-time, after Bloomtide, a stranger came to our sett. His name was Cutter, a har whose mere gaze offered challenge. He was strongly-built, and his face was square with wide cheekbones. His hair, hanging loose to his shoulders, was the colour of dried grass. He had a harling with him called Darys, who was a year or so older than me.

Cutter had been sent, by a convoluted route of well-meaning advisors, to my hostling's hearth. He announced he had need of strong healing or – failing that – strong magic, because his harling was unsound. Darys was weak and often became ill, in the way animals can. Sometimes he could not move from his bed. We discovered fairly quickly that many hienamas had tried and failed to remedy this condition.

How Darys could have been born to a har like Cutter was a mystery to me. Darys was thin and pale, whereas his hostling was robust and tanned. Darys's hair was a burst of blackness, too much for so slight a creature. He wore it braided to his waist, and it was as if the muscular plait belonged to another har entirely; it seemed to weigh him down. He was ethereal, sometimes lovely, sometimes a little grotesque to behold. We could see at once he was sickly, something I'd never witnessed before and found shocking. Corva had heard of such a condition, though; he considered the aruna that had sparked the pearl was to blame, rather than the growing time within the hostling's body afterwards. When he asked Cutter about Darys's see'ver, the har looked blank, until my hostling said, 'Seed-giver?' Still blank. 'Father?'

'Oh, *him*,' said Cutter, and shrugged. 'He doesn't even know about the ling. Didn't realise, and I never wanted him to. We'd taken a dream nostrum; it changed us, but only for short while. Darys was made in that time, but I thought it was a dream. When I found out it wasn't, the other was long gone.' He gibbered a wordless sound of contempt, said nothing more.

Corva drew in his breath through his nose. 'I'll do what I can,' he said coldly, 'although can make you no promises.'

Inevitably, because Darys spent much time in my home, we became friends. But I was wary at first, and in fact used to leave the house when Darys was there. The sight of him unsettled me. He was polite, quiet and appeared eager to please, yet was faltering in his movements, unsure of everything. He was not tiny and wizened, but fairly tall; gangly like a colt or a calf. He did all my hostling asked of him, which first involved observation of his body as it moved, so that Corva could ascertain what it was capable of and what it was not. Then, Corva smelled Darys's breath, his skin, his hair. He examined the harling's faeces and urine, took some of his blood for various experiments. He prescribed a variety of herbal syrups and certain foods. These Darys must consume for a month, then the tests would be resumed. Corva told me all about it, because I was morbidly curious, and my hostling considered this part of my education and held nothing back.

We were eating dinner, about a week after Darys and Cutter had arrived. Balani asked how Darys was responding to the treatment.

'This won't take weeks, or even months. It might take years,' Corva replied. '*If* it's effective at all.' He shook his head, his expression bleak. 'The way he's lived hasn't helped, moving around all the time, no care taken, no proper analysis of his condition. It would have been better if he'd come here much sooner.'

'You *can* cure him, though?' I asked.

'No, because he's not ill,' Corva said briskly, 'merely malformed. There might be a way to strengthen him, so that his body wakes up enough to take control, make him properly har.' He grimaced. 'There's a reason harlings require some effort to create, but even so it seems the feckless can still manage it, somehow.'

'Corva, *enough*,' Balani murmured softly but admonishingly, with a "not in front of Nooni" tone.

'It's right Nooni knows of these things,' Corva snapped. 'It's appalling.' He shook his head. 'Darys is a poor little twig – cursed before he was born.'

'You'll help him,' Balani said confidently.

I believed that too.

The morning following this conversation, Corva asked me to take Darys into the forest with me, when I went to do my gathering. (I'd gather whatever the sett would find useful – wood, fungus, herbs, carrion.) We'd learned that usually Cutter left Darys indoors, wherever they happened to be living, and he rarely walked about. Consequently, he had spent a lot of time alone, or with kind strangers who offered (or were paid) to care for him, while Cutter did whatever Cutter wanted to do. Corva believed the air, the power of the landscape, would be restorative for Darys. I was reluctant to be part of this rehabilitation and complained, but Corva silenced me with a look. 'Don't fear him,' he said. 'And don't pity him, either. Just try to be… useful.'

Cutter had been given a wooden, three-roomed cottage as a temporary home, which still smelled of pine sap. The phyle kept it well-tended for occasional visitors, but Cutter had already managed to make a mess of it. When I went to call for Darys, Cutter was surprised to see me, and said, 'He doesn't usually go out much.'

'Corva said he should,' I answered, aware of my hostling's tone in my voice.

Cutter shrugged. 'As you like.' He called for his son and told him to put a coat on. I heard movements in the room beyond the threshold; an animal stirring.

'Did you live in a city once?' I asked, fairly confident of the answer.

'Yeah, nowhere like this,' Cutter replied, folding his arms. 'I like the old cities. It's too quiet for me here.' He leaned against the door frame. 'Still, I could get no help where we were. Nohar had any idea what to do with Darys. I just kept moving on. But hara spoke good of your hostling. He's the best, they say. Let's see.' He turned into the room. 'Darys, this har's waiting. Get a move on.'

Darys came into the light, slightly stooping, a wry smile on his face. I saw in him then the har he might've been, perhaps the har he would become. We went outside together.

I headed towards the forest. I didn't know how to begin a conversation and the silence became heavy. Eventually Darys said, 'I'm not always ill. You can't catch it. I'm not that different from you. Can we move on from the awkwardness now?'

I glanced at him sidelong. He wasn't like how he usually was, trying to please Corva. 'You like animals? I can show you some.'

'OK.'

We walked in silence most of the time, but it had become less difficult to bear. After a while, Darys said, 'I can feel it waking up… the land. I enjoyed the journey here, although it was cold and made me ache.'

I couldn't think of a response to these remarks and merely answered, 'mmm.'

A stag strode across our path, followed by three does.

Darys drew in his breath. 'Are they real?'

'Is that a real question?' I asked, somewhat tartly.

'It's just they're so perfect.'

The deer ignored us, disappeared between the trees.

Darys's wonder at the world almost made me envious. Aspects of nature I took for granted, he saw as miracles. He didn't know much about the dehara, had heard some of their names, that was all. I told him the story of Eburniel and Elisin, although decided I didn't know him well enough to relate my meeting with Eburniel.

Perhaps, another time, I might tell him.

'In this place, in the silence and darkness, the dehara must walk,' Darys decided.

I said nothing.

'Don't you believe in them that way?' he asked.

I didn't want to tell him just how much I did. 'We all have our own beliefs.'

'So, if I believe that, I might see them. Is that what you're saying?' He laughed. He didn't really believe.

Still, I liked the way he had spoken. Perhaps, if he was lucky, and continued to impress me, I might teach him what I knew. At that age, I was unaware that even the greatest of hienamas may start off proud and vain.

I took him to deep glades where the sunlight comes down through the high canopy like liquid gold. The more we explored, the more introspective he seemed to become – perhaps wondering if the magic of the wilderness had the power to make him whole.

We went out together most days after that. Balani made two pairs of socks for Darys, and we had one of the sett leatherworkers fashion some boots for him – his own clothes were mostly unsuitable for tramping through the forest in the early parts of the year. Cutter claimed to see improvements in his son, and I thought he was right, but when I asked Corva about it, he would still utter grunts, as if he wasn't sure.

There were six other harlings of various ages in the sett, and part of my vanity derived from the fact they looked up to me – because of who my parents were, and I was good at inventing mystical sayings that made me sound wise. (I'd merely learned to parrot some of my hostling's sayings.) As I'd allowed Darys to be my friend, the others didn't treat him badly, but nohar grew close to him as I did. I can recall the exact moment when I realised I was fond of him. It wasn't that I suddenly found him beautiful, or that he uttered profound words that touched my heart. It was simply a laugh.

One afternoon that summer, we were sitting with my best friends, Vixa and Kree, on the banks of a stream that tumbled down a hillside not far from the sett. Vixa had just made a joke – a poor one, I can't remember it – and Darys released this extraordinary peal of laughter. It was so *full*, somehow, so genuine, like a clarion call of nature itself. I glanced at him, startled.

He said, 'What?'

And I realised I loved him, that his restoration was the most important thing in the world. This wasn't a physical love, but something else, perhaps what hara feel for a brother.

Kree once said to me, 'He doesn't seem that ill, just a bit… different. Is he getting better?'

'Yes,' I said. If I believed it strongly, it must be so. He certainly wasn't getting any worse.

There was no indication that Cutter wanted to leave Amberfall. He claimed he was happy to settle there, but as the year wore on, he became restless. Darys could sense this and told me so. 'He'll want to move on,' he said sadly. 'He always does.'

'He can't!' I snapped. 'He can't be that selfish.'

Darys shrugged. 'He won't want to spend the winter here.'

'Do you want to stay?' I asked, aware of a nervousness within me.

'Of course. This is the first time I've lived properly, had friends who really want to be friends.'

Cutter, of course, was also aware of this. He wasn't a bad har, simply a flighty one. He came to speak with Balani and Corva one evening, and from his tense posture, it was clear he had something difficult to say. I felt sick. This was it. He was going to tell us he and Darys were leaving.

My prediction was only part right. Cutter began his clearly well-rehearsed speech by saying he knew Darys should stay here until he was completely whole, but however much he knew about his son and what was right, Cutter knew himself too. He was missing life in a town, he said, and was torn.

I saw my hostling exchange a glance with my see'ver, and sensed the silent communication that passed between them.

'Cutter,' Corva said, 'I can tell you're at the start of a long justification, followed by an embarrassed request, so let's just dispense with all that, shall we? If you wish to leave and take up your previous life, Darys may remain with us.'

Cutter stared at Corva, wide-eyed, clearly wondering what the appropriate response to this should be, other than the cry of relief he was desperate to expel.

Corva smiled, and it wasn't cruel. 'This wouldn't make you a bad hostling, but a good one. You know what's best for Darys isn't what's best for you. You fear you would resent him if you stayed here – so go. Return when you can – and make an effort to do so. That will be a small price to pay. You *did* make the harling after all, nostrum or not. You have a responsibility, but we are happy to share it.'

Cutter uttered a wordless sound and embraced my hostling, who, after a moment's surprise, warily returned it.

I expected my parents to suggest Darys should move into our dwelling, but they didn't. He was sensible enough to look after himself to a large degree. He could remain in the cottage that had become his home, close to everyhar else, should he need help, but distant enough to have independence. It was agreed he would take his evening meals with us, though, so that Corva would have a measure of control over his eating habits. Balani explained to me that these arrangements would give Darys confidence, and make him realise his neighbours respected him, didn't regard him as a helpless freak.

Cutter left before the early autumn festival of Smoketide, and we held a small celebration to show him he would forever be a part of our community and could return when he wished. Not everyhar felt the same about him. Some considered Cutter a shallow, careless creature, but they did what my hostling told them. It was better for Darys that way, to believe the fiction. They didn't know Darys that well, I thought. He wasn't fooled.

The next morning, I went to see him and found him tidying his home. Already, it seemed as if his hostling had never lived there.

'Are you sorry Cutter has gone?' I asked.

Darys expelled one of his beautiful laughs, but it was soft. 'He was never really here,' he said, 'not in the way Corva and Balani are here for you.' He sighed through his nose. 'He's my friend, and I'll miss him, but I'd miss my life here more.'

He looked tired, the skin dark around his eyes, which I thought must be because he'd stayed up nearly all night. For some reason, I felt compelled to say, 'You're so much better.'

He smiled at me. 'I feel...' He shook his head. 'It hasn't just *gone*, Nooni. I'm not like you, never will be. It takes great effort to be anything like you.'

'You hide it well,' I said and hugged him. He remained strangely rigid in my arms, so that I felt I had to let go. 'Believe you are well and you will be.'

He looked at me in a way that reminded me how quickly harlings grow, and that a year between us might soon feel like ten.

Throughout the next year, I told myself Darys was getting stronger. There were moments during the winter, which that year was harsh, when my faith wavered. I saw a har fall sick, which I'd never seen before. I'd witnessed the consequences of accidents – gory wounds, broken limbs – but never this *failing* of the body.

The first time it happened was just after Natalia, when we'd welcomed in the new year. When the sickness struck, it was so severe we didn't know about it until Darys failed to appear for his evening meal. I'd been to Gnarly Root that day with Balani, to stock up on some items that my see'ver needed from the hienama there, so we weren't aware Darys hadn't left his cottage that morning. Corva had assumed Darys had gone on the trip with us. Now, with food cooling on the table, we realised something was wrong.

I went to his cottage and he didn't answer my knock on the door. I went inside and found Darys gasping in his bed unconscious, his body hot and damp, the skin around his eyes a purplish red. He seemed to be drowning. We found out later that the illness had come on suddenly the previous night. Panicking, I ran to fetch Corva, who at once took calm control. Throughout that night, Corva managed to lower the fever, clear the lungs a little.

I was repulsed by it all, part of me reluctant to be near Darys, another part of me screaming inside with terror for a har I loved. I prayed to Elisin, who was strong in the land at that time, newly born. I apologised for my neglect, and for the way I'd not spoken with the dehara all the time about Darys, invoking their different powers to heal him. In my meditation, Elisin, the golden deharling, held out his hands to me and smiled. I took those hands, took his light into me through them. 'Touch him too,' I pleaded, but the deharling only continued to smile at me. I resolved that Elisin had put his power into me to effect healing. This I did – every day – my hands hot upon Darys's chest. Sometimes, I caught Corva gazing at me with an unreadable expression in his eyes.

The crisis passed. My hostling told Darys he mustn't go outside for any length of time until the spring, and could instead work with Corva in the house. He moved in with us, in fact. The illness made a weak attempt to reclaim him in the fortnight before Rosatide, but this time Corva was ready, recognised the signs, and smote the enemy before it could take hold.

'You see,' Darys said to me from his bed, as I sat beside him. 'This is part of me, and nothing Corva can do will truly end it.'

'Bad magic to say that,' I snapped. 'Believe you can heal and you will.'

He took my hand, squeezed it slightly. 'I'm less afraid than you.'

A year had made quite a difference to me too, and as Rosatide drew near I could feel I wasn't the same harling who the year before had met Eburniel in the forest. I had a sense of how I would eventually grow away from Elisin and this saddened me. Still, the end of winter was in sight and Amberfall prepared for the festival. We made plaits of dead rushes we'd gathered from beside forest pools and with these adorned eaves and front doors to our dwellings, so the dehara could find us easily. The hara of Amberfall fashioned a crown of woven twigs, adorned with last year's leaves and acorns, from the sacred oak grove at the heart of the forest. Eight candles were secured to the crown.

The main function of the sett dryadhar was the spiritual life of the community; this har must be close to the earth. Balani would be leading the Rosatide arojhahn, and the dryadini, his grove attendants, came to our house to help him prepare. They clad him in rust-coloured brushed leather, stitched with feathers and leaves, and a long cloak the colour of autumn's gown. As they adorned him, he remained silent, gazing ahead, beautiful and unearthly, his long red hair unbound around him. I sat by the stove, watching the preparations. Corva seemed to fold his wings and take a step back from the proceedings. This was Balani's night, and he must not be overshadowed.

When all was ready, hara lit the candles upon the oaken crown and Balani got to his feet. Now, he would lead a torchlit procession from the sett to the grove. In this place, our most sacred rites were conducted, bondings and namings and words for the dead.

Silently, hara left their dwellings and joined the procession; Balani at its head, followed by his dryadini, then Corva, Darys and I walking just behind them. All of us carried torches that stained the snow a soft, glowing orange. Darys was wrapped in heavy garments, and was still having difficulty breathing freely, but even

Corva wouldn't have prevented him from joining our rite that night. Gradually, we began to singly softly, at first little more than an insect hum, building to low calls of animal and bird, until a wistful melody unfurled within it. Balani walked barefoot, even though the path was hard and cold and dusted with snow. He did not feel the cold, for he was a dryadhar, kin to the trees and the land, more sprite than har, so they said. He talked to the spirits of the land for us and, at the festivals, the dehara talked back to us through him.

As we walked, I searched for Eburniel in the shadows of the trees beyond the path. I'd searched for him earlier too, but he'd not come to me in the forest. Still, I'd found some of his Tears and had murmured a prayer for Darys. I'd taken the flowers home to Balani, who'd sewn them into a linen pouch for Darys to wear about his neck.

At the grove, before a bonfire, Balani called upon the dehara – Eburniel, Elisin and also Panphilien, who was all dehara and more. He asked that our animals might breed, that the fruit and vegetables we grew would be bountiful, that our neighbours down in the valleys would grow much grain and other produce we traded for, that a harling might be given to the phyle, that any accidents not be fatal. Hara threw into the fire round buds of resin and herbs that Balani had moulded that morning. As each bud hit the flames, and hissed, and gave up its fragrance, the one who'd thrown it made a wish. Mine, of course, was 'Make Darys strong and well.' I don't know what Darys wished for; perhaps the same.

After this, Balani lay down beside the fire and opened his clothes to take aruna. Corva stood over him and uttered words in a language nohar knew but him. Then he too opened his clothes and sank down beside my see'ver. This was for our senses, perhaps, but not for our eyes. Their privacy was respected in that way. Hara threw cloaks over them, until all we could see was an undulating mound of cloth. I heard Balani's bleating cries, and then the harsher crow call of Corva as they reached the peak of their pleasure. A wave of energy, like a curtain of invisible light, pulsed out of them, tingeing us all with its glow. They had made me this way, years before, and as their light touched me, so I remembered being made, yet it was a dream, not real. Darys reached for my hand. He was trembling.

After this rite, Balani and Corva rose from their nest of cloaks, and it was time for the feast to begin. At the fire, we drank wine and toasted one another, then wound our way back to the sett, where food awaited us in the communal hall. Darys walked quietly beside me, and I was concerned he was sad. 'What's wrong?' I asked him. 'You should be happy.'

'I saw him,' Darys said. 'Beyond the fire.'

'Who?' I asked.

'Eburniel.'

'Are you sure it was him? Not just a har.'

'No, he looked right into me. I could see he was more than har. He saw me too. He knows me.'

'That's no reason to be sad, surely?' I said, taking his hand. A small part of me was jealous, but I smothered it quickly. 'He'll help you.'

'Yes,' Darys said. He smiled at me, but it was forced. I opened my mouth to say more, but Darys wouldn't allow me to speak, changed the subject. 'You know, of all the outrageous things Cutter did, which I was often forced to witness, I never actually saw him take aruna with somehar. That must be strange for you, seeing that.'

I pulled a scornful face. 'Why would you think that? It's part of life, isn't it? Without it, everything would die and the world would be empty of hara and animals, fish, birds and insects. Then plants would die because we are all part of the pattern. How can something so powerful and fundamental to life be strange to witness? And anyway, we didn't *see* it. We just… *knew*.'

'I don't think aruna is something *I'll* ever know,' Darys said.

I laughed. 'Don't be stupid. Of course you will. Your condition won't stop that, and anyway Corva wouldn't let it.'

Darys didn't answer me. He was melancholy for the rest of the night.

Before we went to bed, Balani raked smooth the ashes in the hearth of our living room so that the dehara might leave a message for us there. He did this every year, and once we had seen what looked like the footprints of a bird in the ashes next morning. There'd been no explanation for it.

Darys now shared my room, and I heard him breathing; a wounded, liquid sound. I don't think he was asleep, but he didn't speak to me.

Come morning, there were no marks in the ashes, although it was if a wind had come down the chimney, blown them out of the hearth, so that what looked like a thin white arm stretched into the room.

As the weather became warmer, Darys appeared to grow stronger. Corva said – to my horror – that if he lived in a warmer climate his health would improve even more. I didn't want Darys to go away, and yet if his body wasn't up to coping with the weather where we lived, perhaps he *should* go. 'But he wouldn't have your care,' I said.

Corva expelled a sigh. 'I'm hoping that when he reaches feybraiha, things will change. One of aruna's functions is healing. Perhaps this will help him.'

'How long until it comes to him?' I asked.

Corva shrugged. 'I would say this year, but it's difficult to tell. He's not like other harlings. In fact, he doesn't seem like a harling at all to me, but a much older har. It surprises me sometimes when I remember how young he is.'

I didn't mention any of this conversation to Darys. I don't know if Corva did.

In fact, Darys's feybraiha began in the late summer. Because of his condition, the symptoms were more severe than they should be – what caused discomfort in an average harling's frame inflicted pain in Darys. His skin became scaly and sore, almost over his entire body. He burned with fever nearly all the time, which was kept only partially under control by Corva's philtres.

Darys always went to bed before the rest of us, tiring easily. He was ready for sleep immediately after eating. One evening, as my parents and I sat around the kitchen table after Darys had gone upstairs, Corva glanced at the ceiling and said, 'If I didn't know better, I'd think he was undergoing a protracted kind of althaia.'

'Couldn't that be a good thing?' Balani asked. 'Maybe feybraiha will normalise him. You'll take him through aruna?'

Corva made a clicking sound and shook his head. '*You* must be the one for him,' he said in a low voice. 'Use all of your magic.'

Balani went still. I could see he wasn't pleased to hear this. 'You can *ask* me, but don't order me,' he said, his tone harder than he could normally manage.

Corva fixed him with a stare. 'All right. I'm asking you. Will you do this?'

'I'll think about it,' Balani replied.

'Think?' Corva rolled his eyes. 'Are you prejudiced, like the harlings?'

'We're not pr…' I began but Balani had got to his feet.

'I don't feel it's the right thing,' he said. 'For me or for him.'

'You're a dryadhar,' Corva snapped, his voice now louder. 'Your spirit is best for him. I'm too *spiky* for this task. Surely you can see that?'

Balani ignored these remarks, pointing to our back door, and therefore beyond it. 'Ask any har out there and they'll say the same as I just did. I understand Darys is your mission, Corva, and your pride wants to make him whole, so in that case *you* should be the one for him.'

Balani dropped his arm to his side. They stared at one another furiously.

'You're a fine one to talk about pride,' Corva said coldly, eventually.

'Is that the best you can manage?' Balani snarled. 'I never put whatever pride I have before the welfare of others. I won't do this, Corva.'

'*I* would,' I said, 'if I could.' But of course, in the frazzling air of their dispute, neither of my parents heard me.

'Fine,' Corva said to Balani. 'Thanks for your honesty.'

'Any time,' Balani said and left the house, pausing only to grab his coat.

Corva looked at me and shrugged. I didn't say anything.

It wasn't a serious argument – my parents quarrelled often and heatedly – but Balani wouldn't change his mind.

Amberfall was – and is – a community of individuals, each member a strong character, about whom you could tell a lengthy tale. But it is possible that even within such a community you can have one who is more individual than others. In Amberfall at that time, this was Yig. He had a rarely-used home within the sett, but also a couple out in the wilderness where he spent more time, when he wasn't travelling. We usually saw him once or twice a year, but he'd been away for nearly two years this time, visiting far away places. He had many epithets – Yig the Bear, because he sometimes lived in a cave, even though he wasn't very bearlike, other than his shaggy hair. He was also Yig the Beautiful, which needs no explanation, and Yig Lightfoot, which other phyles tended to call him. Other names described both his appearance and his skills, among them

Yig Longeye and The Amberfall Cat. Hara said that Yig had a *history*; perhaps was a famous har of the early days, who was a fugitive from an ancient conflict, maybe even had a price on his head. Hara liked to believe this. Yig wasn't a silent type, although not overly talkative either, but he never spoke of his past. An accomplished hunter and tracker, he was regarded very highly, and not just by my own phyle. Despite this, he was essentially an Outsider, appearing unexpectedly and departing quietly, but always causing a stir. It is no surprise, then, that Darys *noticed* Yig, and as sexual awareness unfolded like half-heard songs within his body, this noticing quickly became something rather more meaningful.

The days of Fruitingmoon, the month before Smoketide, were drawing to a close. The sett was occupied by harvesting and trading. Visitors arrived with produce to sell, keen to buy our own. The sett felt busy and strangely larger because of it; there was never any quiet. And, as was quite usual at this time of year, Yig appeared. This was more like a manifestation, since somehar noticed suddenly that Yig was sitting smoking a pipe on the well-mouth at the centre of the sett, his rugged pony dozing on its feet beside him.

Kree came running to find me. Darys and I were chopping wood outside the back door, or rather I was chopping and he was stacking. We'd made rather a mess, or I had, and Darys was attempting to tidy it up.

'Yig is back!' Kree cried.

I dropped my axe at once. 'Where?' I asked.

'The well.'

It was traditional for us harlings to flock around Yig, this magical creature who came from the woods, who brought us gifts from far across the mountains, who would play a bone flute for us, which we were convinced could charm wild beasts to lose their taste for blood.

'Not yet!' A voice commanded from the kitchen – Corva. 'Just finish up, Nooni. Yig won't be going anywhere, except perhaps to our table later for dinner. You'll have plenty of time to be with him. But anyway, when he does come, I don't want him having to walk through a lumber yard to get to the door.'

I grimaced sullenly. Yes, Yig would come to my parents, as he always did, but the moment he first appeared was magical, when we ran to him, then danced around him as he played eerie notes on his flute, singing our wordless hymns to him. I wanted to be part of it.

'Hurry up, Darys,' I said beneath my breath, to ensure Corva wouldn't hear, furiously chopping, so that splinters flew everywhere.

Kree fidgeted impatiently before us for all of a minute, then said, 'Catch me up, Nooni. See you there.'

I swore softly, hacked at a log.

'You go,' Darys said. 'I'll finish up.'

'Are you sure?' I knew I was being selfish, and that Darys's feybraiha made him even weaker than usual, but I was desperate to be with my friends.

'I won't go mad with the axe, like you're doing now,' he said, grinning. 'Just go. I'll be fine.'

I caught up with Kree and we galloped to the well. We were the first harlings to arrive. There sat lean, dark-skinned Yig, smiling his secretive smile. His pony was laden with bulging leather satchels. I was eager to discover what they contained. Yig had put down his pipe and now held his flute, polishing it carefully with a red silk handkerchief. He wore one sparkling green earring that hung in hoops and shimmering threads to his shoulder. The ankle of his left foot rested on his right thigh. He had the legs and arms of a spider, being spindly and long. Since we'd last seen him, his waist-length, normally tangled hair had been made into dreadlocks, which were confined by an emerald scarf. His slanted cat's eyes were painted with kohl and his smile was a sickle. We adored him.

'Hello, cubs,' he said to us. 'If you're here for gifts, you must dance for them.' He played a trill of notes that spiralled up like smoke into the air.

The rest of our friends arrived, and adults paused in their work and conversations to watch. We had no inhibitions about dancing spontaneously to the song of the pipe, nor about raising our voices to sing and shout. Visitors were privileged to witness the arrival of our magical piper, our spider-har, cat-har, creature of mystery. No other phyle nearby had anyhar like him. Those who were here to trade would go back to their own setts and speak of this day.

After only twenty minutes or so, Yig put away his pipe, and bid Kree fetch one of his satchels from the pony. From this, Yig pulled out his first round of gifts, not just for us, but for everyhar, even those visitors who were lucky enough to be there that day. The gifts were small, but wonderful; odd pieces of jewellery, sometimes ancient from the human era, or else newly-crafted, unusual food stuffs and sweet-meats, peculiar little toys, scarves, shawls, combs made of bones, weird perfumes that smelled of the earth or the sea, or hardly of anything but the open sky.

When Yig's eyes fell upon me, and his long hands enclosed one of mine, I held my breath. 'Here's a pretty pin for you, Noonling,' he said softly. I opened my hand and there lay a centipede fashioned of black gems, with tiny, green wire legs and eyes that shone red.

'Thank you,' I said.

'They live in the damp and the dark, and the touch of their feet is venomous,' Yig said.

When he stood up, hara knew he was hungry, and it was time for him to make his way to my home. He put a hand to the back of my neck, and I became giddy with pride as we walked away together.

Corva was alone in the kitchen when we arrived. He and Yig exchanged a look that was actually a kiss, although they did not touch one another. They never did. That was a history too.

'I have something for you,' Yig said.

It was a necklace of ivy leaves carved from wood and painted dark green, or rather a collar of them that would dangle down over the chest. The detail was exquisite. I could see small insects hiding among the leaves. Corva said nothing as he looked at it, then said, 'Put it on me, Nooni.'

This I did.

'Thanks,' Corva said to Yig. 'Sit down. Nooni, fetch the spiceberry liquor.' This was one of my hostling's specialities. He only made one batch a year and it was popular, so didn't last very long. One bottle was reserved for this season, when Yig was likely to appear.

For Balani, who arrived only minutes later, Yig had brought a set of ten unusual glass bottles of dark, rich colours. They were packed in moss and dried leaves, and filled with pungent liquids. A few were perfumes, two were poisons, others were medicines. As I watched Balani hold the bottles up to the window, one by one, to admire their colours, I thought that somehow, the bottles would have been a more fitting gift for Corva, and the necklace for Balani. What had made Yig swap the gifts? (I was sure he had.)

Darys had been at a neighbour's, fetching cream and butter, and had lingered to help with milking the goats. He only came into the house just before dinner was ready. Yig turned instantly to look at the door when it opened, because as far as he knew only three of us lived here, and even the closest friend would knock. Darys stood at the threshold, clearly surprised as well to find a stranger at our table. His plait was loose and stuck with straw, his skin pale. I noticed the red, scaly rash that had splashed up his cheek had faded. He looked frail yet lovely, like a fairy creature, or a dragonfly spirit. Perhaps the labour with the axe had made him so strangely transparent and ethereal.

'Who's this?' Yig asked, with an equal tone of surprise and approval.

'Ah, this is Darys,' Balani said. 'He lives with us now.'

'I hope you've brought the cream,' Corva said sharply. 'This sauce has been waiting half an hour for it.'

'Sorry,' Darys said, loping into the room. He put a package wrapped in leaves onto the work stand by the range and also a jug with a rope handle. Corva opened the leaves and sniffed the butter, then examined the jug of cream. Satisfied he added this to his sauce.

Darys appeared strangely dazed to me, and I hoped he wasn't about to fall ill. He and I sat down with Yig at the table, while Balani and Corva finishing preparing dinner. I explained to Darys who Yig was, and was a little disappointed he didn't seem as excited as I was. He was distracted.

'I don't have a gift for you,' Yig said to Darys. 'Not because I lack the gifts, but because I don't yet know you. Every har has a perfect gift.'

Darys smiled tightly. 'Eburniel's Tears on an early grave,' he said.

Yig raised his eyebrows, and his good humour slunk away. 'An odd request.'

'Darys!' I said. 'Don't say that.'

'I'm sorry,' Darys said, turning to face Yig. 'That was rude of me. Blame this feybraiha crap! Thank the dehara it's nearly over. Any gift would be wonderful.'

They looked at one another then, which reminded me of the way Yig and Corva looked at one another, an attention that excluded everyhar else in the room. It was broken only by Corva placing a tureen of roasted roots rather too violently on the table. The gaze was broken and Darys lowered his head, wild strands of hair covering his blushing face.

'Help yourselves,' Balani said, placing ceremoniously a large plate of roasted boar slices in the centre of the table.

After that, the atmosphere returned to normal, and we spent a lively evening telling Yig all the sett news, listening to tales of his journeys, and then singing and dancing together. The berry liquor was drained, and we moved on to ale. Darys was animated, feverish in a new way. There was a moment during the dancing, while Balani was playing the hand drums and Yig had put down his flute, when Yig pulled Darys to him, tightly. He stared into Darys's face, then let him go. That, I thought, was what he always wanted to do to Corva, every time they met. I remembered the argument my parents had had. I didn't think either of them would be involved in Darys's feybraiha ceremony now.

Darys stayed up with the rest of us until it was nearly dawn. Then we went upstairs together, while Yig ambled back to his neglected house on the edge of the sett. I knew hara would have laid a fire for him there, and put fresh linen on his bed.

In our room, Darys sat on his bed, brushing out his hair.

'You looked lovely tonight,' I told him.

He shrugged, laid down the brush. 'I know him,' he said. He sounded drunk.

'What?'

'Yig. I know him. He's Eburniel.' He frowned. 'Out of season... what does that mean?'

I laughed. 'He's not Eburniel, Darys. What do you mean by that?'

'Just that I saw him that night, earlier in the year, when we held the rite in the forest. Maybe I was mistaken, and it wasn't Eburniel at all, standing there staring at me. Maybe it was always Yig.'

'I can't see how,' I said, somewhat tartly. 'He was away then, far away.'

Again, Darys shrugged and got into bed. Normally he plaited his hair again, but tonight it surrounded him like a soft, dark shawl.

'Is your feybraiha nearly over?' I asked him.

He lay staring at the ceiling. 'Yes. The symptoms went today. I'm ready.'

There was a silence, then I said, 'I know who you want.'

Darys glanced at me and smiled secretively. Then he turned onto his side, away from me.

In the morning, I woke Darys early and said, 'You've got to tell Corva and Balani.' I'd been lying awake thinking about it for an hour.

'Tell them what?' Darys asked, apparently baffled as to why he was lying in a tangled mat of hair. He pulled it off his face.

'About your feybraiha. Yig might stay for a month or disappear today. If you want him, you must tell them now, at breakfast.'

Darys stared at me. 'All that... it was like a dream, just the drink talking. I don't know... not now.'

'Darys, shut up! Feybraiha is a rite of passage. You'll remember it always. It must be right and special and perfect. *Tell* them!'

Darys paused awkwardly for a moment, then said, 'He won't want me. It's embarrassing.'

'He *does* want you,' I countered. 'It was obvious. You know that too.'

I had a romantic vision of Darys going to Yig's dwelling and saying, 'The gift you can give me. I know what it is: it is you.'

This fond imagining was shattered very quickly. Corva and Balani took the news calmly, even though I had to do most of the talking. Darys sat at the kitchen table stiffly, in an agony of embarrassment.

'Is this what you want?' Corva asked him, 'or what my mouse-brained harling has invented for you?'

Darys glanced at him sheepishly. 'It's what I want, but I feel bad for wanting it.'

'Don't be ridiculous,' Corva said briskly. 'It happens to all harlings. If you want Yig to be the one, then he'll do it. I'll go and see him after we've eaten.'

I noticed Balani flick my hostling a brief, questioning glance, then he clearly set aside whatever he'd been thinking and began eating.

I didn't like the way Corva had reduced what should be a magical, mystical event into a function. 'He'll do it' seemed such cruel, cold words to a har shivering on the brink of adulthood, and nervous about it. But as I mulled the situation over, it became clear to me that Corva had mixed feelings about Darys's choice, and one of those feelings was envy. I dared not ask him about his history with Yig. I knew this would anger him.

I don't know what Corva said to Yig, but the outcome was

agreeable. Yig came to talk to Darys later that day, and they went alone together into the forest. Yig would take no liberties; there was a time for their intimacy and it wasn't yet. But I suspected they must've shared breath, because when they returned Darys was again in a daze and couldn't stop grinning. That evening, we had a quiet family meal together, before the rest of the Amberfall hara were informed of the impending event, and Yig was treated as one of our own. Cutter should have been there, of course, but that was impossible.

Next morning, Corva rang the bell outside the meeting hall, and the community gathered to discover what it was he had to tell them. He announced the forthcoming feybraiha rite of Darys, and revealed that Yig would be his guide for this experience. All communities love any excuse for a celebration so the news was cheered loudly. The rite would take place in two days' time.

Before then, the entire sett was decorated with greenery and flowers, the meeting hall so filled with vegetation it was difficult to breathe in there. Balani and his dryadini fashioned a robe for Darys of green cloth stitched with flowers and grasses. Yig presented Darys with a jewelled pin, strangely enough of a dragonfly – as how I'd imagined him that day he'd first set eyes on Yig.

'Is that your special gift?' I asked Darys.

He stared at the pin. 'No, this is just a feybraiha gift.'

'*Has* he given you something?'

Darys smiled at me. 'That is yet to come.'

I'd attended two feybraiha celebrations before, one of them when I was very young and I could barely remember it, but this was the first time it would be for somehar close to me.

At noon on the celebration day, Balani led a ceremony in the open air to welcome formally a young har to adulthood. He proclaimed officially that Yig was his guide, and spoke of this great responsibility. Yig took vows to perform this duty with kindness and sanctity. The entire sett stood in a loose circle around the three of them. After this formal part was done, we sang the airs to awakening, to aruna and to life.

The afternoon was a fete, with hara from nearby phyles coming to sample our hospitality; news of celebration spreads quickly, even in the mountain forests. Darys was heaped with gifts, generally items for his future life, such as tools for work and for domestic tasks, newly-made clothes and boots, and so on. Darys accepted these gifts, and passed them to me. I knew this was only so I could put them in a pile on the table behind him, but even so it felt strangely symbolic.

Then the sun went down into the reaching trees, and candles and lanterns were lit around the sett. Hara played fiddles and flutes as Yig and Darys walked to Yig's cottage, which had been decorated with foliage and flowers. It was customary for the sett to sit in quiet vigil outside the building where a feybraiha aruna rite took place. We had to wait for the cry that signalled the rite was done, that the harling was no more and the har had flowered. I had sat through this twice before, but then it had meant nothing. Now, it seemed to take too long. Was something wrong? Eventually, the cries started, low at first like a lament. I froze for a moment, fearing Darys was in pain, but then realised with relief he was uttering the rising sounds of ecstasy, which eventually climaxed in a scream that was like a peal of bells. It made me feel numb, hearing that, a numbness prior to tingling. Who would be the one for me, when my time came?

Later, once we were home, Balani said, 'I was afraid he would be silent or too quiet to hear.'

Corva nodded. 'My fear too, but he wasn't. It took. I'm sure it took.'

After the night Darys spent with Yig, I was alert for changes in my friend. I knew that in some ways he had left me, because overnight he had moved from harling to har, and had been absorbed into adult life. I knew I mustn't mind about this, and that within a year or so I would catch up with him, so I concentrated on observing his health. Had aruna been the miracle cure Corva had hoped it might be?

Yig stayed in Amberfall for three weeks, and during this time he and Darys were together continually. When he left, Darys seemed to take the departure well. Was he in love? I wasn't sure. He didn't speak of it to me. He did seem sturdier, no longer quite so frail, but he wasn't happy. I could feel this deeply, but there was now a barrier between us that I could neither break nor cross. We might work on our chores together and share jokes. He might accompany my friends and I when we went into the forest, but part of him was now closed off from me.

At Natalia, Cutter made an appearance, which surprised the entire community. He rode in on a large, expensive-looking bay horse and wore luxurious furs. He also had a laden pack-horse with him. Clearly, being free of his harling had helped him secure a better life, undoubtedly involving some kind of benefactor. He'd brought gifts from the coastal town where he now lived, which were more lavish than what Yig had supplied, but nowhere near as meaningful.

'Well, look at you!' he said to Darys in a tone of approval, when they met in our house. 'You're not the same har at all.'

They embraced awkwardly.

'Is my old shack available?' Cutter asked Corva.

'Even if it is, you must stay here,' Corva replied, and if his teeth were gritted, an outsider wouldn't have been able to tell.

Cutter certainly enlivened the Natalia celebrations that year. He was somewhat irritating, a little too loud, but essentially kind-hearted. The produce he'd brought with him made our seasonal meals more sumptuous than usual. He even accompanied us to our Natalia arojhahn, this time held on a hilltop within the forest, where a twisted tree grew out of a single split stone at the crown.

As was the custom, a feast was held in the communal hall after the rite, again augmented by Cutter's gifts. Everyhar treated Cutter like an old friend, probably because of his generosity. Still, it felt genuine and was a joyful gathering.

Near the end of the evening, I was talking with Darys at the edge of the room, when suddenly Darys paused, shuddered and stooped a little. 'Oh,' he said.

'What is it?' I asked. 'Are you all right?'

'Nothing,' he replied. 'Just a strange… twinge. It's nothing.'

'Twinge where?'

'Below my ribs… sort of.'

'Tell Corva,' I said.

'If it happens again I will,' he said. 'I promise.'

He became subdued after that, and about half an hour later asked if I'd go back home with him. We'd had the best of the feast, so I said I would. It would be pleasant to have the house to ourselves for a short while, without the noise – audible and otherwise – of Cutter in it.

We went into the living-room and I stoked up the fire. I poured us both mugs of wine, which was fortified with seasonal spices. Darys sipped thoughtfully, gazing into the volcano caves of the fire. What shapes did he see there?

'You're thinking of him, aren't you?' I said. We'd not talked of Yig since he'd left. The subject had felt taboo.

Darys glanced at me. 'I always think of him.'

'It must be hard that he doesn't stick around. You must miss him.'

Darys nodded. There was a comfortable silence between us and then Darys murmured, 'He knew me too, Nooni. He'd seen me before. At Rosatide.'

'Was he there then, sneaking around the forest?'

'Not physically,' Darys said. 'He can't be here in person for the festivals, but he holds his own rite each time, visualising he's here at Amberfall. At Rosatide, he said it was different, more real. He came right through somehow, into our reality. He saw me and I saw him. The future was set then.'

I wanted this to sound improbable, but found that it didn't. 'So it wasn't Eburniel after all,' I said.

'Oh, not entirely, but Yig told me that although he walks the land the whole year through, he is partly an avatar of Eburniel. He has to be alone in life, most of the time.'

I didn't know what to say, so simply made a murmur of understanding. They had talked intimately, it seemed.

Darys put down his mug. 'Eburniel transforms into Florinel, who transforms into Feyrahni. Yig became Feyrahni for me, the dehar of my feybraiha.'

It *is* love, I thought, somewhat miserably.

'He'll be back,' I said. 'He always comes back.'

'Not in that way,' Darys said. He forced a smile. 'It doesn't matter. He gave what he could and I cherish that. I'll take it with me wherever I go next.'

I froze. 'Go? You're thinking of leaving?'

He waved a hand at me. 'No, no... figure of speech, that's all.' He smiled and it seemed his melancholy had fled. 'When we were together... Nooni, it's the most amazing experience, almost beyond words. The physical side is the least of it. I felt Yig fill me up with light, as if my body was a vessel. I felt that light move through me like a healing wave. I'll never forget it. He knew me... He really tried... But Nooni...' He paused, stared at me, still smiling, but there was an edge to it now. 'You're my dearest, closest friend – my brother. I need to tell you this, and I need you to guard this knowledge. Will you do that?'

I nodded.

'You must promise not to speak of it – for now. You'll know when it's all right to speak of it.'

'OK, I promise,' I said. 'What is it?'

'I was a vessel being filled, up to the brim and more, so that light flowed over and down. It was beautiful. But… we soon realised the vessel was cracked. It couldn't contain the energy Yig fed me. I felt all that light and hope begin to drain away. He felt it too, but I think he knew that would happen. To me, it was as if he was trying to catch with his hands the life blood pouring from a fatal wound. He couldn't mend the vessel. The vessel is my body, marred, malformed, a faulty conception…'

'Darys, no!' I said, mostly to stop him speaking these vile words. 'You're wrong. Look at you. You're not broken, you're mended.'

'I'm not asking for your opinion, merely telling you something,' Darys said calmly. 'I love you, Nooni. You helped change my life.'

This sounded far too much like goodbye to me. Was he planning to kill himself? I was terrified, wondering if I should run straight to my parents and tell them what he'd said. But then, he'd promised me to silence.

He moved in his chair and winced. The twinge again. 'I'm going to bed now,' he said. 'Keep to your promise, Nooni.'

'I'm coming too,' I began, but Darys cut me off.

'No, I want to be on my own for a while. Don't worry. I'm not going anywhere, not yet. But the sickness will come for me, Nooni. It will come vengefully. I want you to be aware of what the future will hold. Remember me how I was that night.' He leaned down and kissed my brow, then left the room.

After only a couple of weeks, the enemy did indeed return. Darys tried to hide the fact he wasn't well, although he did confide in me about it. Superstitious, I dared say nothing to Corva or Balani, because I feared that breaking my promise would invoke a curse, and Darys would get worse. But eventually, after only a week or so, Corva noticed the decline himself.

It was heart-breakingly swift after that. I can't describe how horrifying this was, not only for me, but the whole sett. We believed in our efficient bodies, that we were the future of the world, immune to sickness. The old race had died out partly through disease. We had risen from that, and yet now we were forced to witness what illness had been like. Terminal illness; no hope of reprieve. I thought then, and know now, that the family and friends of victims suffer just as much.

I kept dreaming of the broken vessel Darys had described, seeing it as a sacred cup hanging in the air before me in a snow-shrouded forest. The cup glowed with hallowed light that gradually dimmed. I saw a dead hind on the forest floor, pale flakes slowly covering her body. I saw Eburniel walking between the trees, and where the hem of his cloak dragged, so the snow turned scarlet. Blood and snow. Red and white. These images haunted my days as well as my nights.

Aruna *had* made changes in Darys. It had initiated the flowering of adulthood, and it had met with the faulty vessel. No doubt the body had used the energy of aruna to try and repair itself. Yig's energy had tried it too. But rather than seal the leak, aruna had weakened the vessel further, widening the breach. The harish body now shut down, or tried to. That was the worst part; it was terrible to watch.

A week before Rosatide, Darys asked me to cut his hair. 'It's too heavy,' he said. 'I feel like it'll break my neck.'

I wept as I cut through that thick, silken plait. It was part of him. He could barely sit upright and leaned against me. 'Can I keep it?' I asked him, when I held the rope of hair, severed, in my hands.

'No, you must let me go, all of me,' he said. 'Please burn it.'

Corva had sent out messengers to try and find Cutter at the coast. There were hara among the mountains who'd take on tasks like that. But Cutter could not be found swiftly.

'Do we even need to find him yet?' Balani asked, one morning. 'Darys is an invalid, yet he's far from fading completely. How long will this take, Corva?'

My hostling stared at him for some moments, then shook his head, turned away. 'I don't know. Months, maybe years… who can tell? He's sick but he's har. The body won't give up that easily.'

'It can't go on like this!' Balani said. 'The whole of Amberfall suffers for it.'

'Then what are you suggesting?' Corva said coldly. 'Will you do that, my love? You have poisons aplenty, I know. Will you take a life for your own convenience?'

Balani made a wordless sound and, as he usually did when Corva made a painful point, marched out of the house.

The weeks went on, long, agonising weeks, and Darys didn't die. He could barely eat, and had to be fed soup and soft milky foods by hand. He was too weak to get out of bed to use the toilet behind the house. He soiled himself, so had to wear cloths around his loins that were changed several times a day. I'd had to move out of the bedroom, because it was now impossible for me to rest there. The air smelled sour and stale, as if the sickly emanations of his breath clung to every surface. I slept by the fire in the living room, cushioned by and wrapped in furs, but my back was always cold.

Each day, Darys seemed to fade a little more, but life was tenacious. It was as if he was waiting for something. I didn't think that was his hostling, who still hadn't been found. Yig didn't come. I wished it was over, and prayed for that, for I dreaded waking each day to see my friend – my brother – suffering so, his independence and dignity stripped away. We all suffered because we could not yet grieve.

On Rosatide eve, we carried Darys with us to the forest ceremony on a litter. He was swathed in furs and blankets, and lay within them like a diminished woodland creature. He was so thin, his face hardly more than a skull, his remaining hair dull and patchy. It seemed so cruel he still lived.

I searched the shadows beyond our fire for a glimpse of Yig – or of Eburniel – but saw nothing. Darys's eyes were closed. When Corva and Balani sank down to begin their aruna rite, their faces ran with tears. This sacrament of life seemed such a travesty. The dehara no longer seemed so real to me, because they could allow this to happen to one of their children. We weren't human. I'd been instructed in human history, and knew we were better than them. Our bodies didn't fall sick in the way theirs had. What was the lesson of this hideous experience we were now forced to endure? Wouldn't it be kinder now to leave Darys in the forest, exposed to the elements, so he could be given release? So that *we* could? But instead he was carried home, up to his bed, where he lay gasping for breath. I couldn't sleep in that house. I couldn't.

I walked to Kree's dwelling, where his family were still up and celebrating, happier now they were away from Darys. I stayed there till morning, finally falling asleep in a chair in their living room. As I dozed, eyes half-closed in the dying light of the fire, I saw Kree's see'ver rake the ashes before he went to bed.

Just as dawn broke, I woke in the chair by the hearth. I glanced at the ashes, but they were smooth, untouched. I put on my coat to go home, to face another day of torment. No har was up at my house. The first thing I did was go into the living-room to look at our hearth. Every year I did this. What did I expect to see? But there *was* something this time.

A hand print. A long hand.

I ran from the room and pelted upstairs to the room I'd once shared with Darys. I wasn't surprised to find both beds empty. Not even pausing to rouse my parents, I ran outside again, wondering where Darys would have gone. He couldn't simply have walked, and there were no signs in the snow of him dragging himself. No tracks at all.

I didn't have to run very far.

I found him in the flowers, beneath an oak tree in the forest, his body drifted with snow. Each flower bowed its head to weep for him. Eburniel's Tears. He was dressed in a long coat of magnificent, pale wolf fur I'd not seen before. It had a wide hood, which was drawn up over his head, and hid the fact his hair had been shorn. His slender feet were bare, poking out from the heavy fur. They seemed to be made of marble. His head was turned slightly to the side. He looked exquisite, at peace.

I dropped to my knees, plunging my hands between them, and stared at the body of my friend. I couldn't weep, couldn't speak, couldn't move.

My hostling found me – it must've been nearly an hour later. He said nothing, but put a hand upon my shoulder. Then he leaned down and lifted aside the fur around Darys's body. I saw a crimson stain. The movement of the fur caused a thread of scarlet to spill down over the snow, trickle through it for a short way.

'To the heart,' Corva murmured, and then replaced the fur covering. He lifted Darys in his arms, and that body was limp and supple, not stiff.

'Come now, Nooni,' Corva said. 'Get up. Shake yourself out of it. There are last things we must do for him.'

As we walked back to our home, I glanced behind. The thin

stripe of blood glowed too brightly from the snow.

Death came rarely to our community, and when it did, it was treated with honour, not fear. Corva and Balani laid the body on the kitchen table, and presently several of our closest neighbours came to assist with the laying out. Darys was like a beautiful effigy, his skeletal appearance somehow holy now. There was a mark over his heart like a bruise, with a darker centre. Corva covered this with a cosmetic cream. Nohar commented on it. Nohar said the obvious. The morning light sloped in over the scene from the small kitchen window. Light sparkled from drops of water as they dipped their cloths in a bowl, as they bathed his body and rubbed it with perfume from one of the bottles Yig had brought for Balani. Once Darys had been cleansed and scented, they dressed him in a pale robe, lifting his body as if he were only sleeping. Corva brought the wolf fur coat to the table, and nohar said anything as he fitted it once again to Darys's lean form: his shroud. Corva drew the wide hood up over Darys's head. He no longer looked shorn or sick, merely at rest.

Balani stood at the head of the table, his back to the light, and sang the first of the laments for the dead. Sunlight turned the edges of his hair to a nimbus of fire. To me, the scene was like a painting; a group of hara, in that subtle yet glorious light, laying out the body of a sacred being, a martyr, a symbol. It felt so meaningful, as if Darys had absorbed all the sickness in the world, and had died from it, so other hara might never fall ill.

Once Darys's body was ready, everyhar in Amberfall filed in silently and laid herbs and branches around it. His hands were folded just below the heart and Corva put a spray of Eburniel's Tears between his white fingers. Balani made a crown of ivy, wound with the same blooms, and placed it over Darys's head, around his wolf fur hood. My see'ver sang the second lament.

The body was burned two days later. I wasn't sure why Corva waited, yet he insisted on it. But of course, he was waiting for something – or somehar – in particular.

Yig came back on the second day. He didn't pause in the centre of the sett or take out his flute. Harlings did not run to him. Instead, he came straight to our house. He looked shocked to hear about Darys, but I knew he was pretending. He'd known all along which way the path would lead. He knew everything.

Corva and Balani had laid Darys's body in our small barn and had shut the animals out. Yig went there alone and was gone for half an hour. When he returned, sombre yet dry-eyed, nohar voiced the questions I was burning to ask. Not even glances held accusation. It was a shared knowing between them, my parents and Yig.

You can stop a heart with a long pin, they say. A good tracker leaves no marks upon snow. He'd never admit it, but I knew. I think Darys called to him. I think Yig answered the call. He was not just Eburniel and Feyrahni – he was Shadolan too, the hunter with a fatal dart. The gift – that precious gift.

Yig stood next to me as the pyre was lit, heaped with fragrant woods and resins to mask the smell of meat. We were somewhat apart from anyhar else. I wondered where he'd been for two days. Why had he gone away anyway? Nohar would have thought his actions wrong. How could any kind act inspired by love be wrong? I couldn't ask him outright. Still, he was aware I knew him now, so I felt I could murmur, 'Tell me the story of the crow and the cat.'

He didn't respond at first, then said, 'There were lives before this one, cub. This forest, these mountains; they were rebirth to some of us. We were young once. He had black feathers in his hair and danced with me in the rubble of the old civilisation. But in many ways, it was a bad life. We each had our lessons to learn, our pain to drink, our eyes to open. Our history keeps us apart and always will. And that's all I'll tell you, as that's all I know.'

'Were there hara like Darys then?'

Yig paused, then said, 'No. It might've been better if there had been, reminding us to respect the gifts we'd been given. We were vain and glorious, mad and stupid.' He laughed, and mussed my hair. 'I won't be able to do this for much longer, cub. This time next year, you'll be adult and such an intimate touch might be taken quite wrongly.'

'Or not,' I said. 'Who knows? But then, I'm not a cause, am I?'

Yig narrowed his eyes at me. 'You inherited the claws of the crow,' he said, but without malice. 'Some things are meant to be private, Nooni. Don't pry into what happened. If I ever tell you, it won't be while we say our farewells to him.'

In a dream, I saw Eburniel walking through the snow beneath the tall, silent trees. And where the hem of his cloak dragged across the forest floor, so flowers sprang up, and the world came to life again. Is there a harling somewhere who has the soul of my friend? Does he stretch his small, perfect hands up to the winter light to welcome the rebirth of the sun? The wheel of life forever turns, and sometimes the world reminds us of who we are and what was lost and what was gained. What happened to Darys was once a common part of human life, and just because we are spared it doesn't mean we should forget, or squander our gifts, or not be grateful for the Tears in the snow and their meaning.

Bloomtide

March 21st

This festival marks the Spring Equinox. The ascetic Eburniel transforms (and rejuvenates) into the dashing Florinel, no longer regarded as Elisin's hostling – or even a relative. Florinel begins to woo the maturing Elisin. He is seen as a lissom young dehar, of a similar age to Elisin, dressed in green, with nut brown hair. Florinel conjures flowers to open with the sound of his voice, which is the music heard in the wind, in spring rains and in the surge of swollen streams as the snow melts. His animal is the white hare.

Florinel is a trickster who can sometimes deceive. He leads the unwary into dangerous territory, but can also bestow a change of luck for the better. This youthful dehar is far too full of life to contemplate such dreary concepts as his own demise. He presides over planting and the reproduction of animals.

While Florinel's thoughts begin to turn to aruna, Elisin is entranced by the wonder of being alive. His is the unbounded joy of youth, as yet untarnished by adult cares.

Elisin is coy and rejects Florinel's advances. The only contact Florinel can have with Elisin at this time is to cover his sleeping body with white blossom.

Bloomtide is the celebration of life for its own sake. On the festival night, hara put aside their fears and uncertainties and focus on hopes for the future. The light hangs in equal balance, but only for a short time. From this night on, the days lengthen and the air becomes warmer.

However, these dehara belong to the northern hemisphere. In the story that follows, Nerine Dorman introduces us to harish myths of warmer climes, in the country that in the human era was known as South Africa. What does Bloomtide mean to hara living in a hot land where the rains have not fallen and living is harsh?

The Dreamstone

Nerine Dorman

'Pay attention! You're pulling the net askew!' Orthran's hostling chided.

With a grimace, Orthran straightened from the painful hunch he'd adopted as he squinted over his work.

Ahape's stitches on his side of the tear were neat; Orthran could hardly detect where the old melded with the new, were it not for the newer fibres being lighter. His own handiwork, on the other hand... He peered in dismay at his work.

'I should have you unpick that and start fresh, but you'll probably just make it worse,' Ahape said. 'Go on. Tide's going out soon. Make yourself useful for a change and go see if something's washed up before Jiqua's harlings get there first. And keep an eye out for your father. Maybe you can lend him a hand.'

Orthran bunched up a handful of net and bared his teeth at his hostling, but then Ahape's gaze had him bite back the retort that burned his tongue. His hostling could stop a charging lion through sheer force of will alone. It was a mercy he'd not berated him any more than he already had today.

He ducked his head, and murmured 'Yes, Ahape,' and got up.

As it was, the air in their home was stifling. The light from the slotted windows told him all he needed to know about how hot it was outside.

A mixed blessing then: stay inside and get a crick in his neck from frowning over intricate knotwork or go outside and suffer the late-afternoon sun. He ducked through the beaded curtain and squinted into the brilliance. The southeaster caught him as he stepped over the threshold, and Orthran paused, torn between placating his hostling by putting effort into his mending or taking the relatively graceful exit offered by the act of beach-combing.

He removed the stones that weighted down the basket next to

their home, then hooked it over his shoulder and started to wend his way to the beach. No sane har was out this time of the afternoon, when the sun hadn't quite started its slant to the west. The huddle of dwellings around him stood about like the baked mud fingers they were, small patches of shade doing little to offer him sanctuary as he followed the winding lanes between the structures.

Xindi's yellow hound barely raised its muzzle at his passing, thumped its tail but once, and didn't follow like he usually did when he saw a har heading to the beach.

'Dog has more sense than I do,' Orthran muttered, wishing he'd brought his hat with him. Yet what good would a hat do in this wind? A pointless endeavour. Also, he was loath to turn back now and have Ahape bark at him for not braving the outdoors.

(You're two years out of feybraiha, Orthran. Surely you should be thinking of a trade, developing a skill – something. Your knotwork is atrocious, and your father says you almost stepped on a puffadder last week. When are you going to gather yourself?)

What made it worse were Ahape's constant reminders that he'd find no partner willing to build a home and produce pearls the rate he was going. As if *that* was the be-all and end-all of existence. Then again, what else was there for a har to do in a tiny seaside village like Spitmouth? Here, a har either braved the Girdle of Tiamat for her silvery catch, herded goats, became a hunter or, like Ahape, mended nets. At last resort, he could even become a master thatcher, like his father, who was often called upon to travel as far as Mistsand in the south, or the Aranye River mouth in the north, thanks to his skills. Not that Orthran had any inclination to follow in Cegara's footsteps, for all his father's attempts at making a competent apprentice of his only son.

(It took me a day to fix your sloppy efforts. Tiahaar Kwamma is not to be let down. He is a good client, always pays in good copper.)

More disappointment.

Orthran breathed a sigh of relief as he rounded the ridge and put the village behind him. The wind blew fiercely here, uninterrupted from the sea, and he had to steady the basket with both hands. The ocean was white-capped and cobalt deep; the sky washed out with a salt haze. The fisherhara had not gone out today; their little *bakkies* had been dragged far up the beach, keel up, and now hara hunched beneath their net-shrouded shelters, smoking their pipes and drinking agave from dented tin mugs.

They turned their sun-browned faces with yellowed grins in his direction, but he laughed away their invitations to join them. As much as he didn't mind the sharpness of the liquor coiling around the bitter green smoke he could nearly taste, Orthran could already hear his hostling's bitter recriminations should he allow himself to slide into further dissolution today.

Another time, then.

He cast one last, longing glance in the hara's direction then trod the path between the first line of grass-fuzzed dunes that brought him to the beach.

Miserable pickings. Ahape had misjudged, or maybe plainly exaggerated how late it was to get Orthran from under his nose, for the tide was still high. He hunched along, disturbing surly kelp gulls as he followed the tide line, in the vain hope of finding something other than butterflied white mussel shells pressed into the damp sand. His nose informed him of the dead fur seal a while before he spotted the bloated brown hump, half buried at the high tide mark and seething with sand lice and flies. Orthran stared glumly at the hollow-eyed carcass for much longer than he intended, prodded it with a reluctant toe, but then his gorge rose, and he continued along the crescent of white sand that curved to the headland.

By this stage, he regretted not tying up his hair, for no matter what he did, salt-rimed tendrils flew into his mouth, his eyes, and every time he licked his lips, he crunched sand between his teeth.

Surely there was more to life than this?

He made the mistake of setting down the basket, then wasted precious time chasing after the damned thing when the wind stole it and rolled it end over end, faster than he could run. Eventually, he caught it in the dunes, where, angry at himself and his predicament, he cut away from the beach back inland, into the dune field. Here he found a little more shelter from the incessant wind. Not much. But enough for him to hunker down in a hollow, for long enough to braid his hair back into a tight queue and secure it with a twist of dune grass that he wove into it. There. That would hold for a while.

Orthran sighed, and hated the way his eyes felt scratchy from more than just the sand. He despised the sand. Everywhere in this parched red land, it was just sand, stone and scrub, and if he was lucky, perhaps a stand of quiver trees or an acacia thicket up in the ridges further east. What curse of birth had his pearl suffered, to be pushed out into the world in such an unforgiving place and not elsewhere, where water was sweet and the wind didn't suck the life from the very earth? Why did hara eke out an existence in such a harsh land, when there were other, better places to live?

All questions he couldn't answer, and living elsewhere didn't seem to occur to his parents. In fact, they seemed content, happy even. He thought of Cegara, whistling while he selected thatch, bundling it neatly just so, and Ahape lost in concentration as his fingers knotted fibres into intricate shapes that would later bring in Tiamat's bounty.

Orthran brought his knees up to his chest and rested his head on his forearms, breathed in and out, hating the smell of sweat that clung to him. There hadn't been water enough for him to bathe properly in weeks, and summer's fangs were still buried deep in the land.

He hadn't meant to fall asleep, but perhaps it was a combination of the relative peace of his hiding place, and his own gnawing discontent that chased him into a light doze. He couldn't quite call it dreaming, but he felt as if he nodded on the edge of two worlds, where voices echoed, half-heard, not quite distinct enough for him to decide upon that which was discussed.

Yet by the same measure, he was conscious of the sun's glare, just outside this small patch of shade in the shadow side of the dune, of the way his feet sank into the soft, powdery white sand and the grasses that tickled against his skin.

Tantalising, just beyond his reach, lurked that indefinable *something* outside of snatching distance.

He jerked to full wakefulness with a start. The shadows were gone, swallowed by true dusk, and sand crusted his lips and eyes. The basket had rolled away, and now was captured in the stump of a tree that had died last summer. The gulls wheeled and cried above him; perhaps it was this frenzy of shaking wings and gulping calls that had dragged him fully into alertness. Also, he was *cold* (finally).

The tide would be out by now, surely.

He ran for the basket, then trotted back towards the sea, dismayed to see several harlings already in the distance, bent as they picked through whatever the ocean might've left behind while there was still light in the bruised-plum sky. If anything, the wind had become fiercer, snatching the very breath from his lips as he stalked along the tide line. Where the ocean had receded, the sand was firm and studded with sea snails, oozing their way along on their wide feet. He didn't know the proper name for them, just that their shells reminded him of the stories his hostling had told of unicorns. Except the other harlings had laughed at him when he'd called them unicorn snails. They were just sea snails to the others, with their algae-slick shells. Why was he being so stupid?

Orthran hurried until he passed the furthest harling, pushing on towards the headland. He'd have to cross over to the stretch of shore on the other side now, in order to find anything that might be of value. Which meant he'd take longer on the way back. The way his stomach growled, reminded him that it'd be a while yet before he ate too. And it'd be fully dark by the time he got home.

Almost as if mocking him, a shooting star sailed low and actinic bright, so close he swore he could hear its crackle as it plunged to the earth on the other side of the headland. Perhaps that was a sign from the dehara. As if! Orthran didn't consider himself a superstitious har, but that falling star had been pretty. The tribe's Nahir Nuri would no doubt have many things to say about magical portents. Not that Orthran put any stock in the har's pronouncements. However, he did hurry along, goaded by a peculiar urgency he couldn't quite explain.

Pickings were slim on the other side, though. He found some driftwood, which was precious enough, as fuel for their fires was scarce. Orthran would have liked to carve some of the pieces into fanciful shapes to sell to the tinkers, but as Ahape pointed out, these served no purpose other than to blunt knives and potentially nick fingers. Orthran sighed as he traced the outline of a dolphin, a cormorant, a gull. Then, he placed the pieces into the basket.

The outgoing tide had exposed a reef, where black mussels grew in profusion, so he sought the fattest ones that had shells longer than his hands. That was where he found the stone.

At first, he thought it was a chunk of sea glass, which had tumbled through seven oceans until it was smooth as silk. About the size of his thumb, and roughly the same shape, the object was too heavy to be glass, and gleamed with a nacreous sheen.

A slow smile broke out on Orthran's lips. He'd found many fascinating objects while beach-combing – shards of china glazed with blue-and-white patterns, arrowheads, and even an uncut diamond – but this was truly exceptional.

Suddenly suspicious that he might be observed, he peered around him but saw nohar else, only a few gulls padding along hopefully behind him, in case he turned up anything edible.

Good.

Orthran smoothed the stone with his fingers, then tucked it into the small pouch of valuables he wore around his neck. The little leather bag was immediately heavier, but it was a pleasant kind of heaviness that spoke of an even greater wealth than the few copper pieces and beads it contained. What he would do with the stone, he wasn't yet sure, but he wouldn't be trading it in a hurry until he knew exactly what it was worth.

The rest of his scavenging didn't turn up much of interest – a few more bits of driftwood and a fishing lure attached to a scrap of broken line. Cold, and no longer inclined to endure the biting wind, he turned around and made his way back to Spitmouth.

A flat expanse continues as far as the eye can see, and the ground is powdery, and filled with minute granules as he walks. Each footfall produces a puff of dust, and the sky above is so shot through with stars, it's as if somehar's tossed a handful of ash up into the air and it clings there, glittering. Three moons dance, spinning rapidly about each other along their slow arcs through the sky, so that he feels dizzy watching. One is larger than the other, slightly green. The other two are a little ruddier, their faces pocked with darker welts.

The land about him is brightly lit, and filled with perfectly spherical boulders, which are scattered about carelessly, as if thanks to an abandoned game of marbles. Some spheres are as high as his knee, but others tower above him. He pauses, reaches out for the stone and –

– Orthran blinked, dragged into the present by Ahape banging the kettle with a spoon.

'It's well past sunrise! If you don't get up now, there'll be no breakfast for you!'

With a groan, Orthran pushed the covers from him. His parents' cot was already made up. How had he slept through their waking? Absently, he patted at his pouch with his left hand. It was still satisfyingly heavy around his neck.

A red carpet of fallen leaves is strewn so thickly on the ground that his feet sink to the shins. The mist is thick and cold, and clings to him, dampening his cloak (a burnt umber fabric for which he has no name, luxurious). He cannot see further than a few trees ahead, and the trunks are peculiar, sheathed in a pelt of moss so verdant it can't possibly be real. Also, how is it that the trees seem to curl sinuously upward, around their fellows, like serpents? The steady drip, drip, drip of moisture makes him suck in a deep breath of the gloomy —

— A sharp smack nudged Orthran's head from where he'd rested it on his forearm. He jerked upright with a cry.

His father scowled over him in the shade of the overhang where they were bundling thatch. 'By the dehara's ouna-lims, you are not a harling anymore, Orthran. You can't just nod off like that! We have work to do.'

Somehow, Orthran had pillowed his head on his arm, rested it on a bundle, and had slipped off into dreams. He glanced in dismay at the bundles that still needed tying off, yet he couldn't stop the slow smile that spread on his lips. Ah, but what dreams...

He crouches at the edge of a canyon and, below, a river swirls between countless pillars that rise impossibly, gracefully to the sky, each pale sandstone pylon topped with tufts of greenery. It is as if some giant hand has extruded the rock from the very earth with careless fingers.

Wind buffets him. He watches swifts duck and weave in the sky. Then he opens his arms and embraces the fathomless drop, and is buoyed by some invisible force as he too swirls among the birds, a cry of delight tearing from his lips —

— 'Goodness! Orthran!' Somehar shook him and he startled upright. He was hunched in the leeward side of his family's home, and Luphawe, from the house next door, loomed over him.

'What?'

'You were just sitting there, yelling. What is the matter?'

Orthran blinked sleepily, but managed a smile. 'I was dozing off. I expect I had a dream.'

'Right.' Luphawe stepped back, a frown creasing his forehead.

'I got a bit too much sun yesterday.'

His neighbour's expression suggested doubt, and Orthran couldn't help but feel a weevil of worry. The moment Luphawe's back was turned, he placed his hand over his pouch. The leather bag was still heavy with the peculiar stone, and it felt warm, from more than simply contact with his skin. He supposed he should do the right thing and go speak to the Nahir Nuri. After all, there had been that star that had fallen, shortly before Orthran had found the stone. Yet to share his findings would mean that they'd possibly take the stone away from him, and he had little enough that he could call his own.

And the dreams.

Oh, the dreams.

A week now, and every time his eyes drifted shut, he discovered new worlds. He begged for uninterrupted sleep so that he could spend more time wandering peculiar landscapes, be they rainforest, desert or grassland. Other worlds. Places *other* than this thirsty land, with its stunted trees and too many thorns. Every time he slept, he visited someplace else, could fly, could breathe underwater. He could float among enormous bioluminescent jellyfish, or sprawl across the limb of a massive tree, warm in the light of a distant, binary sun.

His parents worried at him, like dogs might at a bone, complaining of his increased inattention, so he took to sneaking off, sleeping among the dunes during the late afternoons, when he should be helping mend nets. Yet as luck would have it, it was his habit of wandering off to find a place to slip into dreaming that brought him to the wanderer.

The stranger was a tall har, a southerner, with pale skin and long white hair, so that he looked as though he were covered in ash. His wide-brimmed hat sported the iridescent primary feathers of some bird Orthran had never before seen. This har had a haze about him, caught out of the corner of an eye but never detected straight on.

It was the stranger who loomed over Orthran now, as he curled up in the little hollow he'd scraped for himself in the side of a particularly large dune, which did a better job than its brethren of protecting him from the wind.

He blinked up at the stranger, puzzled, and still trying to hold onto the skeins of a dream –

– pearlescent skies, thin wispy clouds and the eerie cries of some unseen creature –

'Tell me, young Tiahaar, is there a village nearby?'

Orthran nodded. The har's accent was peculiar, each syllable carefully pronounced, as though he were speaking to a small harling who might not understand.

'Ah. Would you be so good as to guide me there? It would be

particularly awful if I were to stumble in there unannounced. I am Okiya.' He offered his hand, as if expecting Orthran to touch it. Upon his outstretched palm was a single, bright-orange daisy, completely unseasonal and freshly plucked.

Orthran clenched his hands and kept them to himself. What trickery with that flower? Clearly, this har wanted him to share his name, but he wouldn't. At least, not until he understood this being's motives for arriving without warning.

'Ours is a small village, Tiahaar. I'm sure you will be made welcome,' Orthran said, rising and dusting sand from his clothing. He was immediately conscious of how shabby he was in comparison to the stranger, whose clothing appeared to be finely-tailored. Not a scrap of poorly-tanned hide on this one. And he wore real, honest to goodness leather boots that laced up to the knee. Granted, they bore many scuff marks and scratches, but Orthran hadn't seen boots that fine since some high-and-mighty har from Mistsand had come by a year or so ago on a hunting expedition.

Next to this har, Orthran felt like a miserable savage, and he hated himself all the more as he ducked his head like an obsequious dog. 'Right this way, Tiahaar.'

A faint smile twitched on the har's lips, and it bothered Orthran immensely that this stranger seemed to gaze right into his heart to see its innermost workings. Without even thinking, he placed a hand on his pouch, and was horrified to feel an answering *thrummm* from the stone inside, as if it were pleased to see this stranger and would betray him in short order.

Why was it that the har required guidance? Any fool could see the tops of the mud cones that made up their village, poking up just behind the ridge where the caves were. It stood to reason that anyhar could walk right in and have half a dozen hara begging him to sup with them for the honour of receiving such a fine visitor.

'Where are you from?' Orthran asked grudgingly while they walked.

'Oh, here and there.'

'But why are you here?'

Okiya smiled. 'I think you know why I'm here.'

It felt as if all the blood rushed to Orthran's feet and his breath grew short. 'I have no idea.'

'As you say, but I am looking for an object. About so long.' He gestured a finger-length.

Orthran said nothing, but clenched his hands even more. 'The Nahir Nuri will be glad to receive you.'

'It's not your Nahir Nuri I wish to see.'

At those words, Orthran increased his pace, to the point where the stranger almost had to break into a trot to keep up with him. His peevishness made him smile to himself as he hurried to the village, where their arrival caused the anticipated stir. Hara swarmed out of dwellings and all but mobbed Okiya, some even daring to reach out to touch his leather coat, which he wore despite the heat.

This gave Orthran the opportunity to slip away. He needed to hide the dreamstone, where nohar would find it. But where?

His anxiety carried him out the other side of the settlement, past the palisade and into the riverbed, with its hissing reeds and hard-packed mud. The Spit River hadn't flowed cleanly in two winters, and the only water there was a brackish pool that he skirted on his way across to the scrub opposite.

He kept looking back, but nohar followed, which made him hiss in relief. Yet this still didn't solve his problem. Though the sun was setting, it was still hot, and he had to pause often to remove the thorns that bit into his soles.

He continued until Spitmouth was no more than a few pimples behind him, and the sun kissed the horizon and set the entire western sky aflame. His breath rasped in his throat, and he sank to his knees, still unable to shake the sense he was being watched. He cast about, but saw only a brown hare that hopped away the moment his gaze settled upon it.

The termite mound about five paces from him was perfect for his need, and he hurried to it. Three hard knocks with a stone, and he broke off a chunk that was deep enough for him to fit his hand into. Hundreds of little white insects swarmed out, and he apologised to them under his breath, yet when the moment came for him to place the dreamstone, he couldn't. It felt somehow wrong to secret it in this little space. Try as he might, he couldn't let it go. The stone hummed in his grasp, its song on the edge of his hearing.

What if he couldn't find this termite mound later? What if somehar *had* seen him and marked what he did?

Hot tears of frustration burned in his eyes.

'It's mine!' he hissed and clenched his fingers around the stone.

'Mine.'

For a while he crouched there, the termites crawling all over his hands, biting even. Then, with a cry of frustration, he tucked the stone back into its pouch and made his way back to the settlement.

As he'd expected, there was to be a small celebration that night. The Nahir Nuri even performed a small dedication ceremony to welcome Okiya to Spitmouth, for apparently the har was some sort of shaman himself – or so it was claimed. Hostlings came to ask Okiya to place his hands on their bellies to bless their pearls, and even the ancient human Sindiqua crawled out of his hovel behind the goat pens to ask whether Okiya could do anything about his aching joints. Agave flowed, and a goat was slaughtered, so that all might share of the village's meagre bounty.

Drums were brought out and precious fuel cast upon the village's great hearth, and the atmosphere became festive. Orthran hung back in the shadows, often pressing a hand to his pouch. Distressingly enough, the stone continued to hum, more so whenever Okiya drew near. Each time, Orthran would seek other nooks and crannies into which he could press himself and nurse his mug of agave. The tart spirits did little to lift his mood, but it made his predicament almost bearable.

Yet, when it seemed the entire village was kicking up the dust, ululating and sending their praises to the dehara of the boundless firmament, Okiya found him.

'You saw the shooting star, did you not?' he whispered into Orthran's ear.

Oddly enough, the world about the two of them became muted, as if they stood within a bubble of silence that had somehow separated them from the rest of the village.

Orthran swallowed back a squeak of fright and blinked somewhat owlishly at the stranger. The flames painted ghoulish shadows on the har's face, making him appear somehow feral. He smiled, and his teeth seemed longer, sharper than they had any right to be.

'What of it?' Orthran answered. 'There are often shooting stars here.'

'It wasn't just any star, I think.' The har looked meaningfully down at Orthran's hand that had crept of its own volition to clutch at his pouch.

'I don't know what you're getting at, Tiahaar.'

Okiya sighed. 'I see how things are. You will deny me one more time, and then you'll understand.'

An awful, creeping feeling shivered up Orthran's arms and he hugged himself. 'I don't like you.'

The humour fled from Okiya's features. 'You're not meant to.'

'There you are!' The voice came from his right, and Orthran turned to see his hostling hurrying to him through a knot of dancers.

'Yes?' He nearly sagged in relief then turned back to tell Okiya that his hostling was looking for him, and he must go, but the har had vanished.

For once, that evening, Orthran didn't mind helping Ahape in the menial tasks he had found for him, as it meant he'd remain out of Okiya's clutches.

The stranger remained in the village for three days and nights, and during that time Orthran concocted every excuse he could to be diligently busy, to the point when even his father seemed suitably impressed that this son had turned over a new leaf. Surely, if he was out the entire day with Cegara, cutting reeds for thatch, then he had little chance of bumping into Okiya.

As it was, he hardly dared to sleep in more than snatches, for fear his dreams would draw the stranger to him, like ants to honey. The entire village was abuzz with the quest the shaman had laid upon them; he was searching for a precious stone, he said, that had fallen from the heavens not long ago. Had anyhar seen it? Harlings and others went searching in parties, poking at dune rat holes with sticks. Even the Nahir Nuri was bestirred to take out his divining rod and cast about, though at that point Orthran made himself scarce.

One morning, Okiya announced he'd be leaving, and for a moment Orthran thought himself well rid of the shaman, but he was not about to take risk a chance encounter, so he headed out before daybreak, intending to beach-comb beyond the headland at low tide, just to be certain.

The sky, the sea and damp sands were all tinged with a pearlescent gleam, and the air was still cool before the day's fire. Sanderlings raced ahead of him, their tiny heads bobbing as their feet imprinted tiny marks on the sand. Orthran's exhaustion was lodged marrow deep, but he forced himself onward, realising with a start that he intended to go exactly where he'd found the stone not so long ago.

He'd avoided that third confrontation with the stranger, and he was nearly giddy with the sense that he'd contrived to escape that curse. Yet as he crested the rise, there stood Okiya, by the two granite boulders that stuck up out of the sand like knees. The har was smoking his long-stemmed pipe, and regarded Orthran with thinly-veiled amusement.

Sorely tempted to return to Spitmouth there and then, Orthran was mired in the inevitability of his situation. If he turned his back on Okiya, he would show the har he feared the confrontation, and that he had something to hide.

Well, he did have something to hide, but if the har was playing this game with him – for clearly he knew that Othran knew he knew – Damn. He gritted his teeth and halted four paces before the har.

'You win,' he bit out. 'This is the part where I deny that I know anything about your cursed stone.'

This didn't seem to surprise Okiya at all. 'As you wish.' He drew one last puff from the pipe then tapped out the ash. He tucked it into his hat brim, then shouldered his pack and began to walk away.

'Wait! Is that it?' Orthran shouted. Dismay bloomed hot and angry in his chest. Why did he even care what the har thought?

The har didn't so much as shrug, nor give any indication that he was aware of the rude gesture Orthran made at his retreating back. A savage grin distorted Orthran's lips, and he wanted to crow at the har that he still had the stone. Yet of course that would undo all three of his denials on the matter, so he bit the inside of his cheek, while his hand crept to its familiar caress of his pouch. The leather felt hot to the touch, as if it has rested next to an open flame. A sensible har wouldn't piss about with strange magic, his conscience whispered.

It's mine, not yours, you old jackal.

Fancy har, with his ways that were not *their* ways, down here by the sea. Poking about, creating upheaval.

Orthran gusted out a breath and crouched by the stones, watching as Okiya vanished between the dunes. Well, that was that. He dusted the sand off his hands, yet his feet were reluctant to move.

So, he had the stone now; it was his, fair and square. Yet he didn't know why it gave him dreams, nor why it was so important to the stranger. What else could he have learnt had he given the stone back? It was some sort of test, and he couldn't figure out if he'd passed or failed in a spectacular fashion.

Summer bled into autumn. It hardly ever rained here, but they looked forward to the occasional winter showers. Sometimes, it rained further inland, and then the river would swell and push down its dry bed. A shallow lagoon of brackish water would pool in the marsh, and the weaverbirds would make their basket-nests.

But the rains didn't come, and the dust plumed with each footfall.

Orthran was aware of this on the periphery, and even as he went to sleep hungry, more often than not, he had his dreams to wrap around him with visions of far-off places, where he drank his fill of sweet water and ate strange fruit that stained his lips and tongue crimson.

Such livestock that survived the miserable winter scuffed at the hard-packed earth, licked dust from scrub that had been chewed down to the roots. Hara sat with hollow eyes and bellies, and even the fisherhara lacked the wherewithal to put out to sea. Whenever they did, their catches were meagre. Red tides poisoned the shellfish, and even the seabirds departed. It seemed as if the spirits of the land had deserted them, and the dehara had better things to do than herd clouds and stir rivers from their beds.

All through this, Orthran slept when he could, chasing after phantasms and mirages, and always he felt that Okiya was there at the edges, observing in amusement. Whenever he sensed the har's fitful presence, he'd move on, for he'd become adept in travelling from one dream vision to the next. A door that opened in an old, ruined house brought him to grasslands where massive antelope with spiralled horns grazed. A rock he lifted from the ground became a trapdoor to a cavern, where peculiar crystals were imbued with an inner radiance. If he leapt into a well, he emerged in a river pool, high up in a misty, wooded ravine.

Yet that shadow dogged his heels, coming ever closer, whispering.

It's your fault the balance is out of kilter.

'How so?' Orthran almost asked, but all he encountered was

quiet, mocking laughter and flashes of a barren landscape far inland, where the first mountains slowly humped out of the scrublands and the dry riverbed cut through a valley. It was a land he knew, had seen in the distance.

Come find me.

Then the dreamstone at his neck would offer a small pulse, and Orthran would be aware of the dreams slipping through his fingers like water, and the hardness of his sleeping pallet. Okiya wanted the dreamstone. There was no doubt in Orthran's mind.

Winter's claws dug sharp and dry, and laid a bitter frost on the ground. At night, the sky was so vast and empty, the stars looked like lamps a har could pluck down. There was no fuel for fires, and most nights hara huddled together, in a heap of stick-thin limbs and empty bellies.

At wits' end, the Nahir Nuri enacted a rite, daring to entreat Tsui'Goab, who'd guided their human ancestors and would surely bestir himself at their desperate need, to bring the rains; the entire village gathered at the caves for this, but they had no herbs with which they could smudge the air, no fires to light, for there was no fuel. The gourd from which they poured libations was half-empty, the bitter liquid crushed from shrivelled roots somehar could spare from his foraging. Hara licked dry lips as the greedy soil accepted the offering, but still the rains did not come. Evidently even Tsui'Goab had rejected them.

Much to Orthran's growing despair, even the dreamstone dulled, and such dreams that came seemed wispy, insubstantial.

Hara began to drift away from the village, their jackal-skin karosses swept around needle-sharp shoulders, as their feet plumed up dust. *We'll come back with the rain,* they said. *If the rains come.* The fishing was still good at Dog Stone Bay. The copper mines always needed able-bodied hara to help dig and smelt. Mistsand was constructing a new pier, and they required labourers with strong backs and clever hands.

Soon Spitmouth was a tomb of mud-dauber wasp nests, where the wind sighed and stirred eddies in the powdery sand.

'We are going to Dog Stone Bay,' Ahape declared one night. 'I can mend nets there.'

Cegara had come home with nothing but a handful of

shrivelled corms that they'd eaten raw, for Orthran had failed to find fuel. What he didn't tell his parents is that instead of foraging, he'd sought sanctuary in his favourite hollow in the dunes, where he'd caught a few rays of late afternoon sun and the ghost of a dream. Now he sat chewing the hard corms with his parents, and came to the realisation that like it or not, things were about to change. Out of habit, he placed his hand on his pouch for reassurance, but the stone felt *dull*. Heavy.

'What if I don't want to go?' he asked.

Change was bad. There'd be others there; hara he didn't know. Somehar might find out about his dreamstone; it was precious, and they might want to steal it.

His father merely shook his head, didn't quite meet his gaze.

Ahape sighed. 'You could stay, if you want, though you can barely care for yourself living with us. I can't imagine you'd last long on your own.'

A small, rebellious barb pricked Orthran's heart. 'Perhaps I *should* stay. After all, I am nothing but a burden to you.'

'Orthran!' Cegara exclaimed.

'It's true! I've seen how you trade exasperated glances. If I'm not doing well here, imagine how I'll fail elsewhere. I'm no good for anyhar, anything.'

'If you just applied yourself...' Cegara straightened. 'The dehara know we've tried but...'

'I should never have crawled out of my pearl! Look at the both of you! You're secretly relieved I've offered to stay behind. One less mouth to feed!' The growing despair that had been tugging at Orthran, rose within him, a bleak wave. It whispered of the sweet dreams that awaited if he could but slip away and curl up somewhere quiet. He knew it then: he could sleep forever and perhaps this time he would never awaken. There must be a way in which he could completely untether himself from this bag of bones he animated and spend eternity roving the aethers as a spirit. If he could coax a truly strong dream from the stone, perhaps this might be the case.

'You know that's not true!' Ahape snapped.

'Then what must I do?' Orthran hated how thick his throat was. If he wasn't careful, he'd start crying like a harling. It was always so much easier when he slept; he didn't have to argue, didn't have to feel this constant gnawing hunger in the pit of his stomach, or swallow back the dust in his throat.

His hostling's expression softened. 'Come with us. You know you cannot stay here. There is no food; the well water is thick with mud. Everyhar has already foraged anything edible for miles. The game has moved on. If you stay, you'll die.'

Orthran gave a ragged laugh. 'Perhaps that is for the best.'

Cegara's head twitched, and he opened his mouth to rebuke Orthran, but Ahape's glare shut him up.

His hostling sighed, clasped fine-boned hands in his lap. The myriad little bone beads in his locks chimed as he shook his head. 'I know things have been difficult for you...for us all, of late. We are concerned.'

'What? No recriminations for my words spoken in haste,' Orthran murmured. They were all tired, tested to the ends of their endurance.

'We are all hungry, tired and thirsty. It will do us no good to be angry and let fly with ill-considered words.' Ahape's lips twisted into a thin smile.

'In other words, I'm being irrational.'

'I didn't say that.'

'You certainly implied it,' Orthran said.

'Sleep on it tonight, dear heart,' Ahape said.

He'd not called Orthran *that* in a long, long time, and shame burned Orthran's cheeks. Despite everything, his hostling loved him. Both his parents did.

Cegara reached over and placed a hand on his shoulder. 'My son, we care deeply about you. I wish there was some way we could make things better, but all we can do is be here. We want you to thrive. If I could find the water that would renew your spirit, I would.'

Orthran had to hide his face behind his hands, and he breathed in through his nose so that he could clear his eyes. 'I need to rest.'

Yet when he lay on his pallet, sleep wouldn't find him. He listened while his parents settled for the night, Ahape discussing what they'd pack to take on their journey, what they'd leave behind and hope the field mice would not gnaw. Already, Orthran felt himself putting distance between himself and his parents. This sudden wisdom was the blinding light of a gibbous moon, pressing its face past its misty shroud.

He *should* have found his own way in the world as soon as he was out of feybraiha. He *should* have travelled down the coast until he reached Table Bay, or asked to join one of the caravans headed out into the interior. Instead of dreaming about the mighty forests of the South Coast, he *should* have been there, pressing his hands against the bark and feeling the thrum of life just beneath the surface.

Instead of clutching a dead stone, all its dreams used up.

So many should-haves, could-haves.

Here he was, hungry and thirsty, spread out like somehar half a corpse already, while others made the decisions that affected his future.

That was the crux of the matter, wasn't it? He'd borne Okiya resentment, because the shaman had come stirring in his life, and it hadn't been Orthran who'd been the one approaching him. There was the matter of that single orange daisy, so vital and mysterious, held out in offering, that Orthran had rejected. A mystery, and power spurned.

Perhaps Okiya could tell him now why the dreamstone had grown cold and dead to the touch – despite the wriggling suspicion that the shaman would merely layer more mysteries, more questions, should Orthran seek him. He didn't want to go, because that was precisely what Okiya wanted, and yet Orthran was like one enthralled, with the fear of missing out on greater secrets. The more he resisted the notion, considered that it might not be such a bad thing to go instead to Dog Stone Bay with his parents to start afresh, the more the inherent need to speak to Okiya bloomed in his chest, like that anomalous daisy with its black-ringed eye. For the briefest moment, he even entertained the wild notion of tossing the dreamstone into the sea, to allow the breakers to turn it over a thousand times more, until it was worn away to nothing but a grain of sand. But then his thoughts returned to the enigmatic Okiya and his game.

Desire – that's what it was, and beyond the need for the sharing of breath or taking aruna. Orthran was more than the parents who'd brought his pearl into the world, more than the tiny village where he'd scrabbled about the adobe walls. If he shoved aside this mystery, he would forever wonder what might've happened otherwise.

On silent feet, he rose and slipped past his parents' sleeping forms bundled beneath their shared karosses. Orthran took his own, and wrapped it around his shoulders, although the jackal fur did little to ward away the pervasive chill that made the air heavy. He padded between the silent dwellings, his breath misting before him.

The stars seemed brighter, colder tonight, and though the moon was yet to rise, he could see well enough. The only light in the village came from the gaping maws of the caves, where their Nahir Nuri no doubt held vigil. Orthran felt like telling him that he was wasting what fuel he had, peering into the flames for answers from spirits that'd turned deaf and dumb. Spitmouth was going into hibernation.

Then the tug in his collarbone, the slightest pull, like a finger testing the tension in a fishing line. Eastwards, slightly to the north. A small spike of alarm thrilled through him. What lay in that direction other than expanses of sun-baked red sand and the black twigs of long-dead scrub? There would be no shelter from the sun there, come morning. Even if he followed the riverbed, there was no guarantee he'd be able to find water, even if he dug, nor that he'd uncover the tubers and corms that sustained life when there was little else. He barely knew how to recognise them, despite all the times his father had hoped to instil some sort of knowledge about survival.

Yet cursing his own idiocy at this point was not going to help his situation. Orthran was not prepared to wake his parents now to ask their advice. Harlings on the cusp of feybraiha would occasionally wander off into the wilderness, on some sort of vision quest, but this was something that had never gripped him. Until now, that is.

By equal measure, this entire notion he entertained might be some elaborate suicide attempt, and this caused him to pause, his breath held. He allowed himself one last glance over his shoulder, at the pointed cones of the village that huddled by the caves, and then pushed on between the whip-thin reeds that choked a section of the riverbed. They – his parents, the village – would be well rid of him: the awkward har who didn't know his place. Not a harling, but not quite an adult either.

Yet even that thought brought cold comfort, as he considered how his hostling might send Cegara after him to bring him back, and he grew conscious of the tracks he left in the soft sand. This prompted him to cross over to the veld on the other side, to the first of the many barren plains that lay ahead of him. Here, the ground was hard enough to hide his spoor, and if he was not turned around, he could meet up with the loop of the river as it snaked through the region. At least, that was the theory. This way, his father might assume he'd headed for one of the wagon routes instead.

Nohar would be mad enough to strike off into the hinterlands, away from the beaten track now, would they?

Resolute, Orthran strode along, placing his feet with care so that he might not step on a scorpion or night adder. The stars bathed the landscape in in their ethereal light, and in the distance a nightjar thrust its resonant *chirrrrrrrr* into the emptiness; this was the only sound he heard, apart from his breathing, which was loud in his ears.

The dreams were only holding him back; he understood that now. The same way the few humans he'd encountered were addled by their reliance on weed or spirits, gnarled creatures whose bodies grew twisted and desiccated before they'd seen forty summers. Except nohar could see how twisted Orthran had become inside; or maybe they did, for he certainly bore the fruit of his behaviour.

What would he do once he found Okiya? *Would* he find the har? His own magical senses were as stunted as other parts of him, but Orthran continued doggedly. North, northeast. He'd never gone that far before, not even with his father, but he had tasted that land at the edges of sleep, echoing with Okiya's mocking laughter.

A veiled greying of the eastern horizon was the first hint that dawn would come, and not long after, Orthran found himself drunk-stumbling back across the Spit River's course. Faint with thirst and exhaustion, he continued along the soft, white sand until he reached an outcropping. Here, just as the day's heat began to rise, he crawled beneath an overhang where he fell into dreaming.

Soft rains sift down, bringing with it the sweet water from the mountains. The first tender green spears of river reeds stubble the banks, where the popping and trilling of hidden frogs rejoice at the wetness. Orthran cups his hand in water more crystal than liquid, and when he drinks, he is filled with light to the point where his skin grows tight like a drum. Dizzy, he rises and spins, his extremities forming a fine mist that glints jewel-like in the hazy sun.

Orthran woke gradually, unspooled from his rest, lips cracked and tasting like old blood. The dream was the most vivid he'd had in a while, taunting him with the insubstantial. An affirmation, perhaps? His thirst nearly strangled him. Even in the shade, the heat was stifling, as if he'd been shoved into a bread oven and forgotten. The world outside his tiny refuge shimmered with the glare, and he couldn't help but whimper at his foolishness. What was he doing?

Every part of his body ached, and if he did not find water or nourishment soon, his journey would be over far sooner than he'd anticipated. If he turned back now, and walked at sundown, he could come to the village where the last scrapings of muddy well water would be more silt than liquid. His stomach clenched at the thought, and he whined quietly. Yet to continue? Madness.

You've come this far. Giving up so soon?

He wasn't certain if the voice was his own, and he gritted his teeth.

Return to Spitmouth, shamefaced and foolish, or press further and die? A sane har would give up this fool's errand. He wasn't sure what he was anymore. A sane har would have gone with his family to Dog Stone Bay, and learned to catch fish, cure hides or commit fully to his father's trade. If he was an insane har, perhaps it was a good thing that he walked out into the wilds and never returned.

Orthran struck out, this time following the river. Not half an hour since he ventured from his hiding space, he came to old human ruins that had been overtaken by hara – now gone too – but there was still a small puddle of silty water at the bottom of the ancient rain barrel under the cottage's eaves. This he scraped out with the chipped enamel mug that stood next to the barrel, possibly left here for this exact purpose.

For a while the lukewarm water fooled his empty belly into thinking it was filled, and he stumbled on.

The Spit River was a snake, he realised, as he followed the sinuous curves. The river was life too, for always it provided when he felt pressed to his limits. A patch of damp sand in the shadow of a ridge, where a har might dig and discover just enough liquid to sustain him, or a spot where corms might be uncovered – hard yes, and bitter, but still food. Somehow that dormant part of him, bent on survival, guided him unerringly just when he feared he might starve. Crickets too, could be eaten, and he crunched those chitinous bodies between his teeth without shuddering over much.

When he could catch them, that is, and he had to admit that he was becoming better at it.

Every once in a while, he'd encounter more abandoned dwellings, and he tried not to think too long on where the hara had gone, for the land was empty of all save him, and the nightjar that remained forever further ahead of him. He fancied the bird was now his herald.

Day and night became the inhalations and exhalations of his existence. Sometimes, he rested in a tumbledown ruin or beneath an overhang. On one occasion, he'd wedged himself in an abandoned antbear's nest that still reeked of the creature's mustiness.

I've become a wild thing, hunting shadows, he thought, and allowed himself a feral grin, for it felt good. When he slept, more often than not, his rest was total oblivion and it was his waking hours that felt somehow unreal, hallucinogenic. All the while, the ember within his chest glowed, tugging, whispering. *This way. Go this way. Yes, this is right.* He *is waiting.*

Though he knew not how much time had passed, and the sun had turned his skin from a silty brown to raw umber, Orthran pressed on until the river carved its way between the knees of folded sandstone peaks. Here, hyraxes peered down at him, their eerie alarm calls high-pitched and metallic, echoing on the rocks and scraping through his veins. Pied crows circled, curious, following his progress as he began to struggle on the rocky bed. Still no running water, but by now that was hardly a surprise.

Not much further now, either, and though the exhaustion sucked at his very marrow, threatening to empty him of the last of his vitality, Orthran picked his way between water-polished stones and the fallen limbs of long-dead acacias.

So it was that he eventually came to a shallow valley of red sand and what must have once been a substantial human settlement. Now the mud brick walls were mostly worn away, but the desert had yet to reclaim the faint grid of the streets. A donkey skull grinned at him, set up on a pole as some sort of grim warning – but by whom and why? Orthran stared at the empty eye sockets for a short while, but then pushed on. The sun was already chewing the back of his neck, despite it still being early morning. He tugged his kaross over one shoulder and sweat trickled down his arm.

Of all the structures that had survived, the humans' old church building stood and appeared to have a roof – perhaps others had maintained it, for charred logs in a makeshift hearth outside the structure told him that this was where travellers sought shelter. For a few heartbeats, Orthran remained on the cement steps that bore patches of the slick, brick-red paint he'd often seen on floors of older ruins.

The pointed arch of the door gaped above him, offering him a glimpse of the reed-panelled ceiling within. Somehar *did* care about this place. The walls inside had recently been given a fresh coat of lime.

He was *here*, where he was supposed to be, for that insistent tugging in his chest subsided, replaced by exhaustion and... expectation. But of *what?*

Old pine floorboards, dusty and scuffed, creaked as he set down his foot. The interior smelled strongly of resin, similar to the types that the Nahir Nuri burned for his rites. A holy place instead of a mere waystation, then? But where was Okiya, if this repurposing of old human places of worship was his doing, as Orthran was beginning to suspect? No furnishings, save for an altar, set up at the back. Small spots of guano on the floor in one corner; a rock martin's mud nest stuck to the ceiling, but no birds swooped. Alone then, but all the small hairs on his arms and neck prickled, and he couldn't stop himself from casting about, not quite believing that somehar wasn't there, observing him.

The air here stirred, even though he could detect no breeze, as if somehar was speaking. The words hovered on the edge of his hearing, and his arms and neck continued to prickle.

Despite the growing heat outside, the interior was cool enough for Orthran to shiver as he approached the altar. A simple thing, it was constructed of what appeared to be an old sheet of corrugated roofing set up on four river-round rocks the approximate size and shapes of skulls. Upon the altar itself stood a small collection of glass bottles – artefacts from the humans' era. They contained dust, possibly seeds and beads. He couldn't tell at a casual glance and didn't feel comfortable examining them closer just yet.

The centrepiece was a rabbit skull, its empty eyes leering, and its delicate bones decorated with myriad runes etched into the bone and filled with ochre. What this all meant, he could not tell, and though he found it unsettling, it was, by equal measure oddly compelling, as if he'd unintentionally stumbled onto somehar else's private things.

All the while, the whispers intensified, words nearly intelligible. Grasping shadows tugged at the limits of his vision. Orthran blinked, then noticed the door that stood ajar, behind the pulpit. He stumbled around the macabre display and went to investigate. The smell, when it hit him, was of old carrion, the scuffed linoleum floor littered with thousands of dead insects whose carapaces crunched beneath his feet. The seated figure leered at him, the flesh shrunken to bone where it had not completely flaked away. Strangely, the fine boots seemed unaffected, and a long-stemmed pipe was still clasped in skeletal fingers.

Bitter bile rose in Orthran's throat, and he retched, half turned away with an arm thrown over his mouth and nose – as if that would help. Too many teeth leering at him from papery lips drawn back in a silent snarl.

How this came to be, he could not tell. The har had had a sense of great power about him when Orthran had met him back in Spitmouth, yet even then he'd had the stick-thin limbs of a mantid. Orthran had seen death before, when he'd encountered the corpse of a human male mauled by some wild beast that didn't have the taste of the flesh after the kill. But never before had he seen a dead har. He'd heard stories of elders who'd walked out into the desert, and had never been heard from again. Or those who had allowed the hungry waves to take them. How long gone Okiya was, he wasn't sure. Orthran stumbled back a few steps, his hand pressed to the silent stone around his neck. It all made sense now – the stone was somehow connected to Okiya, and by not returning it to him in a timely manner, Orthran had somehow been responsible for this...

He shook his head. What all this greater mystery was, he couldn't tell, and he wasn't certain if he should rejoice or be bowed down in abject grief. A window had opened for him days, weeks ago, and instead he'd chosen to huddle in his corner. And now the window had closed. Orthran had failed, and he wasn't quite sure how or why.

The ties to the pouch he wore snapped, thanks to his efforts, as Orthran fished out the cursed dreamstone.

'I don't understand, you, old bastard!' he hissed at the dead har.

Those twin black holes burned into him, and no answer was

forthcoming.

The stone itself was leaden in his palm. Whatever iridescent hues had once played across the surface had been rendered to an oily wash that seemed to suck in light.

Orthran didn't want it anymore. Didn't need those dreams. He understood now, or thought he did. 'It was never mine to keep, and I know it's too late, and I've done wrong.'

The moment crystallised, his breath rasping in his throat, as he summoned the wherewithal to step forward. Fearing that this skeletal monstrosity might still be possessed of life after all, he placed the stone in the curled-up palm of Okiya's left hand.

At first nothing happened, and Orthran let out a hiss of breath. Then the grim remains gave a small shudder. A sharp snap, like twigs breaking – and the entire pile collapsed in on itself, until nothing remained but piles of clothing and, incongruously, the pair of boots, still upright. Then a small, green shoot stirred, worming its way up from the remains. It grew faster than any plant had the right to grow, until the bud unfurled to reveal a bright-orange daisy with a black-rimmed eye.

Orthran uttered a small shriek and backed away. By the time he was in the hall again, he sprawled against the altar, and the crash of bones and glass and other small objects shattering and scattering sent fresh jags of fear through him.

The low moan of a hot wind hit him as he tore out of the accursed place, into the solid wall of mid-morning heat.

He came to his senses in the scraggly shade of an acacia that crouched on the outskirts of the abandoned settlement. There he stood, until his heart stopped stuttering and he could breathe in more than strangled gasps of furnace. The door to the church mocked him across the way, but he daren't go back there.

That was when he looked up, and realised that the sky itself had filled with fat, bruised-belly clouds that crowded out the sun. A hot wind blasted from the north-east, bringing with it the strong scent of sun-scorched earth and bitter herbs, and the first, distant rumblings of thunder shook his bones.

Orthran closed his eyes, and he could see it then, feel the slow pulse of *rightness* for his offering, how his feet curved with the hard-packed earth, how the small stones pushed back. His left palm had strayed to the acacia's paper bark and he could detect the faint thrum of the tree's life, its roots clutching deep in the soil. The twin brother crows circling high above, their white chests shocking against the dirty sky. How his lungs were bellows, his heart throbbing the slow river of life through his veins. It was all connected, everything. He'd never truly sensed the life of the land before, until now.

Lightning tore open the sky, and the rains came hammering down, turning the dry dust to murky torrents, washing clean the stones, Orthran's skin, soaking into his kaross and weighing it down. He turned on one spot, his feet sucking into the muddy earth, and around him the desert came to life, the greenery furring the red earth until he walked upon a swaying carpet of bright swathes of orange and white blooms that stretched as far as the eye could see. He could go anywhere, be anyhar he wished, and the paths before him went east, south, west, and north. He merely had to take that first step.

Feybraihatide

Feybraihatide is named for the rite of passage harlings undergo as they enter maturity. It is the feast of aruna, of first love and the deep, spiritual passion that enables harlings to be conceived.

Elisin is now full-grown, a vision of beauty, like a radiant form of his Shadetide hostling, with fiery red hair. His consort is Feyrahni, (a slightly more mature Florinel), but this is properly Elisin's festival, as he is regarded as the presiding dehar. His erstwhile hostling has now fully transformed into his potential lover. They have barely seen one another since Bloomtide, and now Feyrahni steps from the forest, dark of skin and hair, dressed in clothes made of leather and leaves. His sacred animal is the stag. On Feybraihatide eve, Feyrahni initiates Elisin into the mysteries of aruna and together they create a pearl.

Feybraihatide is considered a propitious time for spiritual rites of passage – be that magical training ascensions, namings and bondings. Those undertaking chesna-bonds – the bonding of blood as the formalisation of a life partnership – might wait until Feybraihatide to do so. Should a harling undergo their feybraiha at this time of year, it's considered particularly fortuitous, and the presiding dehara will bestow blessings. Hara might also contrive to conceive harlings at this time, as this is believed to encourage good fortune for their offspring. The coupling of a chesna-bond, along with the sparking of a pearl, is the most auspicious of events, and any harling conceived at this time is believed to be endowed with strong and unusual abilities or skills.

Marked

Wendy Darling

These days, my mark attracts far less notice than it used to. I won't say that nohar notices it now, because certainly the mark hasn't faded with time. In truth, it's darker now, rougher in texture, than it's ever been. And hara *do* see it, don't pretend not to, playing the trick that never works anyhow. Visiting hara certainly seem to find their eyes lingering on the mark. At that point, I'll usually answer their questions before they ask, just to get it over with. But as I meant to say originally, the local hara don't give much notice to it now, as it's just a part of me, and after fifty years I in turn am as much a part of Albion as anything else. There are many here who've never known life without me, and those who were here when I arrived certainly got over the mark quickly enough. And the one who didn't get over it? Well, he's the one this story is about.

It was fifty winters ago that my father and I arrived in Albion, at that time a small town of about two thousand hara. Looking back now, it seems like a village, but arriving on the main road with our cart, I was greatly impressed by the many houses, especially all the shops nestled close together at the centre. I spotted a real tavern with a sign and pointed it out to my father. We'd been living in a *truly* tiny village called Three Creeks some fifty miles off where, yes, there was beer, and mead too, but you went to the neighbour's or made it yourself; you couldn't just saunter into a building and buy it from strangers.

But to the point, my father, named Shore, was a smith, handy in several forms of metal, although mostly iron. He'd decided that there were more options for him, and for us, than life in Three Creeks. Besides, he argued several times, the routes that used to bring hara by the village and give his smithy business had shifted, so he didn't have nearly enough work. He never said anything to me before we packed or as we journeyed, but the death of my hostling three years earlier had made his life lonelier than it once had been. I didn't need to be told that; I was seven years old and my father was my world, and so I simply *knew*.

We had no trouble finding ourselves a spot in town. In fact, a smith had left not a month before to move on to a larger town, and the community was just starting to realise what a problem that was. Shore was able to take up the place, making arrangements with the har who'd bought the smithy. He'd be leasing it until he had enough payment to buy it outright. We also received lodging in the deal, a low-slung house next door, plus a stable with two stalls and a large tree, which though bare in winter, showed promise of lovely shade in summer.

In those first few weeks, Shore took me with him any time he went into town, both because he felt better with my familiar presence beside him and because he wanted me out of the house or smithy, out making new friends. There'd been few harlings in Three Creeks; most of the residents were those who'd decided to take their taciturn, independent natures and live away from crowds – and without offspring. Not that there hadn't been any harlings whatsoever, but I could count them on two hands.

I still remember our first encounter with the townshara of Albion. It was the second day after we'd arrived. We'd slept in a rented room and that morning, as it snowed muzzily outside, Shore worked out his business with the smithy owner, having scoped out the situation the afternoon before at the tavern, leaving me behind in the room to rest. Glad to have come to a satisfactory arrangement, he decided we ought to drop by *The Bridle* for lunch and ale. Afterward we would drive the cart over to our new home and get busy hammering in the stakes, so to speak.

The tavern's main room was quite a lot busier than I'd expected, although what I, a harling from a nowhere village, expected, I can't say. Probably half the hara of Three Creeks could've fit inside! But in any case, it was nicely warm, thanks to a fireplace and a good number of hara. In the corner, a har was playing a stringed instrument of some sort. The lamps, on tables and hanging from the ceiling, were of green glass and curving iron, and my father and I glanced at one another. The product of the last smith? And who had made that glass?

We met many hara that day without even trying to. The har

working the bar had met Shore the day before, but I was now introduced, and from there it was one har after another coming up to say hello. Introductions tended to go something like this:

'Welcome. Shore, is it? I hear you're going to be our new smith. Just in time!'

'Yes, I had no idea it would work out so well. If he were still here… I'm not certain what we'd have done.'

'Well, you don't have to worry about that now. The dehara sent you, I'm sure. Glad you're here. You and your son. What's his name?'

'Garnet.'

'Ah.'

'You see where he gets his name, of course. My chesnari chose it and instantly I agreed.'

'Very well chosen. Pleased to meet you, Garnet. You're a lovely young har. I hope you'll settle in here nicely.'

So there, you've heard me mention it again – my mark. And my name also – Garnet. So I may as well stop here now, as well as anywhere, as it will be pertinent, to say that I have on my left cheek a deep red birthmark that looks something like half of a butterfly. One would have to say a deformed butterfly, but that's the closest shape, and the one I've always seen when I look in a mirror.

The colour is closest to red wine and in fact, in the years since my harlinghood, I've discovered old human books that call this type of birthmark a 'port wine stain.' Only it's not really a 'stain,' it's permanent. A very large half butterfly on my otherwise fair cheek.

My name of course comes from the gem of the same colour. I'm sure neither of my parents ever saw such a gem, just as I have not, but one can see pictures still in old books. It's a good name.

Later, after my father got to talking business and trading news with our new neighbors, I got myself a drink and moved to a table closer to the musician, whose dark eyes gazed up dreamily toward the ceiling as he played. I had planned to enjoy the ebb and flow of the room, along with the music, and did for a bit, until I noticed I wasn't alone. Three quite mature harlings, like me all coming up on feybraiha, were standing a few feet away; close enough that I'd notice them from the corner of my eye, but not so close to startle.

'I hope we're not bothering you,' said one, a lanky redhead. 'But we wanted to say hi.'

Setting down my ale, I extended my hand. Introductions were

made. The redhead was Celci, his companions Slate and Alton. Celci and Alton were easy-going, extroverted, while Slate seemed the type who might not have approached me without the others' company. Slate and Alton's parents were part of one of the town's big businesses, horse ranching, and had grown up together in the barns and fields. Celci's family were farmers, and among the crops they brought in were various feeds for the horses. Accompanying family members on deliveries, he'd met Alton and Slate.

They asked me what things were like back in Three Creeks. I told them the truth; that it was a good place to live, close-knit, but sometimes chafing. That there were few harlings. That my hostling had died and it had seemed like it was time for Shore and I to move on.

We were talking of meeting up the next day, with me going out to the ranch, when we were joined by another harling. He looked more mature than any of us, tall, filled out, not childish at all, but I knew – through innate senses – that he was in fact still a harling.

'Etan,' said Slate, less in greeting but more as a statement.

'Hello,' I said. 'I'm Garnet.' I was about to extend my hand when something made me think better of it. 'My father Shore and I just moved here.'

He sniffed. 'Yes, I know. My father told me when I came in. I was looking for him, wondering why he'd been away from the shop so long.' He looked back toward the bar and directed his eyes towards a har with the same black, curling hair as his own. 'He told me to look for somehar who looked like a *Garnet*.' Etan gave me a significant look. 'Interesting name.'

I noticed my new friends exhibiting subtle signs of embarrassment.

'What was your name before?' he asked.

'*Before?*'

He looked at me as if I were a very dim one-year-old. 'Yes. Before you were cursed. Or accidentally cursed yourself. Was it when your hostling died?'

All the good feeling I'd enjoyed since my arrival in town, and especially in my hour at the tavern, seemed to instantly evaporate.

'What are you talking about?' I said slowly, positioning myself so I could look him squarely in the eyes. 'I was born this way.'

'You're lying,' he stated calmly. 'No hara are born like that. With marks. We're *perfect*. Everyhar knows that.'

Everything inside me began to tighten; I was readying myself for a strike, like a cornered snake. But before I could act on impulse, Celci stepped in. 'I think you should go, Etan. Now.'

'Why should I do that? Because then you wouldn't have somehar to fawn over?' He gestured toward me. 'Nothing worth fawning over. He's marked, and it's not natural, *that* I know. Hara aren't born that way.' And with that he strode away, tilting his head toward the rafters dramatically and sighing.

I sat back down in my chair. 'I... what... do... Who is he? And is he *always* like that?'

'That's Etan,' Slate explained. 'He's our age, though he doesn't look it. Used to be more in line, then a couple of years ago he shot up. We thought for sure – and so did he, I bet – that he'd go through feybraiha early, but he didn't.'

'Maybe that's what makes him so charming,' speculated Alton. 'He's insufferable. His father owns the general store and a few other businesses. Hostling doesn't work at all. They have the biggest house in town. Several hara work there, tending the grounds, cooking, that sort of thing.'

It was becoming clearer to me just what sort of character I'd run into. Not the sort I'd have ever met in Three Creeks.

A month later, my father and I had settled in nicely. The smithy was set up and busy, with work coming in from the ranches, businesses, and hara in town, plus passing trade. We'd taken a bit of furniture with us in our cart and the house had come with some already, but my father took some more, plus household items, in trade for his work, so it was gradually turning into a home. Meanwhile Celci, Alton and Slate seemed to have added me to their friends, and I met up with them several times a week. Slate had a grey roan he would let me ride at the ranch and she'd become another friend. Winter was settling in, but I didn't mind it, with so much to do and friends to get to know.

There was only one matter that caused me trepidation, and that was my coming feybraiha. I knew it would be soon, a couple of months. How would my father arrange it, in a new town? Would he pick the har? Or was I supposed to? Shore and I were close, and had grown more so since my hostling Bri had passed, but we didn't speak of such matters as aruna. It had to do with Bri's death, I suppose. I wanted to bring these matters up, but the time never seemed right.

It was just after our first month in town, as I was struggling with this, when the topic was broached without my father or I initiating a thing. Celci's father Gwen was over at the shop, sketching out ideas for farming tools he wanted made, when he casually said something about his son. Hearing the name, my ears perked up, and so I heard him saying how he hoped Cel's feybraiha would come along in a timely fashion, for the festival of Feybraihatide was only a few months off.

Shore gave Gwen a queer look. 'Festival?'

Gwen studied Shore's face and then mine. 'Nohar's told you about the festival?'

We shook our heads, though I would guess he could tell from our faces.

'Oh, that's our mistake. Somehar really should have, you with a harling of age.'

Shore and I exchanged perplexed looks.

Deciding that this was a matter that concerned me, I stepped into the conversation. 'So, this is about feybraiha?'

'Yes,' Gwen confirmed, speaking seriously as he ushered us towards a bench in the workroom. 'Let me explain to you both.'

I knew Feybraihatide, of course – a late Spring celebration of life's awakening, the flowering of summer, fertility, and the creation of new life. We'd had our own rituals around it in Three Creeks. But what Gwen described to us was something altogether different; not just a few rites, but a town-wide festival meant to honour and serve the community's harlings as they came of age.

About a month ahead of the festival, he explained, all the soon-to-be adults are marked with ribbons about the wrist and hair so they could be easily identified as they went about Albion. Let hara set eyes on them, but let nohar touch them. On the evening of the festival, everyhar gathers in a special field that has been laid out near a hill that has a small amphitheatre built into the side, so outdoor performances can be enjoyed. There's music and dancing as all the initiates – splendidly garbed and as dazzling as jewels – mingle amongst the crowd.

'Then comes the Choosing,' Gwen informed us. 'Throughout the month prior, townshara have been able to apply for the privilege of partnering with the various young hara. Each har may only choose one to ask for. And on this night, the lists have been winnowed down to the top contenders. They are the ones who now vie for the initiates.'

Shore and I had been sitting with our mouths open for a couple of minutes, but at that point my father pressed his lips together and scrunched his eyes shut. '*Wait*. Are you telling me you put them in some kind of whore auction?'

'What? Oh no!' Gwen reached out and patted Shore's knee. 'Nothing like that. What we do is give the young hara a chance to review all the applicants – each is offered up to five by a panel of judges – and let them choose.'

I considered this. 'What is the purpose of this... *Choosing?*'

'Ah, a good question,' Gwen said, nodding. 'There are several purposes. One, to give the young hara more freedom than simply their parents' choice. Two, to find partners who want them and will not reject their invitations. Three, to open up possibilities that otherwise might not be.'

A horrifying thought came to me. And then another. 'Wait! What if the... the har who's just finished feybraiha doesn't want any of the applicants?'

Gwen nodded. 'You forget – they're normally given several to choose from, up to five. And need choose only one. If they reject all suitors, more are found. Nohar is forced to couple.'

My mind was awhirl, but something settled in the forefront. 'And you only do this once a year? Harlings go through feybraiha all year long.'

'We also hold smaller rites a couple of times year,' Gwen explained, 'because of course harlings come into feybraiha throughout the year, but harlings who hit it at springtime experience something grander, as it's tied to the seasonal festival. Sometimes those who arrive in winter will even wait all the way until the festival for aruna.'

I had yet to start my feybraiha but, even so, I could not imagine such waiting. I had watched an older harling go through it and it seemed that from beginning to end, and especially after the end, he had only wanted it to be done with.

'Any further questions?' Gwen asked.

Despite my shock at all this, I found I did have at least one more question I could articulate.

'I'm just wondering... Is this something that all harlings in Albion do? I mean, *always?*' I hoped I didn't sound impertinent, but

I was curious. 'What if, for example, a harling already knows exactly who they want to be with?'

Kell grinned. 'Ah, well, that *does* happen. And that's fine.' He tilted his head. 'Are you asking that for some special reason?'

I flushed. 'No. I was just, um, wondering. Because making your first choice "audition" would be strange. And what if the "judges" didn't approve?'

'Exactly so.' Kell turned to Shore. 'Well, I'm glad I mentioned this or we might have left it too late.'

'Yes!' my father declared, getting to his feet and heading toward the table where he and Gwen had been working. 'Thanks for enlightening us. I'd have been confused if one day some kind of ribbon committee appeared at the house.'

Later, after Gwen had gone, I drifted back to my bedroom, where I took up reading a book on drawing Slate had loaned me. My eyes scanned the pages, without any of it penetrating my skull. I just kept thinking about Feybraihatide.

I was picturing the set-up something like the sale of livestock. All of us would be up on stage, maybe with a sort of rope fence around us. To the side, a har would stand introducing us and extolling our virtues. Hara would call out and raise their hands to bid on us while crowds beyond watched. Gwen had said the process was meant to empower the new hara, but it wasn't having that effect on me.

Celci, Alton and Slate all helped me through this, of course. They had grown up with this "Choosing" and even had older hurakin who'd participated and told them all about it. They were a bit anxious, but not like I was. Alton and Slate at first laughed at my idea of the event as a livestock auction, but then schooled themselves into seriousness when they realised I was truly worried. They assured me nohar would be treated like an animal.

In the weeks following, my panic ebbed to the point I was able to focus once again on settling into town, assisting Shore at the smithy, and pursuing my interest in drawing. All in all, aside from a few snowstorms, from which we dug ourselves out, that winter was fairly uneventful. Lots of cosy evenings at *The Bridle*, afternoons working at the hot forge.

But all that changed when feybraiha struck. And I do mean *struck*, because it was not the gradual build-up I'd been told to expect or seen in the harlings in Three Creeks. I woke up one day and felt sick. My head pounded and my guts were churning. Within an hour I was vomiting into the privy. Shore, who'd been out measuring for a job, found me in bed with a wet towel on my forehead, sweating and pasty.

'Well, now, that was fast, my gem,' he said, sitting down gently on the side of the bed. 'I turn around and you decide it's time to get this over with.'

I narrowed me eyes, unamused. 'This wasn't my decision.'

He got up and after a few minutes, returned with a mug of tea he said would settle my stomach. It was a mix my hostling had brewed frequently.

'I guess now I'll definitely be wearing those ribbons,' I groused.

Shore patted my leg through the blanket. 'It won't be so bad.' He studied my face. 'I thought you'd already decided that.'

I shrugged. 'Yeah. My friends convinced me to go through with it.' I tested the tea in my hands. It was still too hot. 'But I still feel weird about it.'

'I won't say it isn't a bit…'

'*Weird!*' I finished for him. 'But what can we do? It's tradition.'

'Harish *traditions,*' he scoffed. 'Always seems funny to me for us to have such things, but we are creating a culture, I suppose.' He gestured at the tea and I tested it. It was now just cool enough I could take a sip. 'So, what are you worried about? Not the "auction" part, I know – you understand that isn't what it is.'

I thought about it. 'I don't like the idea of everyhar looking at me. Walking around marked like that, with ribbons that say "Look at me! I'm ripe! Like a tomato!"'

My father chuckled. 'That's the point, dear – to be *looked* at. But think of it: You won't be the only harling out on display. And,' he added, patting me on the leg, 'you are most definitely not a tomato.'

By the time I was presented with ribbons to wear, the worst of my discomfort had died down. The side effects hadn't dissipated entirely – I still had headaches, strange nightmares, stomach aches, and general itchiness – but I no longer thought of myself as "sick" and had resumed my usual activities. And once again, my anxiety levels had lowered.

The ribbons were presented to me privately at the house, not in any sort of public ceremony, a fact for which I was grateful. It allowed me a few more hours to conceal what everyhar else in town would soon know. One evening, a group of three hara arrived and asked to come in and speak with me and my father. I knew one of them from *The Bridle*, and my father knew all of them, although he told me later he hadn't known they were involved with the festival.

After a bit of conversation, I was presented with a knitted green satchel that closed with a drawstring. I was told that inside I'd find a set of green ribbons for my hair and wrists. They were of varying lengths and shades and I should feel free to weave them or attach them however I wished, as long as they were visible. I should wear them every day, everywhere I went, until Feybraihatide. My father asked for the exact date on that and, after he had it, offered the committee tea, which they accepted.

Making some excuse, I withdrew into my bedroom. Going over to my dresser, I set down the satchel and opened it. There must've been twenty ribbons in there and, yes, there were many shades of green. I pulled one out, a darker shade, like a mature holly leaf, and held it up against my face while peering into the small mirror tacked on the wall. My eyes are hazel and my hair red, so green really couldn't have been a better colour for me.

Maybe this wouldn't be so bad?

A couple of weeks later, my friends and I were out enjoying the spring weather, sitting on a long bench outside the tavern. All four of us were wearing green Feybraihatide ribbons. I suppose you could say we were out displaying ourselves, but the thought actually had not been that conscious – on my part, anyway – until we were all sitting there and noticed hara looking at us.

'How do I look?' murmured Celci, crossing his long legs and discreetly adjusting his top.

'Marvellous,' Alton responded. 'As always. You and Garnet here have that perfect red hair that sets off the green.'

I couldn't let that statement go unchallenged, of course. 'Oh, but black hair, and so straight, is lovely.' Alton preened, while Slate predictably looked bashful. 'Mine's a mess most of the time!' Mine was, and is still, unruly.

So, there we sat, virtually hara but not, caught in the eddies of good cheer, anticipation and nervousness. Townshara passing by said or nodded hello. And *looked*. Some more than others. I was glad we were all together. It made the examination much easier to take.

After about an hour of our loitering, we noticed a figure approaching from down the street: Etan, coming over from his father's shop.

'Wait 'til you see how many ribbons he has in his hair,' Alton whispered, elbowing me gently. He and the others had grown up with Etan and still dealt with him regularly. I, on the other hand, had done my best to ignore him after the vile things he'd said to me when we'd first met.

'Having fun, displaying yourselves like whores?' he asked, by way of greeting.

Celci huffed. 'We've just been sitting here enjoying this fine weather. If hara want to enjoy looking at us, they're welcome to. They're *supposed* to.'

Alton nodded in agreement. 'It's been nice, all four of us here. None of us get singled out.'

Standing with hands on hips, Etan looked us over assessingly. 'I'm surprised to hear you say that. Three of you are lovely enough – I'm sure many are adding you to their lists – but if Garnet here is getting looked at, it's not because anyhar wants to put an offer on him.'

Here he goes again, I thought sourly.

To my surprise, it was Slate who defended me. He stood up, showing that he was taller than Etan by a couple of inches. 'I think you should leave.'

The brat rolled his eyes. 'Why? Because you want your friend to keep clinging to the illusion that anyhar would want his ugly face?'

Now the other two stood up. 'Leave.'

Etan glared for a moment, then turned his heel in the dirt and walked past us towards the tavern entrance. 'Freak,' I heard him mutter under his breath.

My friends sat down; Alton put an arm around me. 'He is such an ass.'

I was shaken. I really couldn't understand how or why anyhar could be so cruel.

'What is his problem? Where does he get this idea about birthmarks being...?' I struggled to find the words. 'He *hates* them!'

'I think he gets it from his father, Lantik,' Alton explained. 'He pulls off a pleasant enough act when he's doing business, because it's necessary, but my parents have told me Lantik's a backstabber and also very harsh as far as how he judges hara.' He turned to

Celci. 'I've never told you this, but once I heard Lantik saying stuff about your family, how you were no good, not worth much, but "necessary", because we do need the grain after all and "somehar has to do it".'

'Well, if Etan were really confident in himself, he wouldn't be wearing half his ribbons in his hair at once, would he?' Slate pointed out. Etan had managed to weave about a dozen ribbons into his long, curly hair.

'Why does he seem to hate me so much, though?' I wondered. 'Not only does he say these things to me, but when he sees me, he's been giving me dirty looks.'

Alton, whose arm was still draped around my shoulders, gave me a quick squeeze. 'You know what I think? I think he resents you. He was all set for this year's festival and thinking of himself the greatest prize – and here you come in as the newcomer and competition.'

'*Competition?*' I scoffed. 'Me? You all are paragons of harish beauty compared to me.'

Alton pulled back and, twisting half around to face me, placed his free hand on my far shoulder. 'If you're saying you're ugly, cut it out.'

He released me and I fell back on the bench. 'I...' Well, what was I going to say? I had never really thought I looked *bad*, just that I looked *different*. 'I'm not saying that. Just that I'm not quite the ideal. But, no, I'm not saying I'm ugly. And I definitely think Etan is an ass.'

The next week or so proceeded smoothly. I went about my business, either singly or with friends, adorned subtly in ribbons. Once hara in town knew who would be part of the Choosing, it wasn't quite as important to "advertise".

This didn't deter the likes of Etan. He continued to wear a full complement in his hair as well as two woven bracelets. Not that I was deliberately seeking him out for inspection – oh, no, instead he approached me several more times.

After the encounter outside *The Bridle*, he'd learned the futility of attacking me around my friends, so instead had moved to cornering me when I was alone. I don't think it was coincidence that twice he caught me as I was returning from riding with Slate and Alton. He'd probably watched me pass the store and had waited for me to return. Another time, he found me as I was on my way to the tavern. But it was the last encounter, first thing in the morning as I was delivering an order, that unnerved me the most.

'Hey, Garnet, running an errand for your father?' he asked, posing a question to which he obviously knew the answer.

I paused impatiently at the corner where I was about to turn. 'Yeah.'

'Such a good and helpful harling,' he drawled. 'Who's the recipient?'

I wasn't going to put up with this. 'None of your business.'

He stepped forward, verging uncomfortably onto the edge of my personal space. 'On the contrary. It could be for our shop – or a nearby shop. I could deliver it for you.'

I forced myself not to clench the parcel in my hands. 'Thank you, but no.'

With one more step, we were a foot apart. He dared to put his hands on my forearms and squeeze. 'So stubborn. You should really take my advice…'

And that's when I stomped on his foot. His hands flew away immediately. Damn the fact my hands weren't free and that I didn't want him to snatch up the package, or I would've smacked him. 'Get away from me! Just go!'

I tried to make myself look feral, like the wolves Shore and I had encountered on our way from Three Creeks. Naturally Etan just smirked. 'Harling. You don't understand.'

And then he walked away, with a strange look of triumph on his face. It wasn't for a day or so that I understood what it meant.

'Do you think the Choosing is going to be a big deal this year?' I asked Slate as we walked into town about four days ahead of the festival.

'Of course,' he replied. 'It always is.' After a few more steps he gave me a little nudge with his elbow. 'Why, are you worried?'

I was, but I wasn't about to own up to it. 'No. But it just doesn't seem like anyhar's looking at us anymore.' This was true; I'd been covertly checking passersby and was convinced nohar was interested in me.

'Well, that would be normal,' he assured me. 'Everyhar who's going to take part has already made up their mind.'

'Has anyhar been looking at you this week?' I asked.

I paused my steps and let him walk ahead a little bit, so I could judge his body language. He took a breath, in preparation for saying something kind. 'Just the usual. There are a few who keep looking.'

I caught up to him. 'I don't feel like anyhar is going to be interested in me.'

By that time, we had arrived at *The Bridle*. Slate pushed my shoulder towards the door. 'Don't be ridiculous. Let me buy you a drink and tell you why you're wrong.'

But despite the encouragement of my friends and my father, I continued to feel anxious, my mind filling up with worries about the event. And though I'd by and large not fretted about it before, I felt self-conscious of my birthmark. I remember on several occasions turning my face so that passing hara would see the 'good' side. Most unlike me.

These anxieties finally manifested in a nightmare, two days before the rite. I was standing on a stage with the other harlings, and one by one they left with their suitors, until I was the only one left standing. Classic nightmare: I was alone with the crowd staring at me. I couldn't move or speak. Everyhar started to laugh.

I woke up in the middle of the night, shaking and sweating. After getting up for a glass of water, and grabbing a fresh blanket, I settled back in bed. At dawn, I awoke from the same nightmare. I gave up on sleep and took out my sketchbook. It filled up with unpleasant images of leering hara, grabbing hands, and lone figures facing crowds. I tossed the pad on my desk and went to see if my father was at the smithy yet, so I could join him. I needed a distraction.

But that evening, I had to face up to the reality, because all those to be Chosen were to gather at the hienama's home for a preparatory lesson. We'd be learning the specifics of the rite: order of events, a few recitations, parameters of the actual Choosing. We'd also be provided some instruction in aruna, both physical and spiritual aspects. A week earlier I would have been delighted by the opportunity, but setting out just after dinner, it felt like an unwelcome obligation. Tired from poor sleep, and still feeling doubtful of the whole affair, I simply wanted it to be over.

It was a tribute to our then-hienama Kell that the evening turned out far from onerous. He'd prepared plates of delightful sweets along with aromatic tea. Comfortable seating cushions were arranged in an oval on the living room floor, atop a thick braided rug. He had candles lit, set high and low, and the slight breeze through the windows made them flicker pleasantly.

Besides my three good friends and my foe, three others attended. Kell greeted all of us with equal amity and respect. Though Etan naturally gave me a not-so-nice glare as we took our places in the circle, the setting didn't lend itself to his usual cruelties. And so we all settled in to hear what Kell had to tell us.

'Good evening, all,' he greeted us, holding out open palms. 'This is a night of anticipation and preparation. You all have many questions. Some of you hold much anxiety. I can feel it. It is my hope that by the end of the night your questions will be answered and you will have a way to handle your worries.'

He reached out and picked up two framed pictures on the rug by his crossed feet. 'But to start with, I think it's important to refresh ourselves with the story behind Feybraihatide.'

Kell held up a beautifully-drawn illustration of Elisin, the exquisite, newly mature young har: the avatar of each of us. As the dehar of beauty, he would reveal the mystery of his being, Kell said, and through him we would become part of the cycle of the seasons.

Feyrahni was next. Also exquisite, but darker, and dressed in clothes of leaves and leather. A tendril of ivy ran through his black hair. 'He knows the secret glades,' Kell reminded us, 'and at Feybraihatide, he discovers Elisin in one of them.'

Elisin is out walking in the dark forest when Feyrahni spots him. Knowing he is spotted, the young har dashes off to lure the hunter into a chase. And indeed they run down forest paths, sliding in and out of the moonlight, but the pursuit does not last altogether long. Feyrahni "catches" Elisin, and in the soft mosses and grass of a secluded glade, he gives him the experience of aruna for the first time. More than that, Feyrahni makes him with pearl – although that part of the allegory we were not expected to emulate. This pearl will hatch and grow to take his place later in the seasons of the year, but for now Elisin revels in awareness of his own power – his sexuality, his fertility.

While telling the tale, the hienama had passed around the drawings, and as a budding artist I ended up examining them longer and more intensely than anyhar else. Which was fine, because I was the last in the circle, but it did mean that Kell had to pat my knee to get my attention when he was ready to move on.

And move on he did, going over the details of the event at length and providing aruna guidance, mostly designed to boost our confidence. But what I most remember is that at the end of the meeting, he presented each of us with a small iron figurine: Feyrahni. My father had made the lot of them, and I'd had no idea.

Clutching the figurine to my chest, I walked home beneath purple skies, feeling on the one hand reassured by Kell's soothing words and instructions, on the other still plagued by lingering doubts. All the hienama's talk and my own hope was well and good, but – said a voice in my head – the reality was likely to be less pleasant.

When I arrived home, I found my father in his room reading. When he raised his eyes, I held up Feyrahni. 'They're lovely.'

He gestured for me to come closer. '*You're* lovely. I was thinking of you and your hostling when I made them.'

I took his hand and squeezed. 'Thank you. He'd be pleased.'

My father told me he'd left some sandwiches on the counter for me. I ate them at the kitchen table, downing them with a mug of sleep-enhancing tea. The tea would need some time to take effect, and so while I waited, I contemplated the figurine. I needed sleep but I also needed guidance. Studying the work of my father, I hoped Feyrahni would come to me in my dreams.

I was walking down the path of a familiar forest, where I knew the trees, rocks, the bends of the stream. It wasn't far from Three Creeks, and I'd spent countless days there as a harling. But now I was there fully grown, and it was a dream, something a part of me recognised.

Feyrahni. Would he be there? Yes, I saw a flicker of movement off through the trees. The rustle of leaves was my cue to run and for what seemed a few minutes I did, further into the forest. I hopped over the stream and hid behind a massive boulder left behind by ancient glaciers.

No longer hearing the dehar, I let myself consider his intentions. If my situation followed the story, then likely I was being pursued. Feyrahni desired me and would take me in aruna.

I clutched my face, my reddened cheek. No dehar would ever want me. I crouched there still and silent, until I heard Feyrahni approaching once more. Rather than hiding or running, I stood up and walked out from behind the rock.

He stood before me, clothed in magnificent forest splendour, leather and leaves. A tendril of ivy ran through his black hair.

'What do you want, dehar Feyrahni?' I asked him, before he could speak. 'I know the usual story isn't meant to be.'

'I'm here to see you.'

'Me. Right.' How to keep him talking without sounding like an idiot? 'You wouldn't want me.'

Feyrahni pursed his lips and motioned to a fallen tree some feet away. 'Come sit with me.'

I followed, setting myself down an arm's length away.

'You're wrong, young Garnet,' he said forcefully. 'I would want you. *I do*. Yet you are also right. The usual story isn't meant to be. I've come to talk to you, to teach you, to tell you, *two* things.'

His eyes betrayed no deceit.

'First, you *have* been cursed. All the anxieties, all the doubts, all the self-consciousness, the nightmares you've been having – they're nothing to do with you, not really. They originate with your rival, Etan.'

'*My rival*?' I blurted out. 'My rival for what?'

'You have no ego, so I shall tell you that you are a beautiful young har and well-liked. Etan's jealousy knew no bounds, and in the end, he devoted himself to developing a curse to undermine you. And he put it on you last week.'

My mind immediately denied this but, in a few moments, it all made terrible sense. 'He touched me!'

Feyrahni nodded. 'Yes, and in that act, so neatly choreographed, he transferred and activated a curse designed to give you all those feelings you've been burdened with.'

This was a lot to take in. 'He did that to me?'

'He did.'

My next question. 'So, can I do anything about it?'

Feyrahni leaned in conspiratorially. 'Oh, consider it taken care of. In the morning you'll be perfectly fine, ready for the festivities, the ceremony, feeling refreshed and not nervous at all.' He flashed a smile. 'I'm even giving you a little extra boost.'

A dove called in the trees and for a few moments both of us were silent.

'So, you said there was a second thing,' I prompted.

Gracefully he got to his feet. 'Yes. Walk with me and I'll tell you. I also need to show you.'

I followed behind him as he climbed up a ridge and down the

other side. We found ourselves in an area of thick undergrowth, where the bushes were laden with dark purple berries. Here he stopped.

'Now it's time for a lesson.' He reached into the folds of his robe and brought out a hand mirror, which he handed over to me. 'Look at yourself,' he urged softly.

I did, wondering what the lesson would be.

'You know your own face, know it well. And over the short years of your life, you've adjusted nicely to its uniqueness. Yet curse or no curse, I still don't think you appreciate your true beauty. I'd like to show you how to do so, especially how to do so tomorrow.'

After taking away the mirror, he began his lesson – a beauty lesson. A bowl and a masher came out of thin air and suddenly, in the way of dreams, there was a paintbrush – Feyrahni was painting my face with a paste of wine-coloured juices. He was painting the unmarked side. I tried to ask what he was doing, but he stilled my lips with his fingers. I'd spoil the painting, he murmured.

At last it was finished. He asked me to look up and down, right and left, and was apparently satisfied, because he handed the mirror back to me. 'Look.'

What I saw in the mirror was a whole butterfly. Not a half, two red wings, but four red wings – a butterfly made whole, of both flesh and paint.

Feyrahni stood behind me and placed his hands on my shoulders. I saw his face in the mirror as I stared. 'Embrace your mark. No har else has it. Paint yourself this way in the morning, for the festival, for the Choosing.'

He showed me other things to wear, accessories to make. To weave a necklace of tiny spring flowers and green leaves. A belt of woven grass. I could fix my hair up into a bun with a well-shaped twig.

I admit I had never been so dazzled with myself.

But I must have learned all there was to learn, because Feyrahni was suddenly holding me close. 'Think of me tomorrow,' he said, before fading away.

I awoke at dawn, knowing exactly what I needed to do.

When I emerged from my bedroom three hours later, it was to the stunned stare of my father.

I stepped into our small living room and turned around, arms lifted, showing myself off. I'd done everything Feyrahni had suggested and more: twigs of dark purple berries, pinned and woven through my hair, a necklace of delicate blue flowers, a belt of vine, ivy trailing in back. And on my face, the mark of the butterfly.

Taking me in, Shore's eyes began to glisten. Slowly he rose from his chair. Once standing before me, he took my hand.

'I don't think I've ever seen you look so beautiful, not since the day you hatched from your pearl,' he said.

'Do you mean that?'

'I do.' With his other hand, he fingered the side of my face, tracing the edge of the mark. 'Tell me about all this.'

'I went shopping,' I said, and smiled at my own joke.

Shore was now inspecting my necklace, my belt. 'In the forest? In the fields?'

I nodded. 'I went out at dawn, after a dream I had.'

Gently, he put his hands on my shoulders. 'A butterfly. How fitting.' He studied my face. 'And will you tell me about this dream?'

I considered. 'Someday, yes. But not today.'

It wasn't only my father who was impressed with my overnight transformation.

'What's gotten into you?' demanded Alton, as I approached the table where he was sitting with Slate and Celci. 'Not that I mean that in a bad way. Just... wow!'

All of three were dressed with care, as were the other initiates who'd so far arrived. I recognised Celci's gown as a creation of his hostling, who during winter sewed clothes for the family, as well as for sale in town.

'I was inspired,' I informed them modestly.

Celci leaned back in his chair. 'I like it. Especially the butterfly.'

'Do you know who that's going to infuriate?' Alton asked.

'Etan?'

'Naturally.'

'I look forward to it.' At that point I noticed that Slate, who'd been not uncharacteristically quiet, was fingering my belt and looking as if to speak. 'What is it?'

'You got the idea from Feyrahni, didn't you?' he asked quietly.

I nodded. 'Direct inspiration.'

I would have asked how much more he knew, but at that

moment Celci and Alton called my attention to a figure sitting down two tables over. Etan.

It appeared all of us had now arrived. It was surprising Etan had arrived last. One would think he would have wanted to display himself as long as possible.

'He looks tired,' Alton observed.

I silently agreed, noting Etan's strained expression. His clothes were fine quality and his hair and jewellery were as "put together" as always, but he wasn't sitting straight, and I saw him rub his temples.

My friends and I resumed chatting, and as the afternoon continued, there was music, dancing, and games. Young harlings, four years old, even acted out the Feybraihatide story – minus the aruna. It was lovely, something all the townshara as well as all the initiates seem to enjoy.

That is except for Etan. He did dance, he did mingle, he did smile – but the smile never really reached his eyes. And he seemed to have lost his confidence. As a measure of that, he barely seemed to look at me and he certainly didn't speak to me.

I wondered about this until, during a quiet moment, when a single balladeer was singing, it occurred to me Etan could be feeling the way I'd been feeling earlier that week. Earlier that week when I'd been cursed. By him.

Feyrahni.

I realised that not only had he taken the curse off of me… he had put it on *Etan.*

I felt a stab at guilt. Should I tell him? Should I apologise?

But no. I hadn't asked Feyrahni to do it. And I was sure Etan would get through the Choosing just fine. Perhaps the dehar would even be merciful and lift the dark cloud just in time.

All in all, the day was turning out very well.

The Choosing was not at all as bad as I'd imagined.

Toward evening, Kell summoned us all to stage at the front of the small amphitheatre and formally introduced us. This was followed by blessings upon us and a quick reminder of the basic procedures and rules. The three-member screening committee, along with three tents, was set up in the nearby field. One by one, we'd be brought inside a tent and presented with five choices. A judge would be in the tent with us as we interviewed, chatted, or did anything else on the way to determining our choice.

Let me skip over all that.

When I entered the tent and faced my choices, I recognised all of them and was displeased by none. Two of them I'd had my eye on and had hoped had been eyeing me, too. A few days earlier, I had despaired of this. Yet here they were, along with somehar I didn't expect.

On my first visit to *The Bridle*, I'd sat down and watched a dark-eyed musician. Over the course of the months, I'd enjoyed his music many times but had exchanged only a few words. He had at least told me his name: Zelo. And though everyhar in the tent, even the judge, seemed a good choice, I decided straight away it would be Zelo. I chatted with the others for ten minutes, only to be polite, and then Zelo and I were escorted back to town.

Back at his house, which he shared with a half dozen cats, he confessed he'd been intrigued by me ever since I arrived. 'I love interesting faces,' he told me, caressing my cheek. 'But I knew I had to wait to know the rest of your body.'

That night, he took me to the stars and back, as they say. We were both flecked with crushed purple berries by the time we were through; Zelo laughed and said his sheets might never be the same. My painted butterfly wing had smeared and partially disappeared with the force of his kisses but I certainly didn't care. We helped one another beneath the blankets and settled in to sleep, and neither one of us seem to be bothered by the leaves of ivy or bits of flowers that were crushed beneath us.

That night, I was visited by Feyrahni once more. We weren't in the forest, but in the tent where I'd chosen Zelo.

'You are pleased,' he said, seated across from me.

'You know I am. You know everything about me.' He was a dehar; of course he did.

He put his hands on his knees and leaned forward. 'True. Which means I know you have questions. And I know what they are.' He paused several beats. 'Yes, I did put your curse on Etan, but I also took it off him as he entered the tent.'

'Thank you. I don't like him, but I didn't like the idea of everything being spoiled for him either.'

'I understand.' He stood and moved towards the tent flap. 'And now it's time for me to go.'

As he passed through the portal, I murmured: 'Thank you.'

When I returned home late the next day, something I wouldn't have done had Zelo not had an engagement at *The Bridle*, I found Shore in the living room conversing with the town's glassmaker. They looked very comfortable together. I decided I would catch up with my father later and, after some chitchat and well wishes, I retreated into my bedroom.

Flopping down on the mattress I realised I was sore in places I'd never felt sore before. Yet my life had changed irrevocably. Two days earlier I'd been miserable. But that was before Feyrahni had come to me.

I sat up, intending to get undressed, when my gaze caught the figurine standing on my dresser. I went and picked it up, felt its weight. The likeness my father had created wasn't bad, but it came to me that I could draw Feyrahni better, from memory. I'd have to try it.

Off to the side, sat the bowl of red berry paste I'd used to paint my face. There was enough left that standing before my tiny mirror, I was able to draw the outline of a wing on the cheek I'd cleaned off that morning. Truly, I no longer minded being marked.

Cuttingtide

21st June

Cuttingtide marks the Summer Solstice, the moment when the sun begins to decline in strength as it moves away from the earth.

Feyrahni becomes the lord of the corn, the sacrificed one, Morterrius. He is at the height of his potency, and therefore in surrendering his life force at this time, the strongest energy enters the earth. Elisin, now with pearl, sheds his youthful name and becomes Shadolan, the hunter, the executioner. Gone are the cares of youth. The sacred animal of the dehar is the hawk.

Morterrius appears as the golden dehar of the corn, with yellow hair. He wears a crown of barley and poppies and is dressed in red and yellow, symbolising the crop and his own blood. His sacred animal is the magpie.

Shadolan has a darker aspect, dressed as an archetypal hunter. His beauty is fearsome, his gaze compelling.

On the eve of the festival, Morterrius walks the fields as a willing sacrifice. In sorrow, Shadolan must take his consort's life. In a grim repetition of Feybraihatide, the lovers meet in a wild place and take aruna together. But its conclusion this time is death. Shadolan's fingernails have become blades that make a thousand cuts in Morterrius' flesh. The dehar stumbles from their trysting place and as he staggers through the fields, so his blood flows down to fertilise the earth. He eventually falls to the ground, which swallows him up, dragging the dehar's body down into itself. He begins his long journey to the Eternal Plains, the World Beyond, from where he will eventually be reborn as his own son.

As with Bloomtide, again Nerine Dorman leads us away from colder northern climes and its familiar dehara and customs, back into the heart of South Africa, to meet the new dehara that have been dreamed into being there.

Tsangxa's Gift

Nerine Dorman

Everything beneath the sun's jealous eye burns, the grasses bleached blond and whipped into a hissing frenzy by the wind. Even the air shimmers and dances. This is our fourth summer, and Yana and I follow the marsh's otter paths, meander through the dell, then venture past the ruins to the pastures. We're not supposed to range so far from home, but what our hostling doesn't know won't hurt him. He says Father has filled our heads with too many stories, and we'll end up with more than skinned knees. He tells us the baboons will steal us, or the feral dogs will crack our bones so they can lick out our marrow, but the worst we've seen so far is a puffadder – and all it did was lie there on a rock, flickering its little forked tongue.

I am Yana's shadow. He is the summer grass, restless like the sea. I am the coolness under stones with moss-bright eyes. Or so our hostling says when we slip through his fingers and disappear into the bush to North's dwelling place.

This house, Father says, was built a long, long time ago, the stones quarried from the belly of the mountain then shaped by long-dead hands. All the others around it are rubble. Father says the poured rock the ancients used doesn't last; it crumbles quickly if there is nohar to look after it. But North's stone house endures because somehar still lives in it and tends to its spirits.

His home is built from golden sandstone and is surrounded by an overgrown plumbago hedge. The coral tree is so big it casts shade over most of the red-tiled roof. The homestead lies right in the middle of the ruins, where our hostling fears we'll cut our feet on glass or step on rusted nails (we haven't and we always pick up bits of broken glass and put them where others won't hurt themselves). All the windows still have their panes, which is why we went to take a closer look, then saw that the stories about the peculiar stranger har must be true.

The second time we went there it was to steal lemons, but then North spied us before we saw him. At first, we froze like little mongooses caught in the henhouse, but he invited us in, gave us seed biscuits and lemonade, and we've been visiting him ever since.

North is positively ancient, says our hostling, and we mustn't trouble the har in his solitude, for he is not like us. He has been living among the ruins since before our tribe came to settle at Old Station by the Sea. North doesn't look that old to me and Yana, but he does move slower than other hara – careful, calculated, like the chameleons that live in the pink trumpet vine that climbs all over the stone house's veranda. His hair is long and white, and he loves it when we comb it out for him. It is so soft, and we press it to our faces so we can inhale the scent of lavender and mint and damask rose. His skin is almost translucent, and pulled tight over his bones, as if the light inside him would spill out at the slightest nudge. Our hostling says we're making up stories – hara don't have light nearly spilling out of them, but we've seen it with our own eyes and we'll tell you that for truth again and again.

We like it best when we visit and North has stories for us: stories from the time when he came from faraway Megalithica on a windjammer that put in to port at Table Bay. Stories from when he served in the fortress, cupbearer for the *Heer* himself. Stories from when he journeyed, for a time, with the Rakyaska who range along the highways and wildernesses, keeping us safe from the wild things. Stories especially about a har he loved, who loved him enough despite having lost half his soul. North has many stories, and Yana and I gorge ourselves on these tales so that they will take flight from our own tongues one day, and we will not forget the times before.

This is my favourite story, and I will try to tell it with all the right words remembered.

Once, many, many moons ago, when there were still human men and women living on the Flats, between the dunes and the acacia thickets, and there were still fires burning at night, and hara turned on hara, and spilled their brothers' blood, there was a har who rose out of the chaos who named himself Tyrant.

At first, his name was Peacemaker, and he tried to beguile his brothers with honeyed words, that the endless warfare was senseless and that they must set down their spears and guns and blades. But nohar listened to him. Each little tribe, each splintered clan, was content to feed upon their anger, until it sickened them and the earth was crimson with wasted blood. A har couldn't walk from the tip of the peninsula to Table Bay without encountering the signs of violence and death.

Nohar was willing to speak, so this har who would bring peace took up his throwing spear, his bow and his arrows. He took on a new name, and he too went to war. Some hara saw Tyrant was strong, so they walked with him, and lent him the strength of their arms, their blades, their magic.

Hara back then were afraid, says North. This fear was lodged marrow-deep, a shadow on their souls, and if a har could shake his fist at this darkness, and give them a reason to stand together, then this was good.

Yet the feral dogs grew fat, padding after this Tyrant among hara, and the black birds circled above his head. He brought his heel down on the Zhara and the Zhoula, drove back the Ninh until they drowned in the ocean, and the Mebar scattered like chaff to the wind, and we no longer speak their name, unless it is to offer a malediction to the four winds.

It is said that Yash, the lion-headed dehar, who drinks the blood of the cowardly, favoured Tyrant, and gave him a crown of lightning and a sceptre of thorns. At night, it is whispered, the dehar prowled around the fortress where Tyrant sat upon his great basalt throne. All who aimed to stand against Tyrant, faltered, for his eyes were filled with fire and his voice was the roar of Yash Himself.

And for many years, his campaigns reached Mistsand in the north, the great forests of the South Coast, and even as far as the fabled Wytchberg, where it is said that a star fell from the sky and was lodged deep within the mountains' heart.

Within his dominion, there came peace, of sorts, but it was hard won, and it was a peace bought with blood and broken bones, for always there were stirrings and murmurings, and hara who resented their master's heavy hand.

Yash was not a kindly dehar, and his worship required blood, or so it was whispered, when hara were certain the warrior-priests of their Tyrant were not within earshot. And so it was that every seven years, seven hara fresh out of feybraiha were sent to the fortress, never to be heard from again. This was the tithe that ensured the

Tyrant's rule. Anyhar who tried to shirk this sacrifice brought down the wrath of a vengeful dehar. If anyhar refused, entire villages would be razed to the ground, the livestock killed and the earth salted. Everyhar had a story or two, of brushes with the warrior-priests – tall, forbidding hara who always went about wearing masks and robed in black.

Now there were two harlings who grew up by the ancient harbour town of Moon Bay, a place that had somehow escaped the worst of the turmoil when humanity perished. Or maybe the changing of hands went smoother here, for the folks who lived that far south had always been far removed from the madness that had in its grip the ruins of the city centre and the former central suburbs. Luhan and Azra always knew they'd be chesnari one day. The certainty shone in their eyes, and the way they completed each other's sentences, or simply how they knew what the other planned to do even before they twitched a finger.

The Nahir Nuri said they were splinters of the same soul that had somehow become two instead of one. It didn't matter to Luhan and Azra. They didn't need anyhar to tell them what they already understood. Words were unimportant.

But the dehara had tangled their Wyrds with a greater fistful of threads, for the year that they became chesnari was also the one when the warrior-priests came to Moon Bay, claiming that the tithe was due.

The hara were shocked, for their settlement had escaped tithing for many years; it was always something that happened to a town or village half a day's ride away. And it was Azra who was deemed suitable by the masked strangers astride their snorting, foam-flecked horses. No matter how Luhan wept and pleaded, and even offered himself in Azra's stead, his chesnari was spirited away, and Luhan was left clutching at the stones and tearing at his hair.

You will find somehar else, his hostling said. *You are but young. Time heals all wounds.* Then he gave Luhan a cup of red tea sweetened with wild honey, and said Luhan would feel better if he kept himself busy.

Your hostling is wise, said Luhan's father. *His advice is sound.* Then he went back to his woodwork, and bid Luhan continue polishing a table they were finishing.

The Nahir Nuri merely nodded, and offered Luhan a guided

meditation to bring peace into his heart. *There are things we cannot change*, he said, *like the south-east wind when it scours us during summer. Nor can or should we change the shifting of the tides. Nohar has gone against the Tyrant, not when he has a dehar standing at his side.*

Luhan listened to what his elders had to say, and he considered their words carefully, for he did perceive wisdom in their advice, and he was a good, obedient young har. Yet try as he might, he couldn't quell the deep dissatisfaction within his breast, nor shake the nagging sensation that half of him was simply absent. He could not forget that last, lingering look of desperation in Azra's eyes as he was carried away, pale and pinch-lipped, and trying desperately not to cry before the Tyrant's warrior-priests.

How could it be fair that a few should pay such a high price for peace and apparent freedom for all? This thought rested poorly upon Luhan's heart, like a bone caught in a bird's gullet. Surely hara should have the choice to make these decisions for themselves?

So, on the day of the summer solstice, Luhan took a flask of wine and a handful of grain, and climbed the mountain above Moon Bay. The walk was arduous, even though he began early in the morning, before the heat of the day. When he reached the top, where a small marble slab proclaimed the final resting place of a Great Dane and Able Seaman in old-fashioned script, (he couldn't make out the other words, as they had worn away through time), he paused and felt that this was where he should perform his rite. The old ones had thought this an important place to raise a memorial to some great individual, so perhaps here he could reach out beyond himself. Perhaps the dehara might listen to him if nohar else could bring him comfort.

Below him, the sea sparked with sunflashes, and the mountains across the bay were almost as blue as the sky. To the north, the bulk of the mountains swelled, and Luhan's heart was tugged to the port city where he knew Azra had been taken. Even though this was perhaps a day or two's ride from Moon Bay, Luhan had never owned nor ridden a horse, and if he were to undertake this journey, he'd have to walk, and it was a long, long way away, and he knew not what awaited him should he embark upon this quest.

He stood at the precipice of his life; he understood this in his blood, in every breath. It would be simple enough to remain an obedient har, to continue as if having half his soul ripped from him was entirely natural. If he did so, he would forever wonder at how he could have changed his fate, had he taken that first step.

And yet who was he but one young har, to go against Tyrant? This absolute ruler had many powerful warrior-priests to do his bidding, who were in possession of blade, bow and arrow. Luhan had his fists, which seemed small and weak by comparison.

Nevertheless, he drew in his breath, planted his feet firmly on the ground, like the Nahir Nuri had often taught him. He felt his spine straighten, felt the power of the earth travel up through his feet, drew the strength of the sun down, so that he became as a conduit, and every fragment of his body vibrated.

'I call upon the dehara! Who will hear me? I bring forth these offerings to you, this wine, this grain!' He drank of the wine, then poured a libation to the thirsty earth. Of the grain, he placed a pinch in his mouth, then cast the rest out before him.

He felt foolish, standing there, his arms outstretched, an empty bowl clutched in one hand, and at first nothing happened. The wind, as always during the height of summer, was fierce, and pushed his hair into his face, his eyes, his mouth. The grains that he'd spilled scattered upon the gravel of the grave. The wine stained some of the chips blood red, and a small shiver of apprehension passed through him.

His hostling would no doubt chide him for wasting good wine.

How was it that the Nahir Nuri made his own rituals seem so effortless?

Yet just as Luhan was about to crouch and pick up the empty flask, there came a flutter of grey wings. A speckled pigeon landed, cocked its head and regarded him with one red-rimmed eye. It pecked at the grain. Then another flurry of feathers, and another pigeon. And another – until half a dozen speckled pigeons were squabbling for the grain. Sparrows chirruped and flung themselves at the edges, dodging the pigeons' wicked beaks, and within moments, the ground before Luhan's feet became a seething mass of birds.

A chill passed through him, and he cast about, but saw nohar. He was alone up here by the tumbled walls of an ancient barracks, the redbrick mostly reclaimed by a strangling fig blown flat by the southeaster.

If these birds' arrival was a message from a dehar, he wasn't sure how to respond.

As he opened his mouth to ask a question, a shadow passed overhead. The down stroke of a pinion greased the air an inch before his eyes, and then feathers exploded about him. Birds flew hither and thither in their panic to reveal a huge brown raptor that blinked up at Luhan with large, yellow eyes. Clutched in its talons was one pigeon, its neck cleanly snapped.

Luhan took a step back, suddenly and unaccountably terrified of this bird of prey, for his whole being thrilled with the realisation that this was no mere brown buzzard taking advantage of a bunch of foolish pigeons.

Even while he watched, the bird's form grew indistinct around the edges, lost its solidity, and puffed into a plume of smoke that billowed outwards, then coalesced, taking the shape of a har, brown of skin and gold of eye. He was garbed as a hunter, in tan leathers decorated in tassels and feathers, and he had a wicked-looking blade sheathed at his side. When he inclined his head, so he could regard Luhan, the many bone beads in his braided locks clicked and clacked.

It was, for Luhan, all too much, and he fell to his knees, and covered his head with his arms. 'Ai! Ai! What have I wrought?' he cried.

The dehar who stood above him crouched and placed one warm hand on Luhan's shoulder. 'I am Isangxa,' he said. 'Rise, my friend. Your offering is deemed acceptable.'

Shaking and crying, Luhan obeyed, and at the dehar's prompting, his entire story spilled from his mouth like pebbles tumbled by a river.

Isangxa offered yet another hooked smile. 'Tell me, what would you do to free your chesnari?'

At that point, Luhan was ready to promise the moon, the stars, his very soul, if it meant that he would have help from a being as powerful as the one who'd deigned to answer his call. And this he showed to the dehar through pictures in his mind.

'Are you certain?' Isangxa asked. 'The price might be too high, when all's said and done.'

'*Anything!*' Luhan's certainty was a summer wildfire, consuming all in its path. With a dehar at his side, he could achieve his heart's desire. One day, Luhan would grow fat with Azra's pearl, and the sound of their harlings' laughter would echo through the home they had built together.

Isangxa's grin grew broader. 'Very well,' said he. 'We shall seal this with an act of grissecon.'

The first spasm of unease had Luhan pause. 'Grissecon,' he murmured.

Isangxa's nod told him all he needed to know, even as he hesitantly accepted the dehar's hand.

Afterward, with the dehar's fire still racing through his veins, Luhan set out, but he did not go unarmed, for when Isangxa departed in a flurry of brown feathers, he'd left his weapon – a hand-knapped obsidian blade of such fine crafting Luhan had never before seen. The edge was so keen, it sliced the wind, and he took great care to keep it sheathed.

For three days and two nights, Luhan trekked along miles of abandoned highways, where trees and grasses thrust aside the crust of tarmac with their roots, past the rusty wrecks of ancient vehicles slowly sagging into the earth, and between the untold numbers of ruins humankind had left behind.

Such hara that he saw were furtive creatures, unsure of what to make of a single young har marching with such purpose where others feared to tread. The closer he came to the ancient stronghold, the more desolate the landscape. Not even birds sang in the trees, nor did the cicadas share their shimmer-song. Now the fastness from which Tyrant ruled had stood for hundreds upon hundreds of years, a five-pointed structure of dark stone surrounded by a reed-choked moat. It's likely it will stand for hundreds more, and when Luhan approached, even he, a har of little magic, could feel the ancient power imbued in the stones, the watchfulness of the spirits locked into the structure's very foundations. The pennants that snapped in the wind bore the scarlet lion on a black field that he'd grown to hate. He almost fancied that some great beast was stalking his shadow, and he turned often to look behind him, but saw only ancient rubble and rusted metal returning to the earth.

It stands to reason that Luhan's approach did not go unnoticed. After all, a har did not name himself Tyrant without knowing all that transpires within his domain. Half a dozen hara were there to meet Luhan as he approached the gate, and they were fearsome to look upon, garbed as they were in their black leather armour and robes, with the red, snarling masks that obscured their faces.

'I've come to demand the release of Azra of Moon Bay, son of Shianna and Kihar,' Luhan declared.

At first the guards were impassive, their hands on their daggers, others adjusting the grips on their stabbing spears, but when they saw that Luhan was alone, they took his weapon from him and marched him to a cell.

Unbeknown to Luhan, the har who'd removed Isangxa's gift had recognised it for an object of power, and had taken it directly to Tyrant. So it was that Luhan's arrival piqued the har's curiosity. After all, how was it that a mere stripling of a har would walk alone, right to the gates of a dread fortress, and demand the release of one of his new recruits?

The young har was either deluded or completely mad, or so Tyrant mused. He called Luhan into his presence.

'I demand that you release Azra,' Luhan demanded. 'He is not yours to sacrifice to Yash.'

Amused, Tyrant lounged upon his basalt throne. 'Sacrifice him?' he replied, vastly amused. 'Is that what you believe?' Truth be told, Luhan's boldness was refreshing to him, and he was willing to humour this brazen young interloper, for a short while, at least. Tyrant was well aware of the rumours that had sprung up about his seven-year tithe, so he called for Recruit Azra to be brought to the audience chamber, in order that the little trespasser could see for himself.

They waited until Azra arrived, but if Luhan had expected his chesnari to be chained and beaten, the sight that greeted him now confused him utterly. Luhan's beautiful brown locks had been sheared to his scalp, and he was garbed in a dark grey uniform, similar to that worn by the other warrior-priests. Luhan's impassioned cry of relief was met with only a look of cold disdain in his chesnari's eyes.

Luhan started towards Azra, wishing to throw his arms about him, but the two guards who stood by him gripped him hard by his arms so that he swung between them with no more power than a harling. Instead of the sweet tenderness he'd dreamt of a joyful reunion, Luhan tasted the bitterness of cruel disappointment, for he could see how much the other half of his soul had been turned from him.

'Go home, Luhan,' Azra said. 'You can see I no longer need you. I am to be a warrior-priest, not some lowly peasant grubbing in the dirt. I have been called to a higher purpose.'

Horrified, Luhan tried yet again to wrestle out of the grip of his captors, but they were too strong for him, and so he continued to dangle there, between them. His will fled while he contemplated the horrible truth before him – Azra *wanted* to be there. Azra had rejected him. It felt, to Luhan, as if a dizzying black void gaped beneath his feet and he was about to drop into an eternal abyss. He could not fathom a life without Azra. Without Azra, he had no water, no sunlight, no reason to breathe.

'But we have this matter to discuss,' the Tyrant said, holding the obsidian blade Isangxa had given Luhan. 'Where did you find this, young har? From who did you *steal* it?'

Some anger returned to Luhan then, and he fixed his gaze on his enemy. 'I did not steal it,' he spat. 'It was a *gift*.'

'A gift, is it?' Tyrant's smile was slow and lazy

Luhan could see Tyrant did not believe him.

The slow fire that had been smouldering in Luhan's belly all this time roared into life.

'I call upon Isangxa!' he cried, and his voice echoed in the chamber, far louder than anyhar expected from such a slight young har. The guards who held him flinched; one even let go, and a brief struggle ensued, which only stilled when an enormous brown bird winged its way through one of the open windows.

Spears were readied, blades were drawn, as the bird circled once, twice, thrice, yet it was only Luhan who heard Isangxa's voice.

Anything? the dehar asked.

'Yes! Anything for Azra's freedom!' Luhan cried.

Even your heart's blood?

'Yes. Even that.'

With that, the bird vanished, as if it had never been there, and a collective gasp rose from all assembled. Luhan slipped from his captor's grasp and rushed towards Tyrant's throne. He felt as if any moment now he would burst into flame. He felt that his fingers were sharpened into talons, that he had the strength of a dozen lions, and that he could crack the very walls with one blow of his fist. His entire reason for being narrowed down to that one, hateful Tyrant, smug upon his throne.

Yet the Tyrant was prepared for the assault – he might have ascended to a basalt throne, and have others to do his bidding, but he was still mighty in battle. He flipped that obsidian dagger around as Luhan approached.

The blade parted flesh, sighing up past bone to pierce vitals, but it did not hurt, at least not at first. For a moment, solidified in eternity, Luhan and Tyrant clasped like chesnari; Luhan staring up into the Tyrant's dark eyes – eyes that widened as he felt a corresponding pain. The Tyrant looked down to his own abdomen, and Luhan also looked down, saw dark wetness seeping from a wound in the Tyrant that was the same as his own.

As the Tyrant had mortally wounded Luhan, so Isangxa's magical dagger had tasted heart's blood, and had fulfilled the dehar's end of the bargain. While the life flooded from their bodies to mingle on the slate tiles, a great fracturing crash sounded in the chamber, and the massive rock-hewn throne cracked down its centre and split into two halves. Candles guttered in their sconces, and the wind yawned one massive roar that slammed doors and rattled windows.

In this way, the rule of Tyrant was ended. Yash, robbed of his high priest, padded into the wilds to be forgotten, and the warrior-priests, bereft of their leader, their bonds, were as ones who were awoken from a deep sleep.

Azra sat for a long while cradling Luhan's still form to him, heedless of the blood. In his wild grief, he keened, his entire body shaking with the immensity of his loss. But eventually he ran out of tears, and he wrapped his chesnari's body in one of the lion banners from the chamber. He found a horse in one of the stables and returned to Moon Bay. Nohar knows for certain where Azra buried his chesnari's body, but it is said that every summer the poppies grow the thickest in Moon Bay, for longer than anywhere else in the peninsula.

This is how the story finishes. Yana and I often ask North about what happened to Azra. Did he find another chesnari? Did he have harlings of his own? But he shakes his head, and says that some stories are best left finished as they are; the listener can tell their own for whatever happened after.

In Yana's stories, Azra always finds somehar and they live for a long, long time, and they have two sons, and their home is filled with songs and laughter. My stories have Azra taking that obsidian dagger into the desert, where he hunts down Yash and finishes the business Luhan started, even if Isangxa's gift means that Azra deals himself a mortal blow in the process.

I have a last scrap of a tale to share with you, now that you have walked so far with me, and this telling draws to a close. It's an epilogue, Yana tells me, but he is better with bookish things than I am, so I'll take his word for it. I've always been better at finding the words on my tongue. He can squeeze them out of his fingers onto parchment.

One lazy summer afternoon, close to midsummer, Yana and I return to the yellow stone house, lonely in the ruins. I can't tell you whether we want North's lemonade and stories, or whether we are shirking our parents' duties again. I suspect it's a bit of both, because with us it is never a simple desire. We are not obedient sons, much to our hostling's eternal despair. I still remember that day so perfectly, how the sky is almost indigo, the clouds like some dehar smudged them thin across the upturned bowl of the firmament.

The front door is ajar, which is unusual. Usually North keeps the doors shut in case the baboons pay him a visit (they like the contents of his kitchen as much as we do). Our footsteps seem loud on the polished oak floor, and the interior is holding its breath, the curtains drawn, so we are plunged into twilight.

The ancient clock on the wall, which North has gone to great pains to keep in working order, is silent: this in itself is unusual. We hold our breaths, trade glances, then reach out so that we hold hands as we creep from room to room like little mongooses. His bed is made; everything is in its place, but the house is empty in a way that feels…absolute.

Yet it's in the kitchen, with the backdoor swinging slightly on its hinge, where we discover the poppies, blood-red petals scattered in a trail leading out to the back porch and into the ordered rows of the herb garden. By the time we reach the gate in the plumbago hedge, a gust of wind catches us and lifts the petals to the sky in a butterfly dance.

We stand for a while, our breathing laboured, and as quickly as that wind arrives, it is gone. Cicadas gradually fill the spaces between our breaths, and a turtledove offers us its hesitant, liquid call, as if it too is unsure whether it has permission to break the stillness. Only once we return to the house and pass the small altar by the fishpond, do we discover the obsidian dagger placed there next to an empty goblet.

We never see North again. This truth is obvious the day we find the dagger.

As for what has become of Isangxa's gift? Now that is another tale, for another time, for we walk beneath his wings at this time of year, and his gaze misses nothing.

Reaptide

Reaptide is a time when unusual events are likely to occur. Apparitions can be seen in the fields at mid-day. The landscape holds its breath and the hills become haunted. Shadolan becomes the Field Walker, Verdiferel, wandering in solitude through the ripening crops. His hair is dark and he wears a long robe of earthen colours, decorated with leaves, flowers and heads of wheat. His sacred creature is the white owl, which sweeps through the spectral night and even appears during the day at this time.

Verdiferel, like some of the other seasonal dehara, has a trickster aspect. One story concerns a har who came upon Verdiferel in a cornfield, apparently making a crop circle. As the har concealed himself and observed, he saw Verdiferel making talismans from the crop, which he hid around the landscape, in trees and beneath rocks. These talismans were hidden for hara to find, and an audience with Verdiferel could be sought this way. The watching har uncovered a talisman from its hiding place and took it to a sacred site, of two upright stones supporting a vast slab. Verdiferel was already there, and said he knew the har had come to enquire about his future. The dehar bade him lie down on the slab. Verdiferel then produced a sickle blade and sliced the har open. He read the future from the entrails. He said, 'I see you're about to go on a long journey into the otherworld'. He then collected the blood and made a libation in the crop fields. Hara should employ caution when asking boons of Verdiferel.

Another story relates how Verdiferel might appear emerging from the trunk of a tree. He has very long brown hair that comes out of the bark as peculiar strands, and while not as dangerous as other forms, is extremely haughty. He carries a green orb of light, which is called ozaril. It's believed if you chant 'Astale ozaril', then the light of the dehar goes into you, enabling you to see the ghosts that walk at noon.

The Old Fierce Pull of Blood

Storm Constantine

Before I tell you the story, I'll tell you my name. It is Isoldis, which derives from a very old word meaning 'fair'. My brother Senna used to joke that it was really the name of a snake spirit, since its pronunciation is *Iss*-oldis, like a hiss. Am I snakelike? Perhaps yes. I am the only one. My family is otherwise unremarkable. We have three generations of the blood. So far.

I came to *Hart's Cliff* only five years after my feybraiha, choking on the leash of family, desperate to carve a life for myself elsewhere. My hostling told me I was a heartless creature, as cold as Mistmoon rain, and I can understand why he'd think that. I was always apart as a harling; aloof, even. Senna said I was partly dead; it was another joke between us. A snake spirit from the realm of the dead. Senna alone I loved, but not enough. My parents didn't argue when I asked to be found a position somewhere. I liked to grow things. I fancied myself as a gardener of some kind.

So, young in body, feeling ancient in heart and mind, I took up the employment they found for me, in the establishment of an acquaintance of a friend of theirs – not somehar they knew well, but had perhaps met twice. Still, Shademoth har Hernayes came with recommendations, and he owned a vast nursery; it specialised in *rosaceae*, the myth-drenched rose. I knew this shrub was capricious and hard to grow successfully – in some cases it appeared rather to die than please a harish eye with lush, healthy blooms. Its nature appealed to me. I was happy to take the job.

Hart's Cliff lay in the middle of Alba Sulh, around two hours' journey from my home. Back in the human era, it had been the property of a rich family, with its own farms and housing for its tenants. It had lain overgrown and half-ruined since the last days of the Devastation, but over the past thirty years or so had been reclaimed by hara, who had appropriated the estate and transformed it into a thriving village. The old mansion and its vast stable-block housed a healing facility, and a workshop for the crafts centred around the estate's produce. Other outbuildings and the various farms on the estate had become homes, retreats and shops. Around them spread the extensive gardens, which tucked themselves right under the famous, louring rocks that gave the place its name. In the damp shadows, ferns grew prolifically.

I arrived at the end of spring time. The community was far busier than I'd imagined, and its population much larger. The main buildings appeared to be on an island, but this was an illusion rather than reality. An old river cupped the site generously, having been widened into a lake there to feed a nearby watermill. Just above the mill, a broad, decorative waterfall gave the river a riotous voice and turned the waters to foam. The mill was still used, although the building attached to it had been renovated extensively and was now a hotel and restaurant, named simply *The Old Mill*. Hara came to *Hart's Cliff* for its ambience, its ghosts perhaps. For each season here had a strong, distinct mood that tweaked the nerves of a har's spiritual leanings. Whatever you believed, its itch could be scratched in some way within the timeless landscape, which was full of meaning, rife with significant sites, and hidden glades and pools where the hairs might rise on your arms. Phyles brought their impaired hara here – mainly long-standing casualties of the Inception – to be soothed and healed. Strange really, because several of the legends associated with *Hart's Cliff* were drenched in blood – battles, executions and murders – which was partly why it had been left to rot for so long. Yet despite these dark marks in its history, the landscape was restorative. I could feel it myself, brushing against my skin like the tail of a cat.

I was set to work in a precinct of the garden named Hind's Walk, which was devoted to flowers used for remedies, balms and serums. The blooms here were large and showy *rosa centifolia*, of a crimson so deep its abundant petals seemed to suck up the sunlight and draw a strange kind of darkness about them. I was allocated a set of paths within Hind's Walk, for which I would be responsible, at first monitored closely by a supervisor until I learned the character and needs of my charges. The narrow stone paths wound between plots bursting with flowers. The scent was darkly intoxicating, drenching the air, summoning bees and other insects to gorge themselves dizzy on the rich nectar within the pulsing floral hearts. The tasks for early spring were finished and now my job was to wait upon these demanding blooms throughout the summer, keeping them adequately watered and supplied with rich nutrients, as well as attending to their minions – the lavender, mint and wild garlic planted between them as guards to deter or destroy pests. Once a week I must communicate with them encouragingly through meditation. Blooms must be harvested at strictly allocated times to promote the growth of new ones, except for those grown specifically for the medicinal properties of their hips.

Aside from Hind's Walk, there were other gardens across the estate where roses were grown for their use in perfumery, or else in cooking, or for ritual purposes, while others were simply flowers for their own sake – beautiful and heady, designed only to bring grace and fragrance to a room or Nayati. *Hart's Cliff* had its own dehar – Anthara – who must be summoned within a circle of strewn petals.

Hart's Cliff was a thriving centre that attracted visitors as the flowers attracted bees. There were no lonely, mysterious spots around the main house, because even the secluded corners were used for something, and visitors explored everywhere they were permitted to roam. During that first week or so, I could not have imagined the mystery I eventually stumbled into there, nor the darkness that was its veil.

I had a spacious room on the second floor of the main house, in a corridor where many other employees lodged. The room had a basin where I might wash in the morning and evenings, and long, arched windows in the stone outer wall, which framed a view over the landscape to Darkloe Cop. This was a long hill, which rose on the western side of the river and dominated the skyline there. At the end of the day, before I went down to the staff refectory for my evening meal, I took pleasure in washing my hands and face, applying a rose-scented lotion to my skin, while gazing out over the landscape. This became a languorous ceremony for me; my own act of devotion to Anthara. The sunlight seemed always golden in that place and, along with birdsong, and the distant tumble of falling water, there was a low hum of insects on the air. Such a perfect place. No har could remain ill or miserable there for long, I was sure. And yet nothing can be perfect. It is the imperfection of a thing that accents its better qualities.

On the third evening of my occupation, as I stood at one of the windows, I saw a strange sight upon the hill. This was a group of hara – or appeared to be – who were walking along the brow of it, in an area where there were no trees. They were silhouetted against the sky and appeared to me like creatures from a fairy-tale. One was much taller than the others, while his companions seemed to move in unusual ways. I can't explain how exactly; it was simply an impression. Imagination might easily give these figures the guise of animals, some of them hopping or lurching or... *creeping*. I grinned at my own fancy, and as I did so, something cold and damp touched the side of my face. It felt like a strand of silk or cobweb and was gone even before I slapped my own cheek, thinking a spider had dropped onto it. But there was nothing. I went downstairs.

During that week, I glimpsed the motley band upon the hill a few more times. Common sense told me this was a group of friends or workers walking home for their dinner, but I liked to think there was something unearthly about them. They weren't ghosts, I felt, but *representations* of something – creatures or entities from ancient times. I knew it was not uncommon for hara to witness such things, because since the demise of humanity the *other* in nature had crept forth from its banishment. It had been drummed into me during my early learning that the time of ignorant, rapacious Men had gone, allowing the time of magic to return. The figures I saw were only visible for a quarter of a minute at most, before disappearing into the trees, but I felt compelled to look for them. If I was late home I missed them, and that felt like bad luck somehow.

The Hernayes were the senior hara at *Hart's Cliff*, and had been responsible for the bulk of the restoration and cultivation. The family had expanded by adopting hara, and was now officially a phyle of the Sulh. Its phylarch was Shademoth. He had hosted two harlings with his chesnari, Remmayes, and one of these was still very young. Shademoth was a fair and generous har, lacking any hint of ostentation or arrogance. The same could not be said of his eldest son, Sallowbar, who was a year or so younger than me. I quickly came to the conclusion that if there was a blight at *Hart's Cliff*, it was nothing to do with pests that threatened roses, or some malign influence from the past. It was simply this irritating har, who should have been attractive, but was not. The pretty casing around him concealed an ugly grub, I felt, which would not hatch to loveliness, but eventually be revealed for the vile thing it was – *if* there was justice in the world. His parents appeared blind to his shortcomings, as did most of the hara I worked with. But I was aware of my intolerant nature, so thought perhaps my antipathy to Sallowbar was just me.

I met this har at the end of my first week. There was a courtyard to the refectory and, after only a couple of days, I chose to go out there during my lunch break. If I sat inside, other hara felt obliged to join me and put some effort into welcoming and absorbing the newcomer. As I prefer to take my time making friends, the courtyard provided some privacy. I wasn't bothered with company so much out there. It's not that I dislike other hara, but well… I like my privacy. On this particular day, intrusive voices broke into my contemplation as I ate my lunch. Presently, a group of hara emerged from the refectory, carrying their own lunches on trays. Before I'd even taken in their appearance fully, I shifted in my seat a little so as to present my back to them. This apparently acted as a lure. I heard footsteps behind me, then a voice said, 'Ah, the fledgling. I don't believe we've met.'

I knew I had to turn round, preferably after I'd fixed a smile to my face. When I did so, I was startled to find a group of six, five of them standing behind their apparent leader, staring at me. I thought at once: *the grotesques from the hill.* This was rather a disappointing revelation. The leader was fairly good-looking, with pale blue eyes fringed by thick tawny lashes. This gave him a weirdly penetrating gaze. He was of average height, but the majority of his minions seemed smaller than him. While not ugly exactly, they were not well-favoured, being plain of feature and awkward in posture. One towered over them all, an ungainly, hunched creature, with long, lank black hair and a downcast gaze. Were these clients of the care facility? I wondered. Yet they appeared to be third-generation at least, and surely few of those would end up needing treatment at *Hart's Cliff.* I realised some response was in order.

'I've been here a week, if that's what you mean.'

'Fledgling,' repeated the har, grinning. 'I'm Sallowbar. I expect you've heard of me.'

If I had, I hadn't paid much attention, so I said, 'The name's familiar.'

'My hostling is Shademoth.'

'Oh, of course.' My heart sank. I would have to be polite.

'How are you settling in?'

'Fine, thank you.'

'If you need anything, you can come to me.'

'Er... thank you.' My supervisor and several of his staff already fulfilled that function more than adequately. I smiled with difficulty. 'I appreciate that.' I glanced at my meal meaningfully, hoping he'd get the hint.

But instead, Sallowbar signalled to his minions, who sat down around me at the table. He sat opposite me. 'Have you tried the rose wine?'

'Not yet.'

'Allow me.' He presented a bottle to me, which I glanced at. Rose wine is not necessarily red or even pink; this one was greenish white. 'Our best. Some bottles are kept aside for me... and my friends.'

'I don't drink during the day,' I said. 'Not while I'm working.' I doubted this har had to work much.

Sallowbar reached out and grabbed hold of one of my braids. Instinctively, I jerked away, but he did not let go, affected not to notice my reaction. 'Do you cut your own hair to sprinkle around the roots of your roses as protection?' he said. 'It's the colour of a golden-pink rose. Being so fine and pure, I'm sure it'd deter most vermin.'

Apparently, not, I thought, but said in a plaintive tone, 'No. Please, if you would...'

He let go. 'You can have some of mine to scatter about, if you like.'

'I have plenty of horsehair, thank you.'

'But the energy of a horse is not the same as that of a har.'

'You think so?' I was wondering how I could escape this excruciating meeting without giving offence. By my nature, when annoyed, I was bound to give offence. I eyed the remains of my meal. Such sacrifices must be made. I stood up. 'Well, nice meeting you,' I said.

Sallowbar simpered coyly, an affectation that didn't work. 'But you haven't finished your lunch. Are you such a shy little bird that we've scared you away?'

'I'm neither shy nor little, and I *have* finished.' I put my plate and cup onto my tray, softened my sharp words with another smile. 'Good day, Tiahaara.'

Fortunately, Sallowbar gave up at that point and allowed me to retreat.

By the time I went into the cool refectory, I was almost shaking. The encounter had felt threatening, somehow. Most likely because Sallowbar had had the audacity to pull my hair. Unnerved, I emptied the remains of my meal into the allocated bin. *Could* those hara be the figures I glimpsed on the hill most evenings? They were certainly odd enough.

Festival times were always extra busy at *Hart's Cliff*, since entertainments were provided for the local community and guests from further away. Remmayes har Hernayes led the arojhahns at these occasions, which were very colourful, or so I was told. Sometimes, guisers came to add to the entertainment, particularly at Feybraihatide, Reaptide and Natalia. Cuttingtide would be the next festival, but I'd be going home for that. My colleagues advised me not to miss Reaptide, and I said I wouldn't.

By the end of the second week, I'd decided who I wanted to be my friends. I didn't like to have more than two; any other hara I liked would be social acquaintances and kept at a polite distance. My preferred hara were Raephe and Yuroah, dark-skinned hara, Raephe being a few shades paler than Yuroah, and somewhat taller. Around six years older than me, I admired the sense of maturity they had – whether that was because of their extra years or the fact they were naturally mature, I can't say. They were conveniently paired, so could almost be regarded as one har. They were witty and entertaining companions, who were popular, yet did not run exclusively with the main crowd of young hara employed by the estate. I knew they were chesna and lived together, along with their lurcher hound, Leveret, yet they were willing to adopt me to a certain extent. When I wanted aruna, I'd ask one of them for it. I sometimes wondered if they assented to this as a kind of charitable act, as they were kind and innately warm. When they told me I was beautiful and that having me in their life was like adding spice to it, I merely smiled and accepted the compliment, even if I wasn't entirely sure it was true. As for being together with both of them at the same time, I wasn't interested in group intimacy. Far too much can be revealed at such times. Through them, I learned I was regarded as somewhat exotic by other hara at the estate. 'You have your own style,' Raephe said, 'Others will copy you. Just watch. You'll see.'

He was right. I always wore my long, thick hair in a particular way, which was by braiding some of it at the front and winding it round into a coil at the back, letting the tails hang loose, over the rest of the hair. I liked artful messiness, and spent a lot of time experimenting with the weaves. I liked to wear layers of clothing made of different materials – sometimes robes, sometimes tight-fitting trousers and tunics – always embellished in some way. I'd make jewellery out of the weirdest materials I could find; painted and enamelled and carved. After a few weeks, I noticed poor copies of my styles among my colleagues, including a new fashion of wearing thumb rings, as I did. Oh well, exotic style icon was a reputation I could bear. I'd had worse.

Over the weeks, Sallowbar attempted to charm me in various ways, but my wall of resistance held, even if it wasn't particularly efficient at repelling. He'd have to give up eventually. Still, his occasional advances allowed me to inspect his crew. They weren't as hunched and deformed as I'd first thought, but merely rather pathetic in that they didn't have much character. Clearly, they looked up to Sallowbar as a charismatic leader, hoping some of it would rub off on them. The most interesting one was Murarn, because he *made* himself look odd. One day, I saw him without his disguise.

Most mornings, I went into the village heart to make deliveries or fetch supplies. This particular day, I was taking a basket of bottled remedies to one of the shops for my supervisor. The hour was early, so few hara were about. After I made my delivery, I decided I had time for a quick drink at the *Mill*. I could sit on the terrace outside, where wooden decking hung over the water, and provided a picturesque view of the *Cliff*. As I sat in the shade, gazing at the old stones of the house within its cradle of trees, a har walked past me – strangely. He seemed almost a blur and appeared to be taking a short cut to the fields beyond the river: a tall figure, striding purposefully. I realised it was Sallowbar's long-shank minion. He seemed different to how he usually appeared, upright, bolder. Out of curiosity, I called to him. He paused for a moment with his back to me, then turned. The expression on his face was of annoyance. I warmed to him at once.

'It's irritating, isn't it,' I said, 'when hara insist on having your attention and you're unwilling to give it? Allow me my turn.'

He pulled a sour face. 'What?'

'You heard, and I think you know *what*.'

He took a few steps towards me. 'Have I offended you in some way, Tiahaar?'

'Not *you*, no. Will you join me?' I sensed strongly this was against Sallowbar's rules and preferences. A frisson of pleasure coursed through me at the thought of speaking to one of his silent followers without his permission. I knew this would anger him if he ever found out.

'Join you?' said the har. 'Why?'

'A social adventure,' I said. 'That's when you speak to another har of your own volition and say whatever you like.'

He hesitated.

'There's nothing sinister in the invitation, I assure you. I want to ask you something.'

With clear reluctance, he took a seat at my table. I wondered how I could obtain refreshment for him. There were no *Mill* staff about, and if I got up to go inside and order him something I felt sure he would flee. 'What's your name?' I asked.

'Murarn,' he replied, looking everywhere but at me.

I touched my chest lightly with the fingertips of one hand. 'I'm Isoldis.'

At that moment, a har came out from the kitchen door. I signalled to him, asked if I could order another cordial. He complied, and disappeared inside.

'What did you want to ask me?' Murarn asked, clearly fearing interrogation.

'It's silly really,' I said, 'but I must know. Do you and your friends take a walk across Darkloe Cop every evening at the same time, before dinner?'

Murarn blinked at me, pantomimed a double take. 'What? Why do you ask that?'

'Because I think I see you most evenings, from the window of my room, but I'm not sure it's you.'

'No, we don't. It's a strange question.'

'I know. It's a strange phenomenon.'

His eyes widened. 'You think we're strange.'

I shrugged. 'Yes.'

He laughed. 'Charming!' He put his head to one side. 'What do you see, then?'

'A group of hara – well I thought they were hara – as silhouettes against the sky. One is very tall – like you. The others, well...' I smiled. 'This might sound weird, but they appear almost like half-beasts.'

'And you say we're strange!' He paused. '*You* are rude.'

'And your leader isn't? He pesters me.'

He frowned. 'Our leader? You mean Sallowbar?'

I shrugged in assent.

Murarn risked a mordant smile. 'Take your revenge on him, then.'

'I am.'

He eyed me thoughtfully, and I remained silent. I realised his mask was set upon the table: that blank, troubled face. I could almost see it lying there in front of him. The real Murarn was confident and attractive, even if unusual. He had a long face with large dark eyes, which were perhaps too widely-spaced. His cheekbones were high, his brows strong and dark, his rather large nose straight with flared nostrils, and his mouth sensual. Generally, he took care to thin his lips, keep his eyes veiled. What did he fear in revealing the truth of himself?

'I'm sorry,' I said, 'I shouldn't take my impatience with Sallowbar out on you. But the question was genuine. I really do see those hara. Maybe you could see them too, so you know what I mean? I'd be interested to discover whether somehar else actually *can* see them.'

'You want me to look from your room?'

'Or we could go to the hill at the appropriate time.'

He drew back from me a little. 'No, that's not possible. But I could perhaps manage a minute to look from the window.'

I resisted a mild urge to flirt. 'They only appear for a very short time.'

The pothar came out of the kitchen and placed a fruit cordial in a tall glass in front of Murarn. I insisted I pay for it. The pothar went away.

'Perhaps later?' I suggested.

Murarn took a long swallow of the drink, nearly drained the

glass. I didn't think he was that thirsty. 'I suppose so. Which room do you have?'

'Rosa Damask, second floor. The figures appear around 6.40.'

'OK, I'll try.' He finished his drink. 'Hadn't you better get back to work?'

'Are you a spy for my supervisor?'

He expelled a choked laugh. 'No. So... Later, maybe.'

I went back to my room swiftly that day, acutely aware of being nervous and excited. Was I attracted to this tall, dour har because he was Sallowbar's follower or because I genuinely liked him? This was difficult to tell.

One minute before the appointed time, there was a knock at my door. I went to open it and there was Murarn, a dark shadow at the threshold. As I looked at him, I wondered why earlier I'd found him vaguely attractive. He was gaunt, awkward, clearly unsure whether he'd done the right thing in coming to me.

'Come in,' I said, keeping my distance. I gestured towards the window. He followed me.

With a space of two feet between us, we stared at the ridge of Darkloe Cop. Above it, a towering mound of clouds moved across the sun, and a shadow spread out towards us. 'There,' I said, pointing.

The figures were vague in the subdued light, but I saw them.

Murarn shifted in apparent unease. 'Deer?' he said.

'They're not deer!' The figures had already gone.

Murarn shrugged. 'I saw deer.'

I wondered if he'd seen anything. 'Thanks for looking, anyway,' I said crisply. 'It seems I have to live with the fact I might be going mad.'

Murarn coughed out an abrupt laugh. 'Perhaps you're more sensitive to the unseen than I am.' He paused. 'You know the legends of this place, of course?'

I shrugged. 'Not really. What are they?'

'Darkloe Cop is a place of death.' He spoke dramatically, which for some reason annoyed me.

'As is just about every square inch of this land, I expect,' I said. 'You'd be hard-pressed to find a patch where someone hasn't died.'

'But there is death and *death*,' Murarn persisted, apparently not offended by my scathing tone.

'OK,' I said guardedly.

Murarn gestured at the hill. 'Even in the human era, there were stories, including historical facts. There were murders and battles. The man who originally owned this land was a knight, over a thousand years ago. It was believed he brought something back with him from the Holy Land, an evil spirit, whose brief reign of destruction was brought to an end by a brave priest, who died for his interference. The Cop itself was known as a gateway to the underworld, or the land of Faery.' Murarn pulled a sour face. 'But those stories don't concern us.' He waved a dismissive hand. 'After the Devastation, hara put their own imprint here, continued the tradition. Long before the Hernayes, other phyles competed for the land. It was regarded as a place of power. You need only look at the landscape during midsummer to see this is so. You *do* see that, don't you, Isoldis?'

'Yes,' I said. His words had conjured peculiar feelings in me, not wholly pleasant.

Murarn moved closer to the window. 'As summer moves on, the feeling intensifies. It bursts at Reaptide.' He glanced at me briefly. 'There have always been roses here. There was a saying "taken by the briar", which meant the creatures of earth claimed your life. But the briar was also intimately connected with a har named Grisainn har Vulpiers, who was the favourite of his phylarch. A rival phyle, the Lepodarns, took him captive. Eventually, he was found dead and a battle took place on the Cop. Every har died, and none can say they killed each other. In the aftermath, among the broken bodies and the blood, witnesses found the body of Grisainn in a hollow, bound with wild roses, his eyes open wide, unseeing. His was the only body left whole.' Murarn turned and smiled at me cruelly.

'That's a dark romance,' I said, then added sardonically, 'with whom was Grisainn in love?'

'Loyal to his phyle but in love with a har he met on the Cop, who wore wild roses in his hair.'

'Naturally. Is this colourful tale in the tourist information leaflets?'

'Yes, clearly you haven't researched this place very well, but then you don't have to give guided tours, do you.'

'Do you?'

'No. I simply like discovering stories.'

'Then tell me the story behind what I see on the Cop every evening.'

'There's a difference between discovering and inventing.'

'Is there?'

Murarn rolled his eyes. 'Creatures of the land below,' he said. 'Maybe.'

'Not hara mutilated in battle, dragging themselves across the horizon?'

'I don't think so.'

'Why am I seeing them?'

'Time of year,' Murarn said, 'maybe.'

'A pity you can't be more certain about anything.'

Murarn shrugged. 'It's my way. I'm never certain, not about the present, at least. History, I think, is fixed.'

'Us talking earlier is already history,' I said. 'Can we go to the Cop?'

'Not now,' he answered.

'But maybe,' I finished for him.

He nodded, slowly, thoughtfully. 'Goodbye, Isoldis.'

'Goodbye.'

I knew I must go to the Cop. But not yet. I realised I was nursing a fragile hope Murarn would eventually take me there. I mustn't break the magic. His story had roused me somehow, yet it might not even be true. Alba Sulh's corners are soaked in ghosts and tragedies; perhaps everywhere in the world is the same. All hara are youngsters in an old, old house, and its mysterious creakings and phantoms seduce us.

As to what I thought of Murarn, I vacillated between finding him intriguingly attractive and being oddly repulsed, but not so much that I wasn't drawn to seek him out, if only to study him from afar, whenever possible. He avoided me adeptly, and I didn't draw close enough to speak to him, even though I saw him often with Sallowbar and his other friends about the estate. I realised that to pursue him would drive him further away, and my mind still wasn't made up concerning whether he was delicious or rancid.

Sallowbar made reports on the precincts of the gardens to his parents, no doubt a contrived occupation, but he clearly enjoyed what he perceived as its power. Always he had his ensemble with him, faithful pets. Eventually, he came to me.

The day was hot, cloudless, yet a faint breeze blew, scattering perfume in the air. We stood within a sea of roses, which bobbed upon the air as if on water. As Sallowbar asked me officious questions about my work, I decided to address my replies to the shorter hara in his group, who lurked behind him. This baffled them somewhat, and they glanced at him, wondering if they were supposed to respond to my remarks. My eyes I kept away from Murarn, but I was conscious of his looming, hunched form, the shadow he cast.

'Isoldis,' Sallowbar said eventually, in a tone an adult might use on an unruly harling. '*I* am speaking to you. You give the information to *me*.'

'Oh,' I said insouciantly. 'I wondered, seeing as there are so many of you.' I smiled sweetly, ravenously, regretting the expression instantly, since I saw it hit Sallowbar like a missile, which exploded within him. He actually put a hand flat on his chest, above the heart. By Aru, I'd gone and done it now! Stupid, stupid!

'Perhaps I should come alone to you, then,' he managed to say, blinking at me.

I shrugged, frowned. 'Aren't we about done?'

Sallowbar glanced at his notes, held on a clipboard. 'Yes,' he said, 'for now.'

The group moved away, and I applied my attention to my roses, even when I felt eyes upon me. Murarn had looked back. I felt it. I didn't look up.

Two evenings later, I was in my room after dinner, preparing to go out to the *Mill* for a drink with Raephe and Yuroah. As I braided my hair, I gazed drowsily at the Cop, the sun sinking behind it. I'd seen my phantoms earlier, and was wondering whether they ever walked back across the brow of the hill, once their business was done. Perhaps I missed them in the dark. Then I heard movement beneath me, somehar passing by, and glanced down at the path beneath my window. I saw Murarn's pale face, lifted towards me. This moment seemed significant. A har at a window, the evening, the slanting burning light, a har looking up from below. In the background, the thrash of water. In the darkening air, a flicker of early bats. Murarn held a slender, white rosebud in one hand, twisting its stem between his fingers. The window was open. 'Have you stolen that?' I asked archly.

He glanced at the rose. 'Perhaps I have.'

'How wicked.'

There was a silence. Soon he'd move on, but then he opened his mouth, paused, and said, 'You look like a creature from a fairy tale.' Another pause. 'Isoldis, Isoldis, let down your hair...'

I was moved to take a small step back. I don't know why. Shadows of the room reached for my back, comforted me. 'What will you do with the hair?' I asked, lamely.

'In the story, I'd climb it,' he said.

'That would tear it all out, or snap my neck, or else drag me out of the casement and we'd both crash onto the stones below. The request is preposterous.'

'In reality, yes,' he said. 'There are easier ways to reach a har's room.'

'So I understand.'

'Goodnight, Isoldis.'

'Goodnight.'

I walked down the long drive to the *Mill*. I could see the faint, firefly glimmer of candles burning upon the outdoor tables there, between the summer foliage of the trees. Yet I felt alone on the driveway, on one side an uneven wall of dark rock, on the other the front of the house, which faced the mill as I did, while before it lay desiccated lawns, a dry antique fountain. Tree branches hung over me, almost breaking beneath the weight of their leaves. The air smelled of damp earth. I wanted to see a har appear before me, or on the lawn. He would glow in the dimness, his shoulders touched with the last fire of the sun. He would be crowned with roses. I could almost see him. He wasn't black-haired or ascetic-looking like Murarn, but more voluptuous and lissom. His skin would be a mottled green, his hair a greenish brown. No awkwardness within him. A creature of nature, his mouth broad and smiling. But he wouldn't manifest. I couldn't make a ghost – or a desire – appear.

My friends were already sitting outside the *Mill*, having secured a table with the best position for us. As I approached them, I thought about how the immense willows all around the water, the thick reeds, the ancient oaks and sycamores, which looked impossibly huge and ancient, seemed too fecund, too lush and heavy. This was like a dream of summer that might easily turn into a nightmare. You could be smothered by foliage that crawled across the water or dropped down from the high branches.

'You look like a ghost trailing through the dusk,' Yuroah said to me. 'Are you drunk already?'

'Very funny,' I said, sitting down. 'I was thinking. This place. It's changed so much in the past week or so. We can barely see the house from here now. The trees are so big and when they're fully clothed, they hide everything.'

'That's the idea with clothes,' Raephe said, making Yuroah laugh. He lifted a carafe of wine. 'White good for you?'

'OK'. He poured me a goblet, which was a rounded glass cupped in a stemmed nest of dried willow withes and wire, locally crafted. The goblets looked good but weren't that easy to drink from. I'd been told there was a knack to it. I felt I was drinking from a vessel of thorns, but this merely complemented my mood.

'What's wrong with you?' Yuroah asked, smiling, his teeth gleaming almost supernaturally white in the dimming light. 'Found Sallowbar under your bed, did you?'

'If I had, I'd have come to you covered in blood, or partially and ineptly washed of it, but with a wild gleam in my eye.' I took another gulp of my drink.

'Seriously,' Yuroah said, putting his face straight. 'You look bothered. Has he bothered you again?'

'No. I'm fine. Really.'

'If it gets too much, you should report it,' Raephe said. 'It won't be the first time Shademoth or Remmayes has received such a report. Sallowbar often fixates on somehar.'

'It's not that bad, just an irritation.' I drank again. 'What is it with the grub and his band of weirdos anyway? Where did he collect them from?'

'He's one of them,' Yuroah said.

'What do you mean?'

Raephe refilled my glass, which was empty. 'One of the reasons Remmayes and Shademoth added the phrenic therapy wing of the care facility was because of Sallowbar,' he said. 'They wanted to help other hara who might have harlings with... *problems*.'

I pulled a face. 'Are there harlings who need that kind of help? I've never met one.'

Yuroah gestured with both hands. 'Everyhar knows inceptions often used to produce odd results, but pureborn anomalies were rare, still are. However, they can happen.'

'What's wrong with Sallowbar, then?'

'He had a difficult beginning, that's all,' Yuroah said. 'His pearl broke before its proper time, but he survived. Physically, the effects were minimal, but he's known to have difficulties relating to other hara... er, *appropriately*.'

A strange kind of heat swept through me. I felt embarrassed, almost as if I'd been accused, but Yuroah's face was clearly innocent of intent. 'And the others?' I asked quickly. 'What about that tall one?'

'He's just weird,' Raephe said, and took a sip of his drink, shaking his head. 'You have to feel sorry for them, as they can't help their problems. Sallowbar kind of looks after them. I guess they gravitate to each other for support and friendship. Same as we all do. Like to like.' He gave me a sly smile.

I took another long swallow of wine. So, I was intrigued by a freak. What was worse, the situation or the unkind way I'd just described it to myself?

'If you think I'm like you, then I'm scared of what you haven't told me about yourselves,' I said in an arch tone. 'I thought you were much nicer than me.'

'We occasionally turn into wolves,' Yuroah said, and Raephe laughed loudly.

No, they were *not* like me.

I went home early, having drunk too much and concerned I'd reveal confidences to my companions. I lay in bed, restless, too awake. I thought about Yuroah and Raephe, their easy manner, their blissful unawareness of the darkness of life. Or so it seemed. Did I secretly crave their relaxed intimacy? I knew they were whole in a way I felt I could never be, and that to some degree I was deceiving them. Like to like. Freak to freak. No... For a moment, envy of my friends felt almost like hate.

I rolled onto my back, conscious of the heat in my flesh, the need for another beside me. Yet I didn't want anyhar. There seemed to be a strict contract to it all, too much giving. Even beyond the confines of an established relationship, sharing a bed demanded all kinds of other sharing, perhaps with a har you would never see again. What business was it of theirs to know my mind? Why, through my breath, should I spill the blood of my shortcomings into the memories of somehar else? Why couldn't the physical sensations of aruna be enjoyed for what they were; fleeting and ultimately meaningless, like the shadow of a cloud passing over a field?

My blood seemed to roar within me. I needed no other, for I could give my body the release it craved all by myself. And it was Murarn I thought of as I did so. I couldn't imagine him as soume; he was too rigid and scrawny. I could only picture him as an effigy of sticks and thorns that way. Ouana, I could imagine, though, and the images now brought pleasure. And I thought, then, I saw a tall dark shape by my door, watching me. If this was a fetch, I obliged it, whispering his name, writhing wantonly. *Come to me*, I thought, and then the wave washed over me, leaving me gasping for breath, spluttering, until it ebbed away and I panted myself back to normality. I saw that my coat hung from a hook on the door. My fetch. I laughed and couldn't stop for some minutes. This was how it should be, surely? A creature of mysterious delight who turned back into an everyday object once the craving was satisfied.

Cuttingtide was fast approaching, and I would return to my family then for a week. I found I was looking forward to this, because my parents and brother wouldn't bother me; they respected how I was and never pried.

Then, I was given even more reason to escape *Hart's Cliff* for a while.

I'd glimpsed Murarn regularly, as I always did, and now we exchanged glances, small smiles and the occasional greeting of a raised hand, but we did not speak. I felt his eyes on me though, as he no doubt felt mine. I had begun to fantasise about him more and more, but had decided any real encounter between us would shatter my illusions. Fantasy was preferable. Unless, of course, he approached me. I was prepared to let fate take its course in that respect.

Everyhar knew I was going home for the festival and some expressed their disappointment: mainly Raephe and Yuroah's friends. They wanted to be my friends too, I knew, and this irritated me. I believed they saw me as a challenge and therefore couldn't stop trying to reach me. I didn't consider this genuine liking, and therefore it was worthless.

Three days before my departure, somehar knocked on my door

as I was preparing to go down to dinner. I opened it swiftly, expecting Raephe or Yuroah with gossip that couldn't wait, but no, there stood Murarn, as grave and ominous as a sentinel of death.

'What is it?' I snapped.

'May I come in?'

I gestured wordlessly at the room and he walked past me into it. I folded my arms, said nothing.

For some moments, we stared at one another, and I began to hear the surf-beat of my heart in my ears. I put my head on one side, raised my brows.

'This is...' Murarn shook his head. 'You're going away soon.'

'Yes.' Still I wanted to make him suffer.

'There's something I have to say to you.'

I shrugged.

'Would you be free for dinner tomorrow or the night after?'

'I'd better check my diary. I'm very busy.'

He looked bewildered.

'That was a joke.' I relented, smiled, softened my tone. 'I'm sorry. Yes, yes of course. Tomorrow.' Already I was imagining the evening: sharp banter across a table, laughter. Perhaps something later. Perhaps not. The wordplay would be enough to fuel later fantasies.

Murarn smiled uncertainly. 'Thanks. I'll... I'll relay that, then. Somehar will come for you.'

'Excuse me?' I had no idea what he meant.

He frowned. 'The dinner.'

'Why would somehar *come* for me? And why *relay* my answer to anyhar?' I thought he must be referring to a therapist. 'Can't we just *meet*... in private, like hara do?'

Murarn threw back his head rather dramatically, sighed. 'I'm no good at this.'

'It's OK,' I said encouragingly. 'I'd love to have dinner with you.'

He eyes widened. 'No... Oh sweet Aru... I meant to say, *Sallowbar* has invited you to dine.'

'What?' I stared at him in horror.

He appeared confused. 'A dinner... tomorrow or the night after.'

'He sent you here to ask this?'

'Yes...'

'And that seemed perfectly normal to you, did it?'

165

'Well…' He wouldn't look at me.

'He sent you to *procure* me, supposedly because he's noticed something between us, and wanted to make you squirm, since he knows you don't have the guts to say no to him.'

Murarn shook his head, raised his hands as if to ward me off. 'No… not that, no.'

'In what pelking realm is that acceptable?' I said. 'Have you no pride or self-respect?'

He drew himself up, his expression hardened to blankness. 'I don't know what you mean, or why you're angry.'

I took a step closer to him and he backed away. 'Murarn, I accept you might be… unworldly… in some respects, but you can't be blind to what's been going on between us, surely? The interest? I know it's there, so don't try to deny it.'

He blinked at me for a few moments. 'I… Sallowbar sent the request through me, because he thought that would make it easier for you to say no if you wanted to.'

'How thoughtful of him. Go back and say no, then. But before you do, explain yourself to me.'

There was a silence, then he said coldly. 'I don't understand.'

'Do I need to spell it out? I thought *you* were extending the invitation. You must know I have absolutely no interest in that appalling grub, Sallowbar. It revolts me even to think about what's going on in *his* head. How can you not realise it should be you?'

It was beyond Murarn to blush, but two spots of colour had appeared beneath his cheekbones. 'You're mistaken about me. You made assumptions. Whatever you thought, it was only in your head.'

I stared at him for some seconds. From outside, evening sounds drifted in to us: hara walking to dinner, laughing together. I drew in my breath. 'Thank Sallowbar for his invitation, but I decline. You might want to tell your therapist the treatment isn't working. Now go.' I stalked across the room, opened the door and gazed past Murarn, not wanting to see his face for another moment.

He hesitated for a brief while, then slunk out. I slammed the door. I wish I hadn't. I should've closed it softly. As it was, the whole floor of the house shook.

So, there it was: a Cuttingtide rite. The dehar cut down in the fields by the one he loves. An abrupt and deadly cutting. An unmaking.

The dehar expects it, of course. It happens every year. This was the first time it had happened to me. I wasn't in love, but the desire was so strong, it was equally devastating. It makes a har stupid and weak. Open up, and the blade comes for you. I'd been right all along. That night, I vowed no blade would penetrate my armour again.

2

Home restored me and I could forget about my foolish fantasies at *Hart's Cliff*. I'd been influenced by the landscape and the season, but the cutting was past. The time of noonday ghosts approached us now, and soon the perfidious dehar Verdiferel would be sovereign of the season. I would learn about my phantoms of the hill. I'd learn more about Grisainn har Vulpiers. I'd been distracted from these interests by an immature crush, of which now I was ashamed. I had everything I needed in companionship from Yuroah and Raephe. On the journey back to *Hart's Cliff*, I resolved that Murarn must no longer exist for me. Even if I passed right by him, I would not see him. I was relieved to find this resolution worked. I felt no anxiety about returning to work.

Once I'd unpacked, I went to look for my friends. It was a weekend lunchtime, so even if they were on Pelf'sday shift they should be free around this time. They weren't at the refectory, but I came across them eating a picnic meal beside the lake, at the side of the main house. Fortunately, there were no others with them. After the embraces of reunion, I sat down to share their lunch. I'd decided to tell them about my ghost-hunting, which I wanted to experience fully as the season ripened. I related what I'd seen on the Cop – omitting the resemblance I'd perceived to Sallowbar and his minions – and that I wanted to investigate further. 'If a supernatural event plays out every year at *Hart's Cliff*, I want to witness it,' I said.

I was pleased to discover the others were intrigued. 'Now is certainly the time for it,' Yuroah said. 'Verdiferel casts a long shadow.'

I knew he meant that although Shadolan was officially the surviving dehar of the season, Verdiferel already haunted it, a dark shade stretching down from the future.

Raephe and Yuroah already knew about the legend of Grisainn, because guiser troupes who visited the Reaptide festival occasionally performed plays about it. 'Remmayes gave a talk on this subject once,' Raephe said. 'He thinks the whole story might be a parable for a Reaptide rite that the early tribes took part in. Also, he explained how legends have a meaning, a connection, to landscape. That story is part of *Hart's Cliff* and the surrounding countryside, perhaps essential to its well-being.'

I was beginning to wish I'd talked to my friends about this earlier, rather than pin my hopes on the socially-stunted Murarn. 'Have you ever seen anything?'

'Most hara have,' Raephe replied. He nodded towards Yuroah. 'Tell him about your time on the Cop.'

I turned abruptly. 'What happened?'

Yuroah shrugged. 'I saw what I thought was Verdiferel, and whether it was him or not, I did what any sensible har would do and ran away fast.'

'Why did you think it was a dehar? Tell me the details.'

'OK… It was last year, about a week after Reaptide. I was taking a walk with Leveret on the Cop and became…' He wrinkled his nose. '…it's hard to explain although I'm sure you'll know what I mean. The air became *watchful*. I felt disorientated, dizzy, head-achey. Leveret wasn't happy either. He shivered and whined. I knew something unseen was there with us. The trees were so still…' He rubbed his arms, clearly reliving the experience. 'Then a tall har came out from the shadow of the trees, almost as if he'd emerged from one of the trunks. He was dressed like a guiser, or that's what I thought, with a wooden mask over his face that was carved to be beautiful, but was not. It was a caricature of beauty. He was tall and still, just standing there in front of me, one hand on a tree. I thought at first his skin was black, but then I could see it wasn't really skin, but something like bark and roots and moss, gnarled together. Tiny insects were *moving* on it. The long fingers were rootlets. I tried to tell myself this was a costume glove, but that was a lie. I knew who and what stood before me. At any moment, he would beckon to me, and I wouldn't be able to disobey his command. He would take off the mask… He might be kind and beautiful, love me and give me a gift, or he might be hideous and take my mind and ruin my body. I wouldn't gamble with him. I just turned round and dashed off, and so did the dog. We bolted until we reached the gates to *Hart's Cliff.* I ran to find Raephe, half-mindless; that's all I could do.'

'I remember, Ro,' Raephe said, reaching out to clasp Yuroah's shoulder. 'Your eyes were almost falling out of your face and you couldn't speak. I've never seen such terror.'

Yuroah lifted a hand to clasp Raephe's fingers and shook his head. 'It doesn't sound like much when I tell the tale, but it *was*. I'd never felt so close to... I don't know, not death exactly, but *some* kind of extinction. Only a fool tries to take on Verdiferel or believes they're equal to him and his wiles. He's hungry, with a stone for a heart. He's in deep mourning for the death of the sun, but won't acknowledge it. This makes him cruel.' Yuroah laughed, but it sounded hollow, not his usual free expression. 'Light me a pipe, Raephey.'

Raephe took smoking materials from his bag and began doing so. The atmosphere between us was still tense.

'That's an amazing story,' I said.

Yuroah stuck out his lower lip. 'I don't really know what I saw. It *might* have been a guiser playing a trick. They're like that. But... I wonder if that matters really. The feeling of it... I can still remember it exactly. I wish I didn't. Whoever or whatever I met that day, they were dangerous.' He shuddered, but it was mostly pantomime now. 'Verdiferel, we can do without, but I want to see these weird figures you've glimpsed, Issi. You should have told us before.'

'Well, it sounded a bit...' I shrugged. 'I know it *shouldn't* sound mad, because hara see things like this all the time, but... perhaps it was personal.'

'You want *my* story?' Raephe said.

'You have one too? Of course!'

'Mine's not so dramatic,' he continued, packing the pipe with leaf.

'I think it's more so,' Yuroah declared.

'Well...' Raephe ducked his head to one side, pulled a wry face. 'Make up your own mind. Again, it was not long after Reaptide, but some years ago, before I knew Ro or worked here. I grew up in *Hart's Cliff*, so I'd heard all the stories. Like most young hara, I suppose, I was romantic. Grisainn's story appealed to me. Forbidden love, and all that. One afternoon, I was walking in the barley field near home, and saw a har standing upright among the stalks, with his arms held out horizontally.' Raephe mimicked this pose for a moment. 'I thought he must be a hienama or something, because he had the air of somehar spiritual. His head was thrown back as if to acknowledge the sun. I wasn't at all scared. I went right up to him and said hello. He looked at me and said, 'It's beautiful.'

'So was he. He wore a crown of small, dark red roses, wound with ivy. His hair was thick and loose, powdered as if with barley dust. His skin was dusky and his whole being oozed sensuality. His eyes were full of love, but melancholy. I thought it must be Grisainn, his ghost. I said, 'Who are you?' But he only smiled at me. He took my hand, leaned towards me and kissed me on the mouth. I couldn't feel it. I closed my eyes, but I couldn't feel it.' He paused to light the pipe.

'And when you opened your eyes he was gone?' I asked.

Raephe laughed. 'No. I opened my eyes, and he was still standing there, smiling at me. A couple of feet away, though. I'd never seen anyhar so lovely. I think he gave me a gift that day. Joy.' Raephe smiled fondly at Yuroah. 'The possibility of you.' He took a draw from the pipe. 'I wanted to talk with this amazing being, but I was silenced. Before I could force any words out, he bowed to me, and walked off through the barley. I was rooted to the spot, had no hope of following him. Eventually, he passed out of the field into the wood beyond. That's it.'

'Could have been a guiser too,' Yuroah teased.

'Like yours was, of course,' Raephe said scornfully, handing the pipe to him. 'He was like an avatar of Aruhani, aruna incarnate. The first thing I did was find somehar to put out the flames he left burning in me.'

'Utterly romantic,' said Yuroah scathingly. 'I prefer yours to mine. I'm still terrified of Verdiferel and won't go anywhere alone after Reaptide, or even just before it.'

'You're afraid he'll remember you because you ran away?' I said, only part teasing. 'That one day he'll find you to make you gamble with him?'

'Thanks for those kind words,' Yuroah said darkly. 'Now I *will* think that.'

Raephe suggested we go to the Hernayes museum the next day, so I could read all that Remmayes had researched about the Vulpiers and the Lepodarns. I had no idea this information even existed. But we decided that first we would go to the Cop, today, later on. We decided to take Leveret with us, so he could alert us to any supernatural presences our own senses might not pick up. Yuroah was confident Verdiferel wouldn't be around this early in the season, so was happy to take part.

When Yuroah and Raephe went back to work, I returned to my room. Alone, sitting in an ancient, comfortable chair I'd placed by the window, I considered there might be three distinct strands to my story: the legend of Grisainn har Vulpiers and the massacre on Darkloe Cop; the advent of dark Verdiferel and the oppressive ghosts of the ageing summer, and then the figures on the hill. It didn't feel to me as if they belonged to either of the first two ideas. I shied away from including Murarn or his associates in the story. They were peripheral, and if they had melted into the legend it was because I'd poured them there.

Seated so comfortably, I drifted into a doze, but was pulled to full consciousness by the sound of a horse's hooves beneath my window. The path there wasn't wide and, as far as I knew, nohar rode horses upon it. I sat up and looked out. I could hear the hooves moving away but could see nothing. Presumably, the horse had gone out of sight around the building. The air was still and the trees on the Cop were immense and motionless.

'Shadolan, do you walk there?' I murmured. He was the murderer, after all, who had killed his hostling/lover only a week or so before. Yet despite this, and what he'd done, he was not terrifying like his later incarnation Verdiferel was. Perhaps this was because he was still shocked and bewildered by what the season had demanded of him. He had yet to grow bitter and cruel, walking alone with his belly full of pearl and a heart full of spite.

Before dinner, Yuroah and Raephe came to my room. They arrived a good fifteen minutes before the figures were due to appear on the Cop. Our voices were hushed as we took up position at the window. I didn't know what to expect. Like Murarn, they might see nothing, but I knew they'd tell me the truth.

When the figures appeared, I murmured, 'now.'

I heard Yuroah draw in his breath sharply and Raephe make a soft, wordless, querying sound. We didn't speak. Once the figures disappeared into the trees, I whispered, 'what did you see?'

'Movement,' Raephe said quietly. 'Not figures exactly, but a kind of shimmer in the air. Definitely *something*. I felt, if it'd lasted longer, I'd have seen more.'

'And you, Ro?'

His eyes were troubled. 'I saw one figure, that's all,' he said.

'One?'

'Yes. I think it was real. No ghost.'

'What did it look like?'

'Sallowbar's friend,' Yuroah said, 'Murarn. The tall one.'

I stared at him, sure I was displaying emotions that surprised him.

'I mean,' Yuroah continued, 'it looked like him. Too far away to be sure, of course. Just a shape.'

'*When the hare rose up, he stood as tall as a har, and put aside his mask,*' said Raephe, clearly reciting. '*And the lovely vixen within the fox saw the hare was not stupid at all, but something else. And they lay together, in the skins of the jack hare and the vixen fox, beneath the wide eye of the moon.*'

'What's that?' I asked him. I was swamped with a dragging sense of disorientation.

'A fragment that was written a long time ago,' Raephe replied. 'The legend of Grisainn and Fendris, the fox and the hare. Their tribes were named for those creatures.'

'Remmayes thinks the characters were symbols, not actually living hara,' Yuroah said.

I sensed deep discomfort in my friends.

'What's wrong?' I asked them. 'What are you not telling me?'

They exchanged a glance, perhaps more than that in mind touch.

'I think perhaps we shouldn't go up to the Cop tonight,' Yuroah said.

'Why?' I demanded. 'Tell me!'

'The seasons are cycles,' Raephe said. 'Remmayes believes the land seeks symbols to re-enact the past.' He pulled his face into a sour, yet embarrassed expression. 'Don't yell at me, Issi, but... Murarn... that's all I'll say.' He raised his hands to me, as if to ward me off, as Murarn himself had once done too, in fact, in this same room.

'What about him?' I asked, my tone as neutral as it was possible for me to contrive.

'We notice more than you think,' Raephe said. 'We hear things too, unfortunately.'

Yuroah looked mortified. He spoke quickly before I could respond to Raephe. 'Don't be angry. Please, forget it.'

'Tell me,' I said in a gentler tone. 'I promise not to be mad at you.'

'While you were away...' Raephe said, then paused. He began again. 'You upset Sallowbar, by declining his invitation. Upset him a lot. He talked. Everyhar *knows*, Issi. They know what you said.'

'What, that he's a revolting little grub?'

Raephe risked a smile. 'That yes, but also... the other thing. How you wanted it to be *somehar else* inviting you out. How you'd imagined an interest that wasn't there. Sallowbar made a thing of it, because he was upset.'

'You mean he made a joke of it, at my expense.'

Raephe grimaced but didn't confirm or deny that. 'As Ro said, it's stupid, it's nothing. So, you wanted a har. Happens all the time. So what?'

I pressed my hands against my face for a moment, imagining the entire population of *Hart's Cliff* being made aware of my stupidity at the same time, and laughing about it. How could Murarn have repeated everything I said? This was the most hurtful aspect. I could take the rejection, but this? I'd insulted my employers' son, and Murarn had faithfully reported that as well, it seems. What must Remmayes and Shademoth think of me? They'd probably not even thought about me since my initial employment, now I was the har who'd called their impaired son an appalling grub! Murarn must be deranged. I could lie, of course, brush it off as a joke, say I meant nothing by it. I could say I was simply astounded Sallowbar had sent another har to ask me out. How ridiculous. As for wanting Murarn instead, I could claim I said that simply to put Sallowbar in his place, show him he should've approached me direct. Just a joke. That'd be an easy lie, wouldn't it? But then, the faces of my friends, who were astute enough to *know* me. I couldn't do it. Yet, I mustn't show weakness either. I didn't want their concern, their pity.

'I knew it was a mistake the moment those words came out of my mouth,' I said, keeping my voice firm, yet light. 'And while I'm away the gossip starts and grows and... well... Thank you for telling me. It's best I know.'

'We weren't sure whether to mention it or not,' Yuroah said, 'seeing as it's just about died away already as a topic of interest.'

'Will I be in trouble?' I asked, realising this gave me a good reason to appear slightly upset. 'I guess Sallowbar's parents will have heard too.'

'No, no,' Raephe was hasty to assure me. 'They're quite aware Sallowbar gets himself into *situations* this way. You're not the first. Don't worry about that.'

'But...' Yuroah said. 'Do you *like* Murarn, Issi? It's relevant, so please say so if it's true.'

I looked at Yuroah. 'I *did*,' I said, 'right up until the moment he delivered Sallowbar's invitation. Now, I think I hate him. He's right. I read him wrongly, but as he's all wrong anyway, that's not a difficult mistake to make.' I patted Yuroah's shoulder, because he looked so troubled about it. 'Please don't fret. It was nothing, and all that was damaged was my pride. But I don't see how this should affect our plans for tonight. I didn't see Murarn up there, so…'

'There's something else we didn't want to mention,' Yuroah said. 'The last thing we want to risk, in any way, is making potential things *real*, so didn't tell you earlier. Hoped we wouldn't need to, that we could just get into the seasonal mood together.'

'Well, we can,' I said. 'Murarn's nothing. History.'

'Yes, but… the truth is, everyhar knows he's obsessed with the local legends. Maybe it's because he wants to be somehar more confident and fascinating than who he thinks he is. You and him…' Yuroah shook his head. 'You *are* the lovely vixen to him, I'm sure. Dangerous and forbidden, haunting him. Dehara know what he's reading into it all. He *denies* you? A har like him? He's lucky you even noticed him. But he's play-acting, don't you see? Yearning, betrayal? It's all there. Keep away, Issi. Let this season pass.'

'You'll see what we mean tomorrow,' Raephe said. 'At the museum.' He hugged me, a little too forcefully.

'Just one thing,' I said, disentangling myself from the embrace. 'Exactly why is Murarn a guest of Remmayes' therapy wing?'

'He finds it difficult to live in the real world,' Yuroah said. 'Apparently, as a harling he was completely isolated inside his own head. Fantasies are better than reality for him, because he can't function too well in reality.'

'Sad,' Raephe said. 'Anyway, forget it for now. Let's just go to the *Mill* and drink ourselves stupid. Then we'll distract you in the best way we can.'

That night I let down another of my barriers to them. We stumbled, drunk, to their cottage, where they lay me down, insisted I do nothing, and further intoxicated me with their breath and bodies. Fortunately, we were so inebriated, few confidences were exchanged in those intimate moments. They didn't know me better afterwards.

I stayed the night at the cottage, and after a large and lazy breakfast, the three of us went to research the past. The museum of *Hart's Cliff* is housed in a part of the stable-block. A solitary har sat at a desk at the entrance, embroidering a cloth. He asked quietly if we needed a guide. Raephe said no, and in we went.

In the display, throughout a series of rooms, Remmayes has presented the history of the estate. Much of it is hearsay, and he admits this in the first panel of his writing, but states the tales should be preserved. Local artists have created paintings, drawings and collages to accompany Remmayes' blocks of text, which is written large in a beautiful hand. There are artefacts from the first days of harish occupation – clothes, weapons, fetishes. There's little else of interest to display in that respect, since the earliest hara were only scavengers and didn't create or build to any great degree.

I found the rooms of the museum to be sombre in atmosphere, and couldn't repress an urge to hold my breath. They felt weirdly subterranean, even though they were not. Perhaps the small windows and the subdued lighting contributed to that. In fact, it was difficult to breathe and I had to do it consciously. Yuroah, Raephe and I spoke in whispers. And here I began to learn.

The Vulpiers, one of the proto tribes of Alba Sulh, were the first hara to occupy *Hart's Cliff*. Being an early tribe, they did little in terms of renovation or farming. The majority of hara survived during those tumultuous times by raiding and looting what was left of the human population's fortified settlements. *Hart's Cliff* is believed to be one of these communities and, as far as can be established, the Vulpiers sacked and then occupied it for about ten years. Their leader, before the days of phyles and phylarchs, was Malvyen. All the original Vulpiers were incepted hara and there's no surviving evidence to suggest any of them bred.

Savage, disorientated in mind and body, these primordial hara were fashioned like monsters from human young, who had been so desperate and without hope in a cruel and failing civilisation they'd been killing themselves in vast numbers. Until...until that day a miracle happened or a catastrophe. Wraeththu began. Somewhere... As did a different kind of killing.

In the eighth year of their occupation, or thereabouts, the Lepodarns – a new tribe, perhaps created from hara disputing Malvyen's leadership – contested ownership of the territory. The leader of the Lepodarns was Tiernay. The disagreements between the leaders ended in vicious conflict, which lasted for a couple of years. The final confrontation took place on Darkloe Cop, around Reaptide in the tenth year, and no hara were supposed to have survived it. If any had, they'd disappeared or had been absorbed anonymously by other local tribes.

Those are the facts, as much as the history can be verified, which isn't very much. The events took place around a hundred and ten years ago. No written records have been found, and all that remains is what was handed down by word of mouth. I found it unusual, if not unlikely, that every character involved in this drama died in that single, last conflict. Two whole tribes? Even the smallest early tribes had consisted of at least thirty or so hara. And wouldn't at least a few of each tribe have remained at home to defend the domains? Surely, there must still be survivors in the area? Remmayes har Hernayes must have thought the same. He'd investigated but found nohar. There were plenty of first generation hara who remembered those times, but they'd not been directly involved, and in fact had kept their distance from the Lepodarns and the Vulpiers, as both tribes had had a reputation for exceptional brutality. *Hart's Cliff* and its surrounding area, in what was roughly an eight-mile circle, had been off-limits, and whatever had happened there was documented only as conjecture.

Stories, however, persisted. They were perpetuated – perhaps even created and embellished – by hara who had probably never even met the major players. Perhaps they'd caught sight of swaggering Vulpiers riding behind their leader in the countryside, on expeditions to augment their numbers by kidnapping hara who could not adequately defend themselves. Perhaps Lepodarns had demanded tithes from weaker tribes, to be paid in blood and provisions. There are rumours of such things, but no facts.

Within this fierce and unedifying history is the story of Grisainn and Fendris, the archetypal star-crossed lovers. Not real, I was sure. Reading Remmaye's account, I thought – as he did – these hara were simply essential symbols, because stories of rival factions must always include individuals from each side who fall in love.

Remmayes found several different versions of the story, which I won't list here. The most common tells us that Grisainn was the nearest the Vulpiers had to a hienama, in days when magic was as cruel as physical conflict, and rarely used for good, never mind evolution of the self. He was a shaman, who communed with the reawakening spirits of the land; capricious creatures he persuaded – allegedly – to support the Vulpiers. Offerings had to be made to ensure this patronage endured. Harish sacrifice was said to be part of such offerings, generally captives of war. So, Vulpiers sacrificed Lepodarns and vice versa. No wholesome future could flourish from that.

Grisainn was reputed to be the most beautiful har in the area at that time and was the favourite of Malvyen. The Lepodarns had their own shaman, Fendris, who also courted the approval of spirits and elementals. I wondered how young they'd been. Recently incepted and found to be wyrdkin? In their twenties or far younger? No record remains.

The story goes that both the Vulpiers and the Lepodarns regarded Darkloe Cop as a place of power, and it was here that Grisainn and Fendris made their petitions to the spirits. Inevitably, one day, they came across each other. Harsh words were exchanged concerning ownership of the site, but no blows. They parted, hurling insults. But each had *seen* the other, and after a night of invading each other's dreams, they once again met upon the Cop. Here, they mauled each other in a different way. They mauled each other for quite some time, before they were discovered.

To cut the story short, eventually Tiernay became aware of Fendris's relationship with Grisainn, and believed that Malvyen was behind it – a plot to infiltrate the Lepodarns, or to seduce their most powerful shaman away from them. In retaliation, Tiernay had Grisainn taken captive. He sent a message to Malvyen that Grisainn would be sacrificed to the Kindly Ones – their title for the unreliable spirits who were allied with their tribe. Predictably, Malvyen responded angrily and returned a message to inform Tiernay that if Grisainn was harmed, the Vulpiers would slay the entire tribe of Lepodarn. Grisainn must be restored to his hara immediately…. Or else. Affronted by this extravagant threat, Tiernay had Grisainn killed at once. The parts of his dismembered body were left among trees near the gate to *Hart's Cliff*.

After that, it was only a matter of time before each tribe murdered the other. It was said that after the final battle, everyhar was found dead upon the Cop. Inexplicably, Grisainn's body was found nearby, despite the fact it had previously been burned upon a pyre beside the river. Before its cremation the body had been reassembled and stitched together, but the corpse found on the Cop was unmarked, whole. Grisainn looked as lovely as ever, as if he were only asleep. He was covered in wild roses. But if everyhar was dead, who had found his body? In fact, who had witnessed the result of the massacre? Fendris? There's no mention of what became of him. Perhaps, driven mindless by grief and fury, he was responsible for the slaughter, bolstered by the supernatural strength of the spirits. He became the cruel Verdiferel and slew them all. That's what some hara think. It makes sense, I suppose. If any of it was real.

At one time, Raephe – *perhaps* – had found his vision of Grisainn manifesting in a barley field. I doubted Murarn had experienced anything similar. I thought he was still searching – dreaming. I didn't entirely agree with my friends' analysis of the situation between Murarn and me. I didn't think Murarn saw me as Grisainn and himself as Fendris. I believed it was far more likely he simply didn't desire me, or was too panicky about intimacy to initiate anything real between us. That was that.

And yet…

I felt the season swelling around me, its tendrils reaching into every shadowed spot. I could feel the passion of Verdiferel, his tricksiness, his grief, his power, his impatience with stupidity. In this scenario, perhaps I was not the lovely fox, but Verdiferel himself. If there was any truth at all in my friends' suppositions, perhaps Murarn didn't realise what I was, what I might be capable of.

After the visit to the museum, I spent the rest of the day with Raephe and Yuroah, drinking wine in their garden and talking about the old stories. As the day sank into night, I left them, knowing they wanted me to stay. I needed to be alone.

For a while, I walked beside the river, aware of the antiquity of the land. These ancient trees had witnessed so much. The land rang with the cries of the dead. There was blood underfoot, even if it had sunk deep into the earth. I decided I must appear to lose interest in the local legends, in ghosts and visions of dehara. All that could wait for the festival. I wanted hara's suspicions to die down, for gossip to fade. I wasn't sure what would happen.

When I reached my room, I undressed and threw a loose dressing-robe round me. I had wine in my cupboard and drank it, yearning for greater intoxication. The house was quiet around me, as if everyhar who lived, stayed and worked there were absent. I basked in this feeling, fantasising the old house was mine alone. I stood at the window, looking out at the Cop, a goblet of wine clutched to my chest.

As I lingered there, my mind almost empty, I heard once again the sound of a horse's hooves approaching. This must be some kind of acoustic anomaly. Below my room, a path ran around the lake side and front of the building, but at this point was separated from the front lawn by hedges and a low ornamental wall. I could see no horse.

And yet…

I put down my goblet and placed both hands upon the windowsill, leaned out. Nothing. But the hooves still rang, never drawing closer or moving away. Then, silence, and I was sure the unseen creature had stopped beneath my window.

Instinctively, I loosed my hair and let it fall over the casement. Of course, it couldn't reach the ground, but all that mattered was the symbolism of it. *Isoldis, Isoldis, let down your hair…*

Come on, then, I thought, hoping that whatever waited below would hear it.

The being – ghost, idea – hesitated, as if in two minds. I pulled my robe down from my shoulders, let the night scorch them. I became the essence of soume, like a primal goddess. An invitation. *Here I am…*

I stood up, and walked back into the shadows of the room. I didn't light the lamps. I opened the door, just a crack. Then I lay down upon my bed. *Come, darkness…*

I saw nothing, no shadowy shape. I heard nothing. Neither did anything climb onto my bed and leave an imprint on the quilt beside me. But when I touched myself, it was if another did so, and my mouth burned from a kiss I could not feel.

Thoughts came unbidden to my mind, like half-heard dialogue, or as if another spoke through me. *I could take a knife and slice your throat. But instead I will bite it.*

This was too real. I could feel a har upon me, *inside* me, but perhaps I was simply drunk and this was an illusion of desire. There was no throat to slice or bite.

In the present moment, I thought clearly: *Show yourself…*

It didn't.

Another alien thought flashed across my mind: *You dare to come here? They will kill you.*

And he said, in my head, *but I'm already dead.*

I was with a har whose body I craved, whose gaze was like sustenance. Despite my protestations of surprise and warning, I had lured him down to this dangerous spot, my private bower. This was a test of his resolve, the strength of his desire. At any moment, somehar could come across us. But I didn't care. If we were caught, we'd die together. Silent then, hungry and almost grieving, we rode to the peak of our pleasure, until, spent, I realised I was alone, in the present time, short of breath, dazed, shuddering.

Who or what had come to me? The ghosts of Fendris and Grisainn, the phantom of their love, the suppressed lust of Murarn, some other essence or incarnation of desire?

After that night, the invisible visitor did not come again, nor did I hear hooves beneath my window. The invitation had been made and accepted. But this was not simply an invitation to take aruna. Rather, it was letting the past – or *something* – in. I'd made a portal of some kind. Something had stepped through it. Now it was here, waiting.

Raephe and Yuroah were too superstitious. They wouldn't go to the Cop with me, because they feared for my safety. That didn't matter. On Reaptide, I would go alone.

3

The weeks passed as the season deepened. My friends thought I'd changed. I became more sociable, open to establishing relationships with Yuroah and Raephe's circle. I got drunk a lot, laughed. No, I was not the contained, repressed creature of an earlier season. I had emerged from a chrysalis like a gaudy butterfly, perhaps would live only as long, at least in this incarnation.

Yuroah, I think, was least taken in by this display, because I caught him observing me speculatively a couple of times. But he said nothing, and I would merely direct a blazing grin at him in those moments, from which he'd turn his eyes. I became *inhabited*, but not, I think, by an outside entity. I absorbed what remained of the idea of Grisainn, and did, in some way, become him. I knew now he was no fey, gentle thing, but as fierce as any other incepted har. His beauty only made him more terrifying. His radiant smile was really a snarl, the precursor to a deadly strike of one kind or another.

Each day, after whatever evening's entertainment I'd attended, I walked around the base of the Cop, never climbing it. I ran the legends through my mind, and on each retelling, they became more vivid. Now, I believed wholly there was truth behind them, even if that truth was embellished. Hara had died – horribly. The story of the Vulpiers and the Lepodarns was a ghastly, explicit example of how early Wraeththu had been; birthed screaming and bloody, terrible in their fear and confusion, maddened by the changes they had to accept, not only in themselves but the world.

And over it all, wallowing in this gory history, was Verdiferel, rising in power, while Shadolan, I was sure, was aware of being stalked by his future self and hid from it. Once the Cuttingtide festival was past, nohar talked of Shadolan, or revered him. I knew why now. It was because Verdiferel began to manifest shortly afterwards, and before he could reign he must hunt down his predecessor, expunge him. When we welcome Verdiferel at Reaptide, he's been with us – unseen – for quite some time.

All of these influences whirled together like smoke from a summer bonfire, filling the air with sparks and the smell of burning. We danced like puppets before the flames, our Reaptide selves already in place, but waiting.

A week or so before the festival, the guisers arrived at *Hart's Cliff*. They would set up home and give their performances in a shorn wheat field beside the river. I strolled to the site to watch. The name of their troupe was Dog Rose Larks. They arrived in an enormous, covered wagon-home, of two linked carriages, with high sides and colossal wheels, drawn by eight piebald heavy horses. The carriages were decorated lavishly with eerie pictures in tones of red, black and white; scenes of spirits cavorting in black flames or across tree tops, unearthly hara that looked like beautiful demons or vile angels. The vehicle seemed unnaturally big, somehow impossible, as did the stately, gusting horses, shaking the banners of their manes and stamping up clods of stubble and earth as they were unharnessed. Once the horses were seen to, the Larks' band of assistants began to erect a stage upon the field, as well as several pavilions. I was unsure of these structures' purpose; perhaps refreshments would be laid out in them. Meanwhile, the guisers, in costume, strutted around so that hara might come and look at them.

I walked among the gathering crowd, enjoying the feeling the guisers conjured within me, threatening yet exciting, an intriguing reminder of the figures I'd seen on the hill – unearthly and grotesque. They had given up their real identities, at least in public, and had taken on meaningful personae. There were eight major players, along with a dozen or so lesser performers, who took minor roles that changed according to the production or season, or provided music for the presentations. The main characters never changed, even if the story did. There was the Wise Hienama, who was also the narrator of the performances. He was dressed in elaborate robes of ragged cloth, in shades of crimson and tarnished old gold, hung with beads, animal bones and skulls, hanks of fur, braids of ivy and wheat. The Fair Soume was in fact a har of quite ouanic aspect, who wore diaphanous robes, his long cornsilk hair bound with flowers. The Brave Ouana, on the other hand, was a fey, sinuous, soumic creature with a pixie mask and short spiky green hair. He carried weapons that seemed too big for him – a great sword across his back, a massive axe in his hands. He was dressed in battered leather armour daubed in red pigment, or perhaps real blood. A tattered cloak hung from his shoulders. Panphilien was the dehar that contained within him all other dehara of the seasons. He was black and dressed in layers of ragged black cloth, embellished with beads of jet. The ends of his fingers were red, and he wore lavish false eyelashes made of feathers, and a necklace of small animal skulls. He carried a staff. Then there was the Faithful Hound, a har adorned in wolf pelts, the Sweet Serpent, swathed in a sheath of cloth and leather fashioned to look like snakeskin, the Highborn of Tribes, a har with a sovereign's crown, and finally The Friend From Below, a terrifying purple and green demon who was the foe of Panphilien and all surface-dwellers alike. All of the players, except for Panphilien, wore masks. The dehar only donned a mask when the performance began – the appropriate spirit of the season. The assistants could dress up as imps, or animals, or victims of murder.

While more hara from *Hart's Cliff* and the surrounding settlements congregated on the field, the stage hands of the Dog Rose Larks set up stalls hung with ribbons and bells, selling toys, masks and costumes, gaudy cosmetics and sweets. Musicians emerged from the wagon-home, almost naked, clad only in a few thin scarves dyed mottled green. They wore half masks made of leaves and feathers to look like birds. They danced around the crowd, playing on tambourines, rattles, fiddles and pipes; a discordant yet rhythmic cacophony.

I wondered how many hara lived within those immense carriages. There seemed to be so many of them connected to the troupe, more than could be accommodated comfortably. Surely one wagon must be given over entirely to storing the stage, the pavilions and stalls, and the props? And also supplies, I thought. I had a weird image of them lying all tangled together in a heap to sleep, like corpses on a battlefield.

After an hour or so, Shademoth and Remmayes came in procession from the main house to greet the troupe, bearing gifts, as was customary. Tall, gracious and graceful, like idealised representations of a phylarch and consort, the pair of them were balanced of aspect, perfect hara. They were dressed in costumes of summer finery, adorned with flowers, feathers and beads. And with them, of course, their sons – the pretty harling not yet two years old and Sallowbar, chest puffed out, swaggering around as if he was important. From a distance, I could almost feel pity for him. I could sense his parents' fond yet concerned indulgence, always on mild alert for what Sallowbar might do or say.

The Wise Hienama came to the middle of the field, where there was a space between the stalls, and raised his arms. He wore a dark wooden mask, carved into a cruel, lascivious expression, with brightly-painted scarlet lips and elaborate eye makeup. He bowed to the crowd, and removed his mask with a flamboyant gesture. This too was customary. A moment's honesty, perhaps. The Hienama had a bony, quirky face, which was oddly beautiful. His eyes were wide and dark, and his rags of long black hair hung down to his hips in ropes and tassels. He fascinated me. In a loud, thrilling voice, his arms sweeping wide in dramatic gestures, his body sinuous, dipping and swaying, to face all sides of the audience, he cried:

'*Gather round, oh hara dear,*
Gather round in fright and cheer.
Ghosts by day and summer's heat.
Flowers from a dehar's feet.
Death and life and love and fire,
Dancing in the sun's desire.

And when the disc sinks down the hill,
Come, dance and sing to summer's kill.'

He bowed theatrically and the crowd applauded, a fever building up for the performance to come. I considered that this rhyme must surely apply more to Cuttingtide, as Reaptide had no killing – that I knew of.

At this moment, the Fair Soume came forward. His mask was that of soft and expressionless beauty, yet his slender build was powerful and muscular, like a warrior. He wore a crown of roses upon his head and carried a basket of rose petals, which he began to throw into the air. Harlings ran forward to catch them. Adults clapped and whistled. Was this the guisers' interpretation of Grisainn? I was standing in a copse of trees next to the river, away from the crowd, but close enough to witness the proceedings. I thought nohar would notice me, but then the Fair Soume turned his mask in my direction. I flinched from the arrow of his gaze and froze. I didn't want this to happen, but knew it must. He came over to me, his strong bare feet gliding over the stubbled earth, and paused a short distance away from me. It was as if the crowd hadn't noticed. They were still cheering at the Hienama, who was posturing before them. The Fair Soume threw a handful of petals over me. 'Rose from the dead,' he said huskily. 'You *know*.'

Then he skipped back into the sunlight, perhaps had never left it, dancing around the crowd, raining summer down on innocent heads and into tiny hands. I blinked. Petals still fell from my shoulders to the ground.

A minor performance took place that night. I attended with Raephe and Yuroah and their friends. A bonfire had been built in the middle of the field, and the Hernayes were there to light it. After this, the guisers didn't enact a play but offered music and droll recitals. Their stage was more like woodland than a theatre, so thickly was it draped in foliage. The Faithful Hound had a beautiful singing voice and gave us songs that conjured tears and yearning. We ate sticky, overly-sweet confections and drank warm apple wine. In that setting, the repast was perfect, delicious. Torches on tall poles lit the night, their flames hungry and vomiting sparks. Even the earliest hara had celebrated the seasons, drawn as they'd been to pagan ways. It's documented that on these occasions, it had been common for hostilities between tribes to cease for a couple of days, and enemies might mingle warily in the raucous crowds. I felt that Fendris and Grisainn must have grazed each other's auras at events like this one. Perhaps they walked among us still, hidden behind a guiser's mask. I was with my friends, but apart from them, merely observing rather than participating. My performance was convincing enough, so they didn't realise the deceit. I was drowsily content, as if floating on a calm sea. If there were storms to come, they were yet below the horizon.

Near the end of the evening, I glimpsed Sallowbar and his minions, who were making a noise – shouting and laughing. Murarn stood among them, looming and uncomfortable. It looked like the others were mocking him, that his presence there was a punishment, but the truth was his companions hadn't noticed his discomfort. He was, to them, the Tall, Silent One, simply being himself. He would not raise his eyes at all; I thought I knew why. He felt me near and feared me. *You're no Fendris*, I thought, half in pity, half in scorn. Perhaps, in his imagination, Murarn could become somehar powerful and charismatic, but in reality he'd never ride into dangerous territory to claim a har he craved. Fendris had been daring and reckless. He'd crept through the unlit, rubble-strewn passageways of *Hart's Cliff*, sliding from shadow to shadow, to reach that room and plunder it, risking death at every moment, burning up with a desire that scalded and seared him so much, he'd die if he didn't satisfy it. Murarn had no idea. I thought his dreams must be tame and soft-lit, merely a limpid, sterile coupling rather than raging, fierce love. *If only you weren't so weak*, I thought, sadly.

An hour before midnight, I snuck away from the party; nohar noticed. My friends were drunk and chatting up the guisers, who no doubt saw such choice harish morsels as part of the payment for their performance. I didn't want to get that close to the players. They would see through me, unmask me. More than a little drunk myself, I meandered my way to the Cop. Tonight, for the first time, I would climb it. It wasn't yet Reaptide eve, but I looked upon this visit as a sortie. I wanted to absorb the feel of the land up there, as part of my preparations, even if I wasn't sure what I was preparing for.

The moon wasn't quite full, but achingly bright. I could see almost as well as in daylight. As I climbed, my breathing became difficult, as it had in the museum; the air fought me. I clawed my way through bracken, brambles and briars to reach the summit. My clothes and flesh were torn. I could see my arms were streaked thinly with smears of blood, like berry juice. I came to an open space, the spot where the peculiar figures crossed the Cop each evening. Here, the ground was spongey with lichen and deer-cropped grass, strewn with rabbit droppings. A tawny owl called eerily, as if in warning. I turned round and could see the amber glow of the bonfire, down on the field by the river. From here, I couldn't hear voices or music, which was odd, because the field wasn't that far away. It was like being cut off from the world, looking at it through a window.

I thought I heard a movement behind me and froze. Was somehar approaching softly? I welcomed him. *Come to me.* After only a few moments, his fingers were upon my arms, rising up slowly to push my hair from the back of my neck. He kissed me there, nipping the skin. 'Fen,' I murmured and turned.

No Fendris there, dark of aspect, brooding, beautiful. Instead, Sallowbar, grinning at me. Instinctively, I pushed him away with both hands. 'How dare you! Get off me, you little freak!'

Sallowbar appeared not to hear the insult. 'Who are you waiting for, *Isoldis*?' he said, leering in the most disgusting way. 'You *are* waiting for somehar, aren't you?'

I wouldn't answer him, but made to go back down the hill. He caught hold of one of my arms, gripping tightly. I turned and swung with my free fist, which made satisfying contact with his face.

Sallowbar uttered a wordless roar, but I was sure I could defeat him if it came to a fight. I was taller, and believed myself stronger. Blood was running from his nose. Perhaps I'd broken it. 'Don't try it!' I hissed. 'Just back off and run to your hara, grub!'

Sallowbar put a hand to his nose for a moment, then stared at the blood that covered it, which glistened purple in the moonlight. 'Vulpiers!' he cried. 'Come to me!'

I laughed. 'What?'

I saw his creeping minions emerge from the shadow of shrubs to my left.

'Take him!' Sallowbar screeched. He affected not to look at me now, a scorned leader.

I still wasn't worried. Not then. 'Vulpiers? Them? Are you serious?'

He was. They pounced.

I fought them off for some seconds, but eventually I had to accept I couldn't take on four hara at once for any length of time, not even Sallowbar's clumsy minions. One appeared to be missing, though. As far as I could make out, Murarn wasn't with them. After considering my options in an instant, I decided the only thing I could do was run. I tried to wriggle away from those who held me, lashing out as much as possible with hands and feet, lunging to bite. I started to drag them with me down the hill; they clung to me like parasites. They squawked, struggled with me. Perhaps at this point they worked out they'd under-estimated my strength.

Then, I saw Sallowbar pounding towards us. He was shrieking 'Bitch! Bitch! Bitch!' over and over. When he reached us, he struck me on the head with a heavy object, probably a rock. Momentarily, I was paralysed, blinded by white light, then a shooting pain seemed to split my skull. I was dazed, my limbs no longer obeyed me. I knew if he hit me again he might kill me.

I went limp, made no sound, closed my eyes, offered no threat. How far would this idiot go? He didn't think he'd get away with pelki, surely? Things like that didn't happen in modern, rural communities. Aruna was sacred; such disrespect was a horror from the past. But if it wasn't sexual humiliation Sallowbar wanted, the alternative might be worse. Did he think he could murder me and hide the body? Surely, the absences from the guisers' party would be noticed. 'They'll know,' I managed to croak. 'Stop, Sallowbar. For yourself. Stop.'

He must've dropped the rock, but my words didn't reach him. I could hear him panting hoarsely, feel his shaking hands upon me, pulling at my clothes. He was almost sobbing. I could hear strange, snorting mumbles emanating from his followers, whose hands held me down. They were enjoying this; the spectacle aroused them. I must be still, not think about what was happening, merely survive. I must keep thinking that whatever they did to me wasn't aruna, but something else: these pathetic creatures' inadequacy and envy, their warped desires.

Presently, they had me naked.

'Look!' Sallowbar crowed, pointing, and I felt the blaze of their stares on my skin.

Acid rose into my throat, and swallowing it burned me. I prayed to any dehar or spirit who might hear me: *Let them do what they must and be gone, but don't let them kill me.*

Then, a shout in my mind: *Betrayer!*

My body jerked and shuddered as if electricity had run through it. I blinked blood from my eyes and, through a hazy film, saw a face hanging over me. Not Sallowbar's. I didn't know it, and yet I did: Malvyen.

Who were you waiting for, Grisainn?

No one...

Liar.

He struck me – Grisainn – again. I felt my lip split. *I know, you vixen. I know who puts the heat in you. When he gets here, that's the end of it. For both of you.* He moved away from me. *It's yours,* he said to his hara.

This isn't real. This isn't real, I told myself. Yet still I felt what they did to me, to *him.* Mercifully, my mind was removed from the event. Grisainn took it for me, he took it all. Those who assaulted him were young hara, stolen human children, not long past inception, brought to this spot to be shown what happened to traitors. They'd never had a chance to touch him, this remote, perfect being, favourite of their leader. Under normal circumstances, he was forever beyond them, and he'd scorched them with his hard, lovely glances, his sly smiles. He'd flaunted himself to them, these altered, angry, terrified boys, who could not help but see him as a beautiful, teasing girl, because their transition was so new to them. They couldn't believe the change, never mind understand it. They were so young, hardly more than feral children. Now, their leader, their only anchor, had let them off the leash. They could do as they wished, and took revenge for the way Grisainn had made them feel. They took revenge for what had happened to them.

Eventually, Malvyen barked at them to clear them away. He bent over Grisainn, touched his bloodied, beaten face. *Now we'll be together,* he said. *Experience it fully, little vixen. It will be the last time.*

Malvyen... Be kind... Grisainn prepared himself to die, sure his throat would be cut as Malvyen took him for that last wild ride.

But the final violation never happened.

The body upon me jerked violently, and uttered a strange, gargling grunt. I was able to scramble away, on my back, kicking the ground and using my elbows. I saw Murarn standing over me, a raised weapon in his hands, held above his right shoulder. It appeared to be an iron bar. He'd struck Sallowbar. He'd rescued me. I reached up with one hand, caught half in the past and half in the present, dizzy and sick.

I had no time to thank him. That iron bar he held came down on me. Hard. I heard the bone break before the pain in my shoulder caught fire. That's all I can remember.

Hara told me I'd taken a fall down the hill. Foolish of me to try and climb it, drunk. I didn't know the path, was far away from it. A family walking home from the party in the field had found me lying in the lane near the Cop, to which I'd apparently crawled. By the time they found me, I'd been unconscious.

I woke in the treatment facility, being tended by soft-footed hara, who touched me with hands that seemed to have no more weight than a dragon fly. 'Be still,' one murmured to me. 'You hit your head.'

'I was attacked…'

'Hush.' He passed a hand over my eyes and sent me to sleep again.

Next time I woke, bright sunlight streamed into the room. A har was there, reading a book in a chair beside my bed. When he realised I was conscious, he straightened up and put down the book. Wordlessly, he offered me water, which I drank while he held the cup. I could feel no pain, but my entire body was numb, which might explain that. 'What injuries?' I asked the carehar.

'Your head took a bad knock, and you dislocated a shoulder. Bruises, scratches. Nothing that won't be mended soon. There's no great damage to your head.'

'I was hit with a rock,' I said. 'And… somehar hit me with an iron bar.'

'There's no evidence of that,' murmured the har. 'You took a bad fall down Darkloe Cop, that's all.'

'They committed pelki on me.'

The har shook his head, still smiling gently. 'No, Isoldis, we'd have been able to tell. We did examine you thoroughly.'

'And you think I could imagine *that*?' I cried.

The har stroked my arm. 'Hush now. Perhaps you thought that, as you fell, because the fall was so hard it was almost like an attack. That spot is renowned for being weird. Bad things happened there once.'

'I know. I saw.' A headache was starting. Stars pulsed before my eyes. 'Malvyen was going to kill Grisainn, but Fendris stopped him,' I gabbled. 'Yet... I don't understand. He hurt Grisainn too.'

'It's the time of year,' said the carehar soothingly. 'Strange times. Memories linger perhaps, and get confused, mixed up. Nohar knows the truth, Isoldis. Was the old legend why you went up there?'

I didn't answer.

The har sighed. 'So many young ones are drawn to it.'

I found this remark patronising. 'I went to meet somehar,' I said sullenly, 'but he didn't turn up. Instead, I was attacked, violated.'

'No... You...'

'Are you calling me a liar, or a fool?' I interrupted. 'I'm neither, I assure you.'

'Your injuries are consistent with a fall.'

'And somehow during my *fall*, I lost all my clothes?'

The carehar frowned a little. 'You were fully-clothed when you were found, a few rips and tears maybe. Be at rest, Isoldis. You're confused.'

'Don't I at least get my story heard?' I asked, almost weeping. 'It should be investigated. I know who attacked me, and that has severe implications. I want to speak to Remmayes.'

To his credit, Remmayes did come to visit me a few hours later. Clearly, this was partly because of his own interest in local history – the carehar must have repeated what'd I'd said. I'd never been this close to a senior Hernayes before. When I'd arrived at *Hart's Cliff*, Shademoth's assistant had welcomed me and settled me in. I remembered Shademoth had smiled at me from a distance as he'd walked past his office. Pausing at the doorway, he'd spoken across what had seemed like an acre of polished wooden floor: 'I hope you enjoy working with us, Tiahaar.' Then he'd glided away. I'd never had occasion to speak with him again – or Remmayes for that matter – or see either of them close up. Now that I was being given the opportunity, it felt surreal. Remmayes oozed compassion and wisdom, and fair-minded authority. He looked splendid, an ideal to which young hara might aspire. I felt immature and awkward beside him, no longer so confident of my story.

'May I sit down?' he asked me.

I nodded.

He ignored the chair, and sat on the bed close to me, clasping his crossed knees with his hands. 'How are you feeling?'

'Beaten up,' I said.

He smiled wryly. 'Tell me what you think happened.'

I told it as clearly as I could, taking care not to include subjective opinions, just the bare experience. Even to me, it sounded like a fantasy. I'd made my own examination earlier; the carehar had been right. There was no evidence of violation and my shoulder wasn't broken. Still, somewhat wearily, I persevered to the end of my story.

Remmayes did not laugh, or even look particularly concerned about Sallowbar's role. 'I'll make enquiries,' he said. 'You realise this might be the result of concussion, and your interest in the old stories?'

'Yes, but it felt very real.'

'It would,' Remmayes said, 'but your memory might be playing tricks. Darkloe Cop is a strange place. However, since you've made the allegations, it's my duty to investigate. I take this matter seriously, Isoldis, whatever the truth behind your recollections.'

'Thank you,' I said. 'I ask no more than that. I trust your judgement.'

He smiled again. 'Rest and recover,' he said, then paused. 'What you experienced is interesting, because I've not heard that version of the story before. Where did you hear it?'

'I didn't. All I know is what you've put in the museum.'

'Hmm. That site is very powerful, so I'm not going to dismiss what you experienced out of hand. Whether you really were attacked or not, some message might be there for us, some truth wishing to be told.'

I was astonished he took my story this seriously, hadn't expected that, but then I suppose he was as obsessed with the legend as I was, seeing as he'd devoted so much space to it in his museum. He wanted that part of my experience to be true.

That evening, Remmayes returned to me. He told me he'd confronted his son, and Sallowbar had admitted following me to Darkloe Cop. He'd also confessed there had been an altercation and a scuffle, but had denied the attack. Sallowbar blamed the argument on us all being drunk, and claimed it had been "trivial". He'd said that I'd eventually run off down the hill, but neither he nor his friends had seen me fall. They had left shortly after me, taking a different – and easier – route down. The Cop had also been investigated, and there was no trace of blood or other evidence of a fight. No psychic residue had been picked up either, which surely it would have been had my experience been real. Sallowbar's nose was not broken, or even bruised. He was unmarked.

'Have you spoken to Murarn?' I asked, by this time feeling both desperate and foolish.

Remmayes nodded. 'Yes. He wasn't there, Isoldis. Others can verify he remained at the guisers' party until at least 2 in the morning. I think he knew Sallowbar was waiting to follow you, or at least hoping for the opportunity to do so, and wanted no part of that. I could tell by speaking to him he did not lie.'

'I'm sorry for wasting your time,' I said bitterly.

Remmayes clasped my shoulder, the unhurt one. 'No need. I'm aware my son has... an *interest* in you, and I hope you understand his handling of that is down to a condition he suffers from.'

'I know, but...'

'Hush. As I said, that place is strange, and I think that maybe, with all those youthful emotions tumbling about, something was invoked and replayed. You might unwittingly have uncovered some history.'

'If that's so,' I said, 'then how did it end? In the story, the Lepodarns take Grisainn captive, and Malvyen was supposed to be distraught. It doesn't seem to tie in.' I paused. 'Maybe... I should go back there, find out more.'

There was a silence. Oh, how badly Remmayes wanted me to unearth further details for him, but he also knew this conversation was already inappropriate. Any return to the Cop could be dangerous for me in my weakened condition. A har could lose his mind that way. 'Perhaps we could conduct a controlled meditation later in the year,' he said at last. 'I could go with you.'

'That will be too late,' I said. 'Now is the time.'

'And you are injured. No, I can't permit it. Perhaps next year.'

'I feel it's now or never.'

He shook his head. 'I know how badly you want to know more, and I confess I do too. Decades ago, when I was your age, I'd have indulged this compulsion. But to do so would be irresponsible and unsafe. Your parents entrusted you to our care, so I must forbid you returning to the Cop. It's frustrating, I know, but these energies can be very dangerous, and we're vulnerable to them in a way humans were not, or very few humans at least. Younger hara are

particularly at risk, no matter how much that galls you. Perhaps…'
He paused. 'Perhaps Grisainn and Fendris were subject to the same
influences, and they're not the cause of whatever haunts the Cop
but a result of it.'

'I think that's very possible.' I paused. 'I think… I think I have
Grisainn's room… in the house, I mean.'

Remmayes raised his brows. 'Why? What have you
experienced?'

'A feeling. I heard a horse beneath my window, but there was
nothing there. I've felt a presence occasionally. It's what made me
feel close to Grisainn.' I hoped these revelations would make
Remmayes change his mind.

'Interesting,' he said. 'Take care, Isoldis. If anything else
happens, you must come to me at once. I'll make sure my staff
know you can have access to me at any time.'

The next day, I was allowed visitors. Raephe and Yuroah came early
in the morning, before work. They'd spoken to the senior carehar
on duty, and told me I'd probably be sent home later that day. My
injuries had already healed sufficiently. I asked them to bring some
clothes for me, as mine were more or less ruined.

'You've *got* to be healed for Reaptide,' Yuroah said. He was
holding my hand, stroking it. 'What happened up there, Issi?'

I shrugged, invoking a slight twinge in my bad shoulder. 'There
are memories that might not be real. I'll tell you all about it when
I'm out of here.'

'You were crazy to go up there alone,' Raephe said. 'It's almost
like you were lured.'

'Not that,' I said, sure. 'Perhaps sometimes witnesses are
needed.'

'For what?' Raephe snapped, terse in his concern.

'The past,' Yuroah whispered.

I merely stared at him, said nothing.

One other visitor came that day. After lunch, I was allowed to dress
myself in the garments Raephe had dropped off for me. I felt
slightly stiff, light-headed, and still numb from the pain-killing
energy treatment the carehara had given me. Still, my body had
more or less righted itself, which is probably more than could be
said for my mind. I still couldn't credit I'd imagined being assaulted

in that way. It must only have been Grisainn's memories I'd experienced, but still, very strange.

I went out into the facility's garden, where I'd wait until the senior carehar summoned me for a final examination. I found a reclining chair on the lawn, by a wide ornamental pool, and lay back in it, with my eyes closed. A cedar reared like an ancient monument above the garden and I could feel it watching me, but this wasn't unsettling. After some minutes, I sensed somehar approach. I could tell it wasn't a carehar, and for a moment, my heartbeat increased. *Had he come to me at last?*

I opened my eyes, and found Sallowbar standing before me. I was so shocked I couldn't speak.

'My father sent me,' Sallowbar said quickly. 'To apologise for what happened.'

'What *happened?*' It wasn't exactly a question, more an exclamation of disbelief.

Sallowbar thrust a large bunch of flowers at me, which I hadn't even noticed he was holding until that point. I let them lie in my lap, stared at them.

'I didn't hurt you, Isoldis,' Sallowbar said. I looked up at him. He was about to cry, eyes brimming, face red. 'I'd *never* hurt you. I don't know what happened up there, but it's not how you remember, I swear.'

'Well, you followed me up there. Why?'

He shrugged awkwardly, looked to the side. 'I... wanted to speak to you. Change things... I wanted us to be friends.'

'And instead you decided to attack me.'

'No!' He clasped his hands together, as if pleading with me. 'You pushed me and I pushed back. You hit me and I hit back. Then you ran away. I'm sorry. I'm so sorry. We shouldn't have let you go off like that, down that side of the Cop. It's so steep. We tried to stop you, but you were so angry, we couldn't. We should've tried harder. That's the truth.'

I raised my hands weakly. 'Fair enough.'

Sallowbar looked as if he was about to collapse in relief. 'That's it? You forgive me?'

'Forgive what? I was mistaken, drunk. We all were. The apology was unnecessary, but thank you for the flowers. I can't apologise for the accusation, as it still feels real me. I didn't lie. I believed what I told your father. But I accept this is some kind of hallucination or faulty memory.'

'Oh, Isoldis, I…' Sallowbar took a step towards me, and I again raised my hands, with more force this time.

'This doesn't mean anything. We're not friends. Now go.'

He nodded. 'Yes, yes of course. Thank you.'

After he'd gone, I wondered if I'd been too harsh.

4

Reaptide eve. The day was hot, the sky cloudless, and hara were indolent. Everyhar was waiting for the festival to start. The guisers' assistants erected ever more elaborate pavilions in the wheat field. The stage was expanded, more imitation woodland added to it. The guisers themselves were not to be seen, no doubt preparing themselves for the performance that evening.

I had more or less recovered from my "accident". I'd been obliged to go to the facility twice a day for healing sessions, and they'd done their job efficiently. The intensive treatment had left me a little woozy, but the injuries themselves, blasted by the healing energy, had faded.

I went to the field with a group of hara, supported on either side by Raephe and Yuroah. Everyhar in their crowd believed I'd experienced a supernatural event on the Cop, and were eager to hear about it. I kept stalling them, not wanting to share anything yet.

The musicians started playing around half eight, and as most hara were already inebriated, the dancing started then too. I didn't want to dance. I was tense. Something must happen tonight. It *had* to. The story wasn't over. Yet how could I escape? I had no doubt the carehara had instructed Raephe and Yuroah to watch me and prevent me going off alone again, because I *felt* watched and constrained. The only privacy I had was when I needed to relieve myself, and even then one of our group of friends would conveniently stand nearby so I couldn't run off.

The evening drew on. It must've been around half ten when I claimed I needed to pee again. Eyebrows were raised at the frequency of my needs, but somehar said they'd come with me. I went to the trenches that had been dug for this purpose, which were surrounded by linen screens. Somehar came to stand beside me. There was no alert within me. Nothing. A voice said. 'Somehar will take your place shortly. Please, have this.'

I turned my head and saw the Wise Hienama guiser standing there, minus his mask. His face seemed strangely familiar to me; deeply tanned, sinewy, yet also lovely. I felt he was older than anyhar I had met before. His dark eyes were mesmerising and his thick black hair was bound with ivy. Several masks dangled from his hands. He held one of them out to me. I blinked at it. 'What's going on?'

'We turn the Wheel,' he said. 'Take the mask. Put it on only after you've shown it to your friends.'

'Why?'

'You want to know the end of the story, don't you?'

'How do you know about...?'

'How could we not know? Take the mask.'

I took it. It was painted silver and grey, framed by long hanks of white horse-hair. Pale crystals were glued around the eyes and cheek-bones: it was a beautiful thing. 'Is this Grisainn?' I asked.

The Hienama laughed softly. 'Could such a har be contained in hair and stone and wood? No. It is a poor copy, but sufficient for our needs.'

'What do you want of me?'

'Once the exchange is made, the changeling placed, return to the Cop. Grisainn needs you there. You are a guiser yourself this night. You must be afraid, yet in love. Do you understand?'

'Are you going to kill me?'

He shook his head. 'No, lovely. It would be inconvenient should you be killed. Follow your heart.'

'Why me?'

The Hienama sighed through his nose. 'These questions are irrelevant. Time flees before the sun. Do what you're compelled to do. We'll clear you a path.'

Then he was gone. This departure was so sudden, I wondered if I'd hallucinated the whole conversation. Yet there was the mask in my hands.

I came out from behind the screens. The har who'd accompanied me saw the mask and said, 'Who gave you that?'

I shrugged. 'Some har in there. He had a lot of them.'

When we reached our group, I showed them the mask. 'Isn't this amazing? Somehar gave it me.'

Yuroah fastened it to my face. 'It's eerie,' he said, standing back to admire it.

Raephe was staring at me oddly. 'Who gave you that?' he asked.

'I don't know. Some har. Think he's with the guisers. You want one? I'm sure he'll still be around.'

'No, I don't want one,' Raephe said. 'It looks good on you, though.'

Was I afraid? Yes. Did I want to go along with this possibly threatening, mysterious plan? Yes. I had no choice, really I didn't. I can't explain.

The beacon fires were lit across the landscape as was the custom of the season. A bonfire blazed upon the field. I stood in my mask, through which it wasn't very easy to see, squinting at the stage. Everyhar had gathered there now, because the performance would soon begin. I felt disorientated, not really there. Sounds wavered in my ears; sometimes loud, sometimes so soft it was as if I were going deaf. My face felt hot beneath the mask. I could hear my breath rasping in my head. This wasn't good, yet what could I do?

A movement beside the stage caught my eye. I saw a har wearing a mask like mine. Like me, he was dressed in tunic and trousers of grey rough-spun linen, adorned with scraps of finer cloth, the legs bound as if with bandages. He raised a finger to the painted lips. For a moment, we held each other's stare, then he came over to me, flickering among the hara, as if passing straight through them. When he reached my side, he said, 'Now go. Be quick.'

'You're crazy,' I hissed at him. 'They'll know. They can *see*.'

'No, they can't. This is what will happen. They see you watching the performance, then going to a pavilion with one of the guisers. They see you with him there, and because of what you're doing, won't disturb you. Go!'

He pushed me.

I glanced at my friends, who were all absorbed in what was happening on stage, perhaps more so than was natural. Why hadn't they noticed this copy of me arriving, talking to me? Lights had bloomed upon the stage, so that forest shadows lay across the boards. Wistful music had started up.

My path divided. In one future, I tore the mask from my face and told this odd har I wouldn't play the guisers' games. I knew if I did this, the performance would stop, immediately, the performance that no har could see, in which I was an actor. In the other future, I walked away from the party unseen, into the unknown and whatever role waited for me there.

I didn't walk – I ran. I tore through the crowds, expecting at any moment for a hand to fall upon me, pull me back. But nohar did. I felt invisible. Once out on the road beyond the *Cliff,* it was as if I was being led. This time, even though not sure of the way, trusting my instincts, or information that had somehow been put inside me, I took the longer route and found myself without effort upon the easier path to the Cop.

The summit of Darkloe Cop was a temple, its processional way a path through the tall, motionless trees. Its incense was the aroma of earth and foliage, its sacred light the moon. I sat down cross-legged in the middle of the open space where there was a slight depression. Had hara once been sacrificed there? If so, there was no taint left behind. For some minutes, I sat silently as my heartbeat slowed down, not just from the exertion of the climb but the anticipation of what I might find up there. All was quiet and still – the air was soporific. I murmured in a low voice, 'I call to you, Grisainn of the Vulpiers. I summon and invoke you on this eve of the Reaping. I am here to do your bidding, to right old wrongs, to speak hidden truths.'

While nothing moved or made a sound, gradually an increasing listlessness stole through me, as if I was passing into a hypnagogic state. I heard a strange echoing crackle, as of branches breaking in a huge but confined space. The air sighed. The moon blinked.

'I call upon you, Grisainn har Vulpiers,' I said, in a louder voice. 'I summon and invoke you...'

Something was coming. I could sense it.

A sound came from my left, and I turned quickly. I faced a thicket of birch; brambles grew thickly around the silvered trunks. I could see so clearly; the moonlight was piercing. I saw something move and realised it was a pale, dirty hand, coming up from the earth, through the thorns.

I almost jumped to my feet, but willed myself to remain seated. I mustn't show fear.

Another hand clawed through, and then a body hauled itself upwards. I forced myself not to flinch away from whatever might show itself to me.

His hair was matted with earth and hung to his thighs. He was dressed in rotted, colourless cloth, which was like a guiser's costume, somehow too decorative to be authentic rags. He looked very young, hardly more than a harling, but then, he'd been incepted, not born. He looked younger than me, but could have been older. His arms were streaked with soil and the green of crushed foliage, which might have been painted there. His face was beautiful, smeared with gouts of dark earth, that was perhaps only pigment, but with full lips and large, doelike eyes. He wasn't tall, and his body was thin, yet I could see the arms were strong, corded with muscle. He staggered a little, as he walked on bare feet towards me, slightly stooped, curious, as if wondering who I was.

'Are you Grisainn har Vulpiers?' I whispered.

He put his head to one side. 'What are you? What have you come here for?' His voice was croaky yet musical, because of the strange accent he had. It was weirdly clipped, yet lilting. This was not Sulhian, but neither was it any other I'd heard in my comparatively short life. Wouldn't Grisainn have had a Sulhian accent? Would accents change over a century?

'Are you Grisainn?' I asked again. 'Answer me.'

'Who's asking?' he responded. 'Who's come to my bed of earth?' He pronounced the letter "s" in the way it was spoken in my name: a hiss.

'I am Isoldis,' I said. 'Tell me your story, Grisainn, because it aches to be told, and shakes the landscape here.'

He snickered, smoothed his rags with his hands. 'Is that so? Hara never act wisely in the old fierce pull of blood, *Iss*-oldis. How warm you are. I can feel the heat of your blood from here. I want to sit down in you. Let me in.'

'No. Speak to me from there.'

'I can't. I want to show you.' He crept closer on his narrow feet and then hunkered down, his legs poking through the tatters of his robe. His filthy knees almost touched me. I could smell him, and this was not a stench of earth and death but the perfume of roses – old roses, perhaps, that had dried and withered within a shuttered room. He reached towards me and I couldn't move. From one hand, he blew what seemed like a miasma of dust over me.

There were a few moments of hazy confusion, then I was looking out of somehar else's eyes, or somehar else was looking out of mine.

I was uncomfortable, as if wearing clothes that were too small and too stiff, but it wasn't unbearable, at least not yet.

He flexed my fingers, rotated my head, making the neck crack.

Grisainn... I could only speak to him in my mind. *You're not cruel. Don't be cruel.*

'Oh,' he said aloud, through *my* lips, 'I'm very cruel. It's hard not to be.'

What happened to you? I asked.

'You know already. They killed me, cut the head and limbs from my body.'

But Fendris... I saw he attacked you here. Did that happen?

'He had to make it look real, and so it did, but he didn't hurt me. He'd never hurt me.'

Please tell me the story, Grisainn, for it must be told.

There was a sigh. 'Yes, Fen wants it told, I know. He wants *me*. So, pretty vessel, I shall tell you.

'Fen thought that if I went to the Lepodarns, the Vulpiers might not attack them, for fear of losing their shaman. Without me, they'd be nothing, it'd be the end of them.' Grisainn held out my hands in front of him, turned them, as if examining new clothes. 'I was important, *Iss*-oldis. I had power many of them didn't. The Vulpiers would have to listen, to bargain. But Tiernay was a frightened har. He knew the Vulpiers outnumbered his tribe. He knew Malvyen would one day kill him. He saw me as a spy, even though Fen told him I wasn't.'

He got to his feet, *my* feet. 'How stupidly trusting we were. We thought, as shamans, we could change the future, we could bring peace. We really believed Tiernay was more likely to understand us than Malvyen was. We thought our love was the beginning and would make peace happen.' He sighed deeply, and I could feel his sadness — and his fury. 'But of course, it didn't. Tiernay said our love was only lust, and that Fen was being fooled by me. He believed I was there to gather information, to plant poison, cast spells, conjure evil. He gave us one hour together, for Fenris to get what he wanted — or so he thought — then he had me killed. He was merciful. It was a swift blow. The head first.'

I steeled myself for terrible memories, but Grisainn held those back. 'See, this is me being kind. I won't make you live that, little har.' He breathed in deeply, let out a shuddering sigh. 'I thank the sky Fen and I never knew what would come after that brief, final time we had together. We thought it was the start and it was the end, but at least we had that hour of sweetness, so sweet, beyond and above any hour before.'

Grisainn fell silent, and I wondered if he'd left me, but then he stirred again. 'Now is the time. I have taken on flesh. Now we shall kill each other, at last. Then it's done and there will be peace.'

What do you mean? I asked, horrified.

Grisainn raised one of my arms, pointed to the other side of the Cop, where the oaks began. 'See…' he said.

I saw an abnormally tall, dark figure among the gnarled trunks. It was cloaked and hooded, and approaching slowly. Of course, I knew who it was: Verdiferel.

Grisainn, I said, *you haven't told me the end of your story. Your body was found up here, whole and perfect, even though it had been burned by the Vulpiers. How did that happen?*

I was desperate to keep Verdiferel at bay. There must be something I didn't yet know, which would end this enchantment, this curse. Surely the guisers hadn't sent me up to here to perish. How did that help Grisainn? More death? More misery and pain? No! It had to be something else. *Tell me!* I urged. *How did he make you whole again?*

'Hara tell lies in the old fierce pull of blood,' Grisainn said. 'Yes, he saw me here, when it was done, because I watched him all the way through. He said he saw me lying here, in the briars, and in his mind, he did.'

Fendris…

'Yes. He avenged the death of our future.'

How did he kill them all?

'He turned the horses on them, turned the hounds on them, turned har against har, within their own tribes. All they could see was blackened devils, scorched fiends, who were sewn together. He was mad, poor Fen. His grief… This place… it is for magic not fighting. Hara who don't know magic are helpless here. And the one who lives here destroys them…'

Who lives here?

'The Noon Walker, the ghost of summer, who came to Fendris and helped him punish the tribes.'

Verdiferel.

'I don't know that name. He comes as an owl or a black dog. He comes as beauty that can kill. He has been here always, since humans made time and lived by it.'

All the while, the dark figure had watched us from the trees. *Dehara: gods of hara shaped by hara.* I mustn't lose that conviction.

Verdiferel... We call him a dehar, I said. *He exists everywhere. He's an idea, a spirit of the earth, of the seasons. But... he can't exist without us to believe in him.*

'I can't see him agreeing with you,' Grisainn said. He took a few steps towards the trees. 'Shall we ask him? It's time.'

Don't go to him in hate and bitterness, I pleaded. *Grisainn, you'll never be dead. Whatever they did to you all those years ago, you live on in the hearts of hara of Hart's Cliff. You're loved. You're remembered as a spirit of beauty and grace, an incarnation of love. You are crowned with roses, a dehar – a god – of the ripening fields. I know, because one summer, a friend of mine met you in the barley.*

Grisainn shuddered in my skin, but when he spoke, his voice sounded less sure. 'The Noon Walker wants me. He wants your sweet skin.'

No, you're wrong. Verdiferel isn't evil, don't you understand that? He wears masks, but what lies beneath is ours to choose. We make him what he is. Fendris chose the mask of reprisal. You don't have to.

We were only feet away from that shadowy figure now. He loomed over us, immensely tall, as if he'd stepped out from one of the oaks. Then he raised unnaturally long, brown hands, whose skin was like bark, and drew the hood back from his face. Of course, he wore a mask; wooden, similar to the one the Wise Hienama had worn down in the field that seemed hundreds of miles and centuries of time away. I understood then that Verdiferel *was* Fendris and he was also Murarn. He has many attributes and faces, in particular aspects of grief and regret, and beneath these things, sometimes, a thirst for vengeance. He is also a lost soul, mourning the passing of love and innocence.

We were so close now. I could see the wet gleam of eyes behind the eye-holes of the mask. They seemed to be living eyes.

'Kill me,' said Grisainn to this creature. 'End it for ever. Call me back no more. It's done.'

Stop it! I yelled inside myself. *It won't be you who dies! I will! And then you must return again and again in this form. A dead har rising from the earth, lost and alone. For ever! You fool, Grisainn! You can't be my murderer. You're a dehar of love, the heart of the rose, a sacred symbol of Alba Sulh, our land. Be that now! Become what you're supposed to be. Only then can you and*

Fendris be together.

I believed what I said, and most of it was true.

I sensed Grisainn's resolve wavering. It wasn't because I was so convincing, but because some part of this wounded, stranded soul wanted what I said to be real.

Give me back to myself, I said. *Trust me to end it. I was* sent *for this.* And then something made me tell him. *Fendris sent me because he can't come himself.*

Grisainn paused. 'You're lying.'

I'm not. Fendris was attuned to Verdiferel in this place, because the dehar too grieves for a har who died. He grieves for his hostling, his lover, and can never escape it, because his sacrifice is part of the turning seasons. Without him, and what he symbolises, the world dies. So, we must soothe his hurts, hold him for a season every year, embrace him, despite the harsh mask he may wear. Let me show you...

All I could do was reveal to Grisainn, through pictures in my mind, the eternal cycle of the year – birth, death, rebirth – and how our own small lives were reflected in that cycle, part of the whole. *You see?*

'I... Fen...' Grisainn murmured. I felt a loosening within me. Grisainn wasn't gone, but no longer gripped me so tightly.

Verdiferel stood before me – us – not as unnaturally tall as he'd appeared among the trees, simply the height of a tall har. I said to him, 'Take off the mask, for I love you.'

He didn't move; he was like a living sculpture. I reached up and behind his head, undid the ties of the mask. When it came away, I let it fall to the ground. Beneath it, I saw a face I knew yet did not, for in some way it was still masked. Where had I seen it before? I took that face in my hands and stood on tiptoe to kiss him. This was Fendris, every cell of me knew that.

Let him come back, Fendris said to me, in mind-touch, *for my sake. Just for a moment.*

And so I allowed Grisainn to take control once more, allowed them another brief time together.

When the kiss ended, I was alone on the Cop with somehar else, who wasn't Fendris, who wasn't Verdiferel. I looked at him. We were alone.

'Did they give you a mask?' I asked. 'The guisers?'

He nodded. 'Yes. And you too, it seems.'

'Did he… Fendris… *enter* you?'

'Yes.'

'Murarn…' I spoke his name as if it was an invocation. 'We didn't see all of it, did we?'

He shook his head. 'No, not all of it, but enough perhaps.'

'Was it real?'

'I don't know. I can't really remember how I got here.' He rubbed his face. 'Were we drugged, hypnotised? I don't know… But some of it was real, the feelings, at least. The tragedy, the need for peace, for rest.'

I laid my head against his chest. 'I meant what I said.'

'I know.' He sighed deeply. 'Nohar will ever believe this. We mustn't speak of it, Isoldis – *ever.*'

'Not even to each other?'

He smiled a little, stroked my face. 'That's different. What I mean is, I suppose, what we've just experienced is sacred and *ours,* not something for other hara to know, because they won't have the reverence for it they should. It will simply be a story for them, shallow entertainment.' He pulled a face. 'Do you know what I mean?'

I nodded. 'Yes. Remmayes would put it under glass, in a museum. That wouldn't feel right. He's hungry for history, for facts, but… Let's leave it as it is, a story of several guises, and nohar knows which is true.' I was silent for a moment, content to rest against this har, who now felt to me as if he was truly himself, perhaps for the first time. 'The guisers,' I murmured. 'How much are to do with it all? Do they travel the land releasing spirits of the past? How did they choose us for this, or were they chosen as much as we were?'

'Let's hope they tell us.' Murarn pushed the hair back from my face. 'But that's for the future.' He put his head to one side. 'What was it Grisainn said about telling lies in the old fierce pull of blood? I want to tell you the truth now. Listen… I knew from the moment I saw you sitting outside the *Mill*. For a moment, you were *him*. Danger in a harish form. I thought you were a symbol of my death, because the need I felt couldn't be controlled. It was like a sickness. I saw Grisainn and Fendris in us all along, but feared how it would end. I felt we were Verdiferel's puppets, symbols of the season, but also victims of his tricks and illusions. I couldn't tell you how I felt, not only because it sounded like a fantasy, a delusion, but because well... I don't really talk to anyhar that way.'

I laughed softly. 'I understand *that* about you at least, Murarn.'

He grimaced. 'You had it right, though. So simple. Turn grief and vengeance into compassion. Embrace Verdiferel in his season for what he is – or rather, *influence* the nature of his manifestation.'

'I think he made all this happen,' I said, 'an ancient spirit of the land, manipulating events a hundred years ago. I think he'd waited here in the soil, and the water, and the forests, for hara to appear and make him live again. He wasn't originally Verdiferel, but he is now.'

Murarn nodded thoughtfully. 'There are many possibilities, all of it incredible. We'll talk about it further, compare what we know, but not now. It's too overwhelming. I just need...'

Impulsively, I kissed him again, deepening it into a sharing of breath. This was the treatment I felt he needed. Our arms were strong around each other. When we broke the embrace, he said, 'I was going to say "time", but that will do too.'

I took a deep breath. 'Well, now the true trial starts. Are you ready for us to return to the Reaptide festival together? Are you ready to weather the storm of gossip and speculation this will create?'

'No, but... I want to speak to Wise Hienama, don't you?'

'Most definitely!'

I took Murarn's hand. We walked down the Cop together.

In the field, the performance had ended some time before. Murarn and I walked into the crowd. I was looking for my friends, wondering what they'd have to say about my disappearance, or if the guisers' trick had worked completely. We found Yuroah at one of the refreshments stalls. He blinked at us, but managed to control his surprise. 'Issi, I thought... I thought you were... er... somewhere else?'

'Somewhere else?'

'Oh, never mind.' He seemed to shake himself, almost like waking up. 'Hello, Murarn. You two want a drink?'

I was conscious of eyes upon us, the wondering. Everyhar knew the story of Isoldis and Murarn, after all.

'At least have the decency to embrace me in public,' I said to him. 'It will partly make up for making me look stupid all those week ago.'

He laughed. 'OK.'

I wanted them to all to see the truth of it, that I hadn't invented Murarn's desire for me. Such things mattered to me then.

Murarn never got to speak to the Wise Hienama, but I did. At the end of evening, I was alone for a few moments; perhaps this was contrived. I saw him approaching, that familiar yet unknown face.

'Did you lose the mask?' he asked me.

'I must've done.' I narrowed my eyes. 'Now tell me what all this was about.'

'Whatever you want it to be,' he said. I realised he had the same strange accent as Grisainn. 'A rose, a thorn, a fox, a hare, an old mystery, a curse, doomed love. But also…'

He reached out to me, touched my ear. I flinched away, but saw he'd drawn a white rose bud from my hair.

'Illusion,' he said.

'How can you be so cruel? At least tell me something to satisfy my curiosity.'

He gave me a wry look, smiled. 'All right, just for you. After the last battle, when he set them upon each other, he went away, alone, and feasted on his grief for a season. He carried a pearl, but did not know – the fruit of that last hour of sweet delight before the sword fell. At first, he thought a dying sickness was upon him. But nature took hold of him and he guessed the truth. He birthed his pearl, alone, and knew it for an egg, like a bird's. When it broke, he raised his son, alone. Nohar knew. He drifted into memory, into the mist, until nohar remembered him. It's always Grisainn they remember, that fair rose they see in the summer fields. But still… stars align and stars collide, and times will come. The guisers keep the old tales alive, and tell them anew each time.' He bowed to me. 'Adieu, my fair one. Thank you for the kiss. May the dehara bless your union.'

'You're…'

He put the fingers of one hand over my mouth to silence me. 'Respect the dead,' he said.

Then he turned and whistled through his fingers. Beyond him, I saw a lithe form leaping across the top of the wagon-home, which was stationed nearby, beneath a canopy of oaks. It was the Fair Soume, but he was not in costume. He was dressed in clothes like mine and now he perched like a bird on the top of a wagon. He blew me a kiss and was gone.

'That's impossible,' I said, but I was alone.

In the morning, the field was bare, and I knew I'd discover no more. From my friends, I learned the Fair Soume had taken part in the performance, so who had impersonated me? But then, they all wore masks and might not be who you thought them to be. How much of what Murarn and I had experienced on the Cop had been hallucination and how much real? Had Grisainn really risen from the earth, or had he merely been another trick? Had Fendris walked among us, a har of flesh and blood in a guiser's mask, attended by his son? I thought I'd never know the truth and neither would Murarn. But Remmayes added more to his museum, merely what I'd told him of my first experience on Darkloe Cop, making clear it derived from what he called "inspired material".

As for that strange, motley band I'd glimpsed upon the Cop, I never learned more about them, and they never appeared to me – or anyhar else, as far as I know – again. I think they were a symbol of what was happening and what *had* happened – Sallowbar and his friends, Murarn and his lonely fantasies, the young, newly-incepted hara who had witnessed and then taken part in Grisainn's violation. The ill-made ones, but un-made, now.

Murarn and I stayed together for some years and were happy. But ours was a love of youth, which eventually burnt out, once it had had its season. We grew with each other, mended hurts, found our strengths and talents. We parted amicably over two years ago, and are still friends, both working at *Hart's Cliff*. At Reaptide, we shiver to a memory and see the past in each other's eyes.

The Dog Rose Larks have not yet come back to *Hart's Cliff*, although other guiser troupes appear at their appointed time to work their tricks and illusions. Sometimes, in the hot summer days, hara claim to catch a glimpse of Grisainn in the fields and forests, and perhaps that is so. But for me, all the ghosts are laid to rest, and what walks here now is a dehar – imagined, shaped and invoked by hara, an aspect of Verdiferel. The old fierce pull of blood has sunk into the soil, wafted away on the smoke of bonfires. It has murmured its bittersweet farewells and disappeared into the mist, where all things walk eventually.

Smoketide

September 21st

This is the Autumn Equinox and the major harvest festival. The dehar transforms into Prosperiel. He is already a hostling, and in that way fecund. At this time, he appears dressed in garments adorned with autumnal leaves and fruits, and he smells of smoke. He wears a cloak of fox fur, as his sacred animal is the red fox.

Prosperiel, of all the dehara of this half of the year, is the least tricky. Gone are the shadowy aspects of Cuttingtide and Reaptide. He is the expression of fruitfulness, and this is the time of year for hara to make plans for the future, to plant their own seeds of intention that will come to fruit in the New Year.

While Prosperiel lacks the dramatic aspects of some of the other dehara, and his season and folklore are serene and peaceful in comparison to others, he is nevertheless as important a figure in Arotohar as any of its dehara. Verdiferel is come and gone, and his pain laid to rest. Prosperiel, a kinder aspect of Panphilien, presides over the fruit and the harvest, carrying within him the light he protects until its rebirth during the darkest night of winter. He is the dehar of promise, who can grant wishes and make dreams come true. His scent is of apples and earth and the smoke of burning leaves. He walks the forest and the fields, his misting breath bringing final ripening to crops and fruit that conjures greater colour in the berries and apples. Sometimes, it is said, that he walks with the feet of a fox and has a fox's eyes.

Of Promise, Of Plenty, Of Shortening Days

Suzanne Gabriel

'Tell her!' The man shouted. 'Tell her it's not possible!'

I willed myself into stillness, consciously focusing on not wrinkling my nose. I had lived in this community for a week already, but I'd still not become accustomed to the musky odour of human; especially from an unkempt and sweaty older man. This man was one of four humans who had barged into my small office. I could see my assistant trying to manoeuvre his way through the group. I tried to focus my attention on the speaker; he was a barrel-chested man and tall for a human. I could tell his hair had once been jet black, but now it was mostly grey with dark strands peppered throughout. He was currently very red in the face, chest heaving with emotion.

My assistant, Amrat, reached my desk and placed his hand on the arm of the agitated human. 'My dear Miller,' he began in a soothing tone, 'you can't just barge into the Legate's office unannounced and expect him to mediate disagreements on the spot. Perhaps we can schedule a meeting.'

I watched, mildly entertained, as Amrat tried to turn the man and usher him towards the door. 'Perhaps tomorrow,' Amrat continued, 'when the Legate has had time to hear the issues and review them.'

The man was having none of it. 'There's naught to review!' he exclaimed angrily, yanking his arm from Amrat's grip. 'It be a black and white issue. It's not right and it's not possible!'

'What isn't possible?' I asked, my tone set to project a patient calm I did not feel. There had been so much chaos, and talking over each other, when they'd burst into my office that I'd not even remotely grasped the nature of the dispute.

At this point, the elderly man, his hair completely white, stepped forward as he pulled the battered cap from his head. 'If I may, Tiahaar Legate,' he began deferentially. 'The problem is that my granddaughter, Abena,' he turned to look at younger of the two females, 'wishes to go, and some of us reckon it be okay, and some don't.'

Abena's chin rose defiantly.

'You can't keep her here!' exclaimed a white-haired woman vehemently, pushing her way forward. 'She's no prisoner!' The woman was short and lean, but her face was creased with wrinkles and the skin under her chin hung loosely and jiggled slightly as she spoke.

I tried not to stare, but found her appearance distracting. 'She wants to go where?' I inquired patiently.

Abena spoke up, her voice quavering slightly 'I want to leave here and become Wraeththu'

'Don't be a daft bitch!' Miller hollered angrily. 'You can't be one of them. Girls can't get an inception.' He glared at me. 'Go on! Tell her!'

'I would,' I said calmly, 'but I'd be lying. Females *can* be incepted, but not as hara. They're incepted into our sister race, the Kamagrian.'

Abena looked triumphant.

Miller's already red face became redder as he sputtered incoherently for a moment. 'That's not possible!'

'I'm afraid it is,' Amrat said gently.

'Well, it's not right,' Miller repeated. 'The young are needed here. They're good breedin' stock!'

'Breeding stock?' The outrage in the older woman's tone was unmistakable. 'How dare you refer to my baby girl as breeding stock! She's not one of your sheep! She's an independent human being!'

'I'm afraid there's nothing to stop her leaving,' Amrat said in conciliatory tones. 'None of you are prisoners here.'

Miller turned his glare on me once more. He placed his fists on my desk and leaned across until his face was close to mine. 'Are you just going to sit there?' I could feel his spittle hit my face as he yelled, and I pulled back ever so slightly. 'You're supposed to be protecting our population! Instead, you're encouraging our children to become like your lot! Why are you even here?'

I leapt across my desk, grabbed the man by the throat and throttled him. At least, that's what I did in my mind. In reality, I looked down at my desk, a muscle tightening in my jaw, as I weighed the impact of a terse rebuke versus a long-winded attempt at placation. I didn't know these people well enough to know which approach would have the fewest unpleasant consequences. Before I could decide, Amrat took control.

'That's enough, Miller! Everyone go home! Legate Altair has only been in our community for a week. We'll discuss this tomorrow, once everyone has calmed down, and the Legate has had a chance to consider the situation. Out!' He ushered them expertly from the office and pulled the door shut behind them.

Alone, I stared at the closed door for a moment, then rose and crossed to the window. I sighed heavily. Smoketide was next week and I should be looking forward to an open-air ritual at the great Nayati at the pinnacle of the city centre, being caressed by gentle breezes, as the great braziers burned brightly, and day and night hung in equal balance. Verdiferel would be thanked and Prosperiel would be welcomed. After the ritual, the streets would fill with thousands of revellers. We'd feast, drink and dance, and when the skies took on the soft pastels of morning, we'd wander home. Now, instead of looking out of an office window with a view of the grand piazza and its gleaming white fountain bubbling away, beneath the fresh green of palm trees, I stared out of the window of a single-story, grey stone building, known as The Administration Centre, dubbed he Hub by the locals. There were no gleaming piazzas, nor azure blue skies and swaying palm trees. Beyond The Hub lay a rough patch of grass and weeds, a cock-eyed fence, and trees. There were lots of trees, but none of them palms. The surrounding woods were populated by evergreens and varieties of deciduous trees, whose leaves were changing colour and falling to the ground. This year, my Smoketide would be celebrated in a small Nayati, in a remote human settlement, at the edge of a lake in the wilderness; farther north than I had ever been before in my life.

Why are you even here? Miller's question repeated in my head. Why *am* I here? I lamented, allowing self-pity to wash over me. Yet I *knew* why I was here. I was not as good a political player as I'd imagined myself to be, and I hadn't kept my mouth shut when I should have. So, here I was, in the farthest flung edge of nowhere, and feeling very sorry for myself.

There was a tentative knock at the office door and it creaked open slightly. I was expecting Amrat to return, so was surprised to see the face of a har I had not seen before peering around the door; the oval, wide-eyed face broke into a sunny grin when he saw me. The har that accompanied the face was tall, but not overly so, and bundled in a colourful, thick wool cardigan. He was very good-looking in a wholesome, natural way – he wore no makeup and his dark hair hung loose and natural around his shoulders.

'Hi! You must be the new Legate,' he said cheerfully. 'Amrat is outside talking to some people, so I thought I'd pop in and introduce myself.' He paused for a moment before stepping forward awkwardly and extending his hand. 'Hi!' he said again, 'I'm Pipaluk har Cai, the new hienama. Officially, I've been here a month, but I was away this past week at my brother's blood-bonding ceremony.' He paused his rushed speech for a breath. 'So, just wanted to say sorry for not having been here to greet you. Welcome!'

I had taken his hand when he'd offered it and had been all the while gripping it, listening to his breathless greeting.

'Thank you!' I responded as soon as he finished. 'It's a pleasure to meet you. I'm Altair har Nikau, and I am, for what it's worth, the new Legate.'

'Welcome!' he exclaimed again cheerily. 'I don't want us to get off on the wrong foot. I tend to be overly relaxed and informal. I mean, I take what I *do* seriously, I just don't take *myself* seriously. So, I'm checking with you now how formal you want to be – should I address you as Legate? Tiahaar Nikau? I heard the hara who were here before us were both sticklers for formality and protocol. I hope you're not too much of a stickler, to be honest. I say, were you ever told about why the last Legate and hienama were replaced? I wasn't. It's probably bad form, but I confess to being pretty curious. I'd hate to make the same mistake, whatever it was. I did hear a rumour or two, but like I said they were just rumours. Amrat said you came from Immanion, or somewhere close. This weather must be different in the extreme!' He laughed. 'It's different for me too as I also come from farther south. By this time next year, I expect we'll be pros at cold weather survival!' He took a deep breath. 'Sorry! I'm talking too much! I always do when I'm nervous. Sorry!'

I couldn't help but smile. He was disarmingly charming. 'Please, just called me Tair,' I said, 'I don't plan to be too uptight about formality, but I am tasked with maintaining order so…' My voice trailed off uncertainly.

'Good! Good! I'm told this community needs order!' Pipaluk nodded encouragingly. 'Walk softly and carry a big stick!' He winked at me. 'I'd better be off and get Smoketide sorted. Only a week away! I've got to figure out what's already been organised and what I still have to do. Drop by sometime and we'll have tea.' He turned to go. 'Or coffee! Or a good stiff drink! We might both need one!'

The door shut behind him.

It can't be morning already, I thought, as my eyes drifted open, but the sunshine pouring in the window said otherwise. I made a mental note to make sure, in future, the blinds were drawn. I threw back the blankets, but grabbed them again in a hurry; the room was freezing. With concentration and focus, I managed to manifest enough warmth to get me up and out of bed. *I'd better get used to this if I'm going to survive the bloody winter*, I mused glumly, as I shuffled into the kitchen. This room was as tiny as the bedroom, which was as tiny as the sitting room. My whole cabin was probably small enough to fit inside the spacious, airy lounge of the suite I'd shared with a couple of friends in Perrissan, a town half a day's ride south of Immanion. It was there that the Directorate of Human Territorial Administration was discreetly located, away from main, high-profile, Hegemonic agencies. I lifted the metal plate and lit the kindling in the cast iron cooking stove. Picking up the kettle, I crossed to the sink. I suppose I should be grateful that my cabin had running water.

When I reached my office, I was relieved to find it was warm and toasty, as Amrat had started a fire in the small potbelly stove in the corner. I had just sat down at my desk when a woman marched through the door. She was shaped like a bowling ball; about as short as she was round. She strode around to my side of the desk without looking up from whatever she appeared to be examining. 'Good morning Legate!' she announced. 'Welcome to the neighbourhood. We were told you came from warmer climes, so I thought you might need these.' She placed a pair of thick woollen mittens down on the desk in front of me. 'Made them myself!' She reached into the immense basket she carried over her arm and pulled out a matching scarf and hat. She draped the scarf around my neck, and held the hat up next to my head and squinted. 'Yep! That'll fit. Gotta dash! I'll be seeing you later this morning at the community meeting. Don't forget we moved the time of the merchant's association meeting back an hour.'

She turned and started towards the door, stopping in her tracks as Amrat appeared.

'Amrat, love! Tell your beautiful chesnari that I plan to dye that wool this morning, if he wants to come and check the colour. I'm off!' She resumed her course towards the door. 'Toodles!' She called over her shoulder.

Amrat and I stared after her, and when I heard the front door bang shut I turned to Amrat. 'Who was that? And is that...' I cleared my throat slightly, 'normal?'

'I'm sorry,' Amrat said, as he placed in front of me one of the steaming mugs of coffee he carried. 'I was making coffee and I didn't hear her come in. That...' he expelled a long-suffering sigh '...was "herself", one Adelaide Apeldoorn, Missus, widowed. Not so large, but definitely in charge. I'd say she's the top-ranking human in this settlement. She's got the biggest sheep ranch in the area, produces the finest wool, and drives a hard bargain. She's one to keep on-side. And,' he pointed to the mittens, 'it looks like you're still in her good books. That'll come in handy as we've got trouble brewing. Mrs. Apeldoorn is one of the only ones who can singlehandedly contain Miller, and right now he's on the warpath.'

'That big, red-faced goon from yesterday?' I said.

Amrat nodded confirmation.

'Why?' I asked indignantly. 'Because we told him that females can become Kamagrian? He's mad.'

Amrat plunked himself down on the chair across from me and cradled his mug of coffee. 'It seems' he began, 'that Abena is not the only youth who wants to go. We always had male population shrinkage. They reach the age of consent, they leave, and it's never really caused much concern. But now Abena, and three of her friends, want to become Kamagrian. When females start to disappear some of the humans get testy.'

Testy didn't begin to describe it! The auditorium was filled with about a hundred bodies, both human and hara; some supporters of one side, some from the other, and the rest merely spectators. I found myself sitting at a table on the stage with Pipaluk har Cai, Mrs. Adelaide Apeldoorn, and an elderly man Mrs. Apeldoorn had introduced as Kenny. Kenny had nodded amiably, tottered to the table and had sat there quietly ever since. I couldn't tell whether he was quietly observing the proceedings, or was completely oblivious to the drama playing out in front of us. The current performance involved four young females, of whom Abena was one, and three young males, backed by those who supported their right to leave the settlement and be incepted, versus the faction, led by Miller, that opposed their choices.

The initial discussion had started out civilly enough, but once the facts had been presented, and initial arguments made, the emotional discourse had degenerated into yelling and screaming. I banged my gavel and tried to call 'order', but no one paid any attention.

Adelaide cleared her throat and bellowed '*Order!*' At once, the noise level in the room dropped dramatically to a low murmur.

I paused. What I wanted to say to this crowd did not befit my position. I had to find a diplomatic way.

However, before I could say anything, Miller confronted Mrs. Apeldoorn angrily. 'Adelaide, you can't possibly agree to letting the young'uns leave! What about our community? Without the young breeders, we die out!'

'You shit!' one of the females screamed. 'I don't want babies. I want to travel and live my life.'

The yelling started again, and I ran my fingers through my hair in frustration; a quiet office, filled with policy briefs, statistics, and executive summaries for the Directorate of Human Territorial Administration, was more my speed; this nitty-gritty face-to-face was overwhelming.

I stood up and slammed my fists down hard on the table. 'Enough!' I roared.

For the most part, the din quieted down, except for Miller. 'And you,' he rounded on me, pointing a finger at me in accusation. 'You, Legate, are supposed to be protecting us! This is a Wraeththu plot to kill us humans off! Death by a thousand cuts!'

'Miller,' I said, as evenly as I could, 'I and my team are here to protect you. We provide you with lands on which to live freely and safely. We protect your community from violence at the hands of those who might still wish to harm your kind, and we advocate on your behalf. However, freedom and safety are extended, not just to the community, but to each individual member of that community.' With that, I sat down again.

If looks could kill, the one Miller gave me would have dropped me in my tracks. He turned his attention towards the elderly man. 'Kenny!' Miller entreated, 'I don't care – the males can go. We got too many lads anyways! One ram can serve a whole herd. But you must agree the girls have a duty to remain.'

Kenny's watery eyes blinked several times, but his voice was surprisingly strong, given his frail appearance. 'If you forced them to stay, can you guarantee off-spring? I have two daughters. Only Rachel managed to produce a child, and that child, Alice, has, in twenty years of marriage, produced nary a *bairn*. None of Adelaide's children have produced offspring. It's been almost ten years since any women in this settlement gave issue. I say let 'em go.'

A murmur rumbled through the crowd as both sides reacted to the man's words; it was quite apparent that this was not what they'd expected to hear.

'But Ken,' Miller objected. 'We're dying out. The human race will vanish.'

'Oh, for heaven's sake, you fool!' Adelaide barked in exasperation. 'There are no virgins here. All these kids have been *at it* since their early teens. Not one pregnancy has resulted! Not one! What makes you think that forcing these girls into a life they don't want will result in something that's not happened so far?' She made a harrumphing sound. 'The whole lot of them! At it like rabbits and no issue! There you go! End of discussion.' She waved her hand with an imperious flourish.

Pipaluk leaned to me and whispered into my ear. 'Ken serves as a kind of spiritual wise-man to the humans. He and I could offer counselling and educative sessions, if you think that'd help.'

I nodded and rose to my feet again. The babble of voices began to subside, and I waited until most spectators were quiet and focused on me.

'The Gelaming Directorate of Human Territorial Administration is tasked with protecting and advocating for the remaining human populations. We protect them, but we cannot lose sight of the fact that any population is made up of individuals with inherent rights. The Directorate supports the rights of any individual wishing to leave. However…' I paused as the crowd reacted, 'arrangements will take time. The Directorate will organise the safe passage of all those wishing to leave at the Spring Equinox. Until then, Tiahaar Pipaluk and Mr. Kenny will counsel not only those planning to leave, but anyhar… er… any*one* who wishes to understand further.'

Miller roared in anger. 'No! No! No!'

'This meeting is adjourned!' Adelaide's' voice rose above Miller's.

I walked down the stairs from the stage to the floor. As I did so, Miller charged at me, coming to a halt with his face barely an inch from mine.

'You!' He growled ominously. 'I hold you responsible for the death of my people! Of my race! You will pay for this! Mark my words! You! Will! Pay!' He emphasised each word, his finger jabbing towards my face.

I met his stare and his tirade unflinching and stony-faced.

The stand-off ended when Kenny, who'd finally made his way down from the stage, put his hand on Miller's arm. ''Tis not our way, lad!' he murmured. ''Tis not the way!'

I left the auditorium and stepped out on the street. I had no stomach to head back to the office; I was done. This was not what I wanted to be doing, nor where I wanted to be. I went for a walk.

Elakrel Lake was vast, and the settlement radiated up and out from its edge. I'd been stranded in this place a little over a week, but I had yet to go down to the beach. Now, that was where I found myself heading.

My idea of a beach involved gentle fragrant breezes, hot white sands slipping under warm waters, for which the descriptive terms "azure", and "cerulean", applied. I surveyed this beach with chagrin; there was no sand, only pebbles, and the choppy waters were a dark blueish grey. There was no gentle breeze, only a cold wind that blew down across the lake from the snow-capped mountains opposite. I sat down dejectedly on a log near the water's edge and stared at the distant shoreline, the mountains beyond.

'Did you know it apparently takes three days to walk around this lake? I plan on trying it next summer!'

I hadn't heard the hienama arrive. He sat down next to me on the log and stretched his long legs out in front of him. 'Don't let that meeting get to you,' he said. 'It's some pretty emotionally charged stuff to deal with, so soon after you arrive.'

Pipaluk looked around, drew a deep breath, and exhaled a happy satisfied sigh. 'It is so amazing here. Look at it all! The town behind us, and then around here, and over there, those pastures...' He suddenly pointed 'Look! Those white little puffs are the sheep.' His laugh conveyed pure joy. 'And would you look at that lake!' he exclaimed. 'Those far hills, and the snow caps behind are stunningly beautiful. I'm beyond thrilled to have been given this posting. I came here once and thought it was beautiful, so when I heard this position was suddenly available, well, I jumped!' He sighed happily, then he leaned forward to rest his elbows on his knees. Turning his head, he looked up at me. 'I'm going to go out on a limb and say that this was not *your* idea of the ideal job.'

I met his gaze. 'No,' I had to admit.

'So why did you end up here? Have you worked with humans before?'

'Sort of,' I responded. 'I've worked *for* humans for a long, long time, working my way up the ranks in Directorate of Human Territorial Administration, where I excelled at organising, policy writing, and reporting. But I haven't actually seen many humans since I was incepted, and that was eons ago. I'm here because I got frustrated that certain high-level policy issues were deviating from their original mandates. I let those frustrations erupt in the worst possible way, at the worst possible time, and in front of the completely wrong officials. And so, instead of a sun-soaked, cushy city life of policy meetings, gala events, and luxurious schmoozing, I got "reassigned".'

'Ah,' Pipaluk said, brushing his hair away from his face, 'you shot yourself in the foot?'

I shrugged. 'Basically.'

'Is it so bad?' Pipaluk asked. 'Being here, I mean?'

'This is not where I want to be. It's all so alien; the wilderness, the cold, and the humans. I don't know how to deal with humans face-to-face! I'm a policy-writing, pencil-pushing bureaucrat. I don't belong here. I don't fit in.' Even to myself, I sounded whiny. 'Come on! Even my most casual outfits look like I'm going to a fancy formal function.' I tried to end on a joke.

Pipaluk chuckled. 'Nah, you've just upped the ante! We're all going to start dressing better. I put on a clean shirt today!' He grinned.

We sat in silence for a time, listening to the waves lap the shore and the birds calling overhead.

'Sometimes,' Pipaluk mused out loud, 'we're where we need to be, even though we think it's not where we want to be. This settlement has been without a decent Legate for a while. If you're good at organisation and policy, then you are exactly where you need to be.'

I grunted in response.

'I get it,' he continued, 'change can suck! It's not always about surging forward, is it? No matter how much a change is wanted, or *not* wanted, time is always marching on; nothing ever stays as it was. Even things that appear not to change *do*, because *we* have changed. Something must give way to allow that change to happen; it's your choice how you react.'

I said nothing.

'As it's almost Smoketide, and because it's my job as a hienama,' Pipaluk went on in a chipper tone, 'I like to couch my advice in the narrative of Arotahar. This is Smoketide, when the dehar becomes Prosperiel. He's hosting a pearl, and is both happy at the prospect of its arrival, and resigned to the cycle of birth, death and rebirth that follows. At this time, I advise we all reflect on sacrifice, and reaping what we sow.'

I heard his breath catch suddenly, followed quickly by a gasp. I looked up in time to see the sun emerge suddenly from behind a cloud. Long, slanting rays hit the snow-capped peaks in the distance, then travelled rapidly down over the foothills, and across the lake, until they reached us: the colours changed, the lake shimmered, and we felt the sun's warmth.

'Wow!' Pipaluk exclaimed happily, 'that's just … wow!'

I had to agree. It was indeed a spectacular moment.

Pipaluk was grinning as he turned to me. 'Can you imagine what our lives would be like if we'd not been here to see that? And ask yourself this, Altair har Nikau, how you would feel if you knew you would never see it again?'

I held his gaze for a few moments, before I turned back to look at the lake and the mountains.

'Come on!' Pipaluk said getting to his feet 'we'd better get you back in time for the Merchant's Association meeting.'

Later that evening, once I was back in my cabin, I sat down at the kitchen table to compose a letter to the committee that had reassigned me here, asking them to reconsider their decision. This wasn't the first letter I'd tried to write since coming to this settlement, but I'd yet to send one; they always sounded too whiny and pathetic. An hour later, I crumpled tonight's attempt and threw it into the grate. I couldn't focus properly. My mind kept going back to that moment by the lake with Pipaluk. His words about being where we were meant to be, and that moment when the clouds had let the sun shine across the landscape, kept floating into my consciousness and interfering with the flow of my thoughts.

The next day, after a blessedly uneventful morning involving paperwork and statistics, I walked to the Nayati, as Pipaluk had invited me over for lunch. I arrived to find him outside the door, standing between a tall angular woman, with auburn hair twirled into a bun at the nape of her neck, and a very soume-looking har whose long blonde plait hung over his shoulder.

'Good morning, Legate!' Pipaluk called out. 'Allow me to introduce Mia and Perun. They're organising the Smoketide feast this year. We're just...' He cleared his throat meaningfully, '*discussing* the menu.'

The woman turned to me with a thin smile. 'A pleasure to meet you, Legate,' she said. 'I'm trying to explain to Perun that it's traditional to serve goose at this festival feast.'

'I'm sorry, Mia,' Perun responded rather shrilly, 'but it's traditional to serve mutton.' He turned to me and batted his eye lashes. 'Perhaps our new Legate can settle this dispute?' he said sweetly.

'So be it!' Mia responded, raising her chin defiantly at Perun. 'Which would you prefer, Legate? Goose or mutton?' She tilted her head coyly in my direction.

'Well,' I began carefully. 'Personally, I do not eat meat. However, I see no reason you can't prepare both.' I hoped that was the right answer.

Mia and Perun blinked at me for a split second before Perun exclaimed, 'You don't eat meat? Oh! Well, never mind, there'll be plenty for you besides the meat, what with the squash and nut dish

Ula makes…'

'And the goat cheese tart, and the mushroom stew…' Mia jumped in.

They both turned and hurried off, discussing non-meat options.

'I'll be back in a flash!' Pipaluk whispered and hurried after them.

The Nayati was a cavernous, red brick building. Within, the huge timber frames that supported the vaulted ceiling had been left visible and unfinished. It felt colder in here than outside, despite the huge windows that flooded the room with sunlight. Heavy wooden benches lined the walls, but the rest of the space was empty, save for a raised dais at the centre. I walked to the dais. Upon it stood a table, with a jumbled assortment of empty candle sticks, gourds, and a folded tablecloth. I smiled – clearly the decorating committee still had work to do. I closed my eyes – the space was large and echoing, but I could hear the stillness. I took a deep breath and noted a faint hint of incense lingering. I nearly jumped out of my skin when I opened my eyes to find a large red fox sitting on its haunches directly in front of me, its tail wrapped primly around its front paws.

'Whoa!' I exclaimed involuntarily. 'You startled me.'

At the sound of my voice, the tip of the fox's tail twitched, and it tilted its head to one side. Suddenly, it sprang to its feet, darted across the floor, and out the front door. I hurried after it, but by the time I got to the door the fox had vanished

'What are you looking for?' Pipaluk called as he came ambling back toward me.

'I just saw a fox!' I exclaimed. 'Did you see it?'

'How very seasonal!' Pipaluk grinned.

'What do you mean?' I asked, confused.

Pipaluk laughed. 'Smoketide!' He exclaimed heartily. "It looks like I have my work cut out for me!' He chuckled. "You can't have forgotten that the dehar Prosperiel's sacred wee beastie is a red fox. Come on to the house!' He headed off towards the tidy cottage that stood a short distance behind the Nayati. 'I'll have lunch on the table in a second.'

'Oh, yes, of course.' I felt my face flush, as I followed Pipaluk, then said a little louder, 'I really did see a fox – it was big! You must have seen it!'

'No!' Pipaluk shook his head. 'No foxes around here, not with those goons around.' He pointed to three large dogs by the porch of his house; one had his leg in the air busily cleaning himself, while the other two played tug-of-war with a stick. 'No foxes around here,' Pipaluk repeated. 'Those nutters would be after it like a shot. They'll chase anything that moves; rabbits, squirrels, chipmunks! They've never caught a damn thing, though.' He chuckled. 'I don't think they'd know what to do if they ever did catch something.'

He stepped up onto the porch. 'This,' he said, picking up an enormous orange cat, 'is who you must have seen. Allow me to introduce Mistress Tara Mousekiller, aka Cuddlebutt, aka Stupid Cat. Her name depends on my mood.' He grinned. 'Also on hers.'

No, I thought resolutely, as I followed him into the house, *I definitely saw a fox.*

I returned to my cabin that afternoon to find a group of people assembled outside, diligently working to clean up what appeared to be white paint, which was all over my door and the porch. Kenny stood watching them, leaning heavily on a staff.

'Good afternoon, Legate!' he called out as I drew closer. 'It were Miller.' He jerked his head in the direction of my cottage. 'He threw a bucket of paint at your place. But never you mind, Legate, we're dealing with him. It's the drink, you see.' Kenny shook his head sadly. 'We got him locked up in the drunk tank. I'm hoping you'll be able to...' He cleared his throat. '...see past this, as it were. We'll sober him up and have a good chat with him, if you catch my drift.'

'As you wish,' was all I said.

That evening I took another stab at writing my letter to the Directorate of Human Territorial Administration, but my mind kept wandering to thoughts of the fox; the letter sounded sad rather than persuasive. I crumpled it up and threw it into the cast-iron stove.

Next morning, I woke up very early and couldn't get back to sleep. After tossing and turning for a time, I gave up and shuffled groggily into the kitchen. I congratulated myself for having gotten out of my warm bed more easily this morning. Grabbing the kettle, I crossed to the sink. I was about to turn the water on, when I glanced out the window and froze. On the porch, a large red fox sat on its haunches, its tail once again wrapped primly around its front paws:

it stared through the window at me. I dashed to the door, but by the time I'd gotten outside, the fox had gone, yet I could see his wet foot prints on the wood. I scanned the misty predawn area surrounding the cabin, but saw nothing. I inhaled deeply; the air smelled earthy and damp. On a whim, I dressed quickly and headed out the door.

The trail I chose to follow was called Fire Tower Trail; it had been recommended by several hara, including Amrat, as a great hike with a phenomenal view. The trail alternated between an easy path meandering through gentle woodlands hills, and energetic scrambles up steeper rock bluffs. Despite the chill of the early morning, I was hot and sweaty by the time I stood at the foot of the fire tower. From the ground, the tower looked formidably tall. For a few minutes, I debated whether to climb it, as the narrow metal beams, held together with rivets, and the steep stairs that more closely resembled a series of ladders, made it appear quite daunting. Even so, I started up, and - oh! - the climb was worth it. From the semi-enclosed cabin at the top, you could see for miles; it took my breath away. The sun, only recently risen, shone low on the countryside below me. I could see the settlement, and the pastures laid out around the lake. I could see the rolling hills of forests spreading out into the distance; the trees a brilliant array of dark greens, bright reds, and flame-like oranges and yellows. Mist still hung like low wispy clouds in some of the valleys. I looked towards the lake; it sparkled in the new light. The foothills beyond were shrouded in mist, but the snow caps of the mountains glowed orangey-pink in the light from the rising sun.

Can you imagine what your life would be like if you'd not been here to see that? And how you would feel if you knew you would never see it again?

I closed my eyes and took a deep breath. The air was crisp and cold, and the breeze carried the smell of pine trees and wood fires.

I was smiling as I headed back home down the trail.

Just after lunch, Amrat entered my office. I didn't look up from my work, but announced pensively to him, 'I don't like the way our policies refer to the reduction in human numbers as "shrinkage" – we aren't discussing inventory. We're discussing living breathing individuals.'

When he didn't answer, I looked up to find him hovering in

front of my desk. He clutched a letter and looked deeply troubled.

'What is it?' I asked.

He stepped forward hesitantly. 'This,' he said holding out the envelope. 'It was delivered "express". It must be important. We don't get special deliveries here.'

I took the letter from him, broke the seal, and removed the document. I reread the letter twice.

'What?' Amrat said, agitation high in this voice. 'What is it?'

'We're being asked to absorb eight orphans into this community,' I stated matter-of-factly.

'Human orphans?' He exclaimed. 'Eight of them? Here? What are we going to do?'

'We'll take them,' I said simply.

'But how?' He asked.

'We oversee a large human settlement, it will be fairly easy to fit a few small creatures into our numbers, and since we are about to lose seven, a gain of eight will...' I paused awkwardly '...even things out'.

Amrat nodded slowly 'Yes,' he agreed 'That might go far to mollify the faction that wishes to prevent the young adults from leaving.' He stopped and his brow furrowed. 'Does it say how so many humans ended up orphaned? It seems like an unusually high number for one settlement.'

'It is a large number, but according to this,' I began, scanning the letter to find the relevant paragraph, 'these children were already orphans, and being housed at an institute west of Breva. The building was old, and badly in need of repair, as is much of the infrastructure in that area world; when the roof finally failed, the Directorate decided that it was more... I cleared my throat, '...*cost effective* to move the eight remaining orphans into an existing human settlement.'

'I guess that makes sense,' Amrat said. 'But why here?'

'Well,' I said, 'our is a large, stable community; it's prosperous, and has a good balance of old and young. That's how they think in Human Territorial Administration circles.'

'I see.' Amrat nodded. 'Of course! But may I recommend that we don't mention this matter publicly, until all the details have been worked out? I wouldn't want to raise any hopes. You know, "just in case".'

'Agreed,' I confirmed. I was well aware of how the bureaucracy in the Directorate works.

That night, when I sat down, as I had almost every night since I'd arrived, to compose my letter to the Directorate, I didn't manage to write anything beyond the greeting; my mind was too preoccupied with the potential new arrivals, and their impact on the humans for whom I was responsible. Also, I couldn't shake the exhilarating feeling of seeing morning's first light from the top of the fire tower.

In the morning, I woke up early on purpose and headed out for another hike. Today, I took a different trail that cut through some woodland areas, and then skirted the pasture lands that ran up from the lake. Shafts of pale, early sunlight slipped through tree branches, mist floated low along the ground, and leaves fell silently from the trees. The trail ended at a fence around a field full of sheep. I stood watching them for some time, long after they'd realised I had no treats to give them and had lost interest in me. As I turned to head back home, I caught sight of something scurrying through the undergrowth; it was a fox. It kept darting ahead of me, then it would stop and glare at me until I'd almost caught up, before sprinting a little way ahead again. I couldn't tell whether it was annoyed because I appeared to be following it, or annoyed because it had to stop and wait for me.

The morning at the office passed uneventfully enough, given the community's excitement about Smoketide and the Autumnal Equinox. Other than the secretive paperwork regarding the human orphans, the only issue arising was a request to add an item to the agenda of an upcoming meeting. However, around the middle of the afternoon, the relative peace and quiet of The Hub offices were interrupted by the sound of breaking glass. Miller, along with a couple of rather inebriated-looking men, could be seen outside, bellowing and shaking their fists, while a hefty rock sat amid shattered glass in the foyer. As I watched the community peace-keepers hurry to deal with the situation, I worried that this might be the start of trouble. I'd have to confront Miller soon, before the bridges were irreparable.

That evening, I'd just sat down at my kitchen table for another attempt at a letter, when I heard a knock on the door. I opened it, to find a very distraught Adelaide on my porch. She brushed past me and sat herself down at the table.

'Did I do the right thing, Tair? Did I do the right thing?' She sounded despondent.

'Did you do the right thing about what?' I asked her gently.

'About agreeing to let the young ones leave? I've done nothing but think about this since that meeting. My head says *of course* they should go. They're free, and they need to live their own lives.' She paused and sniffed. When she started to speak again, her voice wavered. 'But my heart worries. We're getting old, and our numbers are dropping, and... oh!' She started to sob quietly.

I reached out and put my hand over hers. 'Yes, Adelaide, you did the right thing. You know you did. Besides, you also know that I wouldn't allow anyone to stop them, anyway. We must protect the rights of everyone in the community. As for getting old, that happens to us all, day by day, but we'll never allow anyone here to suffer because of it.'

She nodded, drying her tears. 'Yes. Yes, I know. Thank you! I just needed to hear someone say it.'

'I do have news for you. I haven't announced it officially yet, but, as I will need your help, I feel I ought to tell you.' I paused, knowing full well that by spilling the beans to Mrs. Apeldoorn, I was effectively making the announcement official.

She looked at me expectantly.

'I have,' I began slowly, 'agreed to accept eight young children into our community. They're human, and now orphaned, so that's where I will need your...'

'Children?' She sat up straight and her eyes widened. 'Here? When? Are you serious?'

I smiled. 'Yes, children. Yes, here. Yes, I'm serious. They'll be here about a week after Smoketide.'

'Oh my!' She exclaimed. 'Oh my! We have so much to do! You said eight, correct? What do you know about them? How old? Boys or girls?'

Her whole demeanour had changed; she now sizzled with energy.

'Eight,' I confirmed. 'The oldest is eleven years old and the youngest is six months. As for whether they're boys or girls...' I shrugged. 'I have no idea. Does it matter?'

'No, of course not!' She clasped her hands together, a big smile on her face 'Oh Tair!' She gushed, 'this is fantastic!' Suddenly her eyes widened in horror 'Oh no! I didn't mean that! It's tragic, really isn't it?'

Adelaide stayed for a bit longer before she took herself off home. I wondered, as I shut the door after her, how long it would take for news of our impending new arrivals to spread.

A cold steady rain prevented me from heading out for a hike in the morning; I was oddly disappointed.

When I got to the office, Amrat confirmed what I had suspected; Adelaide had not been able to keep the news quiet. Between the buzz surrounding the arrival of the children, and the excitement about tomorrow's celebrations, there was not much work I could get done. Instead, I sat down at my desk and wrote my letter to the Directorate asking for a reassignment. This time the letter was perfect. I packed it away carefully into my carry-all bag before I headed for home that evening.

The rain had continued to fall all day, and I was thoroughly soaked by the time I reached my cabin. As I delved into my pocket for my key, I noticed wet paw prints on the porch next to the door. I bent down to examine them. I'm not an expert, but I could tell they weren't cat prints, and they were too small and delicate to belong to any of the local dogs, so I figured they must be the prints of the fox I'd been seeing around the area. I left a raw chicken breast out on the porch, just in case.

After I'd changed into dry clothes and eaten a quick bite of dinner, I went into the sitting room. I took the letter out of my carry-all and placed it carefully on the coffee table, and then turned to the fireplace. Once a cheery fire crackled away, I sat down in one of the two oversized armchairs that occupied nearly the whole of the cosy room. It had become tradition for me, on the night before Smoketide, to meditate on the dehar Prosperiel, the lessons of the season, and to set my intentions for the future. I was determined that this year, despite all the things that had happened, would be no different. I made myself comfortable, took a few deep breaths, and tried to clear my mind. But I couldn't. I had a bad case of "monkey mind"; it chattered, and jumped, and refused to focus. I kept thinking about Miller, and the young humans who wanted to leave. I thought of the logistics of integrating eight new arrivals into our settlement. I thought about the view I'd seen from the fire tower, and down by the lake, and Pipaluk asking me to think about how I would feel if I never saw those things again. I thought gratefully about how hard Amrat had been working to make me feel welcome in my new role. I also kept thinking about the fox.

Eventually I gave up; it didn't seem likely I'd be able to meditate properly that night. My eyes still closed, I heaved a deep exasperated sigh, and leaned back heavily in the armchair. That's when I heard it; the crunch of somehar taking a bite from an apple. My eyes flew open. A har I'd never seen before sat opposite me in the other armchair. He lounged back casually, with one foot on the coffee table. The apple he held had a large bite taken from it. He stared at me as he chewed. His tunic was a dark green, and over that he wore a heavy hooded cloak of dark brown. The hood was thrown back, and his long auburn hair spilled across his chest.

You must learn to embrace change, he said in a voice I felt, rather than heard; like a mind-touch, but so much richer. *Nothing that is can stay as it is. The moon waxes and wanes. The seasons change. Day becomes night, which becomes day again. It's a cycle in which we all play our parts.* He took another bite of the apple, as he rose to his feet and stepped towards the fireplace. He stood there watching the fire for a time, before turning towards me. *When will you realise*, he asked, *that it's not only about you? You, like me, are merely part of a Universal narrative.* Then he sprang at me. I tried to get away but my limbs felt leaden. As I tried to struggle free, I found myself awake, sunshine pouring in through the window. I lay sprawled in my sitting room, on the same chair as I'd been in last night.

Whew! What a dream, I thought as I started to push off the comforter, but I paused in confusion mid-way through the motion. How had the comforter from my bed ended up covering me on the chair in the sitting room?

The air in the room smelt uncommonly smoky, so I got up a little stiffly to check the flue. I noted, with annoyance, that an unusually large amount of ash had blown out of the grate onto the flagstones in front of the fireplace. I squatted down and reached for the brush to sweep it away. It was then I noticed that the ash was covered with paw prints, exactly like those I'd seen on the porch last night. How on earth had a fox gotten in? I stood up and looked warily around my sitting room. My comforter lay on the chair I'd been sleeping in, and my letter sat where I'd placed it on the coffee table last night. But when I looked at the other armchair, a chill ran up my spine. This was where, in my vision, the strange har had sat; a partially eaten apple balanced on the arm. I stood rooted to the spot for quite some time as my mind tried to process the events. My eyes dropped to my perfectly written letter. *It's not about me*, I thought. I picked it up and turned back to the fireplace. Crouching down again, I stuck a corner of the letter into the pile of ashes where the embers still glowed; the corner of the paper began to smoulder, and eventually a flame began to race across the sheet. I let the paper fall in the fireplace.

At dusk, the community, both human and Wraeththu, gathered in the Nayati. Standing shoulder to shoulder, we watched as Pipaluk, stripped to the waist, and Kenny, carrying his staff and wearing long grey robes, stood together and each in turn, call the corners to create our sacred space.

Then Kenny retreated from the dais and the humans stepped back.

Pipaluk drew the sign of Verdiferel in the air and called out to the dehar, thanking him for walking amongst us during his season, which had now come to an end. Pipaluk turned to the table, and raised a bowl of smoking incense as he murmured sacred words. He blew smoke over the gathering. Then, he raised his arms and began the invocation to the dehar, Prosperiel.

Prosperiel, Dehar of Plenty
Dehar of Promise
Heart of the Shortening Days
Walk among us...

The drums beat, the chanting began, and the gathered hara sent their visualisations into the Nayati; we shared the energy of life and its harvest, warm fires in the hearth, and the changing trees. Visualisations of sheep with their thick woolly coats, squirrels gathering acorns, and smoke rising off bonfires helped the energy build. I shared the sights of my early morning hikes, the view from the top of the fire tower, and my fox sightings. Throughout it all was the presence of Prosperiel; he appeared larger than life, long robes, a hooded cloak, long flowing auburn hair, and bedecked with garlands and flowers. His features however were fluid; he looked like everyhar, and nohar, at the same time as each har present projected their own visualisation of the dehar. At a signal from Pipaluk, the community released the amassed energy to work its magic on our community and wherever else it was needed.

Once the Smoketide arojhahn was complete, hara stepped back. Kenny went up to the dais and there performed an Autumnal Equinox ritual with and for his fellow humans. I had noticed some of the young, hara and human alike, had taken part in both rites.

I found a spot along the wall near the main door of the Nayati; I found leaning against the cool bricks grounding after the intensity of the arojhahn. I shut my eyes and let the echoes of the ritual course through me. I had shared much of my seasonal thoughts with the community, but I had not shared my experience of last night. I speculated that my vision had been conjured by the presence of Prosperiel. All the pieces fit; the seasonality, the description of the dehar, and my sightings of the red fox, but I didn't want to share the experience, at least not yet. I let my eyes float open; the Nayati was lit by the candles on the dais and the torches in sconces along the wall. My gaze moved casually over the celebrants until my eyes fell on one figure; he stood alone in the Nayati doorway, tall and straight, with an oak leaf garland draped across his shoulders. The hood of his cloak was up, but I could see his long hair flowing down across his chest. There was a quiver of movement at the bottom of his cloak, then a large fox emerged from the folds to sit at the har's feet, wrapping its tail neatly around its paws. No har, and no human, seemed to notice this figure with his fox. I found that my limbs felt too heavy to move; time felt suspended. The figure turned his head and looked at me; this time I knew. I was sure this was the dehar himself, and that he had visited me last night. Abruptly, Prosperiel turned, his cloak swirling around him, and left the Nayati. The fox trotted after him, out into the night. I closed my eyes again, conscious of the cool bricks against my back, and the world felt as if it moved in time again.

After the ceremonial part of the evening, the community left the Nayati and headed to the field that that lay just to the south, which served as the community commons. There, on the edge of the field, a large tent had been set up. Within, tables groaned beneath the weight of the feast dishes; we helped ourselves, and dined together, as neighbours do.

Pipaluk had approved the accumulation of a huge pile of wood for a bonfire, and after careful considerations of "safe distances", a spot farther south in the field had been chosen. Shortly after the meal, this huge bonfire was lit and the drummers began drumming again.

I stood with Kenny watching the bonfire. The man leaned on his staff, a big grin on his face. 'It went well, din' it?' His voice was full of deep satisfaction. 'It were the first time we tried a joint celebration. I liked it.' He nodded to me and set off back in the direction of the tent.

I remained watching the group drumming and dancing by the fire. The Smoketide arojhahn here had been every bit as substantial as those I had attended in the massive Nayati in Perrissan, but I found myself incredibly energised by the more organic observance here. I was also awed by my encounters with the dehar and his fox, sure that I'd never have experienced anything like that back in Perrissan.

I looked past the bonfire and saw Miller sitting alone on a picnic table, smoking a cigarette and staring at his boots. I grabbed two mugs of cider, then squared my shoulders and walked towards him. He looked warily at the mug I offered before accepting it.

'Miller,' I began, 'we got off to a bad start. I don't want us to be enemies. I do understand your concerns, but I hope you can understand that I have a sworn duty to protect the human interests of both community and individual.'

Miller shook his head. 'I don't hate you Wraeththu,' he said grudgingly. 'In fact, I coulda' even been one of you at one time. But I'd already met my lady, and I loved her; couldn't imagine a life without her.' He cleared his throat. 'Still can't imagine it. I just have trouble sometimes 'cuz I can remember the "bad ol' days". You know?'

I shrugged my jacket off and pulled up the sleeve on my left arm, holding it forward for Miller to see. In the firelight from the bonfire, the old scar was still visible; white and slightly puckered.

'I also remember the bad old days,' I said quietly. 'Some of us weren't given a choice – not that I have any regrets now.'

In the silence that followed, Miller nodded. 'That's why you believe in personal choice, then?'

'I don't hate humans, Miller.'

'I know,' he said heavily. 'I know. It's just Abena is my baby girl. I don't want her to go.'

'You've given her deep roots here,' I said. 'Now let her spread her wings and fly. Change doesn't always sit easy on any of us;

myself included. We're all just playing our parts in a Universal narrative. We can't choose the hand we're dealt, but we can choose to play it the best we can. There's great strength in letting change happen, and there's great freedom in going with the flow.'

Miller didn't respond, so we sat together in a slightly awkward silence.

'Thank you,' Miller said, rather abruptly. 'The orphan kids, I mean. I know you could have refused and had them sent to another settlement, so, thank you.'

'*Miller!*' The woman's voice could be heard calling over the drumming. '*Miller!*' I looked up and could see an arm waving in the crowd. Miller got up and put his mug down carefully on the table.

'Looks like my lady wants to go home now.' Miller hesitated. 'Sorry about the paint, and the window. I can get stupid worked up and the drink don't help.' He then made a fist and held it out. 'No hard feelings, Tiahaar?'

I made a fist and tapped my knuckles against his. 'No hard feelings,' I responded.

I watched as Miller and his lady left, then made my way to where Pipaluk stood, leaning on a tree, observing my interaction with Miller.

'I have,' I announced, 'hopefully made peace with Miller. At least for now, although I'm sure we'll lock horns again at some point, about something.'

Pipaluk smiled. 'So, are you staying?' he asked.

'I took your words to heart,' I responded gravely. 'I thought a lot about how we end up being where we're supposed to be.'

Pipaluk nodded.

'I'm sacrificing a hypothetical career in the Directorate for the opportunity to do important work in the trenches and make a real difference. So, yes, I will *not* be requesting a transfer.'

Pipaluk uttered a scoffing sound. 'Well, I already knew *that*. I knew from the moment I set eyes on you. Once you got over whatever injustice you felt had been done to you, I knew you'd recognise what needed to be. And anyway…' He grinned impishly. 'What I meant was – are you staying *tonight?*'

Hours later, as I lay in the bed next to Pipaluk, listening to the gentle rhythm of his breathing, I tried to visualise the face of the har I had seen last night in my sitting room, but the details had faded; I wondered about the foxes I'd seen – the sacred creatures of Prosperiel – and about my choice to remain. I wondered about all these things, not frenetically, but in a slow serene way, as sleep began to take hold. We all had our parts to play in this universal narrative, and I was, for now, content with mine. Just before sleep claimed me, I heard the shrill, yipping call of a fox close by the window. I smiled.

Walk as you will, in this world and all others.

Shadetide

This is the last of the harvest festivals, and traditionally a time when the portals between different levels of reality become unstable. It is the time when the veil is thin and discarnate entities can make contact with the living.

At this stage, the dehar transforms into Lachrymide (La-CRIM-ee-day) the Keener. Heavy with pearl and alone, Lachrymide stalks the bare earth. In nature, he can be unpredictable. His tears bring floods and the coldness of his heart brings snow. Only at his festival time does he really show any lighter side, and that is when, compassionate with his own sense of loss, he leads lost souls to the light. It is a night of trickery and feasting, of carnival and costume. Lachrymide is one of the most intimidating and fearsome of the seasonal dehara, but he is appeased by merriment and feasting.

Lachrymide can be petitioned to give glimpses of the future or news of lost loved ones. After being invoked, he appears at the threshold as a tall har dressed in black with long red hair. Often, his face is veiled – in red or black, or simply in flames.

As Lachrymide presides over the dark weeks between Shadetide and the solstice, he is asked to provide warmth, food and shelter, to keep animals healthy through the cold months and to preserve the stored grain. His animal is the black cat, cats being invaluable in guarding grain stores from rats and other vermin. Often, during his reign, tall dark figures are spotted in the fields or at crossroads, or beside lonely tracks. If a har comes across Lachrymide in the dark, they should offer him a gift. If he is pleased with it, he will grant them fortune.

Certain of Panphilien's aspects are associated with smiting. Lachrymide, along with the hunter Shadolan, may be petitioned to deal with enemies and injustice.

He Who Stands at the Crossroads

E.S. Wynn

The weather is turning cold. The forests are quiet and empty. The deer have moved on for the season, and the first frosts of the coming winter are already glazing the morning dew, browning the dead and fallen leaves.

My tribe is hungry. Naten, my chesnari, is hungry. Lailae, our harling, who Naten carries in a sling as he grinds the last of our grain into bread, is restless, as if he knows. As if he knows what promise tomorrow brings.

It is three days before Shadetide, and our fields are barren and brown. The dead stalks of corn and tangled tomato vines have been cut down and fed to the woolly goats that weather nights by the communal firepit in the centre of our settlement. There's talk of a feast on Shadetide night, a dumb supper of roasted meat, honeyed pumpkin and salmonberry melomel to chase away the ice of the settling dark. There's talk of honouring ancestors, but in a vague and general sort of way. Honouring the creators and visionaries among the lost tribe that called itself *Human,* so that we do not forget where we came from, or the many mistakes that were made before we became har.

And there is talk of fire, of a bright and vibrant bonfire to welcome in the future, to light the way for our hopes and dreams to find us. As one tribe, we will rise and dance and sing and rage against the settling darkness, the bitter months that are to come. As one, we will stoke the fires of will and pleasure in defiance of the night, fill our bellies with meat and mead, and believe that we have plenty, that the winter months will be warm and fruitful, and that our luck, our pride, and our stockpiled reserves will carry us through to spring.

It is these thoughts I focus on when I stalk the straggling deer in the deep woods three days before Shadetide. It is these thoughts that carry me over the new-born ice with supple bow in one hand and a clutch of chert-tip arrows in the other. Even one deer would be enough to carry us through for a week, perhaps more. Even a handful of squirrels or quail would take some pressure off our herd of goats. For three days, I'm hopeful, quick and optimistic. By dawn on the morning of Shadetide, I'm exhausted and starving. I imagine the sad look I'll see on my chesnari's face when I return emptyhanded, and it hits me deep inside, leaves me feeling defeated.

But after three days of eating nothing but a handful of withered berries gathered from vines the deer have missed, I feel as if my belly has caved in on itself. By noon, I give up on the hunt, make my way back to the settlement and turn my thoughts to the feast still to come. In my mind, I imagine my neighbours setting up tables and kindling for the evening. I imagine the smell of roasting meat, and I imagine my chesnari smiling, his long blonde hair falling about his face, Lailae in his arms, bright and bouncing, pointing at me as he babbles. I imagine sharing breath with Naten, feeling his bright spirit, his relief at my return, imagine him happy to see me, even if my three days of hunting have yielded nothing.

The stories my mind spins, the hopes, the smiles – I see none of it when I arrive. The first har I see is Cauren, one of my neighbours, but when I raise my hand and hail him, he only turns and hurries away. Worried, I pick up speed, call out for my chesnari, but nohar answers. Nohar comes out to greet me, and when I reach my shack, I sprint up to the door, clear the steps between me and my home two and three at a time.

'Naten!' I shout, and the hara gathered in my home turn as one to regard me. In the silence, I hear quiet, desperate sobbing, and I practically tear my way through my neighbours to reach my chesnari, my love, my mate.

What a terrible surprise it is when I find him missing. On the floor before me, a pair of hara I've hunted with in the past hold my harling, try to comfort him, but he only cries harder when he sees me. Lost, confused, I sweep him up as he reaches for me, pull him close.

'Lailae.' I whisper his name, brush an edge of hair out of his wet eyes. 'Lailae, what happened?'

He's so distraught that he can only shake his head, press his wet face into my shirt. When the words come, he howls only one thing. A name. *Naten! Naten!* Over and over again, he cries out for my mate, for his hostling, and his pain tears through me like ice, like the claws of a raging bear.

'Lailae.' I want to shake him, demand more, but I can't. I'm too wounded, can't muster even a sliver of rage, couldn't turn any of it on my harling even if I had it in me. 'Lailae, tell me what happened. What happened to Naten?'

'Jelse.' A voice catches my ear, brings me back to the wall of neighbors crowded around Lailae and I. Hara part, and then somehar steps up to stand next to me, extends his hand in a gentle gesture of empathy. I look up, recognise the face immediately. *Brekand.* The closest thing our settlement has to an elder, a leader.

'Brekand.' I take his hand, hold it. In his eyes, I see traces of tears, a wetness barely restrained. His touch is warm, tender, and in that moment, I feel waves of compassion flowing from him, a sense of unity, of understanding, flooding through our touch and into me. He knows. He understands.

'What happened?' I ask him.

'It was the Nulytep,' he says. 'The Nulytep took your chesnari.'

I squeeze his hand. 'Show me.'

Brekand watches me, his eyes searching mine. In his touch, I feel his worry, his doubt, but he doesn't hold out on me for long. Nodding, saying nothing, he places his hands along the sides of my face, his thumbs over my eyes, gently urging them to close.

Darkness, then flickers of colour. That's how it always starts. Strange shades and afterimages coalescing into a rushing haze. Voices, and then a pinprick of light, of something familiar, growing until it becomes everything, until I'm sitting in the stream of Brekand's memories, seeing everything he has seen.

'Kenadri,' he says, and the har he's facing is tall, fierce-faced and ominous. He isn't somehar I recognise, isn't somehar of our tribe. *Nulytep,* I decide. *Must be.* His leathers are black-dyed and rough on the inside from miles and miles of riding. The sheen and thickness of his leathers is unusual, doesn't strike me as cow or goat hide. Something else, perhaps. Something...

'It has been a long time, Brekand.' When Kenadri speaks, it pulls my attention completely to him. His voice is rich, deep, seems to carry notes of magick within it, glamours to hook and pull at the mind. Behind him, shadows shift and gather – other Nulytep, a pair of them, maybe more, and dressed in the same strange leathers as Kenadri is. 'Your settlement looks much the same as it did when last I saw it.'

'We live in harmony with the land,' Brekand says, and there is pain in his voice, an old pain. 'As much as we can, even still.'

'That is why your tribe is small.' The notes of superiority in Kenadri's voice bring all kinds of feelings up into my chest. Anger, sickness. One of his long-fingered, pale hands comes to rest on his thigh, absently stroking the leather there. 'That is why you starve, even after the harvest.'

'We do well enough.' Brekand pulls in a deep, steady breath, and I can feel his defences rising, the pride welling up within him. 'It is Shadetide. Shouldn't you be making preparations for your own festival? Why have you come to our settlement?'

'You remember Morton Creek, don't you?' Kenadri asks.

'The human settlement twelve miles east of here.' Brekand nods. 'How could I forget? We were both born there. Many among my tribe and yours were born there.'

'It's a ruin now,' Kenadri says, picks at his glistening red nails in the pause. 'The last of the humans there have struck out into the wilderness. They're gone, and they burned everything when they left.'

'They were probably tired of being treated like livestock by the Nulytep,' Brekand says, and when his eyes go to Kenadri's garments again, I suddenly recognise the unusual texture of his leathers. *Human skin,* I realise. Kenadri, indeed all of the Nulytep in the vision, are dressed in well-cured and dyed leathers of human skin. Simmering in the realisation, I feel a new tide of revulsion and rage as it wells up within me, washes through me.

'Meat should know its place,' Kenadri muses, and the look within his eyes is hungry, disturbing. 'We are the superior race. All others are merely fodder.'

'That's the same attitude that caused the rift between my tribe and yours, Kenadri.' I can feel Brekand's fists clenching, the pain rising in him again. 'We were one tribe once. With the temptation of the human settlement gone, we could be again.'

The grin that Kenadri gives him is sharp and sneering. 'Meat should know its place,' he says again, slower this time. 'With the humans of Morton Creek gone, we have no meat for our Shadetide feast, and we have so many hungry bellies to fill.'

The silence that falls between the two hara is cold, palpable. Kenadri's stare is intense, but Brekand stands firm in spite of it. He's strong, so strong, unwilling to bend, even under the full force of Kenadri's pressing mental influence.

'How many are there in your tribe these days, Kenadri?' Brekand asks. 'If you're hungry, I'm certain we could spare a goat or two in trade for a promise of labour in the fields come spring.'

'My tribe isn't hungry for goat.' Kenadri reaches out, runs one cold hand across Brekand's cheek. 'The feast of Shadetide has always required something more in line with the season, something of more meaning to the forces we invite into our rituals.' He pauses, looks up for a moment, as if listening for some distant voice, then turns his eyes back to Brekand again. 'Something we've already taken.'

Realisation hits me like a bucket of ice water splashed down my back. In the vision, Brekand slaps away Kenadri's hand, then pushes past him and sprints to the door of the shack. Standing on the deck just outside, he surveys the settlement, and as I follow his eyes, he spots a pair of shadows darting into the woods, each carrying a squirming, wailing bundle.

I count them mentally, right alongside Brekand. Five in all. Naten and four others. Through his eyes, I see Lailae fall to his knees in the centre of the settlement, hands held up as he howls wordlessly at the sky. It hits me, like a sledgehammer to the heart, it hits me, and then Kenadri is suddenly beside me, beside Brekand, his voice like honey in our ear.

'Don't do anything foolish, Brekand,' he says. 'We outnumber you ten-to-one. Even now, there are a dozen hara with hunting rifles watching you from just within the treeline.'

Within Brekand's memories, I feel the fear, feel the ice eating into him, spreading through skin in a cold sweat as he turns his eyes to the forest, searching for signs of movement, for shadows, finding nothing.

'You should be grateful,' Kenadri whispers, that sharp smile so close, taunting me. 'The hara we took were some of the weakest and slowest among your herd. They would have been a drain on your reserves during the coming winter. I've saved you the trouble and waste of feeding them and keeping them alive.'

'You can't do this,' is all Brekand can say.

'Meat should know its place,' Kenadri says again, and it stokes such a fire of rage in me that I nearly explode out of the vision. 'See you next Shadetide, Brekand.'

And then, in a flicker of roiling shadow, the three Nulytep are gone, darting for the forest, leaving only the fear, the hate, the tears and the wailing in their wake.

'Jelse.' *My name.* There is light, a movement within the vision, and when I turn back toward the shack, I find myself in my own body again, Brekand standing over me, regarding me with his deep, worried eyes.

'They are strong,' he says. 'We do not have the means to fight them, Jelse.'

'No.' The hot tears rimming my eyes are barely restrained. 'Not yet.'

'You have a plan?' somehar asks. A neighbour, somehar who hasn't lost their chesnari to the Nulytep, somehar who doesn't know the pain that's eating me alive. 'Don't let rage take you. Think this through.'

'Today is Shadetide,' is all I say. With the elements of a plan still coalescing in my mind, I stand, meet the eyes around me evenly, returning worried stares with firm iron will and fire. There's something within me, a wave of intent, a river of energy that carries a colour, a scent, a flavour. *Lachrymide, the widower.* 'I need to leave.' It comes suddenly. 'I need to seek guidance.'

'You're not making sense,' Brekand says. 'Jelse, take a moment. I know how much this must hurt—'

'Nothing hurts.' I cut him off. 'Take care of Lailae.' I untangle myself from my harling, from my flesh and blood, my only physical connection to my chesnari. It's so painful, pressing him back into the arms of my neighbours that I have to squeeze my eyes against the ache, the tears. Terrified, he starts screaming for me, scrabbling with tiny nails bared like claws. Doing everything I can to ignore him, I turn my eyes to the door, focus on the hot wave of energy already rising within me like a snake, and I want so badly to seize it, to pull it into myself and ride it all the way to the Nulytep camp.

'You'll die if you pursue the Nulytep,' somehar says. It doesn't stop me. Resolve builds, and I stoke the current within me like a flame, gather it as it grows. As I start toward the door, words find their way to my tongue, words that I know aren't mine.

'The veil thins.' I reach up, pull the pair of picks holding my long, red hair in place, let it fall loose about my shoulders. 'Anything might happen at the crossroads. Anyhar might wear the mask of The Keener, given sufficient need and sacrifice.'

The other hara are silent, gravely so. By the time I'm outside again, I can feel the spirit of the season rising within me, filling me like water barely restrained by a dam. *Astale Lachrymide, dehar of Shadetide. Come to me.* I call out wordlessly, letting the thoughts echo in my mind like a litany, until someone reaches back through the abyss, grips my mind in cold, sharp-nailed hands.

And as I surrender my body to The Keener, I feel him blossoming within me, so at home with the rage and pain I'm feeling. It's familiar to him, all too familiar. My hands rise up before me as I step back within myself, let the dehar take control. It's an exchange, a willing sacrifice of life and time for something more. *You know the pain I feel,* I tell him, and his agreement is blinding, palpable. *This body is your horse. Ride it, but please, see my pain, my fear. See how it is like yours.*

Please, save my chesnari.

No words come back to me, no fight or agreement. For a moment, Lachrymide seems only to soak in the world around me, but the instant my hands drop back to my sides, we're running as one, sprinting toward the treeline with supernatural speed. In seconds, we're in the woods, and the dark branches close in around us like doors, like the halls of another world entirely.

We cover maybe a mile before I realise that I've left my bow back in the settlement, that I have no weapons, not even a blade. *We won't need them,* Lachrymide whispers, and his voice is like smoke, sad yet sultry, strangely alluring. Riding backseat in my own body, I try to trust the dehar driving us deeper and deeper into the woods, but the fear, the worries creep up anyway. Lachrymide makes no effort to coddle me, to reassure me or quash the emotions chewing at me. He wants me to feel them. He wants me to understand, to learn and overcome.

How do you cope, Widower? I ask him, letting the words coalesce in the mind-space we share.

I don't, he says. *I live within the loss. I've let it consume me, define me. Even in moments of hope and sweetness, there is still the bitterness. Even in the midst of celebration, I grieve for all that I've lost.*

Supple branches whip at my skin as the trees close in around us, tighter and tighter. Guided by Lachrymide, my body moves like a knife, cuts between the green and the black as they become a wall through which only we may pass. *The veil thins,* he says, but all I can think about are the words he has breathed into my mind. *I live within the loss. I've let it consume me, define me.*

Does my chesnari live? I ask the dehar. He doesn't respond, so I push harder, try to force an answer from him. *Will I suffer as you do? Will my future be shaped and ruled by the pain you feel?*

That is up to you, Lachrymide says, and in the spirit-spun words, I swear I hear the traces of a coyote smile, the grin of a trickster.

And then, all at once, we're squeezing into the tree-coloured membrane separating realities, popping through to somewhere else. Hues of shadow green and sky-blue cling to my skin like slick slime, run down my arms and legs in brilliant rivulets, as we step into the dry ash and monochrome twilight of the place Lachrymide has led me to. Stunned, I try to soak in as much of the world around me as I can, try to understand it, comprehend its weird rules, but the dehar only rests long enough to brush the colours from my skin. Turning his eyes toward the horizon, he starts off across those ashen plains, jogging toward a tiny point of light hanging in the sky in a direction I assume must be West.

Where are you taking me? I ask him.

His response is simple. *To your chesnari.*

What is this place? I try to get him to look left, look right, take in more than just the light line where grey ground meets grey sky, but he's firmly in control of my body.

Somewhere familiar, is all he says. *A place between. Time and distance are different here. Think of it as a shortcut.*

Curiosity pulls at me. The air is thin, and warm but for the occasional icy gust that comes suddenly, cuts right to the centre of my being. Nothing stirs the ash beneath my feet, nothing, not even the quick winds, not even our sprinting stride as Lachrymide hurls us toward the horizon. Briefly, I consider wrestling control back from the dehar, even if only for an instant, even if only to stop, to reach down and feel the ashes between my fingers, but the sensation he sends me in return is quick, almost disciplinary.

Don't, he says. *To move through this realm requires a great deal of focus. Were we to stray or slow even a little, you might find yourself trapped here, lost here, emerging too late to help your chesnari, if indeed you emerged alive at all.*

It's just a barren, empty expanse of ash and dust. I turn my attention completely to the dehar riding within my body. *How could anyhar get lost here?*

This place is more than just what you see around you now, he tells me. *It is full of the ashes of everything that was. Spirits get lost here. To them, it is a twisting maze of impassable memories, cast in mist and spreading in every direction. To them, it is as deep and terrifying as it is featureless and oppressive. Words cannot easily shape a description of it as I see it, and to fill you with the essence of it might drive you mad. Better to leave it be, and only observe what you see passively. Soon enough, we'll emerge back into the world of the living.*

In his words, there is enough detail to chill me, to intrigue and worry me. Instead of pushing him or trying for more, I let him keep his focus, let him guide us without interruption. Time moves without a way to track, and Lachrymide drives my body across the featureless landscape, as if he carries a map in his heart, as if he knows the land well.

And when he stops, it happens suddenly, without warning. Curious, I turn my attention on him as we crouch, press hands into the cold ash. There's a sensation, a strange sinking, and then the ground becomes the sky, and he's pushing against it as if trying to shove the entire Earth out of the way. It's confusing, the way everything bends, the way gravity suddenly seems meaningless, and then we're sinking into the ashen earth, hands sliding, clawing, dragging as much as parting, swimming into ash, soil and stone. Cold earth rises up and swallows my face, swallows me as if my body were a burrowing worm. *Another membrane,* I realise, and Lachrymide fills me with a sensation that feels like confirmation. *Then, on the other side...?*

I feel the wet and frigid air before I see it, before I see sky or take a sucking lungful of forest air. Eyes open as I brush the dirt from my face, take in the grey and blue above me, the green and brown of the woods, of the low side of a mountain. With practiced ease, Lachrymide extracts us from the earth, stands among the stones and fallen leaves for a moment to catch his breath. *Where are we?* I ask, and in response, he shows me. Turning West, he points toward a plume of smoke, barely visible in the sky above the trees.

The Nulytep? I ask, and feel my body nodding in confirmation. I've never been to their settlement before, but somehow I know. Because of Lachrymide, because of the dehar wearing my skin, I know. *They're close.*

We must go around, Lachrymide says within the vault of my brain. *Around?* I ask. *How far around?*

243

Without answering, Lachrymide sends me a feeling, a sensation, and I dismiss it immediately.

That far? I demand. *Surely there must be an easier way! The sun will nearly be at the horizon by the time we reach that side of the settlement!*

Again, there are no words, only images, sensations. In my mind, I see a hazy image of Naten standing in that featureless grey plain of twilight sky and ashes. Desperate, he calls out for me, but there is no sound, nothing reaches me, and no matter how hard I run toward him, he never gets any closer. For days, I could run and never reach him, only see him as if he were trapped on the other side of an invisible wall. Slowly, the message coalesces, comes as a warning. *Death.* Death, and the dehar's commitment to helping me avoid it.

I am here to guide you, Lachrymide says, and I know that he is right, that I can trust him.

Is that place, the words take a moment to form in my mind, *that field of ashes that stretches on forever... is that the land of the dead? The spirit realm?*

It is a realm in which the dead wander, he says to me. *But then, the dead wander through many realms, including this one.*

There's something in his words which sends another chill through me, a depth to his meaning, which I know will take time to comprehend completely. Lachrymide doesn't wait for it to sink in, but instead starts off again, toward the Nulytep settlement, skirting a wide line around it, aiming for a spot I cannot see, can only *feel.* There's something there, I know. Something important to Lachrymide's unspoken plan.

The rough-hewn trunks of an ominous palisade wall rise up out of the trees as we approach, and the closer we get, the quieter the dehar causes us to move. Even trying to trust him, I worry as he slows. I worry more when he stops, as if to rest, and presses his hand against one of the stout beams of the wall.

Why are we stopping? I ask the dehar. Ahead of us, I see only trees, only the curve of the wall as it wends its way steadily away from us. If I strain, really focus to separate the sounds around us, I can pick out little noises in the distance, the traces of muffled conversation, laughing, the sounds of civilisation, but none of the voices are anywhere near us. It's nearly night, and that worries me. Meat takes time to cook, and with no way to know when the Nulytep will hold their Shadetide feast....

There's a gate just ahead, Lachrymide says, brushing aside my fears. *Jelse, listen to me. To go further, to do what must be done, I will need more.*

More? I hesitate. The dehar has my body, has control of my muscles, my senses, everything he would need to fight, to kill. *What more is there?*

Intent, unity, fluidity. He offers concepts, fills my thoughts with elements that seem disparate, unrelated, until he pulls them together suddenly, stitches them into a solid whole.

Up until now, it has been enough for me to become you. Now, he says, *to survive the trials that lie ahead, you must become me.*

The images that flood me then are deep and intense, even terrifying. A loss of individuality. A surrendering of the soul. More than just giving up my skin to The Keener. More than just giving him a vehicle and expecting him to achieve my desires for me. What he wants is so much more, and yet, looking at it, understanding the nature of the change, the power it would grant me to save my chesnari, it is also so very tantalising.

Are you ready? he asks me.

It takes me only a moment to respond, to quash my fears and force myself to take the necessary step, to move forward without doubt, without looking back.

If this is what it will take to save Naten, I tell the voice within my head. *Then I am ready. Show me, Lachrymide. Show me how to take on the mantle of the Dehar of Darkness and Fire. I am ready to become you.*

Even as I think the words, something uncoils and opens within me. *Remember the field of ashes,* Lachrymide tells me, and on some level beyond the physical, I close my eyes to sight, find myself there in the darkness, facing him. Standing before me, he is the black-robed widower I've seen in dreams, in vision meditations led by Brekand on past Shadetide nights. He is The Keener with crimson hair spilling down his shoulders. Taking in the details, I see the mask of tears he wears, the glistening wetness that runs from eyes I cannot see, eyes hidden beneath the hem of his shadowy veil. *Do you feel what I feel?* He asks me, and when I shake my head, overwhelmed by the emotions he practically radiates, the grief and fire raging within him, he smiles ruefully.

Astale, Jelse. He hails me as if I were an equal, as if I were a dehar, then reaches out with one cold hand and presses it against my cheek. With the other, he reaches up, catches the edge of his veil, holds it in place. *Welcome, har of the forest and of the hills. Welcome, chesna*

*of Naten, sire of Lailae. Welcome, hunter and seeker, brave and burning bane
of the Nulytep. Be here now, be here now.*

When he yanks up the hem of the veil, something happens.
There's a change, drastic and sudden, a change that strikes me down
to the core of my being with all the searing fire of a lightning strike.
All at once, I feel the weight of the shift, let my cold fingers fall
from the edge of the shadowy veil hiding my tear-wet eyes. I'm so
shaken by the flash, by the memory of a single burning, crimson
eye staring back at me, filling me with a penetrating ray of soul and
heat and pain, that it takes me a moment to realise I am alone, that
nothing remains of Jelse. As if expecting to see something else, I
look at my hands, see only the long, pale fingers of Lachrymide
spreading out before me.

And that is when I think of Naten. That is when the fear of
losing my mate mixes with the pain of having lost him already, long
ago. The feelings are mine as much as they are Jelse's, only Jelse
hasn't lost his chesnari yet. There is an icy, heart-shaped void in my
chest, an unquenchable, sucking hole where my love once rested,
bright and beautiful. For me, it is too late to be spared the feelings
that come with loss, with deep loss, but for Jelse, there is still time.
There is still time to protect him from the kind of scars I wear,
from the pain that has cut me so deeply that I see myself as
disfigured, forever defined by a deep-running current of despair.

In Jelse's realm, it is Shadetide, and nearing dusk.

There is still time.

When I emerge back into the forest, the sun and brilliant blue
sky have darkened. Light yields to night, casts long inky shadows
over everything. I close the distance between myself and my goal in
the space of a blink, skip across the skin of the otherlanes like a
smooth stone over the surface of a lake. The Nulytep har standing
at the Western gate of their sprawling settlement doesn't even sense
my presence until I'm beside him, rising over him like a silent,
staring omen.

There's a shiver. I feel it in him as I reach into his spirit, pluck
something from his soul. A memory, packed away, but still rich with
pain. 'Tomal is waiting for you by the bend in the river, where he
died.' I whisper it into his ear, and the har's eyes widen as he turns
to face me, takes in my towering, veiled visage with terrified eyes.

'Astale, Lachrymide.' He recognises me, regards me with awe
and fear. 'How can this be?'

'It is Shadetide.' I breathe a verbal venom into the words, a knife of intent that makes him anxious, unmoors his senses from the physical world. 'The veil is thin. Anything might happen at the crossroads.'

The har says nothing more, only turns his eyes toward the woods. His heart is full of thoughts of a young har he once loved fiercely, an ebon-haired beauty with daisies woven in around his ears, and as he thinks of Tomal, I feel the spirit of Tomal somewhere else, manifesting, thinking of him.

'Go to him,' I tell the Nulytep har. 'He misses you.'

The har nods absently, and without a thought given for his tribe or his post, he hurries off into the woods, intent on finding Tomal, on finding that bend in the river that he remembers with so much lingering pain.

Alone again, I set my eyes on the collection of shacks ahead of me, search for signs of Jelse's chesnari, for signs of any of the hara who were kidnapped.

When I walk amidst the Nulytep, I move with all the casual grace of a welcome guest. Gathering firelight shadows about my face and arms, I muddy my features with shifting shades of darkness until I blend in, until I'm easily mistaken for one of their tribe. Most of the hara barely glance at me as I go by, as I search, run my hands across the bars of heavy steel cages stained with blood. *Old blood. Human blood.* Only once does a har approach me, seem to see me as something else, something other than one of his kin. A few well-placed words laced with intoxicating venom are all I need to turn him away with a yawn, send him stumbling back to his cabin, convinced he's only dreaming.

And then I hear a shout and everything changes. Sliding into thicker shadows, I move through alleys and under awnings with a singular speed, stealth and sleekness. Pinpointing the source, I close the distance between myself and the sound within seconds, slither to the last lip of darkness and peer out, staring. Almost instantly I spot Naten and the others. Five in all, and each of them lined up in the centre of a squat platform of adobe brick. *An altar,* I realise, and every one of the stolen kin of Jelse is positioned upon their knees atop it, bound at the wrists and ankles with coarse rope, displayed before a crowd of perhaps two dozen Nulytep.

Excitement, hunger, something like bloodlust. It's in the air, grips the crowd of Nulytep and drives them to shout and dance at the base of the platform. The executioner and his assistant stand on the altar with the kin of Jelse, the older of the two sharpening a long blade made for slashing throats.

Time is short. Reaching out for the two Nulytep atop the altar, I search their psyches for thoughts I can turn against them, trigger them with. One of them, the master, has grown cold and closed, but the younger one, the apprentice…

I pull in a deep breath as I send part of myself leaping into the executioner's assistant, overriding his thoughts and turning his attention toward a splinter that's been festering in his mind for months. All at once, it grows, expands, blossoms into something larger, sharper, something too important, too intense to deny, even now, mere moments before the meat of the meal to come is butchered for all to see.

'Hasay!' He blurts the executioner's name, startles everyhar to silence. Undaunted by the attention turned suddenly on him, he licks his lips, steps toward his master. 'Hasay, I – I have to tell you how I feel.'

'Save it!' The executioner rasps his blade against his boot, starts eyeing the hara I've come to rescue. Desperate, I force more of my will into the younger har, and he responds like a puppet on strings, consumed by need, unwilling to back down for anything.

'I love you, Hasay!' he shouts, and throws himself at the executioner. It's all the older har can do to toss the knife away before his assistant tackles him, bears him to the ground. There's a tussle, shouting, and with a little push of will and intent from me, the crowd rushes toward the platform, chases the two wrestling hara as they roll off into the dirt on the other side.

Naten and the other four look bewildered, stare after the crowd of Nulytep, but a flick of thought from me brings their eyes right to mine, lights me up in their vision. *Lachrymide.* Naten mouths my name, sees me as dehar, not as a mortal, not as flesh. In the space of a breath, I am among them, easily loosening their bonds, guiding them toward the darkness, wrapping them up in shadows as they go. By the time the Nulytep recover enough awareness to realise that their captives have escaped, Jelse's kin are well past the gate and on their way back to the village from which they were stolen.

But the deed I've done isn't enough. With their magicks, their mastery of shadow, and their skill in quickening the blood with a driving internal fire, the Nulytep could easily catch up with the fleeing hara I've set free. More of a distraction is needed if Jelse's kin hope to reach their homes tonight, and so I stay while they dart deerlike through the woods beyond the palisade. I stay, and one by one, I pick at the Nulytep from the shadows, confuse them, set them into arguments and affairs that sweep up whole groups of them into screaming, shouting, wrestling knots. Reaching out to hara at the edges of the settlement, in the kitchens and cellars of the Nulytep, I give them sudden spikes of intuition that it's time to serve wine, to roll out barrels of mead and bring forth the dancers that are scheduled to entertain the tribe after the sacrifice. Searching for triggers, hitting them at just the right moments, I play the entire tribe like a piano until the whole mess devolves into chaos.

I don't linger long after that. Hitting enough mental splinters among the Nulytep to keep the chaos self-sustaining, I turn my thoughts toward freedom, slide through the shadows and make my way to the Western gate. The way is clear, feels clear, but the moment I slip into the blotchy firelight that frames the threshold, an oily shape rises out of the shadows and trees just beyond. Uncoiling like a snake, the figure stands straight and tall, and I catch a glimmer of light on the blade of the long knife in his hand.

'Astale, Lachrymide,' he calls out to me, and I recognize his voice immediately. The har from Jelse's vision, the memories imparted from Brekand. *Kenadri*. 'I suppose it's true what they say, that anything might happen at the crossroads on Shadetide.'

'You've brought a great deal of strife into this world, Kenadri.' I say it without malice, without venom. He smiles a little at the magick in my tone, at the taste of the intent lightly infused within my words. Confident, I spread my arms, show my palms, stride toward him. 'It is Shadetide. It is a time for feasting, for merriment and for reflection. Now is a time for visions, for scrying and seeing what may come in the year ahead.'

'Have you brought me a vision, Lachrymide?' His grin turns sharp and wicked as he steps toward me, knife held low but with the flat of the blade displayed, flashing, like a threat. 'Who are you under all that shadow and magick? Who are you really?'

'Don't you recognise me, Kenadri?' I match his sadistic grin, turn as he turns, circling each other like jackals.

'Are you one of mine? Are you Nulytep?' He shifts the blade in his eager hand. 'Name yourself, har!'

'Name myself?' I laugh, loud and mocking. 'You've already

named me!'

'You're a pretender, a charlatan!' He shouts back at me, angry, but there's a crack in his resolve, a tiny fissure of fear and doubt that excites me, thrills me. 'No more games! Show me your true face, imposter!'

In one quick, desperate motion, he reaches for me, reaches for the veil hiding my eyes. Anticipating his move, I lean in, let him catch it, let him tear it from my face. My grin spreads as his eyes widen, as his hands start to shake with fear. All at once, he recognises me, opens himself to me, and I use it against him, lever him open with willpower, until I'm wrapped around his mind, his soul, tightening around him like the coils of a snake.

'Lachrymide.' He breathes my name, feels it, knows it to be true.

'You've seen this moment in your dreams,' I whisper against his ear, every word wet and paralysing, worming deeply into his psyche.

'I have,' he says. 'Every night, I have dreamed of this moment. Every eve since Brekand incepted me, I have dreamed of your coming. I knew that you would end me. I knew that encountering you incarnate, I would die.' Tears start to gather at the edges of his blankly staring eyes, then break and run down his cheeks in thick rivers. 'Thank you, Lachrymide. Thank you. I am grateful.'

'I am not here to end you,' I whisper back, soaking in the fear that spikes within him at the sound of the words. 'What you have seen in dreams is not death. It is deliverance, penance.'

'What are you saying?' Kenadri asks, tries to turn his face to look at me. He starts to panic when he realises he cannot move, that he is bound and paralysed as much by my words as he is by my shadows, my body.

'Meat should know its place.' I offer him his own words. He recognises them immediately, starts to shake. 'The veil is thin, and I have need of something *more.*'

'More?' His heart is racing against mine. 'You have me at your mercy, Lachrymide. I am ready to die. What more is there to give?'

'Intent, unity, fluidity.' I reach into him with my mind, fill him with concepts, with images of joining, of two souls merging, becoming one. It hits him hard, leaves him breathless. 'I can think of no greater penance than this, no greater deliverance than for you to become me.'

He's struck by the power of it, I can tell, and blind to all else. 'I accept,' he whispers hurriedly. 'To become one with the Dehar of

Darkness and Fire, to see all that you see, know all that you know—'

'Feel all that I feel,' I add, cutting him off.

'Yes, yes.' He swallows, tries to nod. 'I accept. I am ready. Take me, Lachrymide. I am ready to become you.'

Something opens between us then, a conduit triggered by his consent. An uncoiling, familiar. For a brief moment, I remember the field of ashes, remember Jelse, remember the moment of joining, the moment I became Lachrymide. It hits hard, passes quickly, and then my focus is on the har in front of me again, the meat that I am about to make mine.

'Astale, Kenadri!' I hail him as an equal. Reaching up with one cold hand, I press it against his cheek, turn his face until his eyes meet mine evenly. 'Welcome, Chief Har among the Nulytep. Welcome, Bane of Morton Creek. Welcome, Lord of Grief, kin of those you would kill on Shadetide eve. Be here now. Be here now.'

Lips part, struggle to form words, but nothing comes. I run my long, pale fingers over his face, take his head in my hands, then lean in and breathe life into him. My life, my essence, all of my heat, all of my pain, all that I am, all that I know and all that I battle with. His soul twists, burns in the rushing current of my breath, is tossed about and dissolved as the grief and scars I carry devour him, scatter his memories among countless others. For him, it feels sudden, like a searing bolt of lightning arcing through his body, electrifying him as it obliterates him. For me, it is a process, a translation of all my nonphysical elements into a new physical body. A new incarnation of Lachrymide.

I feel hollow when the last of the dehar pours out of me. Stumbling away, coughing and shuddering, I fall to my knees in the grass, dry-heave foamy spittle as I claw at the earth. It's painful, frightening, but also oddly relieving. The weight of all the woe of the world is gone from me, and with it, all of the wisdom such suffering could grant me.

'Astale, Jelse.' I hear Lachrymide's voice somewhere above me, turn and wipe at my lips. It takes an effort to stagger back to my feet, but when I do, I take in the dehar before me, his pale hands, his tear-wet face, his veil and the wry smile spreading beneath it. Kenadri is gone. We're alone in the woods, far from the gate, as if we somehow drifted there on some unremembered current.

'Astale Lachrymide,' I whisper, voice quieted as much by awe as it is by exhaustion. 'Kenadri? It's finished?'

'Kenadri is part of me now.' The dehar reaches up, places one palm flat against the centre of his chest. 'The hara you saved are nearly home again. By the time you arrive at the settlement, your chesnari will be waiting at the doorway for you with Lailae in his arms.'

'And the Nulytep?' I ask.

'They will no longer be a threat to you or your tribe,' Lachrymide says. 'Kenadri was powerful in the arts of mind manipulation. Many of his kin were thralls to his will.' Lachrymide makes a sharp gesture. 'No more.'

'And what of you?' I regard the dehar evenly. 'Will I see you again? Will you leave or stay now that you have a body?'

'I have always had a body, and I am always here, and everywhere, and nowhere.' He smiles at me. 'There is no difference between meat and mind except what you think you see to define and separate one from the other, Jelse.'

'I don't understand.' I shake my head.

'Take time to consider my words,' he says, and as I watch him, he starts to fade, starts to drift apart into shifting shadow. 'Anything might happen at the crossroads when the veil is thin. Remember that, Jelse. We were never separate, you and I, and yet never a single soul either. You will find me whenever you look for me, and forget me whenever it serves you to.'

'I could never forget tonight, Lachrymide,' I tell him, glancing back toward the Nulytep settlement, the distant flickering lights shining amongst the trees. When I glance back toward the dehar, he is gone, and I am alone again, standing at a crossroads in the woods where one deer path intersects another.

'Farewell, Lachrymide.' I breathe the words into the settling silence. Hugging myself against the cold, I let my eyes rove among the trees around me for a moment, then half turn, suddenly eager to return to my home, to Naten and Lailae. 'Farewell, Dehar of Shadows, Hostling of the Pearl of Hope. Walk as you will, in this world and in all others.'

No answer comes, nor do I expect one. Shivering, I cast one last look around the crossroads, then turn and start in the direction of home. As I go, I think of all that I have, all that I am grateful for. I think of my chesnari's warm smile, and of the soft hands and playful laughter of our harling. I think of Brekand, and of the settlement our tribe has built under his guidance. I think of the future, and I think of the pearl that is just starting to grow within me. I'm a week, maybe two along, and I think of how Naten will smile when he knows, when I tell him, perhaps over a plate of roast goat and honeyed pumpkin. It is the night of Shadetide still, and back home, there will be a feast. Everyone will be celebrating the turning of The Wheel of Arotahar and the approach to Natalia.

Especially now, especially with the return of the hara they thought lost forever.

Adkaya

December 7th

This minor festival, two weeks before Natalia, is not one of the major celebrations, but still an important part of the seasonal calendar.

Adkaya observes the time when the dehar Lachrymide drops the pearl of the deharling and transforms into Solarisel, the presiding dehar of Natalia. The pearl of the deharling takes two weeks to mature before it hatches, so hara uses this time to perform magical rites associated with planning and preparation.

At Adkaya, harlings might craft a representation of the pearl and imagine within it all their hopes and desires for the future. They might keep this object in a bower of light, adorned with seasonal foliage and berries, until the solstice, when their creation might be burned upon an arojhahn bonfire, or in the hearth at home.

For adults, Adkaya is a time to plan for the future, to fine-tune the wording of boons that will be asked of Solarisel and Elisin at the solstice. Majhahns held at this time – a rite of Adkaya is rarely referred to as an arojhahn, unless for some reason a community makes a big event of it – will be used to prepare the ground for the new year. Participants will concentrate upon the forthcoming re-arrival of the light and its limitless possibilities. For some, this might involve casting off all the cares and problems of the year that is nearly done, leaving a serene 'blank slate', capable of soaking to the full the benign and expansive influences of the forthcoming solstice. For this reason, Adkaya is sometimes referred to as the Feast of Purification.

Solarisel's Covenant: A Sequel to Summer

Storm Constantine

The town had been taken by Wraeththu during the Devastation, and those intent on claiming it had found it abandoned, empty of human lives, half-eaten meals left on dining-tables and other such trappings of mystery. It had been named Shroomtown back then, because of the high amount of psychotropic fungus that grew in the fields around it. The name had stuck and Shroomtown it still was, over a hundred years later.

Positioned near one of the old highways, which still acted as an artery between the north and south, the town's visitors were therefore transitory, mostly accommodated by *The Falling Star*, the vast old coaching inn. In the human era, it had been renovated so its stables became part of the main building. Now, its previous function had been restored, the enclosing walls pulled down. As in the past, wagons and carriages trundled beneath the great arch to the yard beyond. Tonight, the area had been brushed of early snow and a brazier roared in the eastern corner. The inn was filling up because, in two days' time, the first festivities of Natalia would be held nearby, in fields between Shroomtown and the larger settlement of Irran's Thumb. Accommodation was cheap at *The Falling Star*, hence its popularity. There were two weeks yet until the major festival, but Adkaya was nigh, that time of possibilities, which lurked unseen within a pearl.

In the stable-yard, Isoldis har Mesrier dismounted stiffly from Minx, his winter-grey mare. He had been riding since mid-morning, through light flickerings of snow that while seemingly benign had somehow managed to soak him to the skin. His clothes were damp, despite his heavy coat, and his ears numb, despite his broad-brimmed hat and the scarf he wore beneath it. His gloved fingers could barely operate to unfasten his saddle bags, and he was grateful to the stable-har who offered to care for his horse.

'Get to the fire inside,' said the stable-har. 'Have a drink, a big one. Beef pie's on today, too.'

'Thank you, Tiahaar.' Isoldis bowed politely and entered the inn through its yard door.

Inside, the air was humid and hot, filled with the scent of cooking beef, and the somewhat less arresting reek of boiled greens. In the main bar, hara were smoking pipes of herbal mix, which added to the general fust in the air. Isoldis was too tired to care. He hoped there was a room left to hire, and he wouldn't have to spend the night trying to sleep in the bar. He still had another half-day's travelling to endure, to attend a growers' muster in Larmer Marsh. He was representing *Hart's Cliff*, the estate he worked for, being a custodian of its gardens. His employers expected him to return with trade alliances in place, and possibly new strains of rose for the garden precincts. It was the first time he'd been sent to represent the *Cliff* at the event and – he thought glumly – this wouldn't be the last. Not for the first time, as he clawed his way to the bar, Isoldis thought sourly about why a growers' muster was held virtually at mid-winter. The answer he'd been given back home was that growers were less busy at this time of year. Perhaps that was true, or perhaps the organisers were just stupid. Everywhere was busy, owing to Adkaya and the approaching Natalia. If it was up to him, he'd move the muster to mid-summer. Surely every establishment could spare at least one representative then? But no, its date had apparently become a tradition and could not be moved. Perhaps, for some, the socialising aspect of the event had become part of the Natalia celebrations.

Realising the folly of attempting to wait his turn for attention at the bar, Isoldis yelled at the young pothara concerning available rooms, until one took notice and said, yes, there were a couple left, overlooking the yard. Isoldis said he'd take one. He didn't care about the view. He'd be gone in the morning.

He was obliged to go to a reception area beyond the bar, where somehar would take his coin and allocate him a room. This area seemed unnaturally quiet after the raucous atmosphere in the bar, and was no doubt a relic of human occupation. Few coaching inns, in Isoldis' experience, had anything resembling a formal reception area. A young har sat behind the desk, writing up what seemed to be accounts. His green and black braided hair was held back with a spangled scarf. He had a small black star painted over his right cheek bone. Isoldis said he'd like a room.

The young har yawned and stretched. He glanced at Isoldis. 'You're back soon, aren't you?'

'Sorry? I've not been here before.'

The har took a key from the board hanging on the wall behind his desk. 'But you have. About two nights ago.'

'How much for one night?'

'Ten stoats.'

Isoldis put his money on the counter.

The receptionist took it and said. 'It was definitely you. I'd know you anywhere. You spoke to me here, just as you're doing now.'

'No, you're mistaken.'

The response was indignant. 'I'm *not*.'

Isoldis was not exactly a stranger to such inconsistencies in reality. 'Well, perhaps it was a fetch,' he said, smiling. 'Might I have my key?'

The receptionist appeared put out, rather sulky, and certainly disbelieving. He slapped the key into Isoldis's outstretched hand. 'You must know the way.'

'Actually, no, but I expect the rooms are numbered coherently and that this...' he glanced at the key, '... number 7 will be found between rooms 6 and 8.'

'Breakfast starts at 6.30,' said the har in a surly manner.

'Have a meal and some ale sent to my room, would you?'

'Two stoats.'

Isoldis handed over the coins. 'Thank you,' he said dryly, then climbed the wide, creaking stairs to the left of the desk.

The meal arrived with surprising swiftness, and after consuming it Isoldis felt much refreshed. A fire was laid in the room, and he took off his clothes so he could dry them before the flames. He hung them over the backs of two chairs that had stood to either side of the window and which he'd dragged before the hearth. He stood before the mirror naked and brushed the ends of his hair. The whole lot needed unbraiding and restyling, but he lacked the mood for the task. He'd have time for such things in the next inn he'd be staying in, before the muster started.

Soon, the fire had warmed and dried his body. He had a change of clothes with him, so dressed himself once more, then lay on the quilted bed, staring at the ceiling for some minutes. Weird how the receptionist had been convinced he'd been here before. Must have been somehar who looked similar, that's all. He was too wide awake to sleep, but the thought of the raucous crowd downstairs wasn't appealing. He could go and see Minx, make sure she was stabled adequately. Her comfort was as important as his own.

Dressed in boots and coat once more, Isoldis went downstairs and left the inn through the front door. The receptionist was no longer on duty, or had perhaps left his desk for some purpose or another. Whatever the reason for his absence, Isoldis was relieved. He realised the earlier encounter had unnerved him more than he'd thought.

The stable yard was quiet, so the crackle of the brazier could be heard, with snowflakes hissing upon it. The snow was falling heavier now, quite early this year for Alba Sulh. But the signs had been there in autumn; the hips upon the roses had been fuller and redder than normal, a sure warning of a harsh winter to come.

Was anything more beautiful than thick, falling snow? Isoldis thought, throwing back his head to catch the cold kisses on his face. He stuck out his tongue to drink the winter. Such snow was for walking through, over fields and hills; it would crunch beneath the soles of thick boots. It was the dais for the low winter sun, the pastel sky, the inky scrawl of rooks across the muted colours. It was the mantle of a stag patrolling his domain in the forest. It was a shame snow could be such an inconvenient thing too, making travelling difficult, cutting isolated communities off from the wider world.

As he bathed in the falling snow, Isoldis became aware of the twinge deep within, a soft cry, as if heard from afar, a plea. Only at certain moments would he allow its voice to be heard, and this was one such moment. He could give into what felt like grief and weep into the dusting flakes, or he could swallow hard, breathe deep and shrug it off. He chose the latter, putting aside the flicker of pain, silencing the distant voice. This phenomenon had assailed him sporadically since the incident in his youth, when he'd tripped into an alternate reality for a while and fallen in love with a ghost, an idea. Fendris: there was the name. He was not afraid to think its shape. Fortunately, Verdiferel, that duplicitous dehar of the season, had administered a balm in the form of Murarn, a har who'd resembled the ghost of desire. This had healed Isoldis's wound and given him joy, for around five years. But that passion had fizzled out over ten years ago, the burning adorations of youth had long been dampened and swept away, and the absence of this warmth allowed, sometimes, an old scar to throb and leak.

But Fendris was never a ghost, Isoldis thought, against his will. *He's out there, somewhere.*

He shook his head, managed to laugh a little at his own foolishness. The sun was dead, but soon would be reborn. These were dying feelings he was experiencing, emanations from the land. They would vanish with the solstice sun – or so he must convince himself. He'd done a fairly good job of that over the years.

Isoldis went into the stable and Minx murmured to him in greeting, coming to the gate of her stall. She pressed her head against his chest and he scratched her ears obligingly. He kissed her hard brow and rested his cheek upon it. Was Murarn similarly haunted? he wondered. Was there a ghost for him too when the season shifted? They never spoke of the past now; if anything, they skittishly avoided it, even should they find themselves alone together and in the presence of wine. Murarn was now a hostling and had a chesnari who knew nothing of what had happened during that summer. Their harling – nearly adult – was black-maned and beautiful, and had done much, Isoldis supposed, in the way of exorcism.

Isoldis had remained close friends with Yuroah and Raephe, who were still together and always would be, but they too never broached the subject, not even at moments that provided a perfect cue, such as Reaptide Eve, or when the guisers came to raise their pavilions on the river's field.

Isoldis had no chesnari, no special somehar to banish old memories. He chose to be alone, because he knew he was difficult to live with and had little patience with others. Besides, he'd never met anyhar who could compare... With what? A childish wish – ultimately. The Fendris who Isoldis remembered had never really existed. There was, in fact, nothing to remember, only an ideal, a sketch in his heart of the perfect har. Yet even now, that ghost could rattle its chains and moan, and bring feelings to the surface. An exhumation: Fendris would stay neither dead nor buried and for somehar who'd never existed that was quite an accomplishment.

I should hate him, Isoldis thought. *I go through life feeling very little, and the only feelings I do have are thwarted.* He kissed Minx's brow again and decided to nose around the yard, and perhaps even go for a walk, before going to bed.

Opposite the long main stable block was a wide covered area, where carriages and wagons were housed. Tarpaulins were thrown over them and fastened with narrow ropes. Isoldis walked among these hunched, sleeping vehicles. He could imagine their dreams, all of smooth roads, where the wheels could turn fast and horses gulped the miles. A couple of lanterns were left burning in this area, presumably so that owners or passengers of the vehicles could visit them easily, should the need arise. But the shadows cast by the lamps were long and eerie. Isoldis felt watched, and perhaps somehar did stand hidden nearby. He decided to return to the inn.

Just as Isoldis was about to retrace his steps, a lamp flared up for a moment, making the area brighter, and he noticed an enormous humped shape behind the coaches. A ripple of heat went through him, which felt something like recognition. Curious, he went to this shape and lifted aside a corner of the tarpaulin that shrouded it. At once, the face of a demon stared back at him, and he dropped the canvas in surprise, frozen for a moment. Then, impulsively, he pulled more of the covering aside, revealing scenes of cavorting supernatural creatures, twisted trees, pale ghosts, skinny cats and mad-eyed ravens. He knew those paintings, and even though it had been fifteen years or so since he'd last seen them, they appeared as new, freshly-painted. This was the wagon-home of the Dog Rose Larks guiser troupe, who'd been an intrinsic part of the eerie visitation during that long-ago summer, the lost season that still sang mournful songs in Isoldis's memory.

He put his fingers against the red and black face of an exquisite demon, ran them over the contours of the thick paint. Could this be the Larks' wagon? For a moment, he imagined the guisers inside, hanging like bats or folded up like discarded skins, hibernating in the darkness. He choked back a nervous laugh. Ridiculous. He remembered the masks, both sinister and beautiful. The wagon creaked.

Isoldis laid the covering back down, patted it straight. He was compelled to bow and murmur, 'Astale,' as if whatever might hide within the wagon was a magical creature, and he must welcome it, and also excuse himself for imposing upon it, by uttering that simple word conveying respect and reverence. He backed away from the monstrous vehicle, and soon the heavy snow flakes all but hid it from his view. He must go inside.

Before he reached the threshold of the inn's back door, he heard a low, musical sound, barely audible beneath the crunch of his boots on the rapidly-thickening snow. In the silent pause, he heard again the sound: a two-toned whistle, somehow out of key, yet clear as the Natalia bell that rings in the birth of the sun. When hara call to animals, they often employ such a whistle, high-pitched, then low. This was the other way around – low, then high; it sounded unearthly in the otherwise silent world. Not even noise from the bar intruded into the yard. The whistle came from beyond the arch, somewhere near the road.

Isoldis knew his path had just divided. If he took the safest, most sensible path, he'd go back into the inn and forget what he'd seen and heard. If he took the dangerous, unpredictable path, he might discover something that had been waiting for him to find it. There might be danger, but that was the gamble. *Do you take it, har? Like before?*

Isoldis walked beneath the arch.

The road was now covered by snow, unmarked by tracks. Across the road, forest began, which had not yet become ancient but followed the pattern of the old Sulhian woodland, expanding once more across wild acres. In some areas, whole towns could be found within the boscage, the remains of humanity's depredations being smothered, pressed into the earth, as into a mass grave.

The greenwood here was comprised of deciduous trees, oaks, beeches, sycamore and birch, and no doubt hid a dozen groves where families paid their respects to Panphilien in his many guises.

Isoldis stood upon the road, glanced back at his tracks that led to the inn yard. The *Star* was full of life, golden light falling from the windows onto the snow. Inside, hara celebrated the season, preparing for greater festivities still. As the night progressed, and ale and wine flowed, the party would become rowdier. There would be laughter, and fondness expressed in kisses and embraces – even for strangers. There would be voices raised in joyful song, and dancing to the jabber of fiddles, the heart-thump of hand drums.

Yet Isoldis felt apart from it all. He often felt that way. *What ill-making am I?* he thought. *To be such a ghost among my own kind?* There was no accounting for it, no troublesome pearl-bearing for his hostling, no maladies in infancy, no accidents. As a harling, he'd been contained and well-behaved, if aloof. Where his brother had run to hara's outstretched arms, eager for attention and praise, Isoldis had hung back, uncomfortable with such attention. And yet he was not completely without finer emotions. He felt close to growing things, to animals, to the spirits in the land. There was simply a block inside him, where amiability and love for his fellow hara should bloom.

For what had seemed a brief time, and so long ago, Isoldis knew – or was fairly sure – he had experienced love. He had for a short time been like other hara, or at least how he assumed other hara to be. Life had felt bright and warm: a summer of the heart. But, inevitably, as summers are doomed to pass, eventually the leaves fell, the fields became bare, and darkness closed in, along with the cold. He'd lived in this winter of the soul ever since. And for some reason, in this place where he was a stranger, far from home, in this time of approaching renewal, the past had come back to him, stronger than ever before.

The whistle came again. Isoldis followed it, into the embrace of the trees, the rimy kiss of the snow.

A path ran ahead of him, narrow but clear; he was ankle-deep in pristine drifts. He heard the whistle twice more, always ahead of him. There was no sense of threat, although he was aware he was holding his breath for seconds at a time. As he walked, the snowfall eased off, perhaps unnaturally quickly. The clouds hugging the moon swam away across the sky, revealing a sickle of brightness moving to dark. The glistering starlight seemed hard and sharp.

Isoldis saw ahead an opening in the trees, beyond it a glade. This would be a place of reverence. As he approached, he realised hara were already present, no doubt enacting some ritual of the season. But there was no laughter and singing, not even soft chanting, merely a silence. He could see moving shapes ahead. And then the movement ceased.

He stood at the threshold to the greenwood chamber and saw he had come to a guisers' play. He knew them: Dog Rose Larks. He knew their characters, who were dressed in seasonal finery and elaborate masks. Was this performance for him alone? Had they *rehearsed* this, brought him here before, in some strange way? Perhaps even two days before? Isoldis shivered, but not in fear.

Panphilien, dressed in robes of spangled gold and white, sat upon a rock that was like a high altar. His black skin had been rubbed to a glowing sheen with golden powder to mimic the sun, and his braided hair was gilded with sparkling dust. His beautiful, sequinned mask was shaped into an expression of pain. The Sweet Serpent and the Highborn of the Tribes supported him, and he leaned back against them, his robes hitched up, his legs spread. This was Solarisel, in the moment before the birth of the sun's pearl. The Friend from Below hung back, watching, one hand to his carved red mouth. The Brave Ouana stood behind Panphilien-Solarisel, his weapons sheathed. The Fair Soume knelt at Solarisel's feet, his hands raised as if to catch the pearl when it emerged. The Faithful Hound lay shivering at the dehar's side. Half a dozen other hara, in costumes of green and white tatters, were ranged in a semi-circle behind the main players, their pale mossy masks set in rapt expressions. The entire scene was a tableau, a second caught in frozen time.

And then Isoldis saw another har approach. *He* was coming through the trees to the right of the scene, dressed in an enveloping cloak of the deepest, darkest crimson. The hood pooled around his shoulders, hid nearly all of his face but for the mouth and chin, so artfully fashioned. No mask. Not for the Wise Hienama, who took in his strong brown hands the wheel of the year, and turned it.

He paused before he reached the group and appeared to notice Isoldis for the first time, although Isoldis doubted this was so. The Wise Hienama beckoned: *come forward.*

Without hesitation, Isoldis did so. He stood some paces behind the Hienama, who now raised his arms and spoke:

> '*Gather here, in the white kingdom,*
> *Where the hounds are silent,*
> *And the sun's pearl comes forth in blood.*
> *Take the pearl, beloveds,*
> *And guard it closely,*
> *Until the night of revelation*
> *And the rebirth of the light.*'

In response, the company breathed 'Astale', and Solarisel uttered a groan that managed to sound both agonised and sultry. His body heaved and from it fell the pearl, into the waiting hands of the Fair Soume, who rose slowly to his feet and raised the pearl to the sky. His hands were reddened, dripping with blood. Scarlet trails nosed slowly down his arms. Solarisel lay in the embrace of his attendants, his mask now smiling. Isoldis had not seen him change it, but... deception, sleight of hand... Blood ran from Solarisel, down into the snow, and then soaked right through it, vanished, leaving no stain.

Solarisel got to his feet and his attendants straightened his robe. He beckoned to Isoldis. 'Come, harling, take my blessing.'

Isoldis obeyed and knelt in the snow that should have been red but was not. 'Astale, Solarisel, you are welcome in your season,' he said.

Solarisel reached down and placed his hands on the crown of Isoldis's head. 'Walk in light, beloved,' he murmured. 'Take my gift and nurture it. Now, rise.'

Isoldis stood up, dazed. He was part of the performance, and this did not feel strange or awkward, but entirely natural and comfortable. The Fair Soume offered Isoldis the pearl, which he accepted. It was warm in his hands, pulsing with life, still sticky with blood, and fluids of the cauldron within Solarisel's body. A faint light gleamed inside its leathery skin. Was it a real pearl? Had the guiser who played Solarisel really birthed it?

'What must I do with it?' he asked.

'Break it at Natalia,' Solarisel answered, 'for it holds promise inside, and promise will walk at the solstice.'

'But...' Even as Isoldis began to speak, he realised that what he held was not a gourd-sized living pearl, but a small acorn. Illusions. Tricks. That was their way, of course. 'Thank you, Tiahaar,' he said, and bowed.

Isoldis turned to look at – to drink in – the features beneath the red hood of the Wise Hienama. So often he had imagined them meeting again and had dreamed of it. The Hienama raised his hands and drew back the hood from his face. His hair fell forward over his breast.

Isoldis was breathless. He closed his hand over the acorn. 'All these years,' was all he could say. 'All these years.'

'Everything in its season,' said the Wise Hienama.

'Are you Fendris?' Isoldis asked. He was aware he had perhaps only moments to find answers, resolution, and must therefore be blunt, perhaps brutal in his words.

'I was,' said the Hienama, 'for a long time. Until my son brought to me a different name that had no darkness in it. I am Levallier.'

'What am I to you?'

Levallier tilted his head slightly, laughed.

'I was *him* to you, for a while,' Isoldis said, a trace of bitterness leaking from his voice. 'I was Grisainn. When you came to me in my room... and on the Cop... that night...'

'It is, in my opinion,' said Levallier, 'a mistake to live in the past.'

'Perhaps so, but some are trapped in it, unless somehar brings them a name of light.'

Levallier stepped forward, curled his hands over Isoldis's own, which gripped the acorn. 'Break the pearl at Natalia,' he said softly, 'for that is when potential breaks into reality. I promise you.'

Isoldis looked into this har's eyes for some seconds, consumed by sadness and longing. 'But it will not be *you*,' he murmured plaintively.

'Grisainn lives in more than one har,' Levallier replied. 'As does that which you perceive me to be.' For a few moments, he stroked Isoldis's face, his hair, with his thumbs. Then he clasped Isoldis's hands once more. 'The beloved is an airy spirit, always moving from body to body.'

'If that is so, why has this happened?' Isoldis asked. He shook his head. 'No, I don't believe you. I wasn't simply *possessed* for a time, if that's what you mean. There's something still in me, maybe only myself – and it's always been that.'

Levallier didn't answer.

'Did you know I'd be here at this time?' Isoldis said. 'Have you been waiting, as I've been waiting? Why didn't you come back to *Hart's Cliff*, Fendris? Why? You woke me up, and cursed me to sleeplessness, then left me awake, alone.'

Levallier closed his eyes. He was still holding onto Isoldis's hands and now raised them to his brow. He sighed. 'Time is different for us,' he said. 'I'm sorry you were alone in the dark and cold for so long.'

Isoldis uttered a choked laugh, pulled himself away. 'I don't want your weird sayings. I deserve to know the plain truth. I served some purpose for you once. Tell me, why are you here? Why now?'

Levallier, Fendris, the Wise Hienama – all of them – stared at Isoldis. 'If I said I had a dream of you, or a star fell from the sky and spoke to me about you, or a blackbird sang your name, or I saw your name written in frost on a window... would that suffice?'

Isoldis exhaled through his nose, then said, 'Your pretty words mean nothing to me. They won't mend anything. Come to me at Natalia, *Fendris*. If I was called here tonight for this, you care enough.' He stared into those eyes as deep as an ocean, non-reflecting. 'Do you dare to share breath with me?'

Levallier held the stare. 'No, I do not.' But he leaned forward and breathed upon Isoldis's eyes. 'Luscious dreams for you, beloved.'

'How can you be so cruel?' Isoldis said coldly, backing away. 'I don't want dreams to torment me. I'm a different har now, and won't be fooled by your tricks. I'll stay awake all night.'

'Valla,' said the Fair Soume, in a warning tone, clearly keen to interrupt the conversation. 'Come. We must go.'

Somehow, without Isoldis noticing it, the rest of the Dog Rose Larks had left the grove. The Fair Soume had taken off his mask and was staring in a hard fashion at Isoldis.

We look alike, Isoldis thought. *But then, his father, Grisainn, looked like me.*

'Valla!' The Fair Soume was more insistent, almost afraid.

Levallier pulled the hood of his cloak over his head once more. 'Break the seed,' he said to Isoldis. 'Trust me.' He made an elaborate, sweeping bow, gesturing dramatically with one arm. 'Astale, spirit of snow.'

Suddenly and completely, Isoldis was alone. There was no sign in the grove of anything that had occurred. The snow appeared unblemished, not even the tracks of a deer through it. Yet the seed of the oak was still clenched in his fist. They must have drugged or entranced him, as they had before, but why? Simply to absolve an old guilt?

Isoldis stared at the acorn in his hand for a few moments, then put it in his pocket.

Back at *The Falling Star*, Isoldis went up to his room. He hadn't bothered to check the yard before he went inside, because he knew the wagon-home would no longer be there, and probably never had been.

Downstairs in the bar, hara were still in rampant party mood, but the noise didn't disturb him. Rather, it was like a screen, behind which was privacy. 'If I dream,' he said aloud to the room, 'then so will you, Fendris. A new name can't unmake you. A truly *wise* Hienama doesn't fear, like you do. So ensure that the promise, when it hatches, is you.'

Isoldis closed his eyes in the silence that was beyond and apart from the cacophony of celebration below. He imagined himself back in his room at *Hart's Cliff*, lying on his bed.

The window is open, and from a distance come the sounds of Natalia celebrations. It is midnight. Hara are welcoming the hatching of Elisin's pearl. In the field by the river, guisers cavort and dance, music and fireworks blaze in the night, and everyhar feels the future actually happening. But at the main house, all is quiet, but for the breath of the har upon the bed, and the soft clop of a horse's hooves beneath the window.

Glossary of Terms

Adkaya – a minor festival of the year, when the pearl of Elisin is dropped by its hostling Solarisel on 7th December.

Aghama – (*ag*-am-ah) the first of all Wraeththu, regarded as a dehar.

Agmara – (ag-*mar*-uh) natural energy, equating to chi or ki, used for healing and manipulated to affect reality.

Althaia – (al-*thay*-uh) the process and period of change from human to har following inception.

Almagabra – (*al*-mah-*gab*-rah) lands corresponding roughly to what was once Mediterranean Europe.

Archon – the overall leader of a tribe, who has a number of phyles under their custodianship.

Arojhahn – a ritual or rite specifically associated with a seasonal festival.

Arotohar – The Wraeththu name for the Wheel of the Year and its festivals.

Aruna – (a-*roo*-nah) sexual union between hara that is both spiritual and physical.

Arunic – pertaining to aruna.

Astale – (ass-*tah*-lay) a term of respect, generally used in invoking dehara or other spiritual entities.

Bloomtide – the festival of the Spring Equinox, corresponding to Easter or Eostre in human traditions.

Chesna – (*chez*-nah) a close relationship, a chesna-bond can be equated to marriage.

Chesnari – (chez-*nah*-ree) a partner in a chesna-bond.

Cuttingtide – the festival of the Summer Solstice, around June 21st

Dehar – (*day*-har) a Wraeththu deity. pl. *Dehara*.

Devastation, the – one of many terms used to describe the final days of humanity, when the world was in turmoil, and there was catastrophic conflict between hara and humans. The days of change.

Dryadhar – a har who communicates with the spirits of the land for his tribe, who is more than usually attuned to the natural world.

Elisin – the 'Child of Light', the infant deharling whose pearl is born on the 7th December, and which hatches at the Winter Solstice, 21st December. Elisin presides over four turns of the Wheel, the only dehar to do so. He transforms into Shadolan at Cuttingtide, the summer solstice.

Eburniel – the dehar of Rosatide, along with Elisin.

Feybraiha – (fay-*bray*-uh) a period of time equating to puberty in humans when a har matures sexually. The term also refers to a day of celebration for this. At the end of his feybraiha, when he is physically ready, a har will take aruna with another for the first time. This is regarded as an important rite of passage.

Feyrahni – the dehar of Feybraihatide, along with Elisin.

First Generation – hara who were became Wraeththu by being incepted as humans.

Feybraihatide – the festival that was once Beltane, May 1st.

Florinel – the dehar of Bloomtide, along with Elisin.

Gelaming – (*Jel*-uh-ming) the most influential tribe of Wraeththu, whose tribal home is Almagabra.

Har – a Wraeththu individual (pl. hara).

Harakin – a term used by a har to describe members of their family, or within small phyles, other phyle members. Also *kinshara.*

Harhune – (har-*hoon*) a ceremony during which inception takes place, the transfusion of blood that turns a human to har.

Harling – a young har not yet at feybraiha.

Hienama – (high-en-*ah*-mah) equivalent of a priest/teacher/healer within a community. In the early days of Wraeththu, hienamas also incepted humans to become hara.

High-harling – harish equivalent of a grand-child

High-hostling – harish equivalent of a grandmother.

High Rehuna – a har who acts in a priestly role within a community, but is below the status of hienama.

Hostling – the harish equivalent of a mother, a har who hosts and carries the egg, or pearl, in which harlings grow.

Househar – a har employed in the household of another, or in a hostelry.

Hura – a relation within a family who is not father or hostling, corresponding to the human terms uncle or aunt. Can also apply to extended family. See *surakin.*

Hurakin – members of an extended family.

Immanion – principle city of Almagabra, founded by the Gelaming tribe, regarded as a centre of culture and learning.

Inception – the process by which a human becomes har, involving a transfusion of blood.

Kinshara – members of a phyle, sometimes blood family.

Lachrymide – the dehar of Shadetide.

Majhahn – (mazh-*ahn*) a ritual

Megalithica – the landmass once known as North America.

Morterrius – a dehar of Cuttingtide, along with Shadolan.

Muster (n) – a gathering for a specific purpose. Official meeting.

Nahir Nuri – the third and highest tier of the harish magical system. This term also refers to a har who trained to that level; they can also be known as hienamas.

Natalia – the winter solstice festival, around Dec 21st, presided over by Solarisel and Elisin.

Nayati – (nigh-*ah*-tee) a temple or sacred space for spiritual work

Ouana – (oo-*ah*-nuh) the masculine aspect of Wraeththu

Ouanic – pertaining to the attributes of ouana.

Panphilien – the dehar who represents the Wheel of the Year. He has different aspects who preside over the different festivals and seasons. From Adkaya to Cuttingtide, he is represented by two dehara, the Child of Light and his parent and lover.

Pearl – the egg or sac within which a harling forms. Hara carry pearls within their bodies, which are expelled or 'born' some weeks before the harling reaches to state to emerge. Pearl is also a term of affection used by harish parents for their offspring. (*With pearl* – a har who is carrying a pearl.)

Pelki – the harish term for rape, which is regarded with the deepest disgust by the majority of hara who believe aruna is both a sacrament and a blessing.

Phylarch – leader of a phyle

Phyle – a distinct community within a tribe, a sub-tribe

Pothar – a har who works in a bar. Pl. *pothara.*

Prosperiel – the dehar of Smoketide.

Pureborn – a har who has been born to harish parents rather than inception from human. A second-generation har and beyond.

Nahir Nuri – a har of high spiritual rank, who has undergone all caste training.

Reaptide – the festival that was once Lammas of Lughnasadh, on Aug 1st.

Rehuna – a har who pursues spiritual training in a serious manner.

Roon (v) – slang word for taking aruna with somehar.

Rosatide – the festival of what was once Imbolg, on Feb 1st.

See'ver – seed-giver, father.

Sett – a short term for 'settlement', generally a rural or forest community.

Shadetide – the festival of what was Halloween, October 31st.

Shadolan – a dehar of Cuttingtide, along with Morterrius.

Smoketide – the festival of the Autumn Equinox, around Sept 21st.

Solarisel – the dehar who presides from Adkaya to Rosatide. He is the hostling of Elisin.

Soume – (*soo*-mee) the feminine aspect of Wraeththu.

Soumic – pertaining to the aspects of soume.

Spark (v) – to provide the ouanic aspect in pearl-creation. To spark a pearl means to father it.

Surakin – harish term equivalent to a cousin.

Tiahaar – (*tee*-ah-har) a polite form of address, pl. *Tiahaara*

Townshar – a har belonging to an urban community. Pl. *townshara*

Unneah – (oo-*nay*-uh) a Wraeththu tribe of Megalithica.

Unthrist – hara who belong to no tribe.

Vakei – a ritual knife used in ceremonies to conduct energy, and for cutting magical herbs.

Verdiferel – the dehar of Reaptide.

Woodshara – small tribes who choose to live in wild, forest areas rather than in larger towns, or be part of a greater community.

Wraeththu – (*ray*-thoo) androgynous race that came to replace humanity.

About the Contributors

Storm Constantine

Storm is the creator of the Wraeththu Mythos, the first trilogy of which was published in the 1980s. However, the influences and inspirations for the Wraeththu world go much further back than that, and continue into the future as she plans more stories for it. Storm is the founder of Immanion Press, created initially to publish her out-of-print back catalogue, but which evolved into the thriving venture it is today. She has written over thirty books, including full length novels, novellas, short story collections and non-fiction titles. Her interests include magic and spirituality, Reiki, movies, music and MMOs. Among her many occupations, most of which are unpaid, she runs a Reiki school and a guild called Equilibrium on the EU servers of World of Warcraft. She lives in the Midlands of the UK.

Wendy Darling

Based in Atlanta, Georgia, USA, Wendy Darling is co-author of *Breeding Discontent*, published by Immanion Press in 2003 as the first *Wraeththu Mythos* novel. She has been involved in Wraeththu in many different capacities, including editor of the revised *Wraeththu Chronicles*, webmaster of the *Inception* and *Forever Wraeththu* fan web sites, and staff at several Wraeththu conventions.

With Storm she also co-edits the Wraeththu Mythos story collections. Her full-time job is as a web projects manager at Emory University, but she engages in many side projects and hobbies, including photography and blogging about Art Deco architecture. She has also forged relationships with Wraeththu fans around the world and has been fortunate to meet several authors whose work is included in this collection. At home she is ruled by two cats, cats she did not have in her life until she met and visited with Storm, who as usual had a strong influence on her. Wendy enjoys international travel and tries to visit Storm and her husband Jim as often as she can. Connect with Wendy online at about.me/wdarling.

Nerine Dorman

Nerine Dorman is a South African author and editor of SFF currently residing in Cape Town. Her short fiction has been published in an assortment of anthologies, including the *Midian Unmade: Tales of Clive Barker's Nightbreed*; *The Endless Ages Anthology for Vampire: The Masquerade*; the Wraeththu mythos; and *War Stories: New Military Science Fiction*, among others. Her YA fantasy novel *Dragon Forged* was a finalist in the 2017 Sanlam Youth Literature Prize, and she is the curator of the South African 'Horrorfest Bloody Parchment' event and short story competition. In addition, she is a founding member of the SFF authors' co-operative Skolion.

Suzanne Gabriel

Born to nomadic Canadian parents, Suzanne grew up in Canada, the UK, and USA. She is a wife and mother. She completed a Master of Science degree in Food Science and Nutrition and spent time working in the food industry and currently works in a university as a budget officer. Suzanne is fascinated by antiquities museums, old cookbooks, old etiquette books, and documentaries about old things.

Even when there isn't any music, Suzanne is likely to be dancing and she will go out of her way to hug a tree. She adores animals, travel, historical re-enactment, science, hiking, yoga, and way too many other hobbies.

Fiona Lane

Fiona was born and brought up near Glasgow during the Time of The Flared Trouser and Unfeasibly High Platform Shoes. By the time we all came to our senses, she had relocated to Aberdeen, and spent several years waiting for a number six bus, in a horrible collision involving the nature of time and the Aberdeen weather. During the eighties, while she was waiting for the Internet to be invented, she acquired a husband and a couple of replacement units, and they all now live in a field full of sheep in Aberdeenshire, along with the odd cat or two and Fiona's posse of obsolete computers, many of which she has single-handedly restored to a completely non-functioning condition. She once kept chickens, but they were messy and she couldn't use them to buy vintage shoes from Ebay. The eggs were good though. She likes gin and hats, and dislikes the oppression of the proletariat. Her hobbies include cooking, gardening, and staring into the abyss.

Ruby

Ruby is the official artist for the Wraeththu Mythos, who creates all the covers for the Immanion Press editions. She started drawing from her imagination long before she could or indeed would talk. Still heavily influenced by the fairy tales and myths absorbed from her childhood, Ruby has grown into a multimedia illustrator interested in exploring the darkly sensual, symbolic and surreal undercurrents of life. Ruby's illustrations blend perfectly the mythological, the classical and the future fantastic and are also evocative of Beardsley and Mucha. She is now a much sought-after cover artist and interior illustrator for books across many genres, and is the creator of the ongoing Wraeththu Tarot project.

Ruby is up for designing anything as long as it fits in with her bohemian aesthetic and animal-loving ethos (her dream is to run a combined cat sanctuary and art gallery by the sea). On any one day she might be fleshing out a tattoo design and then the next sketching concept art for a theatre set or perhaps sourcing unusual props for a photo-shoot.

E. S. Wynn

E.S. Wynn is the author of over thirty books, the chief editor of Thunderune Publishing (and the associated magazines: *Daily Love, Weirdyear, Yesteryear Fiction, Farther Stars Than These, Linguistic Erosion,* and *Smashed Cat Magazine.*) He has written two Wraeththu Mythos novels in The Gold Country series – *Whispers of the World that Was* and *Echoes of Light and Static* – and is currently working on the third.

He manages dozens of websites, has written hundreds of articles and short stories for a number of publications, has taught classes in literature, creative writing, marketing, math, spirituality and guided meditation, voiced fifteen albums as a voice actor and even spent time working as a model for stock photography. He has a bachelor's degree in English, has been trained in Reiki and other forms of energy healing, and is a proud Freemason.

Storm Constantine's Wraeththu Mythos

Also published by Immanion Press

By *Storm Constantine*

The Wraeththu Chronicles
The Enchantments of Flesh and Spirit
The Bewitchments of Love and Hate
The Fulfilments of Fate and Desire

The Wraeththu Histories
The Wraiths of Will and Pleasure
The Shades of Time and Memory
The Ghosts of Blood and Innocence

Wraeththu
(omnibus edition of the Wraeththu Chronicles)

The Alba Sulh Sequence
The Hienama
Student of Kyme
The Moonshawl

Blood, the Phoenix and a Rose: An Alchymical Triptych
A Raven Bound with Lilies: Stories of the Wraeththu Mythos

Other Mythos Novels and Anthologies

Paragenesis, edited by Storm Constantine & Wendy Darling
Para Imminence, edited by Storm Constantine & Wendy Darling
Para Kindred, edited by Storm Constantine & Wendy Darling
Para Animalia, edited by Storm Constantine & Wendy Darling

Breeding Discontent, by Wendy Darling and Bridgette Parker
Terzah's Sons, by Victoria Copus
Song of the Sulh, by Maria J. Leel
Whispers of the World That Was by E. S. Wynn
Echoes of Light and Static, by E. S. Wynn

Visit http://www.immanion-press.com for details of these and
other Immanion Press publications

IMMANION PRESS

Purveyors of Speculative Fiction

The Darkest Midnight in December: Ghost Stories for the Winter Season, edited by Storm Constantine

The ghost story is a Christmas tradition; shadows looming over the brightly-lit tree in a room where logs crackle in the hearth, and the smell of spice and brandy fill the air. Outside the weather is chill; perhaps snow is falling. And over the festive season, as people gather to celebrate and welcome in the New Year, eerie breath might be heard in a dark corridor, hurrying footsteps overhead, a sigh in the depths of a stairwell. When all are supposed to be happy and secure, the intrusion of fear, grief or sadness are alien, and yet bizarrely integral to a time of celebration whose roots lie in ancient, pagan festivals. What stirs in the darkness? Previously unpublished tales from: *J. E. Bryant, Storm Constantine, Louise Coquio, Wendy Darling, Nerine Dorman, Rosie Garland, Jessica Gilling, Suzanne Gyseman, Misha Herwin, Rick Hudson, Rhys Hughes, Hannah Kate, Fiona Lane, Fiona McGavin and Adele Marie Park.*
Papaperback. ISBN: 978-1-907737-83-1 £11.99, $18.99

Madame Two Swords by Tanith Lee

An unnamed narrator, in the French city of Troy, finds an old book of the writings of the revolutionary, Lucien de Ceppays, who lived and died in the city two centuries before. She feels a strange bond to the life and thoughts of this long-dead man – what is the mysterious truth behind her obsession? Perhaps she did not find the book at all – perhaps it found her. Some years later, impoverished after the death of her mother, the narrator – in a state of desperation – find herself inexorably guided to meet the peculiar and unnerving Madame Two Swords, an old woman with a history, and her own enduring bonds to Lucien – as well as the book. For the narrator, reality seems to unravel, as she begins to penetrate just how intimately she is connected with Madame Two Swords and Lucien. Previously only available as a limited-edition hardback in 1988, the long-awaited new edition of this vintage-Tanith novella includes illustrations by Jarod Mills.
ISBN 978-1-907737-81-7 £11.99, $15.50 pb

Salty Kiss Island by Rhys Hughes

What is a fantastical love story? It isn't quite the same as an ordinary love story. The events that take place are stranger, more extreme, full of the passion of originality, invention and magic, as well as an intensification of emotional love. The stories in *Salty Kiss Island* are set in this world and others, spanning the spectrum of possible and impossible experiences, the uncharted territories of yearning, the depths and shoals of the heart, mind and soul. A love of language runs through them, parallel to the love that motivates their characters to feats of preposterous heroism, luminous lunacy and grandiose gesture. They include tales of minstrels and their catastrophic serenades, dreamers sinking into sequences of ever-deeper dreams, goddesses and mermaids, sailors and devils, messages in bottles that can think and speak but never be read, shadows with an independent life and voyagers of distant galaxies who are already at their destinations before they arrive.
ISBN: 978-1-907737-77-0, £11.99, $15.50 pbk

The Lightbearer by Alan Richardson

Michael Horsett parachutes into Occupied France before the D-Day Invasion. He is dropped in the wrong place, miles from the action, badly injured, and totally alone. He falls prey to two Thelemist women who have awaited the Hawk God's coming, attracts a group of First World War veterans who rally to what they imagine is his cause, is hunted by a troop of German Field Police who are desperate to find him, and has a climactic encounter with a mutilated priest who believes that Lucifer Incarnate has arrived…*The Lightbearer* is a unique gnostic thriller, dealing with the themes of Light and Darkness, Good and Evil, Matter and Spirit.
"The Lightbearer is another shining example of Alan Richardson's talent as a story-teller. He uses his wide esoteric knowledge to produce a story that thrills, chills and startles the reader as it radiates pure magical energy. An unusual and gripping war story with more facets than a star sapphire." – Mélusine Draco, author of "Aubry's

A Raven Bound with Lilies by Storm Constantine

Androgynous, and stronger in mind and body than humans, sometimes deadly, and often possessing unearthly beauty, the Wraeththu have captivated readers since Storm Constantine's first novel, *The Enchantments of Flesh and Spirit*, was published in 1988, regarded as ground-breaking in its treatment of gender and sexuality. This anthology of 15 tales collects all her published Wraeththu short stories into one volume, and also includes extra material, including the author's first explorations of the androgynous race. The tales range from the 'creation story' *Paragenesis*, through the bloody, brutal rise of the earliest tribes, and on into a future, where strange mutations are starting to emerge from hidden corners of the earth. With sumptuous illustrations by official Wraeththu artist Ruby, as well as pictures from Danielle Lainton and the author herself, *A Raven Bound with Lilies* is a must for any Wraeththu enthusiast, and is also a comprehensive introduction to the mythos for those who are new to it. ISBN: 978-1-907737-80-0 £11.99, $15.50

Dark in the Day, Ed. by Storm Constantine & Paul Houghton

Weirdness lurks beyond the margins of the mundane, emerging to dismantle our assumptions of reality. *Dark in the Day* is an anthology of weird fiction, penned by established writers and also those new to the genre – the latter being authors who are, or were, students of Creative Writing at Staffordshire University, where editor Storm Constantine occasionally delivers guest lectures. Her co-editor, Paul Houghton, is the senior lecturer in Creative Writing at the university.

Contributors include: Martina Bellovičová, J. E. Bryant, Glynis Charlton, Storm Constantine, Louise Coquio, Elizabeth Counihan, Krishan Coupland, Elizabeth Davidson, Siân Davies, Paul Finch, Rosie Garland, Rhys Hughes, Kerry Fender, Andrew Hook, Paul Houghton, Tanith Lee, Tim Pratt, Nicholas Royle, Michael Marshall Smith, Paula Wakefield, Ian Whates and Liz Williams. ISBN: 978-1-907737-74-9 £11.99, $18.99

Immanion Press
http://www.immanion-press.com
info@immanion-press.com

NEWCON PRESS

http://newconpress.co.uk/

The very best in fantasy, science fiction, and horror

Tanith By Choice by Tanith Lee

Tanith Lee is one of the finest writers ever to grace the field of speculative fiction. Tanith has left one heck of a legacy. I would never dream of attempting to compile a 'Best Of' collection, so instead I've let others do so for me. This collection features many of her finest stories, as chosen by those who knew her. With contributions from *Storm Constantine, Craig Gidney, Mavis Haut, Stephen Jones, John Kaiine (Tanith's widower), Vera Nazarian, Sarah Singleton, Kari Sperring, Sam Stone, Cecilia Dart-Thornton, Freda Warrington, Nadia van der Westhuizen* and *Ian Whates*, each story is accompanied by a note from the person selecting it explaining why this tale means so much to them. Available as a paperback and a numbered limited-edition hardback ISBN: 978-1-910935-57-6 (hardback) 978-1-910935-58-3 (softback)

Visionary Tongue edited by Storm Constantine

When founding Visionary Tongue magazine, Storm Constantine and Louise Coquio determined to produce something innovative. They recruited a rolling cast of guest editors and set about finding the very best in new dark fiction. *VT* gave early exposure to the work of emerging writers such as *Justina Robson, Tim Lebbon, Katherine Roberts, Liz Williams, Jaine Fenn, Fiona McGavin* and *Ian Whates*. In compiling this anthology, Storm has revisited all those old issues, and selected a host of gleaming gems from amongst the content. With some three dozen stories (and the occasional poem) in the paperback edition, and four bonus stories in the hardback, this truly is a volume to savour. ISBN: hardback: 978-1-910935-59-0 Paperback:978-1-910935-60-6

NewCon Press Novellas, Set 2

Case of the Bedevilled Poet ~ Simon Clark

His life under threat, poet Jack Crofton flees through the streets of war-torn London. He falls into company with two elderly gentlemen who claim to be the real Holmes and Watson. Unconvinced but desperate, Jack shares his story, and Holmes agrees to take his case ISBN: 978-1-910935-47-7, hbk, £14.9; ISBN: 978-1-910935-48-4 pbk £6.99

Cottingley ~ Alison Littlewood

A century after the world was rocked by news that two young girls had photographed fairies in the sleepy village of Cottingley, we finally learn the true nature of these fey creatures, involving a harrowing account written by a village resident laying bare the fairies' sinister malevolence. ISBN: 978-1-910935-49-1, hbk, £14.99; ISBN: 978-1-910935-50-7 pbk £6.99

Body in the Woods ~ Sarah Lotz

When an old friend turns up on Claire's doorstep begging for her help, she knows she should refuse, but despite her better judgement finds herself helping to bury something in the woods. Will it stay buried, and can Claire live with the knowledge of what she did that night? ISBN: 978-1-910935-51-4, hbk, £14.99; ISBN: 978-1-910935-52-1 pbk £6.99

The Wind ~ Jay Caselberg

Having moved to Abbotsford six months ago, Gerry reckons he's getting used to country life and the rural veterinary practice he's taken on. Then a strange wind springs up to stir the leaves in unnatural fashion.... ISBN: 978-1-910935-53-8, hbk, £14.99; ISBN: 978-1-910935-54-5 pbk £6.99

This set of four novellas is also available as a limited edition lettered slipcase, containing all four signed hardbacks with the combined artwork as a wrap-around. For details of these and other novellas sets: visit http://newconpress.co.uk/

www.ingramcontent.com/pod-product-compliance
Lightning Source LLC
Chambersburg PA
CBHW020418260626
47156CB00007B/2448